# The Air Between Us

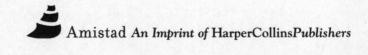
Amistad *An Imprint of* HarperCollins*Publishers*

# *The Air Between Us*

## DEBORAH JOHNSON

THE AIR BETWEEN US. Copyright © 2008 by Deborah Johnson. All rights reserved. Printed in the United States of America. No part of this book may be used or reproduced in any manner whatsoever without written permission except in the case of brief quotations embodied in critical articles and reviews. For information address HarperCollins Publishers, 10 East 53rd Street, New York, NY 10022.

HarperCollins books may be purchased for educational, business, or sales promotional use. For information please write: Special Markets Department, HarperCollins Publishers, 10 East 53rd Street, New York, NY 10022.

FIRST EDITION

Designed by Gretchen Achilles

Library of Congress Cataloging-in-Publication Data has been applied for.

ISBN 978-0-06-125557-1

08 09 10 11 12 OV/RRD 10 9 8 7 6 5 4 3 2 1

*To my son, Matthew Thurman Schumaker,*
*with love and gratitude,*
*and*
*to my brother, Derrick Anthony Johnson, M.D., who shared*
*with me many stories of our father's life as a surgeon*

*A reporter once asked Eudora Welty why she felt there were
so many writers coming out of Mississippi.
To which Miss Welty replied,
"I imagine it's because we have so much explaining to do."*

# Acknowledgments

Without Harvey Klinger, my agent, and Dawn L. Davis, my editor, there would be no book. I am extremely grateful to them both and to everyone else at Amistad and HarperCollins who has worked so diligently on this project, most especially Christina Morgan, Bryan Christian, and Gilda Squire. Wilbur O. Colom was a tremendous support throughout this project; indeed, his insight and tales of life in Mississippi were fundamental to it. Dr. and Mrs. Charles Miles, Mrs. Fran Ivy, and Barry Stidham unselfishly shared their stories and answered my many questions. I thank them. Dr. Connie McCaa of Jackson, Mississippi, was a godsend at a crucial moment. Truly, this book could not have been written without her. Cathy Guerrasio, JoAnn Zautzik, Beth Spirrison, Jacqueline Exum-Petty, and Valerie Dodson were always there, through good times and bad. Last, but certainly not least, I want to thank my son, Matthew, and his dear wife, Malena Watrous. You two are the joy behind the words!

*The Air Between Us*

## Chapter 1

THE BATTERED 1952 FORD PICKUP jolted against the curb, bounc-
ing the driver just high enough so you could see the tip of his head,
making him look for all the world like a teeny ghost, a low-riding
specter. The sight froze the two men—Charlie Symonds and Butter Bob Latham, standing at the coloreds-only emergency-room entrance to Doctors Hospital—stock-still. They watched a cloud of
dust cover the truck as it started bumping its way onto the gravel-
rock parking lot. Amazed, the men continued to stare as the pickup
emerged from the gritty fog and honed in on the door right behind
them. The head did not bob into view again, and for an instant each
man thought he'd imagined it. This false comfort did not last long.
The truck was there, and it was coming straight for them. Their
minds told them to dive for cover and quickly, but their bodies were
locked in place, like the gears of a car. Both men thought they were
dead for sure.

The truck jerked to a halt—"three feet from my kneecap," as

Charlie would spend his winter down at Carter's One-Stop Barber Shop telling anybody who cared to listen—"and that truck must have been coming fifty miles an hour if it was comin' at all. You can bet I saw them Pearly Gates."

Thus this first of many strange events that were to occur that autumn in the town of Revere, Mississippi—population twenty thousand and diminishing rapidly—naturally became famous. With each telling, the truck's speed increased and the distance to Charlie's kneecap decreased until one was up to sixty and the other down to no more than two inches—one, if Charlie had spent time in some juke joint the night before. Within a matter of days, most everybody in Revere had heard the tale at least once. No one questioned if that old rattle-trap truck could even have reached sixty miles an hour, which it could not have. Instead the Reverites all nodded, impressed and sobered by Charlie's choice of biblical allusion. This was later, after all, and right then he wasn't thinking about any implications whatsoever, other than those that had to do with protecting his life from destruction.

The truck stopped so thoroughly that a puff of dust-following billowed around it. Ghostlike. It was seriously dawning on Charlie's mind that he should be hightailing it on out of there and right now. The man remembered that quick glance of bobbing head, and he remembered how thoroughly it had disappeared again. Beside him, Butter Bob had already started a slow turn toward the driveway. Then, through the haze, both men heard the driver's door crank open, heard a thud and the paddle of small, bare feet running toward them along the packed earth. Stirring up the dust.

The owner of the feet pulled up short. Coughed. Tried to speak, coughed again. The men couldn't tell if it was the excitement or the dust. Both black men—strikingly dark in their white, emergency-room uniforms—rushed forward, one to the truck, the other to the child. Charlie Symonds, the older of the two, bent down eye to eye with the youngster. The kid looked to him to be about ten. No wonder they hadn't seen him over the wheel. Charlie shook his head.

"Boy, what you doing driving this—"

Before he could finish, he heard Butter Bob's whistle and then his carefully articulated, "Shit."

Charlie Symonds was an elder deacon at the Mount Union Missionary Baptist Church and did not normally feel at liberty to use such language; but in the context of telling a *real* story, like being in court, you felt called upon to present only the unvarnished truth. And the unvarnished truth was that he took a certain naughty pleasure in shocking and eliciting gasps from whatever womenfolk happened to be hearing him. "Pardon me, ladies," he would say as an aside when he retold his tale again and again, "but you all know what kind of man Butter Bob Latham is, as well as I do—one of them Latham men from over Brooksville—and you know he really is capable of using such language."

Everybody could agree with him on that.

Now, however, in this run-down driveway, Charlie stared at the boy jiggling around in front of him, then glanced over at Butter sidling away from the truck. Charlie got up very, very slowly. He sure did not like the sound of that one word, "Shit." This part, of course, would be left out of the eventual tale telling at Carter's, but this *was* 1966 and this *was* Mississippi, and no God-fearing, right-thinking, common-sense-having black man wanted to be dealing with any kind of "shit" after sundown.

"It's Mr. Billy Ray. He done shot himself!"

The boy had finally recovered his breath, and his words got Charlie's immediate attention. He hurtled over to the truck, pushing burly Butter Bob aside like a feather.

"Oh, my God."

Blood was everywhere: seeping from a pale white man slumped over in the cut-up passenger seat, dripping down onto the running board, soaking into the dirt.

"I got him here as quick as I could. His hunt stand done fall down, and the gun went off. Shot a hole right through him. I tried to tell him he was doing it all wrong. He don't read, you know. None of them Pucketts do, except maybe Miss Ruth Ann. A little. I tried to tell him, but he said . . . Well, I don't want to tell you what he said, but now he's bleeding himself to death." The boy was babbling. Charlie could not have shut him up if he'd wanted to.

"Blood or no blood, he can't come in here. No way. No, sir." Charlie Symonds stepped back so smartly that he almost trampled the boy, who'd come up close behind him. "You gotta get this man on over to the other side of the building. This is the entrance to the coloreds-only emergency room—cain't you read?—and ain't no white folks can come in this way. We cain't touch 'em. I'm not gonna do it."

"Of course I can read," said the boy, offended.

Butter Bob now took it on himself to step up between the child and the truck he'd driven in on.

"Get on around to the other side," he said, and pointed. "Go on, now, get. They made the rules, and they got to be followed. I for one ain't losing my job over some white man. He's not dying in here on my time."

They heard a moan from inside the truck. Charlie couldn't tell if the bleeding man had heard them or not. It didn't matter. Rules were rules. White folks had to abide by segregation just as much as black folks did.

The child stood still for a moment, looking from one tall black man to the other, but even at ten—a country boy dressed in overalls and a checkered shirt—he was smart enough not to waste any more of his time arguing here. Without another word he scooted back into his truck and turned the key in the ignition. Naturally, the motor sputtered and refused to start. The boy released the key, kicked the damn floorboard, then tried once again to fire the truck. This time the motor whined, but still it didn't hold. Charlie saw the boy slide a glance over at the white man and see what the hospital attendants had already dutifully noted—that the blood oozing from Billy Ray Puckett's chest had hardened and turned black. This was not a good sign. They all knew dying when they saw it. The boy, like just about everybody else down in some poor backwoods, had probably been killing to eat since he was five. Probably he wasn't superstitious and didn't believe in haints and coming-back people and all, but under no circumstances would he want to be stuck with a dead man, especially a dead white man, in his daddy's truck. He was starting to suspect there might be a whipping lurking in all this for him. Charlie could read this recognition in his eyes.

"Shit," the boy said under his breath. He tried the key again, and this time—thank goodness—the engine flared. The attendants jumped back as the boy jerked the truck around the side of the building toward a new-looking entrance that reigned at the end of a paved parking lot. It sat less than fifty yards from the door he'd first pulled up to, but to the boy its lights and its calm brightness had taken on all the luster of the New Jerusalem.

The boy's name was Willie B. Tate Jr., although he was known as Critter by everybody but himself. He was exactly ten years old and would have to give his name, his given address, and his age—and worse, his daddy's name, *his* given address, and *his* age—eight more times before his ordeal was ended. And while he was still a little ways away from comprehending the true meaning of that old expression "No good deed goes unpunished," comprehension was coming, and it was coming fast.

Critter stopped his daddy's truck for the second time, got out, and ran up to yet another emergency-room entrance. This door was wide and modern, built to hustle people efficiently inside. Looking up, Critter read the little sign that said Whites Only. He knew that a Whites Only sign meant exactly what it said—it was serious business—and he paused, but this was no time to fiddle around and get literal. Too late for that now. There was a man leaking blood all on the inside of his daddy's truck, his daddy's source of livelihood. Critter picked up his courage and thrust forward. He headed straight to the two women who were staring at him bubble-eyed from behind the nurses' station.

"Ma'am, I'm sorry, but I need some help. Mr. Puckett done shot himself, and I drove him here." Critter was proud to hear that his voice did not shake. It was the only part of him that didn't.

One of the women inched a beady gaze down him. The look was meant to browbeat far stronger souls than the dark little one she had currently before her, and she had it down pat.

"Boy," she said, "cain't you read? This part of the hospital is for white folks only—and that means *only white folks*. Get on back around the corner where you belong."

She was a heavyset woman, and she'd been cooling herself off on this hot night with a palm fan. She motioned Critter away with this as the other nurse looked on, smirked, and shook her white-capped head. *My goodness! These people! Must be all that civil rights nonsense in the air.*

Pointedly they turned away and started talking to each other again, as though by ignoring him they might get this pesky colored child to remember his place and get on gone.

But Critter had no intention of going anyplace anymore. He had his daddy's anger to think about, and there was nobody, black or white, who could intimidate Willie Tate Jr. more than his daddy. Willie Tate Sr. was a big black man whose hand tended to get a little heavy when he was teaching his son a lesson. Critter had to get Billy Ray Puckett out of that Ford truck before he up and died in it. The boy did not even want to think what would happen to him then. There was not good blood between the Tates and the Pucketts.

*Stupid dumb-ass. I told him he was doing it all wrong.*

Aloud he said, "Yes, ma'am, I can read. That's why I brought Mr. Billy Ray on around over here. He's a white man." Critter added, "Ma'am," again for good measure.

This got their attention, if just barely. Critter watched as one of the nurses, the skinnier one, shrugged, eased slowly across the lobby, then strolled on out the door and over to the truck. Three attendants had come up to see this little no-account colored boy get just what his uppity behavior deserved, and one of them followed her, taking his time. Critter waited patiently until he heard the nurse shriek out, "Y'all move your lazy butts on over here and get this man out this truck! Get on, now. Make it lickety-split. This here is a *white* man over here."

The mood in the hospital changed dramatically, and suddenly activity sluiced all around Critter. He gaped wide-eyed as white uniforms appeared out of nowhere, bearing stretchers, everybody acting like they had to be the first one on the scene. Commotion everywhere. Even the telephone started suddenly ringing off the hook. To Critter the whole place had changed into something right off television, one of those shows like *Ben Casey* or *Dr. Kildare*, and he was amazed by it.

The nurse dropped her smart-alecky ways and started sounding urgent. "Better send somebody over to get Dr. Connelly—there's a party at his house tonight, Senator Connelly's up from the legislature. And, Luanne, you probably better go on and put through a call to the sheriff. Looks like this man's been rifle-shot, and the bullet darn near tore him up. Probably made it here in a nick of time."

*And I'm the one brung him in.*

Critter puffed up—a ten-year-old, well aware of his starring role in this unfolding drama and eager to get himself put on the credit line. But rescuing could be thirsty work; little Critter Tate was finding this out as well. People would surely soon want to know what had happened, how he'd got here, and he'd need a wet mouth to get out his tale. He snuck a quick glance around, saw everybody was still rushing, and then angled over to the drinking fountain—Whites Only—where he took himself a man-size swig.

You'd have thought the earth had ruptured. Hero or no hero, this infraction of rule and tradition was not going to pass without notice in Revere, Mississippi. From behind him rang out a sharp, "Child, have you lost your mind?" No need to say more than that.

To Critter the woman's sharp voice sounded eerily like the retort from Billy Ray Puckett's Carcano, and he jumped at the sound of it, just as he had jumped back there in the field. Death coming, and he knew it. He started to shake. Tears welled up in his eyes. Then he focused once again, saw bright lights around him and the Whites Only sign. Things that were familiar to him. He turned, very slowly, and faced the burly night-shift nurse, who had looked straight at him, talked to him, even, then pretended not to see him when he'd first come in. She was all eyes now, though, and they were both staring straight at him, looking at him hard as BB-gun bullets.

"Night crew's just been through cleaning, but I'll have to call down and get them back up here to disinfect that spigot, and they are not going to appreciate that one bit. What's your name, boy?"

"Willie B. Tate Jr., ma'am."

Critter was way into trouble once again, and he knew it. He tried smiling at this huge white woman, while he squinted at the name tag she wore pinned to a lacy white hankie at her impressive bosoms. Miss Lucille M. Bobo, it said. Critter's smile broadened. He showed some teeth, and tried once again. "My name is Willie B. Tate Jr., Miss Lucille."

The woman softened a bit at this show of respect. Obviously, somebody had taught this child some manners. For a moment the two of them, Critter Tate and Miss Lucille Bobo, were an island of civility in the midst of the hustle and the bustle that was Billy Ray Puckett's slow dying. She nodded at him. "Well, just don't you be doing it again."

Lucille Bobo had already made up her mind about what had happened and had made sure the police were dutifully notified, but, like Charlie Symonds, she wanted to have something to say at her own weekly social gathering, in this case a Thursday-evening bridge group held at the house of neighbor—a Presbyterian—out off Highway 69, on Holly Hocks Lane.

*I was standing right there with that little black child. I was the first one heard his whole story.*

"Tate? I didn't know there were any of your people named Tate in Revere?"

By "your people" Miss Lucille meant colored people, and they both knew this.

"I'm not from Revere," said Critter, lighting his most winsome smile directly on her. "Billy Ray Puckett and us lives down in Macon, over near Short Cut Road. I brought him on up from there."

"You mean you drove that rattletrap thing all the way from Macon, Mississippi?" The woman cocked her head, looked out the door. "Why, Macon's close to thirty miles south of here. How old are you, boy?"

"Ten years old," said Critter, yet again.

"Ten years old!" echoed Miss Lucille, brows arching. "And you *drive?*" The word came out *du-raaah-ve*, slow and trisyllabic. Miss Lucille was making her point.

Critter, now the incarnation of misery, nodded. "Tractor mostly. I been doing it since I was seven. But when I saw Billy Ray—I mean, ma'am, when I saw Mr. Puckett laying there and know'd that he'd shot himself, the only thing came to hand was my daddy's truck."

"A colored child able to drive thirty miles," said Miss Lucille, shaking her permanent wave and obviously not believing a word of it. "I never heard such a notion in my life." She layered every vowel she uttered with a strong Alabama-accented *aaah*. She was revving herself up to put this lying Nigra child in his place.

And as if that weren't bad enough, at that very and precise moment the hospital's revolving door started flapping once again, and in walked the sheriff. Critter felt himself starting to really shake. The sheriff could not possibly have anything good to say to anybody named Willie B. Tate Jr., and Critter knew this. The boy had been in Revere barely twenty-five minutes, and already he'd got kicked out of a coloreds-only place by colored folk, ventured into a whites-only place and just about got himself booted out of there, then got caught swigging water from a whites-only water fountain with his coloreds-only lips. Critter watched enough news on WLBN to know what complicated troubles a black boy could get himself into, performing even the most simple of acts. Especially simple, defiant acts. They brought out the cattle prods and the dogs on you for less—at least that's what his folks said about goings-on over in Alabama. When his big sister, Rayette Louise, wanted him to behave, she only had to threaten to call out old Bull Connor, the police chief over in Birmingham, and Critter invariably knuckled down and did what she wanted. After all, Birmingham was just barely over the state line, a mere hop, skip, and a jump away for Bull Conner should his services be needed.

*And,* on top of everything else, Willie Tate Jr. now needed to get to the bathroom. Bad.

The sheriff—a huge guy, "healthy-looking," as Big Mama politely put it—was aiming right for him. Critter couldn't tell about his face, because he was too scared to look up into it, although he knew he'd probably have to once the interrogation began. He just hoped they wouldn't torture him too hard. He didn't want to start crying and disgrace his daddy and his family. Critter's bladder really started to serenade him now, and with a depth of feeling he was not again to fathom until, fifteen years later, he held his first son in his arms, Willie Tate Jr. found himself thinking, *I wish I'd left that damn, stupid, silly-ass, no-reading, Negro-hating peckerwood for dead. Them Pucketts mean nothing but trouble for us black folks, just like my daddy always told me. Why didn't I listen to my daddy when God gave me the chance?*

But it was no good going over that kind of stuff now. Not with Billy Ray Puckett's blood all up in his daddy's truck and Billy Ray himself laid out flat on a stretcher and the night growing long and the sheriff involved.

"Hey, boy, come on over here. I got to ask you a few questions."

"I tried to tell him he was doing it all wrong." Critter started babbling out his side of things before he even got near the sheriff. "I tried to tell him that stand wouldn't hold together if he did it like that."

Critter was still too scared to raise his eyes, but even from his low vantage point he could see that the sheriff was wearing both a gun and a billy club. The boy imagined he must have left the cattle prod and the raging German shepherd in the car. They'd be close to hand, though. He'd want them nearby so he could get to them when they were needed.

It was a toss-up now whether Critter's bladder would go before or after the torture began when—Blessed Assurance!—there was another ruckus at the door, and it opened up and everybody, including the sheriff, stopped what they were doing and looked that direction once again.

"It's Dr. Connelly!" whooped out Miss Lucille. In her excitement she forgot the little colored boy beside her, which was certainly fine with Mr. Willie Tate Jr., who hoped the sheriff would soon do the same. "Dr. Connelly. He'll take care of all this mess."

Critter was glad that somebody would. He looked over and saw Billy Ray still stretched out on his hospital gurney; in all the commotion nobody had thought to move him out of the hallway. *That's strange*, thought Critter. *They shouldn't just leave him. Even Mr. Billy Ray—they ought to see to him, give him some dignity.* The doctor must have thought so, too.

"What's this man still doing here?" Dr. Connelly's voice was quiet, but there was enough authority in it to bring immediate hush to the hallway. After all, thanks to his daddy, Cooper Connelly owned Doctors Hospital, and everybody knew it.

A young nurse cleared her throat. "We're waiting for his next of kin to come up and sign him into the hospital. This boy"—a curt nod in Critter's direction— "says his name is Billy Ray Puckett, that he comes from round Macon, but there's no name like that in the Noxubee County book. You know how folks are down there. We're lucky if they got six phones among them. And that's talking about white folks. The sheriff sent one of the deputies to scout out his people. Can't do a thing without their permission. Can't start to work on him. It's the law."

"Don't matter about the law," said the doctor, who knew what he was talking about. "Look at all the blood. This man should have already been prepped for surgery. Please get him on into the examining room. Cut his clothes off. Call my team while I take a look at him. I want my OR ready, stat."

Miss Lucille shrugged her shoulders and said real low, "Well, you own the hospital, and it's your daddy's town."

If the doctor heard this, he gave no notice. He strode straight over to Billy Ray Puckett, his newest patient. As he did, the waters, so to speak, parted around him, and when they flowed together again, Critter had managed to edge up close. He watched as Cooper Connelly bent over Billy Ray. The doctor's handsome brow furrowed, but he didn't touch his patient, not yet; instead he talked to the young nurse, one Critter had not seen until then, who hovered at his side. He asked her questions. Scissors, antiseptic, gauze, other attendants arrived at the doctor's side as though by magic; the doctor asked for none of them. Billy Ray was unconscious now; he did not say a word. Neither did the doctor. Cooper Connelly motioned, and Billy Ray Puckett was whisked efficiently out of sight. His doctor did not immediately follow.

Critter was glad about that. He tugged at him.

"I'm the one brought Mr. Billy Ray in," he said. "I was there. I know all what happened."

Connelly hunkered down, just like Charlie Symonds had done before him, until he and Critter were looking at each other eye to eye. He did not seem at all amazed at what this little colored child was telling him.

"Brought him in," repeated Critter. "All by myself."

"Well, that was a mighty fine thing you did, then," said Dr. Cooper Connelly. "You probably saved this man's life."

*Saved this man's life.* Critter beamed at that, ear to ear. He gave this wise man his full attention.

Growing up in the country, living there, Critter Tate had never seen anything resembling Cooper Connelly before in his life. Tall and strong-looking, without being muscular, dressed in a black jacket made out of some shiny-dull material, with a bow tie and a wide burgundy belt stretched over a starched white shirt. And that smell! It was heavenly and reminded Critter of the way his mama smelled on Sunday mornings as she got herself ready to spend the day over at Holiness Chapel. Critter was used to men coming in from a hard day in the fields, men who went into the washroom stinking sweat and emerged humanized again by nothing fancier than Dial soap. Anything else would have been considered sissified to them and caused a great deal of gentle, and not-so-gentle, speculation among the neighbors. But Cooper Connelly didn't look like a sissy to Critter Tate. With his crisp blond hair and blue eyes, he looked almost godlike, like something or someone you read about in a book—though Critter would be smart enough never to say this out loud at home. Opinions as to white people might vary according to time and occasion within the Tate household, but any hint of blasphemy was always speedily punished. Critter didn't care. Cooper Connelly's was the only friendly face he'd seen all night, black or white, and he thought Dr. Connelly might be the first one to finally ask him what had really happened, and Critter needed to tell it. He needed to sort through things. He needed to talk to somebody about Billy Ray's shooting, because there was something that troubled him, something that wasn't quite right. The boy thought he could get this man to listen, make him understand that all this had happened because Billy Ray couldn't read. Critter, taught by his father to be responsible, swallowed hard and opened his mouth.

But Miss Lucille turned out to be quicker than he was.

"I cannot believe my own eyes! Boy, what you still doing here!" She whirled indignantly to the sheriff, who had been hovering at a respectful distance. "Mr. Trotter, remove this child from these premises right now! Cain't y'all see we have an emergency going on? We cannot have random children underfoot! Dr. Connelly needs to get in and examine his patient!"

And indeed Dr. Connelly did get up and move off, leaving Nurse Lucille's as the voice of command.

Without further ado, Critter found himself once again—and definitively this time, as it happened—thrust out into the dark night air. Brought face-to-face with his daddy's truck.

If anything, it appeared even more beat-up-looking than it had been when he started out. Was that possible? Unfortunately, yes, it was. A new, deep dent on the left front fender radiated trouble. Critter knew it would not be missed, would not blend into the general misshapen landscape. Worse yet, it had been the sheriff's car that had done this terrible deed. Critter knew this because it was still sitting there, bright as day—a shiny black-and-white sentinel blocking the truck in. And there was something else. A slip of official-looking paper waved back and forth against the cracked windshield, beckoning him. Critter squinted closer. A ticket! He had brought his daddy's truck to rest in the hospital's emergency no-parking zone!

He wobbled down until his butt touched the cold flagstones of the entrance portico. He would have sunk on into the ground if he could have, not stopping until he came through in China, but he knew he didn't dare move that far away, because pretty soon now he'd have to go on back into that shitty hospital, find the shitty sheriff, and get him to move his shitty car out of the way so that Critter could get on home and face the whupping that surely waited for him there. He had ruined the family's only means of livelihood, and not even his mama, sweet as she was, would be able to save him. Willy Tate Sr. would surely feel it his duty to kill his only son.

As his bowels started to twitch, Willie Tate Jr. felt exactly like Job.

Right then Critter thought he heard someone say low, "Everything's going to be just fine, just fine. Nothing at all to worry about." But he was too concentrated on his own misery, on his impending death and on his daddy, to pay much attention.

"Critter, boy, what in God's earth are you doing up here in Revere? Your folks must be worried sick. Your daddy's gonna beat your butt."

Critter hadn't heard the man come up behind him, couldn't see him, but he knew who this man was, and he jumped up, instantly full of hope. At last there was somebody who knew him, somebody who could handle things. All his life Critter had been watching this man—this *particular* man—work miracles. If anyone could save him, this man could. The boy turned around, his face now wreathed in its first genuine smile of the night.

Reese Jackson was coming down the whites-only entrance of Doctors Hospital toward him, and for just a second Critter thought he saw the other man, the one they called Dr. Connelly, watching them. But Critter was through thinking about Dr. Connelly. It was Reese Jackson who could actually save him, and he knew it.

"I said what are you doing here?" Dr. Jackson was not used to having to say the same thing twice.

His voice had grown irritated, as it always did when he had to repeat anything. Spencer Reese Jackson was venerated in this part of Mississippi—its only black doctor. But he was not known for his patience. Critter started talking fast. "I was out in the fields, and I was just about to go out and hunt me down some squirrel when I saw Mr. Billy Ray putting up his deer stand on some of my daddy's land. You know that meant trouble. I went on over and wanted to talk to him and I saw—"

*What was it he saw?*

Memory bubbled up again, forcefully this time, almost making it to the surface of his mind. Critter stopped. He frowned. One little thing niggled at him, had niggled at him off and on since that terrible, slow-motion moment when he'd run across to the collapsed deer stand and discovered white-trash Billy Ray Puckett, stinking of cheap stillwhiskey, fallen out over his own damn gun. Bleeding. Dying.

"Dr. Reese," Critter began, "I think there's something wrong."

But, like everybody else at Doctors Hospital in Revere, Mississippi, Reese Jackson was in no mood to listen to a little black child's speculations. He reached a strong, firm hand under the strap of Critter's bib overalls, almost dragging him down the last few steps into the glow of the hospital's brightly lit parking lot.

"You run on over to my house and have Miss Lyle Dean give you something to eat. She'll let your people know where you are. Tell her I said to send Rufus on down to do it. Tell her I said you should probably sleep on up with Skip tonight. The two of you haven't played together all summer. Tell her to tell your daddy I'll take care of getting you and this truck back down to Macon first thing in the morning. Tell her to tell your folks that."

Critter nodded and kept on nodding, much relieved. Dr. Reese was in charge now, and everything would finally be set right. The child let go of everything else except this sure knowledge. Besides, he'd get to spend the night with his best friend, Skippy, and there was always good food waiting for him at Miss Lyle Dean's house. She'd fix up something strange, something Critter had never eaten before, with recipes she'd brought with her from up north. He'd finally get to go to the bathroom, too, without having to mess on himself like a baby. And at this moment those were the only two things that really mattered. Critter straightened himself up, brushed off his overalls. He started to feel like a hero once again.

To his credit, before he rushed off into the safe night, he did look back one last time for Cooper Connelly, who might need Critter's help to set his patient, Billy Ray Puckett, straight. He'd been the only one to seem really *interested* in what Critter had to say. But Dr. Connelly had disappeared, and his hospital now seemed deserted. Besides, Dr. Reese, visibly impatient by this point, was pushing him on. In the end Critter put his hand in the hand of the man who had "brought him into the world," as Big Mama phrased it, forgot all about Billy Ray Puckett, and ran on over to Reese Jackson's house. Just like he'd been told to do, because now that Dr. Reese was here, Critter knew that everything was going to be just fine.

# Chapter 2

REESE JACKSON HEARD ABOUT Billy Ray Puckett's death on the morning news two days later. Just about everybody else in Revere, black or white, had already known about it for hours by the time Dr. Jackson found out. Folks got up early, and the gossip circuit had been wearing out the telephone lines since dawn. *My goodness! Well, anybody could have seen it coming. Trash like that! Living out in the woods, in a trailer! Wife and kids and all! I bet he never stepped into a church in his life!* Reese wasn't much of a churchgoing man himself, and he could certainly sympathize, at least with this last.

The official report went out on the five-minute, early-morning television news. Reese Jackson heard it there—but just barely. Nobody had bothered to call him up and tell him. Dr. Spencer Reese Jackson was a god to the people around him, and everybody just assumed that somebody else had gotten to him first. Or that he already knew. Been told by the Spirit. This last was more than a conjecture, considering who his next-door neighbor was.

But the fact is, Reese almost missed it. As usual, he was too busy keeping an eye on his wife, Lyle Dean—known as Deanie to everybody but him—as she snuck a quick glance out the breakfast-room window and on over toward Madame Melba, busy out with her roses. Melba waved back fingers that had been freshly tipped in Revlon's Cherries in the Snow, as they were every morning, transmitting the unspoken message that, within the next hour, once Reese was safely out of the house and about his business, the two of them would get together.

They did this each and every day and, like blind fools, hoped that Deanie's husband would not notice. But Reese Jackson had a very precise sense of his surroundings. He rarely missed a thing, especially if that thing was going on in his own house and involved his own family and its acquaintance with Miss Melba next door.

Deanie knew this, but she couldn't help herself, and Reese knew *this*; she was enticed by Melba and her gossipy ways with the gluttonous self-destruction of a june bug drawn to a fig tree. When she turned back and caught his warning head shake, Lyle Dean Jackson had the good sense to blush. But they both—husband and wife—knew that red cheeks did not mean reformation, not as far as Madame Melba was concerned. Still, Reese was bound to lecture and Deanie to spar back.

They had opened their respective mouths to do just that when, luckily, their ten-year-old son, Skip, called out through a mouthful of Trix cereal, "Hey, isn't that Critter?"—drawing everybody's attention, including his daddy's, to the television screen. Much to his mother's relief.

The television was housed in its own glass-fronted cabinet, just beneath Reese's basketball trophies from high school and college and the everyday dishes, which were by Noritake. Their small pink flowers exactly matched the wallpaper, the plastic seats, and the frilly curtains at the window of the Jacksons' sunny breakfast room. Reese Jackson had grown up on a dusty road down in the Delta, and he sure did want some brightness around him now, and some color. Only one thing seemed out of place in this lovely, perfect room, and that was Skippy's crutch. His mother kept it propped against the wall in case he might need it. He never had. His daddy did not like him using his crutches.

"This suite was the most exclusive, expensive, out-of-this-world thing in the whole of the Furniture Mart down in Jackson. True provincial French," Deanie had proudly announced to her family, before she learned better. With all the brightness surrounding it, they still had an old black-and-white in the breakfast room. Deanie had brought up the subject of color television once, maybe twice, but hadn't really gotten around to pushing for it yet. You had to be careful with Reese. He could be a generous man, and he was devoted to his family, but you had to catch him just right. This was something she repeated to Melba all the time. He'd worked hard for what he had and didn't want to overspend it. Part of him still lived in the Delta, and the rest of him was determined not to go back. At breakfast, which was usually the only meal he shared with his family, his medical bag held pride of place on the chair right beside him. The medical bag had served as a passport, and Reese was known for being good to what had been good to him.

Deanie could tell that black-and-white wasn't going to make a bit of difference today, not with this story. She looked over at Reese.

"Turn the sound up for me, son." His deep, rich voice demanded obedience, and he generally got it. Skip jumped to attention but, as usual, just a tad too late. Poor Skippy. Before he could reach over, his best friend, Critter Tate, had disappeared.

Floyd Sobczak—pronounced "Subject"—was WLBN's all-around newscaster. He took his position in town seriously, took pride in getting the news out to folks. And you could tell he had a case on his hands today. A real tearjerker. Six people—all ages, all sizes, all eyes swollen, all so white they looked like snow about to melt, and all huddled together within his protective shadow. Probably some underpaid photographer had called himself arranging a scene of Southern misfortune. A grieving family. Struck down, as it would turn out, by fate. Reese, paying close attention now, first picked out a mama and a daddy, then what looked like an older daughter and four scrawny little children. The unblinking eyes staring straight out at the wealthy Dr. Jackson were that pale, milky color that always seemed to bring poverty to mind. Actually, this picture was deceiving, the truth not quite what it appeared to be. And Reese Jackson knew it.

"Peckerwoods," whispered Deanie.

"That is ignorant prejudice!" cried out Brendan, their daughter, right on cue. She was sixteen years old and not willing to let a single word Lyle Dean said go unchallenged. Her proud parents took this as part of the expensive boarding-school education they were paying for and accepted it, even reveled in it. Still, it could be disconcerting.

"If a white person said that about a Negro," Brendan continued, up on her high horse now, "you and Daddy'd be beatin' it on up Highway 45, making straight for the NAACP."

Brendan was a lovely girl; she took after her mother, and so she was very pretty. But she was still young enough that her parents, her school, her position protected her. She would learn how things really were soon enough. Of this Lyle Dean was certain.

"Not if they said it within the privacy of their own home," perked out her mother. "Anybody can say anything they want to, as long as they say it in private."

"Hush, y'all!" shouted Reese. "I want to hear this."

The Jackson children and their mother, their mouths dropped open, swiveled as one toward the head of their household. Alarmed. Reese Jackson could be stern and stiff, but he rarely ever raised his voice to any one of them, and certainly not at breakfast. He didn't need to. Normally Reese paid no attention to morning television; he was devoted to the sacred, silent reading of the day's *Times Commercial*. Pages of it lapped all over the table; his wife and children had to continually move them off the dishes so they could eat. Any change in Daddy Reese's behavior did not bode well, especially if he were frowning, as he was surely frowning today. Something must be up. They followed his lead, as they did in so many things, and fixed their attention on the television. Skip reached with stealthy, pudgy fingers for yet another piece of toast. Brendan left off eating. Both children studied the barometer of their daddy's face and decided that storms were brewing. Maybe big ones.

But over what? They stared, confused, at the television set. These were poor people, poor *white* people, and there usually wasn't a lot of interest in or sympathy for them within the Jackson household, especially from Reese, who had suffered quite a bit at white hands and still did. That he was paying so much attention to this story was a puzzle to his family. Now they all followed his lead yet again and frowned.

One thing about being poor and black was that you wore your excuse right out there for everybody to see. All you had to do was look in the mirror, and there it was—a reason for all life's problems staring back as you, big as you please. The same thing didn't work if you were white. If you were poor and white, you didn't have any excuse for failure in this world, and everybody knew it, even other poor white people.

"I said turn up the sound."

"But what are people like this doing on TV?" asked Skippy of his daddy, but looking at his mama.

"Shut up," said Reese Jackson—another first—"and we'll all find out."

It took a minute for his family to realize what Reese already knew: that the oldest girl was really the mama. She sat side by side with another woman—her mother-in-law, as it turned out—in front of the studio's cheap-looking silver-colored curtain. Each held a quiet baby. In fact, nobody fidgeted a bit. They all stared into the camera with the intensity you normally saw in faded daguerreotype prints. The lone man wore pressed trousers and a matching khaki shirt. A workingman's clothes; you could see the script of a name on his pocket. Beside him were two older children, one boy and one very skinny girl, who clutched at whatever piece of their mama or their granny came to hand. They had obviously been carefully dressed. No little girl, even in Mississippi, wore an enormous ribbon threaded through her hair on a school day; no little boy sported a bow tie. The women—bless their hearts—had on light cotton dresses, which, like white, were not the kinds of things one put on after Labor Day weekend. Reese, married to the *Vogue*-reading, Memphis-shopping Lyle Dean Jackson, knew this.

Floyd Sobczak was speaking. "Tragedy struck two days ago in Macon, Mississippi, when Billie Ray Puckett, late of Wicket Mill Road, fell from a flawed deer tree-stand onto his 6.5 Carcano. The rifle discharged a single bullet into his side. Mr. Puckett was rushed to Doctors Hospital here in Revere and was immediately operated upon by our own eminent Cooper Livingston Connelly but passed on unexpectedly early this morning. We've asked Mrs. Puckett here to tell us . . ."

What really and truly amazed Reese—and he would think over this again and again—was that none of these people seemed particularly surprised by what had happened to them. Stunned, maybe, but not surprised. He looked from one face to another, trying to find an emotion or reaction he could understand, and found neither. There was none of the crying and screaming and weeping that normally accompanied death, whether it was black or white, in rural Mississippi. Not even a trace of feeling from these children's mother, who must surely be aware of the quagmire she'd now be called upon to navigate, and without the aid of a supporting man.

Deanie must have seen exactly what Reese saw. "Peckerwoods," she repeated, as though this explained everything to both him and herself. "Different from us."

"No fight left in them," commented her husband, a born scrapper.

They looked up at each other, shook their heads, and smiled briefly. Their disagreement was over; Madame Melba forgotten. They'd been married a long time, and Reese Jackson loved his wife.

Floyd Sobczak turned with solicitation toward the young widow. "Mrs. Puckett, could you please tell us what happened with your husband? Take it easy now. Just use your own words."

What "own words"? Reese wondered. The woman didn't look like the kind who really owned anything, not even the thoughts in her head.

It appeared as though Mrs. Puckett herself might share his opinion. She started, and then her shoulders hunched. The Jacksons watched gravity slump them down again. Next she tried edging a little away from the microphone, but this proved just as futile. Floyd Sobczak was right on her. This was *his* story of the day, and he would not be denied it.

Mrs. Puckett finally conceded. "Well, I don't rightly know. Billy Ray didn't come home for supper, and I thought . . . I mean, I just figured . . . he'd gone straight on out deer hunting. He did that sometimes. At least lately he did it."

Ruth Ann Puckett had a sweet voice, but with an accent you had to have grown up a little farther south than Jefferson-Lee County to understand. Even Reese had a hard time with it. But she looked like a nice enough woman. As they leaned in closer, the Jacksons could see this. Of course, it was very important that she appear to be kind, sweet-spoken, and nice—the very picture of frail, defenseless southern womanhood. No one would donate to the upkeep of a whiner or a whore—and what was going on, on this broadcast, was most definitely about money. Reese Jackson knew this, his family knew it, and everybody else in the three-county area who didn't already would soon know it as well.

Not only had Billy Ray Puckett died last night, but he'd taken their livelihood with him. Now this little Puckett family needed help, and they needed help bad. This was an integral part of Floyd Sobczak's story, the part that would give it appeal.

"But you didn't *know* he'd gone hunting, did you?" Floyd said. He was angling shamelessly toward the pathetic. Sympathy always made for good television. "Hunting at night being against the law and all. He didn't *tell* you he planned to sit on out there with his gun, with it loaded. He could still have been just working on his deer stand, for all you knew."

"Yes, that's right. I didn't really know what he was doing." Again gravity responded to a faint lift in Ruth Ann's shoulders. "He didn't *say* he planned to stay out there once the stand was up. Maybe he decided during the day. He wanted to do things his own way. Didn't like a lot of questions. Didn't like what he called 'interference.' Last time he lost his job was when we moved down from the hills and over outside Macon, near his folks. There weren't that many people living near us, only a couple of colored families. He could do what he wanted out there."

Sobczak said, "Your husband wasn't working at the time of his demise?" He was milking this piece for all it was worth.

"He'd been hauling pulpwood to the lumberyard, but y'all know about the trouble been goin' on with that. Striking and all. Not been much real work since they started up that new union. Things were supposed to get better though. In the end." Ruth Ann Puckett paused.

Beside him Reese felt his wife twitch. Lyle Dean could hardly contain her excitement. It was Madame Melba up between them again, and Deanie had to concentrate real hard to keep her eyes from wandering over to the window and on out the door. Obviously, she was itching anew to hightail it over to Melba's to get the inside scoop on this pulpwood workers' mess. Because of her last boarder, a white boy down from Dartmouth College, who was running that volunteer school over in Macon, Miss Melba—as Reese called her to her face—knew all the inside scoop on Revere's latest unfolding civil-rights drama: poor whites and colored folk striking together. The mayor, the city council, the county board of supervisors, and all the white business leaders acted like they were up face-to-face with Armageddon. "What else could he do?" said Ruth Ann Puckett from the television screen. Reese thought the whole thing was a pathetic mess.

"What else could he do?" echoed Brendan, her tone entirely different from a few minutes before. Now that they had served as a means for her to put her mother in her place, Brendan Lenore Jackson was rapidly losing patience with these people. "He could work, like the rest of us. *That's* what he could do."

After college Brendan planned to go on to law school and then into practice—before she settled down with a baby or two—but so far, at least according to her daddy's recollection, she'd never yet worked a day in her life.

Reese waved her to silence, wanting to hear more, but, as it turned out, Miss Ruth Ann had little else of interest to say about the sudden and totally unexpected death of her husband. She tried once or twice, stammering over words and phrases, making a mess of things, before a smooth Floyd Sobczak stepped in. His seconds were ticking.

"Butter wouldn't melt in that man's mouth when he's after an exclusive or he's got a good story," said cute Deanie, referring to Floyd Sobczak, "but Melba told me he's the stingiest damn man in Revere."

"And she should know," Reese replied, "considering her main occupation."

His wife let that silver bullet slip right on past.

The drama continued, Floyd Sobczak looking newly aggrieved. "At seven P.M. that night, a wounded Billy Ray Puckett was driven by ten-year-old Willie Tate Jr., the son of a Macon neighbor, to Doctors Hospital. Although he was admitted and operated upon immediately, Mr. Puckett never regained consciousness and died without saying good-bye to those he loved, the people who needed, and still need, his support the most. His family."

The newscaster paused as the camera moved in for a close-up of Ruth Ann Puckett. This proved to be a mistake. The new widow shook her head as her eyes flashed and narrowed. For an instant, Reese Jackson had the alarming sensation she was staring directly at him.

Just a shadow of rebellion, but even the cameraman caught it. He swiftly shifted the focus of his lens onto an always-reliable Floyd

Sobczak. "Your television station, WLBN, has started a community fund to help Mrs. Puckett and her family through this extremely difficult time. Y'all know what's been going on down in Macon with the pulp haulers and their strike. If any of you would care to contribute in helping to better this poor young woman's situation . . ."

A sponsoring bank and account number were mentioned, a mailing address given. WLBN would see that all donations were passed on.

The end of the segment was fast approaching. Floyd Sobczak gave a last bit of information about their pitiful plight—"the eldest child barely ten years old!"—and twisted his face into even more of an appropriately sorrowful expression.

That's when disaster struck. On some impulse—misguided, as it turned out—he reached down to pat the oldest girl's head. It was just a gesture. She was scrawny, like her mother and her brother and her baby sisters. Reese did not expect much of a response. But when that hand and its unspoken condescension descended upon her, that little thing reached right up and slapped it away. The microphone picked the slap up loud and clear.

She shocked Floyd Sobczak silly. He remained stock-still, his fingers tangled in the rayon tiara of a bow that had crowned the girl's hair. He tried to be civil—after all, he'd just spent one minute and fifty-eight seconds painting these people as needy and helpless—but, desperate over airtime, he finally had to just go on and attempt to yank his hand away. This only made bad matters worse. The thick, pale ribbon must have been two feet long if it was an inch. Now that it was unraveled, it was much bigger than the girl's little, peaked face—dwarfed it, even. Until the only thing you could see glaring out were two mean-looking, spite-spitting, contempt-holding eyes. All the Jacksons gasped as one. Reese was staring right at the mother, curious as to what she would do. Reese knew he would have been very upset, somebody manhandling his child like that. Lyle Dean, too.

But Ruth Ann Puckett continued to look out straight into the camera. She even tried a little smile. She did not even glance at her daughter. Catastrophe again, her passivity seemed to be saying. Anything could happen. Nothing for it. Along with practically every other household in Revere, the Jacksons watched, mesmerized, as the skinny little white girl, who probably answered to some silly name like Scout or Ruby Rose, reached up and very slowly and very deliberately pulled the ribbon back from her face. She hated Floyd Sobczak. You could tell it.

WLBN rejoined the *Today* show immediately after that.

"That girl's going to cost them folks some money for sure," said Deanie. She was in awe of such bad manners.

Still, the Puckett family's plight, though briefly interesting, was not vital to the Jacksons and their plans for the day, and they were soon back at their orange juice, their newspaper, and their cold eggs. The *Today* show began to air a segment on plans for an upcoming walk on the moon.

"Suicide," said Brendan as she reached across the breakfast table to turn the sound down again. "I bet that's what he was up to."

"What?" Reese's voice sharpened up once more.

Skip plucked up his courage. "Bren said that Puckett man probably tried to commit suicide," he repeated. "He sure had reason enough to do it, with that wife and all those kids. No real help from his parents. No money."

"And no education," chimed in Brendan. Education was the acme of Jackson achievement. "When he fell off that deer stand, he was doomed before he hit the ground."

"*Dead* before he hit it," corrected her daddy. "Billy Ray Puckett was a walking disaster. He'd been brain-dead for years."

"You knew him?" Brendan was deep into a row of vitamin pills. She swallowed eight of them religiously every morning—C's, E's, and every B type known to man—even though Reese kept telling her they didn't do her one bit of good. "He was white, though. Couldn't have been one of your patients."

"He wasn't my patient. But I might have seen him once or twice, maybe hanging around the hospital," answered her father as he reached across to snap his medical bag shut. "You know how everybody knows everybody in Revere."

This was not quite the truth, but it was true enough so that nobody could really argue against it. Products of the South, though not all children of it, the three other Jacksons nodded their heads in complete agreement.

*Poor white folks.*

And yet—once again Deanie saw that little girl with her wide, crowning bow. Once again she saw that child reach up and snatch her head away from Floyd Sobczak's patronage. Deanie smiled, giggled almost, and then looked up to see her handsome, successful, Mississippi-bred husband staring over at her.

"Nothing," she answered to his unasked question, then quickly amended this to, "I wasn't thinking anything at all."

But of course she *was* thinking. *That one's trouble. Revere's not heard the last from that child, and that's a damn fact.*

Reese wiped his mouth with a folded cloth napkin, which he then precisely positioned back beside his plate. "Skip, get your books, and I'll drive you up the hill. This is the first day of school, and I want you to be on time for it." Something he wouldn't be if he were left waiting for his mother.

Lyle Dean had never been on time for anything in her life. "Two weeks late for her own birthing," Miss Hinkty, Reese's own dear, dead mother had once said. "Been running to catch up ever since." While it was true that Miss Hinkty had always harbored a powerful-great prejudice against Lyle Dean—Reese was her only boy, and he'd made good, and there was no woman on earth could be the match for him—still, you had to admit she had a point.

But Reese never displayed disappointment in Deanie before his children, at least not with words. He shrugged into his suit jacket, jerking it away just as Deanie reached over to help him. He realized, too late, that he'd offended her and hadn't meant to do this. He never meant to hurt anybody, especially his family. It's just he had so much to think of, so much on his mind. There were a lot of people depending on Reese Jackson.

Brendan blew a kiss at her daddy and headed for the spiral staircase. She was impatient to pack up the last few things she needed so she'd be all ready tomorrow, early, when her mother drove her up to Greensboro. She was starting her last year at Palmer Memorial Institute. Reese loved his home state, had given up a lot to come back to it, but he knew that his daughter couldn't wait to be out of Mississippi. Even North Carolina—proclaimed by an article in *Ebony* magazine to be the most prejudiced state in the Union—was better than here.

Reese hurried out the door, and Skip rushed out just behind his father, clutching at both his gym bag and his new gym uniform, not that he'd get much use out of either one of them. Unfortunately, Deanie's own baby boy wasn't much of a sportsman.

"Well, I guess I'll go on up and get dressed," Deanie said to the passing breeze. Reese was already behind the wheel of his enormous, gleaming Lincoln Continental—bought newer and bigger and better each year. He gunned the engine. She waved him off over the pots of geraniums on her back porch, watched him disappear through the extravagant blossoms of their backyard rosebushes. She did not allow herself even one little peek toward the fence and Miss Melba. She waited patiently while the car rolled down the carefully bricked driveway, out the elaborate wrought-iron fence, and into the rugged streets that lay just beyond. She smiled and waved and waved and smiled. She kept her face just as bright and clear as the sunshine that streamed over it. Just as brassy, too. He might not seem to be paying attention, but Deanie knew her husband. Reese Jackson never missed a thing.

"Lots to do today," she added, to no one in particular.

At least that much was true.

The moment Reese's car was truly and completely out of sight, she was running up the stairs, picking clothes out of her closet, getting ready to go over to Melba's next door.

# Chapter 3

MADAME MELBA OBRENSKI, late of New Orleans, opened the door to her little cottage to such a searing of morning sunshine that it forced her eyes shut.

"Almost into October and must still be a hundred degrees." She never had been one for the heat. Eyes closed down tight, it was what she heard and what she smelled that told her she was really outside. *Her* outside. Mockingbirds sang through the giant magnolia tree that was the bane of her garden, bees buzzed through her various rosebushes. She could even hear butterfly wings brushing against the leaves of her late hydrangeas, or at least she thought she could. Melba breathed deeply, taking in a scent that had the fine kick of good bourbon. All this activity. All in *her* garden. *Hers. Hers. Hers.*

Nothing—not one whiff—from that manicured dreadfulness Reese Jackson had built up, then walled up, next door. As if anybody wanted to see what was going on over there, or cared what was growing. Who ever heard of purple tulips? Who ever heard of orange cabbage roses that looked like they were made of Naugahyde and smelled like it, too. Melba knew this because she'd nosed on over there on an occasion when she knew that Reese Jackson wouldn't be around to catch her and gain the satisfaction from having done so.

Melba and Reese Jackson did not get along.

Her cat-green eyes open now, Melba raised a fair hand to shade them from the glare coming out of the east. Barely 8:00 A.M. and already a scorcher! In her own garden, all was in order. She kept it old-fashioned, and she kept it lush. Yellow mums gave way to flashes of daylilies and an occasional bright flame of geranium, skillfully placed. Hydrangeas that had managed to hold on in the heat nuzzled against the last, lusty gasp of a gardenia bush. Her garden would flower on like this through autumn, even on into deep winter. If there was a flower able to grow anywhere in Revere, it would be showing itself at Melba Obrenski's. She saw to that.

But Melba had more on her mind than daffodils this morning. Reese needed waving off, and she was right there to do it. She raised her sparkling fingertips.

"Bye, Skip," she called.

"Bye, Miss Melba."

"And bye to you, Mr. Reese."

Always "Mr.," never "Dr.," because Melba knew this got on Reese Jackson's last nerve.

Yet there was nothing for it; he had to answer, had to be polite. He couldn't be mean as he wanted to be with his son, the miniature Spencer Reese Jackson–in–the–making, standing right there beside him, all ears.

"Good morning, Miss Melba. Hope you have a productive day."

Just knowing she wouldn't.

"I'll be sure to do that."

Melba kept her smile stunningly bright.

She'd been born lucky—or at least lucky enough not to be given over to useless ruminations—and to this day she remained a brightly perky woman, a woman with an exceptionally knowing eye. It was quick enough this morning to notice just how swiftly Reese Jackson bundled Skip into that huge white Lincoln and careened off. And how nervous Skippy looked, trying to surreptitiously stuff a last corner of toast into his mouth and wipe the crumbs off before his daddy saw.

Melba nodded. "Something's up." Her late geraniums, bloodred splashes in the garden, nodded on the morning breeze right along with her.

"Wouldn't want to be little Skippy," she added, "in more ways than one."

Her flowers agreed with that as well.

Not only did he have Mr. Dr. Perfect for a daddy, but this would be Skip's last year at the old Hunt School. Integration was coming, plans were already on the table now that the federal government was involved, and Reese Jackson had fought hard for the change. But the whites were upset because Cooper Connelly, though he had never said as much as "boo" to any black person not directly under his employ, was showing himself to be a little unpredictable on the subject of racial integration—a little fiery, even.

As president of the Revere School Board, he had flat-out said city money was not going to be given to the White Citizens' Council for the funding of private academies. He said these were "nothing more than public schools for white children." Naturally, most white people were offended when they heard him say this.

Melba had read all about the segregated academies, had heard about them on the television. They were springing up like Topsy all through the South. But Cooper Connelly said—loud and clear and in the *Times Commercial* newspaper—that Mississippi was too poor a state to be courting nonsense, and if Mississippi wasn't, Revere sure enough was. Integration was coming, and everybody just better get used to it.

Only somebody as rich and educated as Dr. Cooper Connelly could get away with talking like that, and Melba had heard, because she made it her business to hear as much as she could, that even he was starting to have some trouble. That he was getting calls. Rumor had it that his own daddy was upset with him and had come up from Jackson while the legislature was still in session to give his son a piece of his mind. As if State Senator Jack Rand Connelly had any mind to spare.

Melba sighed. Everybody knew that people like Cooper Connelly could take care of themselves; it was poor, overweight, over-wrought Skippy Jackson she grieved for. It mustn't be easy being Reese Jackson's child. Reese would make certain his son would be one of the first black children to transfer over from Hunt Elementary School to Robert E. Lee Junior High School—should that become necessary—where the people wouldn't want him and where they'd not be one bit bashful about letting him know this. Poor child might be sneaking more than Snickers for comfort before that ordeal was through.

Brendan was lucky—she was older, and she was a girl. Her daddy was already sending her up to North Carolina to Palmer, where well-off colored children could get an education without all this fuss. It was barely six city blocks from the Jackson house to Lee Junior—the school was actually a few yards closer to here than Hunt was—but next year, when Skippy scrambled out of Reese's car and into the cold embrace of educational progress, he would be entering a whole different world.

Melba, on the other hand, liked this world just fine. Indeed, she was partial to it. She stayed on her porch, waving off the doctor, longer than his own wife did. That didn't matter. Deanie might have disappeared, but Melba knew she'd be over in twenty minutes flat. It took her that long to make herself ready. Lyle Dean never left her house unless she was turned out and perfect. It was one of the reasons her husband loved her. He had an image to maintain.

Melba knew she always looked perfect, too, only in her own way. Not just anybody could understand the need for rhinestone clip earrings at breakfast. Or black crepe turbans when it was 103 degrees outside. Or long, flowing caftans in daytime. But then Melba had her own profession and her own image, not to mention her own sign, to live up to.

She settled back into her big swing, waiting for Deanie to call her or, better yet, show on up. Melba loved her front porch, no doubt about it. It was probably the most comfortable room in her house and the one she spent most time in, when she wasn't working. There was all kinds of big, white wicker furniture with down cushions on them, a rotating fan that hooked into an outlet in her hallway, a notable collection of blue-and-white china-doll cats, and, of course, the books. Piles and rows of them, whatever she and Deanie happened to be reading or had read in the past. If her day chanced to be slow, Melba stayed out here, watching the world go by and attending to everybody else's business. Making sure people minded their manners when they passed her by.

Folks sure better speak to Miss Melba. And if they didn't, it didn't matter to her if the offending party was black or white. People might harbor their suspicions about her, they might even have formulated opinions, but one thing was certain: Nobody was going to ignore Melba Obrenski, at least not anymore. If they tried to, she was apt to sing out, "Hey there, don't I know you? Don't I know your people?"

Not everybody wanted to be known by Miss Melba or have their family matters known by her. Not with that sign out front.

Melba sighed at that notion, pleased as punch.

At this point in her life, hovering steady at forty, it didn't take much to pleasure Miss Melba. She was tickled with the few old-time clients who remembered her fondly from what she called "a previous life" and still bothered to look her up when they passed through, and with the more numerous ladies who showed up at her door during the day. It tickled her to have time to spend on her lucky lantana beds and on her prized harvest mums, time to waste with getting on Reese Jackson's nerves and what she called "serious spells" with his wife, Deanie. Melba was still thrilled with not having to work so long and so hard.

She loved sitting on her porch, especially in the morning. For most of her life—both adult and child—she'd been forced to miss day lighting up. Going to bed, if she were fortunate, at its dawning, struggling up again when its fullness was well on the wane. She knew she'd missed a lot of light and a lot more of life when she was younger and a working girl down in the Quarter. Now she was determined not to miss a thing—and she didn't.

She'd started out at twelve, and so by thirty she was already getting a little long in the tooth for her profession—this was the "previous life" she referred to, when pressed—the night she'd met Stefan Obrenski. He'd shipped in with the navy. It was his first time away from home, his first time in the South. And he was young, a good ten years younger than she was. Probably more. Melba had a keen eye for such differences.

Unfortunately, she also had an eye for a serious drinking problem when she saw one, even in a twenty-year-old. But Stefan swore he truly loved her. This was the first time anybody had put those words together in her hearing. And he promised her marriage and a home. The idea of home had always intrigued her. He'd said, "You're just gonna love Ohio—it's a whole lot cooler than here, less humid—and my mama's gonna love a little sugarplum like you." Even ever-hopeful Melba had her doubts about that, but at her age she was sure game to find out.

Like her betrothed, she'd never been out of her home state a day in her life before she left it, knew nothing about geography but had high hopes that New York City lay on the road to Columbus, Ohio. Unfortunately, she was not to find this out, at least not then. They'd made it only as far north as North Mississippi before Stefan sobered up enough to notice the looks they were getting. Melba may have talked all-American and looked as white as Shirley Temple, but the skintight dresses she favored and the gardenia stuck in her hair told a slightly darker tale, at least to those primed to recognize it. There was also the fact that no matter where they traveled in Mississippi on their march northward—in Picayune or Gautier or Canton or Macon—Miss Melba definitely preferred staying in the black part of town.

One day Melba went out for cigarettes—"Gone all of fifteen minutes," she would later tell a fascinated Deanie Jackson—and came back to find Stefan totally disappeared—"I mean *everything*"—from the Queenie Anne Hotel. Melba had been neither surprised nor displeased.

Fate had dumped her smack in the center of Revere, Mississippi, about four blocks away from where she now stayed. What a place! She'd walked out of that hotel door to mosey along its crepe myrtle– and magnolia-lined streets, admiring the cleanliness of it—so different from New Orleans—and loving the way this small, quaint place filtered life through time. It was the fifties, and trouble was already brewing in other parts of the country; *Brown v. Board of Education* was the number-one topic on the evening news with Chet Huntley and David Brinkley. But trouble, especially racial trouble, seemed a world removed from Revere, Mississippi, where everybody seemed to have been born knowing his or her proper place and had decided to stay put there. It was a good life, at least it was if you were white.

Natchez and Vicksburg, with their big old houses and their big old families and the graceful flow of their shared river—the river for which the state was named—were considered Mississippi's reigning beauties, but Revere had its own particular charms. For one thing, it had been planned out; it hadn't just popped up, helter-skelter, along some waterway, in this case the middling-size Tombigbee. For another, Revere was one of the few southern cities that did not share in the proud distinction of being Civil War wounded. Its complete history could still be told in its streets and outlined in the façade of its houses, which marched along in stately architectural progression, without a disconcerting and disheartening break.

Next to the Baptist religion, gardening was Revere's great passion, and this also helped to make the town a beautiful place. Melba, by nature a spirited if untutored horticulturalist, recognized this. But it wasn't really the town's flowers that had attracted her, and she knew it. It was the straight streets, the hedges and fences, the clear differences that made one place recognizable and bound and differentiated it from another, and the river with its slow and edging ways. Melba, a working girl, open to all, had been intrigued by the notion of boundaries for all of her life.

Laid out in a grid from its Main Road, or First Lane as the old families still called it, Revere's numbered streets ran south to north and its numbered avenues east to west. One could, and Melba did, find whole sections of town that remained untouched and where houses moved serenely through the ages, making it a veritable cornucopia of architectural history. Massive antebellums, the city houses of rich planters who grew cotton along the Tombigbee, gave way, without fuss, to brightly painted Victorians, built by merchants and city officials early in the century, and these in turn made way for the unobtrusive bricked structures of the present day. And all of this could be happening on the very same stretch of Fifth Street. The Lockhart House, the Pickett-Billups House, the Carrie Barrows House—each had its name discreetly lettered in white on a small, black wrought-iron garden sign, stuck out front. In Revere, designations and flower borders were everywhere, making it possible to recognize easily when you had moved from one place to another. This was reassuring to Melba, who had doubts about how she'd actually done this—gotten from one place to another—in her past.

Property being cheap, she bought herself a trim, white-painted wooden cottage and named it The Haven, just so she could fit in. She made sure its green trim went well with her green eyes. She threw a picket fence around the place just to show that she owned it, planted her flowers, and put up a sign. And even though she had not quite managed to take him as husband, this small particular did not stop Melba from taking Stefan Obrenski's last name as her own. She kept a framed photograph of him in a place of honor on the mantel, over the living-room fireplace, which didn't work. She liked the idea of memorializing a man who had once joined the words "I" and "love" and "you" together and spoken them to her. It made for a happy memory in her past.

Through the years since then, Melba had grown a wee bit fatter—she was a size six now—and a great deal more content. Her business was good. Her flowers spectacular. Her place in her community, though awkward, still assured. It was only some years later, when Reese Jackson moved in, that she found that the whole of her worldly possessions stood smack in the shadow of his imposing antebellum, spoiling that uppity Negro's view of the river and giving him stiff competition for growing the best roses in this part of Revere. And Reese Jackson was not used to competition. He did not take to it well.

Waiting for Deanie, Melba settled back on her swing, fanning herself with a Black Jesus fan that came from Southside Missionary Union Baptist Church. One of her regular clients had left it by mistake. Miss Melba glided back and forth, killing time, staring straight over, eyes narrowed, from her own awfully little house to Reese Jackson's mighty big one—named appropriately, Jackson Manor. That man put his name on everything.

Not that it had always been the Jackson house, but there had always been a doctor in it lately—at least that's what Melba gathered from her clients, and in a town like this they were the kinds of folks who would know. The kinds of folks who were acquainted with things from much further back than when she had first met Reese Jackson, or even heard about him, and everybody had been hearing about Reese Jackson for years. Like most of the old places in Revere, the Jackson house had been put up by slave labor, but this particular slave, Caleb Sykes, had been a little more enterprising than most, a little more cunning. He'd built the place for himself, and not for some rich white man, and he'd managed to hold on to it as long as he could.

A freed black, in a state where these had been pitifully few, and a master engineer, Caleb Sykes had started out building quality bridges for the Confederacy during its Glorious Revolution and had been smart enough, and capable enough, so that he could demand his money up front. In gold. When General Nathan Bedford Forrest lost Mississippi to the federals, Caleb Sykes had smoothly changed his allegiance and continued building the same sturdily well-designed bridges for Ulysses S. Grant, for which he was still paid handsomely. In gold.

Through it all, Daddy Sykes raised a family and continued to prosper quietly in a poor time and in a poor county and in a poor state where there were even few whites doing likewise. And his children turned out to be just as canny and hardworking as their daddy. Mainly boys—Daddy had six sons—they stayed together, they did not fight among themselves, and they almost never left home, usually only to go up to Virginia or Maryland—rarely over to Louisiana and never into Alabama—to find their light-skinned wives. Mainly the Sykeses kept themselves to themselves, and they tried their best to pass unnoticed. They knew what could happen if they didn't. In Mississippi, things could turn down mighty quick for a black man if he was not careful. But their beautiful house, with its columns and crenellated balconies and its gleaming white outbuildings, was too much of a beauty to pass unobserved in reconstructed Mississippi. Jim Crow and high taxes soon managed to wrest it out of the Sykes family's hands.

Not that many white people would want to live in a black man's house; they just didn't want Daddy Sykes's kin to have it, and so the house lay fallow for years. But when Melba first showed up, the house had belonged to Dr. Earle Ray Shelton, called "Chance" by all his new friends over at the Revere Country Club. He didn't know what the name meant, but they did.

Dr. Shelton's people were originally from Muscle Shoals, Alabama. This was not considered to be a place where decent people should be from, but he'd been born and brought up there. When Dr. Shelton fell in love with the house next door to Melba and bought it, he had not known its history, had not realized that it had been built by a black man and that the whole of his black family had lived in it for years and years. And the folks he knew, his new friends in Revere, did not go out of their way to enlighten him. He was from Alabama, after all. Dr. Shelton was a tolerably good doctor, at least when he wasn't drinking, but nobody in Revere knew his people. This meant they didn't really know him.

"Let him buy where he wants" seemed to be the general opinion. They'd let him do what he pleased.

Needless to say, Chance Shelton had not been particularly pleased when he found out he was living in a colored man's house, especially a colored man who'd broken all the conventions and gotten real, real rich off white people.

Nothing for it, though. The house was a beauty, one of the best built in the state. By the time he learned out its history, Dr. Shelton was in love with it, obsessed by it, and determined to bring it back to its glory days. He sanded off the last of its peeling paint with his own hands, then had fine white layered on its graceful boards and columns, pulled up the rugged concrete and swirled a brick drive in its place. Laid out the original rose garden and cleaned the delicate Venetian cut-glass chandeliers. All in all, he remade the Sykes House magnificently.

But there was still the problem of its location—smack in the middle of Catfish Alley, between Third Street and Fourth—the colored part of town and surrounded by colored folk on all sides. Dr. Shelton didn't seem to mind; in fact, in the end he joined in the joke against him, especially as he got older and lonelier and bolder in his opinions, and once Melba moved in, he took to drinking his bourbon with her on her front porch in the still light of the late afternoon for all eyes to see.

Dr. Shelton hung on to his home until his dying day, but his family was having none of it. They were Reverites now and knew what was what. It might have been the house they'd grown up in, might well have been the biggest, prettiest, best-preserved place in town, but even they didn't know how they'd managed to endure the shame. Their daddy was barely two hours in his grave and they'd found a real-estate agent and put him on the case.

Once again the house sat on the market for years, falling apart but still gracefully beautiful, because no white folks would buy it and no black folks could. Until Reese Jackson showed up. Much to their credit, the Shelton heirs recognized a savior in this newly rich, striving Negro just come back from up north. They asked him over. Let him in the front door and made him an offer.

Neither party dickered much over particulars. Wayne Shelton lowered his asking price, Reese Jackson wrote out a check. Everybody, on both sides, became immediately cordial, gratified, and content. Especially Melba.

In fact, she'd been in a particularly happy state ever since she'd first seen cute little Deanie Jackson stroll up to have her first look at her new house—on the morning after her husband bought it. Melba even remembered the date—June 13, the Feast of St. Anthony, traditionally one of her lucky days.

She'd been sitting on her porch swing, creaking back and forth and minding everybody's business, much as she was doing now, but paying particularly close attention to what was going on next door. She watched Deanie Jackson climb gracefully out of Reese's big Lincoln—it had been a baby blue one back then—and walk up to the house she was soon to turn into even more of a legend and a showplace, at least in the black part of town.

Deanie was that nice, uppity-Negro color, more coffee in cream than cream in coffee, and peaking out from beneath that perky pillbox was chestnut-colored hair that had just enough curl but not too much. It was obvious to Melba, who knew all about the important nuances of color, as only people born in Louisiana could, that deep, dark Reese Jackson had considered himself marrying up when he took on Lyle Dean Campbell as his wife.

That had been six years ago, when Jackie Kennedy was just becoming the fashion, and Lyle Dean had been turned out to make her proud. Pink mohair suit, matching hat, long kid gloves—all this at noon in Revere, Mississippi. Deanie had the whole thing down pat, including Jackie's look of total adoration as she gazed up at her difficult husband and held on to his arm for support.

For a brief second, Mrs. Dr. Jackson looked up and caught Melba's eye. She stared longer than she should have, then flicked her gaze on over to the sign and brought it back again. Once she was sure she had Melba's full attention, Deanie smiled at her and winked. Melba winked back with that same solemn silence, which for her was very strange. But then, of course, she'd heard about Skippy, what had happened to him, and whose fault it had all been. She thought maybe Miss Lyle Dean might be happy living next door to somebody who knew how to soothe.

Reese Jackson, however, was not as enthusiastic about his new neighbor. Melba realized this immediately, not half an hour later, when she caught him staring down at her from the upstairs back veranda door—the same door she was soon to see Brendan Jackson sneaking out of almost every night, at least before her parents sent her off to boarding school.

Melba watched Reese's eyes snap over her little haven. And you could tell those eyes never missed a thing. They made short work of her sign, sashaying back and forth in the sunlight, of the sassy red rayon curtains at her window, her pride and joy; then he took in Melba's turban—slowly this time—and her long, purple silk peony-printed gown. He did not seem one bit fooled by the grotto to the Virgin that she'd put up and prominently displayed among the roses in her garden. Revere was a small enough town, and Reese Jackson cut what they called "a figure" in it. Everybody told him everything—trying to impress him, trying to get on his good side, or just because they liked hearing themselves talk—and so Reese knew, not just suspected, how Miss Melba Obrenski had once made her ends meet. Lots of people from Revere had spent time in New Orleans. Not that Melba minded. She didn't really need Reese Jackson, and she could have cared less about his good opinion.

But she did care about his wife's friendship.

She and Deanie had hit it off right from the beginning; they hadn't needed time to sniff each other out and to snoop. Within hours after the Jacksons had actually moved in—and she was sure Mr. Reese was safely at his office—Melba had shown up at their house with a truly glorious coconut cake. Deanie dropped everything to head on back over to have herself a sizable piece at the Obrenski kitchen table. They'd started talking, found out they had more in common than people might suspect, though on the subject of Reese Jackson they were of quite separate opinions.

"What a husband!" said Deanie.

"What a husband!" echoed Melba, though in an entirely different tone of voice.

Deanie might have been the daughter of dignified school teachers, might have met and married Reese Jackson right out of college—"still a virgin," she whispered—but underneath, she and Melba were just alike: two bright, light-skinned girls who read books and talked some French and, once upon a time, had caught on to what the oldsters politely called a "narrow chance" and had held on to this chance for dear life.

It turned out that Deanie had grown up in a small town in Iowa, a place that perplexed her southern-born parents but where they were determined to fit in. The one thing that baffled them more than the town was the behavior of their only daughter. Always buried in a book, and yet so pretty! Reading *Vogue* and sewing slim gray skirts and wearing white blouses and red berets when every other girl they knew was decked out in felt poodle skirts and crinolines. Lyle Dean was different, and they could see this difference for themselves. After all, they taught in the high school. Then, on top of everything else, here she was, their little black daughter, wanting to take herself off to the Parsons School of Design in New York. This far-fetched notion truly frightened her parents. They had both started life down in Little Road, Georgia. They knew, firsthand, how dangerous this world could be for a little colored girl who might not know her place.

"Distracted," they called her. "Flighty and light-headed." All of this for her own good.

When she met Spencer Reese Jackson on a University of Iowa trip to Washington, he'd looked her over once, long and slow like, and proclaimed her "artistic." He was the first one ever called her that, and Lyle Dean Campbell had made up her mind, right on the spot, that she'd just met the love of her life.

Deanie and Melba were both outsiders and different. Always had been, always would be. This was their main binding bond, that and the fact that their minds worked just alike and they were very slightly devilish, and each of them had managed to hold on to her perky ways. Even Deanie. Maybe especially Deanie, even though she had that tragedy behind her, a tragedy they rarely mentioned but one that Melba staunchly and completely believed could not possibly have been Lyle Dean's fault.

"We're evil twins," said Melba.

Stretched out at opposite ends of Melba's green sofa, drinking cool, sweet tea in her dim little house, they filled each other in on everything: gossiped about married life and Melba's customers, read Balzac to each other out loud because they thought they should, then talked about what was going on over in Birmingham and down in Jackson and wondered if Reverend Streeter was ever going to be able to integrate the River Café.

"Worst food in town," said Melba. "That's one thing I know for a fact."

Talked on and on about everything—except the one thing. And Melba had seen to that right away.

Once, during the very early days of their friendship, as they sat in Melba's shaded living room sipping their cool drinks, Deanie had said, "What race are you anyway, Melba—black or white? I've always wanted to ask you that."

By then "always" was all of six weeks.

Sometimes you just had to forgive Deanie. She didn't mean any harm, but she was from up north, had been brought up to be more forthright than what Melba was accustomed to. No one had ever taken the time to teach Lyle Dean what a polite person could ask and what she could not. Melba knew this, and so she made allowances. She just continued to tinkle the ice cubes in her tall glass and smile and not answer. Pretty soon they moved on to talk about something else.

This was because no matter what she might say or what she might know—and Melba had once met her daddy, so she knew what color she was—she did not talk about race. Wouldn't do it. Maybe it had something to do with her helter-skelter upbringing, where what color you were seemed to be the last thing on anybody's mind and where mean and nasty, and good and kind, came in all shapes and sizes and shades and sexes and configurations. But whatever the reason, over the years Melba had taken on being raceless as her own personal protest and crusade. Let folks make up their own minds, think what they wanted. And with her the subject, as something personal to speak over, came up rarely, a lot more rarely than one might expect. People, even a good friend like Lyle Dean, could easily be kept at bay if you used their good manners against them. You just had to clam up, and pretty soon they shut up as well.

In fact, through all her long experience and her life's many changes, Melba could remember only one man, a client, who had insisted and had brought up the question of her race more than once.

"Tell me now, just tell me. What is you anyway, white or colored?"

He'd been a good customer, regular and wanting nothing fancy, and the last time he'd asked this, he'd been firmly in the saddle but not yet fully trotting out. Melba had smiled up at him as gracefully as if they'd been strolling hand and hand down Canal Street. And she'd decided to answer him, something she had never done before and would do only one more time in her life.

"I'm a chameleon," she said sweetly.

There was a skip of the rhythm at that. "What the hell's a chameleon?" he demanded, though being from New Orleans, that's one animal he should surely have known.

"It's a creature," replied Melba, who was a great reader, even back then, "that takes on the color of whatever it's near. And tonight I'm near you—at least my body's near you. So the question becomes, more appropriately, what are *you*?"

The man shook his head, got back down to business.

"Chameleon" had once been her word for the week, and she remembered it, but not him, when she came to Revere, put down her roots, and put up her sign. She smiled. She studied it now.

*Madame Melba Obrenski!*
GENUINE CREOLE CARD READER!
STRAIGHT OUT OF LOUISIANA!
THE REAL THING!
KNOW YOUR FUTURE!

And she thought, as she always did with great pride of ownership, that hers was a sign and a half.

# Chapter 4

"MISS MELBA LOUISE, come on in here and see these folks on TV."

It was Deanie, hollering out to her from inside Melba's own house. They did that each day, when they first got together—formally called each other Miss Lyle Dean or Miss Melba Louise and giggling. Right from the first, Deanie had known enough not to call her friend "Madame Melba," which was solely her professional name. They could laugh about most anything else, but not about this. Melba took her calling seriously.

"I was just seeing to my 'seven sisters,'" said Melba, hurrying on into her house. "Can't let Reese Jackson get the notion that his roses are nice as mine are. Wouldn't be good for his humility, if he started thinking that."

Reese was always "Mr. Reese" or "Reese Jackson," never "your husband" when Melba talked about her neighbor to his wife.

She plopped down on the sofa. Deanie had gotten her own coffee out of the kitchen and was settled in, watching television. As usual, she was fully made up and had put on the new B. H. Wragge suit she'd picked up in Chicago when she and Reese had gone up there for the National Medical Association convention last August. It was a nice yellow color, bright without being too bright. Under Deanie's tutelage Melba was starting to learn the distinction, though she still mostly favored too-bright.

Like most other sets in Revere, Melba's was tuned to WLBN and the local news segment the Jackson family had tut-tutted about through breakfast was replaying yet again.

Deanie said, "Look at these people."

Melba said, "That Reese Jackson. Roses big as that are an abomination to nature."

Miss Melba could certainly go on and on about her neighbor in the huge house next door, but his wife was having none of it this morning.

"Look at these people," repeated Deanie, over the rim of her cup and pointing to the television set. "It's some poor family from down in Macon. I think it's one of the white ones that joined up with that pulp haulers union—the one your old boarder was involved in instigating."

This got Melba's attention. She reached into the folds of her caftan and laced her rhinestone-rimmed eyeglasses in place beneath her red turban. She was quite a sight, and she knew it, and the delicious thing was that Deanie, her only real friend in the world, knew it as well.

Melba peered closer. "Why, I'll be. Isn't that Willie Tate's oldest boy, Critter—the one's always over at your house playing with Skip? Can't say I know these white folks, though."

Deanie thought this a little incongruous. No matter what Melba actually might be, she *looked* white, and when she mentioned race, it could be a bit disconcerting.

"I know them," she said, folding her napkin back onto the palm-treed TV table Melba laid out so nicely for them each morning while she waited for Deanie's husband to leave. "Or rather Reese knows them. He said they belong to somebody named Billy Ray Puckett. His family. They're on because he died last night, over at Doctors."

"Died?" Miss Melba raised her glasses and peered closer, trying to make out what was happening on her little black-and-white through all its snow. "I declare, those folks look too young to have anybody that close dying around them. Is that his wife over there or his mama? Look at that little girl, batting at Floyd Sobczak—you know they should have cut that child right off the screen. She's going to cost them a pretty penny, not acting right. What happened to him, the dead husband? Was he likkered up, or did he just go on out and suicide himself? Or was he murdered?"

"It was an accident," said Deanie, with a shade of sanctimony. She had long ago discovered that her friend could be morbid, that "suicide" and "murder" and "awful happenings" were words that could just pop into Melba's mind for no reason, and that she sometimes had a decided tendency to think the worst.

Melba stared at the Puckett children harder and said, "Bless their hearts," as Deanie shook her head and glanced around.

Inside her little house, Miss Melba was a firm believer in the blessing of "adumbration"—a word so obscure that Deanie had had to look it up. In fact, Melba kept things so closed up and gloomy she needed to leave a little red-shaded lamp glowing all day long on her mantel. The only brightness in the whole place came from Melba herself. By now Deanie knew that fixed habits made Melba rise, in summer, at 3:00 A.M. to air her house for precisely one half hour before she shut things up tight as a tick again in an effort to keep out as much as she could of the moist Mississippi air. This caused her tiny Victorian cottage—with its drawn, heavy curtains, its dated antimacassars, its claw-footed furniture, and its books—to be perpetually dark, almost spectral, the kind of place where, if your eye were quick enough, it might be able to catch strange movement or your ear the tinkle of some unknown sound. At first, early on, Deanie had put all this down as artifice, slightly macabre but probably good for business. Now she wasn't so sure this was the reason. Tight, closed, and dark places seemed to make Melba feel secure.

"Must have been operated on by Cooper Connelly," said Melba wisely, talking about Billy Ray Puckett and shaking her head. "He may own the hospital, but he sure can't hold a candle to Reese Jackson, not when it comes to cutting up on people. Bless his heart. Too bad Mr. Reese is black."

Deanie couldn't quite figure which of the two—her Reese or his rich white counterpart—needed blessing, but she knew one thing for certain: She didn't want to get started talking about her husband with her neighbor and only true friend. Melba and Reese had been bad-mouthing each other to her since the first day they'd met.

"He's a phony," said Melba.

"She's a hooker," said Reese.

Over and over. And Deanie knew deep down that these were not words the two of them would get over; deep, deep down they meant what they said.

Floyd Sobczak faded away and was followed by *Brighter Tomorrows*, their favorite soap, but Deanie had a full day ahead of her. She got on up.

"Thanks for the coffee, Melba," she said, "but I just came over for a minute. Got to start planning my trip up to North Carolina with Brendan. Somebody told Reese construction's going on up along U.S. 11. That means I've got to work out an alternate route."

Melba nodded. You had to plan your stops carefully if you were black and your aim was to make it safely from one place to another in the South.

"Better get out *The Green Guide*," warned Melba. "Lord knows that's the only thing, except Jesus, gonna see a colored person through."

Deanie nodded. "Reese mapped out my route last night. He worries about me. Doesn't want anything to happen to Brendan." The last said too quickly, and with a sigh.

"Skippy going? Missing school?"

"Skippy goes everywhere with me."

Melba flashed her bright smile. "Take care of yourself, honey," she called out. "Hurry on back over if you get any news. I'm not going anywhere. Be here all afternoon."

After the back screen slammed shut, Melba cleared the coffee cups and washed them. She fluffed up the couch pillows and rearranged her living-room knickknacks just so. Then she carried fresh coffee out onto her porch. She left the television running so she could keep up with hearing her story if she wanted to.

As it was, she didn't want to. She was still thinking about those people she'd seen, the family of Cooper Connelly's dead patient, staring out at her from seventeen inches of silver screen, the snow on it making their stiff faces strange and alien. It made them look like they came from some unknown world—a world a lot farther away than Macon, Mississippi.

*Poor children*, thought Melba. *Especially that girl.*

UNTIL JUST A FEW DAYS AGO, she'd had a boarder. His name was Josiah Chamberlain Bixby. A white boy, he'd come from up north. Melba'd been fond of him from the beginning. She loved the way he spoke to her, the sound of his strange voice, the way he formed his words. He'd come down to organize the pulpwood haulers over in Macon—the dead Mr. Puckett had belonged to their group, if Melba remembered right—and eventually Josiah Bixby had moved down Noxubee County to "be with his people," whatever that meant, but his summer had been spent with Melba, and he'd been quite comfortable in her back room with its "adjacent screened porch and separate entrance."

The pulp haulers were an integrated group, a true union; they'd been started up that way by the young carpetbagging Bixby. He'd studied history, up at Dartmouth College, and was of the firm opinion that poor whites and poor blacks should finally learn to get along. It was in both of their best interests. Naturally, not everybody in Revere felt the same way, and most folks would have been scared to take in a civil-rights worker, what with the Klan and the Citizens' Council and the burning crosses and the lynchings and the riots flaming through the South. But Melba was her own woman. She could do as she liked, and she usually did.

And Josiah had shared a great love of her sign. While he was with her, he'd sent at least ten letters home in which he minutely detailed it to his parents and to his brothers, to friends who had graduated with him that spring from Dartmouth College and who had scattered. He'd told her so himself, and he'd shown her parts of the letters.

It was obvious to Melba, whose fortunes rose or fell on her ability to fathom what was going on in people's minds, that Josiah Bixby found describing her sign a whole lot easier than he'd found describing her self. He was not only white but pale white—light eyes and light hair—and he came from a long line of liberal thinkers. Congregationalist ministers and their mates, they might applaud his stand on civil rights and even, Republican though they undoubtedly were, understand his labor-organizing work with the pulp haulers' union. Still, Madame Melba and her activities might be a bit much for them. Better to let the sign speak for itself.

And talk it did, squeaking back and forth on any breeze that blew up from the Tombigbee River.

### *Madame Melba Obrenski!*
#### GENUINE CREOLE CARD READER!

Plus all the rest.

On top of its elaborately scrolled message was the portrait of some exotic, dusky-skinned, turban-headed woman, her black eyes flashing, her long, crimson-tipped fingers spread wide over a crystal ball. These bright protuberances were the only thing this woman had in common with Melba, who had actually clipped the photograph from an old issue of *True Confessions* magazine and had it copied. The woman was dark, much darker than Melba herself.

Dark could be good for some businesses. Melba had learned that a long time ago.

# Chapter 5

REESE JACKSON DIDN'T SEE the woman, at least not at first. He was too busy doing what he did every single time he drove up to his spanking-new clinic: admiring it. Long, sleek, yellow-brick, and modern; he'd designed it himself to be nothing like *Gone with the Wind*. His own building, right here smack in the middle of town. In the *white* middle of town and not along its black outskirts. Hot diggity!

Even the sign reassured him, his name spelled out in big, bold, capital letters.

DR. S. REESE JACKSON, M.D.
PRIVATE PARKING

He had originally thought of adding "Jackson Medical Building" in bright gold beneath his own name but then decided that might be too much. Actually, it was Deanie who'd decided this. Instead the architect—somebody whom they'd imported all the way from Los Angeles, though it was Reese who had come up with the main design—had placed this discreet, polished-steel marker out front. It was what he called an absolutely unnecessary accoutrement. Everybody in Revere knew this building anyway, and everybody knew that it belonged to Reese.

He edged his Lincoln in between the crisply painted outlines of his very own parking space, entering at the same time into one of the most pleasurable moments of his day. Physically pleasurable, almost as important to him as caring for his patients, and nobody could say that Reese Jackson did not know how to take care of his patients. He was a man born to be a doctor. He thought of himself as a healer through and through.

Reese reached into the backseat and pulled out his worn medical bag, a wedding gift from his in-laws that he kept meaning to replace. His car door shut behind him with a whoosh of luxury. He paused and took one last look at his sign and then, automatically, at the building next door, the one that dwarfed his. Doctors Hospital, 300 Main Street. Reese was at 316. As usual, Doctors still smiled benignly down on him in all its fake, neatly kept-up, antebellum glory. Well, it could grin on all it wanted. He, Reese Jackson, had built himself up right here, right beside it. The city fathers had tried every trick in the book to keep him on the other side of Main Street— everything from redlining to sending out the Kluckers to burn a few crosses at night—but Reese was not one to be easily intimidated. He aimed for the last laugh, and he usually had it.

Hey, he'd already made it this far, all the way to Main Street, the first black professional to head out of Catfish Alley, bringing all sorts of black folks with him. Just like white folks had been scared he'd do.

From the shelter of his clinic door, Reese looked up and around him, seeing nothing too fancy. Not many specialty places, what you might call deluxe shops. People liked going up to Memphis or over to Birmingham to get what they needed, and if you were black, you had to. No colored people got to try on clothes in Miss Pearl's Dress Shoppe. Not that they minded, at least not openly. It gave them a chance to get out of town and visit their people. Southerners, black and white, had kinfolk all over the place.

Revere's own brightly painted storefronts housed Penney's and Woolworth's and a Piggly Wiggly grocery store, all of these linked together by an optimistic row of florists, lawyers' offices, gift shops, and one or two small, white-owned restaurants where Reese's friends sent their secretaries to get carryout lunches for them at the back door. Not Reese, though. Each noontime, he got in his car, big as you please, and drove the short distance over to Catfish Alley and Sallie's. She kept a booth for him right at the front door, where he could greet everyone who entered, all his patients, and where he wasn't too close to the Delta Blues that wailed out of her jukebox night and day. Old, sad, dirty songs that Reese pretended never to remember, even though he'd been hearing them every day of his life.

Turning now, Reese continued on into his office. *Ebony* magazine had recently done a major article on this building—Reese and John Johnson, its publisher, were fraternity brothers and friends. Reese still kept copies of that particular edition on every table in his oversize waiting room, even though the folks who spent any time here had more than likely already read it. This was Mississippi, his practice was a black one, and everybody, even poor everybodies, already had *Ebony* coming to their own houses. Reese kept the magazine there anyway, Just in case, he told himself. But mainly because, like having his own name on his own parking space and caring for his patients, this article made him feel good. He wanted to share it.

SURGEON MAKES MAJOR CONTRIBUTION
TO EASE "BURNING" MISSISSIPPI.

And there he was, smiling right in living color from the cover, surrounded by blurbs for recipes and the latest fashions coming next spring with the Fashion Fair. Inside, placed strategically near the front of the magazine, were photographs of his rambling brick structure, shots of his patients in his chock-full waiting room, boldfaced accolades from people he had helped—people whose lives he had saved. And then, near the end, a small black-and-white photo of white people going into Doctors Hospital's main entrance and of black folks, *sick* black folks in need of medical attention, snaking around to the back door—as cautionary a sight as Reese had ever seen.

Looking around, Reese was calmed by the peaceful nature of the space he had built, pacified by it, and so he didn't really hear the woman when she entered, didn't really pay any attention as his clinic door whooshed shut. But when he looked up, he recognized her. And knew instantly why she had come once again.

LATER HE WOULD TELL THE STORY—or at least most of it—to the one person he believed he could truly trust.

"I have this patient," whispered Reese Jackson to his friend. They were down by the river, on a night that was way too quiet for late September; not even the crickets and frogs were singing. They, the two of them, had always liked the river, the night, and the deep, rich smell of Mississippi that the river and the night called forth. Reese apologized for talking so low but continued on whispering, urgently telling his tale. Neither he nor his friend were aware just how far his voice carried, over the water, on the still air. They were not aware that someone was listening.

# Chapter 6

COOPER CONNELLY, WHO WAS SHORTLY to become identified with Billy Ray Puckett and remain so for the rest of his life, found out about his patient's death through normal administrative cycles. He could have cared less. He was dealing with other problems.

In the instant before he called out that it was okay for Ned Hampton to come on into his office, the body washed through Cooper Connelly's mind yet again. Bloated and gray, it floated on the waters of his memory, looking for all the world like the sack of discarded garbage that, of course, it had been. Lately the body invaded him whenever it wanted, which seemed to be all the time now, and it had taken on a life and a presence and an authority of its own. Cooper never knew when it might show up. It would just be there: threatening to swallow him up and spit him out again, back in time, back in space, back onto the byroads of the Tallahatchie River. Back where they'd first become acquainted, him and his body, when he'd been fourteen years old, deep in the woods on a moonless night and frightened half out of his wits that this *thing* might somehow follow him home. Which it had.

In the beginning the body had mostly slunk up on him at night. Cooper had learned to live with that. He'd grown up since then, hadn't he? Become a man. He'd just stay up all night to avoid the nightmare and go on the next day as though nothing had happened. But lately the body had taken to catching him off guard. Popping up anytime. Out of control. When he was younger, he'd used the sheer activity of life to keep it at bay; after that had come the bourbon. But he was no longer young, and he no longer drank. So there was nothing between the two of them now. No time, no space. Nothing but memory.

The thing was, it wasn't even his body. The man had not been his responsibility. He, Cooper, had not done anything wrong. But he had been the first to see it, no doubt about that. He had discovered it, set it loose, and it was coming for him, breaking away from the bank and bringing with it the dank, musty smell of the backwoods, the strangled croak of the frogs, and, of course, the fear. Always the fear. Almost three decades of fear.

In the orderly elegance of his corner office, and without even realizing he was doing it, Cooper began his chant. "I am Dr. Cooper Livingston Connelly. This is my hospital. I belong here." The sound of his own voice reassured him, as it always did. His voice. His place. Indeed he belonged here.

"Cooper, you in there? It's me, Ned."

"Come on in, Ned," called the doctor. He was already out of his chair, on his feet and extending his hand before the compact little man bustled through his door. "Care for some coffee? I think my secretary's got some made up fresh. Doughnuts, too, from Shipley's, if you want one."

As usual, when he was upset, Coop lost his carefully cultivated up-country accent, and his voice took on the singsong cadence of the Delta region where he'd been brought up. He himself could hear the change in him but couldn't do a thing about it. Nothing made him forget his manners, though; his daddy had drummed them into him from birth.

"No coffee, Cooper. I've had three cups of Folger's already, and it's not even nine in the morning yet. My heart's knocking around in there like a crazed mule with all this caffeine. They're starting to say it's bad for you."

They'd have been strong cups, too, thought Cooper, black ones. He watched with no interest at all as his administrative assistant— Doctors Hospital's true chief executive—plunked a sheafload of papers on the corner of the large mahogany desk.

Dressed in his summertime trademark, a sky blue seersucker suit, one of the two he ordered fresh each April from J. Press in New York, Nathan Bedford Forrest Hampton was a small, freckle-faced man with thinning ginger hair and pale, pale eyes. The eyes looked sleepy; they could fool you. Considered dapper by most folks in Revere—a distinction in which he reveled—Ned Hampton sported a perky red carnation every day of his life. He also possessed a melodious voice that was, and probably always would be, the topic of much lazy afternoon gossip in Revere. Like the legendary children of Hamelin, Ned Hampton had been led by the Pied Piper of his voice along a singular path.

He perched down on, but did not settle into, one of the oversize leather armchairs that flanked Cooper's desk. He never did—settle comfortably, that is. Maybe this was because it was Cooper's daddy, not Cooper himself, who had hired him, and everybody knew this. Ned had come, along with the hospital itself, as part of Cooper's graduation present when he managed to make his way out of medical school at Tulane. "Ned's a real firecracker," Jack Rand Connelly had said, and then laughed out loud, right in front of Evelyne Elizabeth, his son's new, up-country bride, something even he rarely did, he was so in awe of her. "He can run the place, leave you free to operate, do the surgery. Ned'll make sure you look real good."

Back then Cooper had smarted under the notion that he might need anybody to make him look good. But that had been a long time ago, twenty years. Now he was truly grateful for any little help with polishing his luster, and Ned Hampton was a sharpie, all right, and good with laying on the veneer. There was absolutely no doubt about that.

"Brought you your mail and the newspaper, too," Ned said. "Thought you might want to see it. Your wife's picture's in Miss Dabney's column, some political luncheon. Even the ladies are all fired up about this school-integration thing. Naturally, they know it ain't right. They're frightened for their children. Your daddy's leading the charge, like usual. His piece is on page three."

*Jack Rand Connelly writing up from Jackson to save Mississippi from the scourge of federal gov'ment.*

"Thank you," said Cooper, but he did not look down. "Evelyne's always at her best and most charming when Miss Dabney's around."

He didn't say a word about his daddy, didn't want to open up that can of worms with Ned, at least not yet. Besides, he was starting to relax, starting to feel like himself again now that the ghost was receding, and he didn't want to mess with this good feeling. Coop had to admit that his wife was a marvel, at least at a distance. Hell, he'd once been awed by her himself, and so had his daddy. Jack Rand still was.

As was Ned. He really admired Evelyne and her society ways.

A true southerner—born and raised not a hundred miles away, up in Tupelo—Ned was gently obsessed with family connections. He knew all his own Hampton, Sykes, MacKay, and Dismukes cousins, six times removed, and there was no doubt but that he reveled in the dynastic implications of Cooper's marriage to the former Evelyne Elizabeth Dunaway of Roanoke, Virginia. Usually his morning meetings with Cooper were begun with a gentle discussion of kinfolk coming and going in Revere, who was about to marry whom, and how this would or would not affect first their family bloodlines and then, secondarily, their economic situations.

Cooper watched Ned glance, as always, at the silver-framed photographs arranged on the polished mahogany table behind his back and out of his sight. But Cooper knew they were there, knew *he* was there, in his Ole Miss uniform, clutching tight to his football and smiling broadly for his daddy, and that Evelyne Elizabeth was there as well, posed in white tulle on the night of the Richmond Cotillion. And then the two of them together—looking smugly out from their official engagement portrait and then Evelyne in the lace veil that once had been special-ordered and handmade by lace makers at Jesurum in Venice, the veil that had been in her family for generations and which she had worn on her wedding day. Cooper remembered how shoddy it had seemed when he first saw it, how consumed. Why, the patching worked through it was in plain view. The Dunaways had insisted on keeping the family veil, but they'd let Jack Rand's money pay for everything else. And everything else had been spanking new.

His new bride—"mighty tired of all this," as she'd put it, meaning the genteel poverty, the making things do—had left Virginia without looking back. She viewed Jack Rand Connelly as her liberator, and she'd been grateful to him ever since. And to his lawyer,

Meade MacLean, Cooper's contemporary and friend, who'd come to the wedding, who managed his money, and who could be counted upon to give Miss Evelyne Elizabeth everything she might want.

Ned said, "You and Miss Evelyne Elizabeth are both so attractive. Hard to know which one looks the best."

On a normal morning, the pleasantries could flow on for more than ten minutes; today they barely took up one.

"Bad news," said Ned, without further warning. "Your patient died."

Cooper, taken off guard, felt the river smell ooze through him, dank and cold.

"Not my patient," he said quickly. Just like that, back to being fourteen years old again and living on the Tallahatchie. "I didn't know him at all."

Ned shook his head, puzzled. "Of course you knew him. Billy Ray Puckett. That man the little Nigra boy carried over here in his daddy's truck the other night. You operated on him. Called your personal team over to the hospital—got your nurse, Miss Billy, up out of her bed, she came on over still in her curlers—and took him right in. Two nights ago. You *got* to remember Billy Ray."

A gentle harking-back to the days when Cooper had been drinking heavily and on some mornings found it hard enough to remember his own name.

"Yes, Mr. Puckett," Dr. Connelly said. His heart still hammered, but he had managed at least to bring his mind back to the present and to Ned. "A pretty straightforward chest wound, nothing much wrong with him. He lost a lot of blood, and so there was danger from that, but he stabilized pretty quickly, at least once we started working on him. I sure wasn't expecting him to die."

"Apparently not," snapped back Ned, but then he thought better of it—this was Jack Rand's boy, after all—and toned his voice down. "Tragic when something like this happens. Four young children, they say the littlest two are still in diapers. It makes my heart bleed just to think about it. When folks up north hear about poor Mississippi, they only think about the Nigras, but people like Billy Ray Puckett . . ."

Cooper nodded. *People like Billy Ray Puckett are a problem unto themselves.*

Ned leaned close. "His chart says he was forty-six years old, almost forty-seven. His wife is barely twenty-five. Their oldest child is ten." He paused so Cooper could do the math and draw the conclusion. "Hill folk. Poor whites. Seems like they come up from Choctaw County a few years back, looking for work. Old as Billy Ray—Mr. Puckett—was, he still has a daddy who's alive and kicking. *That* Mr. Puckett called first thing this morning, said he and the wife would like to speak with you, but not right now. Later, after the funeral is past. He says they just want to make some sense out of what happened. He says you told the wife not to worry, assured her Billy Ray was going to live."

"He *was* going to live," said Cooper flatly. "I didn't see any problem at all. There *were* no problems."

"Of course we don't know what went wrong. Not yet, at least." Ned shrugged. "Billy Ray Puckett just . . . went on. Sudden like. The hospital's all abuzz. It was on the news, but I didn't think you'd catch it. I guess his wife was the only one with him when it happened. From what I gather, the family's planning to ask for an autopsy. That's legitimate, at least under the circumstances. Hopefully, it won't lead to anything more. We don't need an inquest right now. Folks in Revere are already riled up enough as it is, what with this school-integration mess going on and you being on the school board and all. . . ." Ned let his voice trail off.

They heard a train taking the track on Tenth Street, the engineer staying on his horn the whole time. Noisy, thought Cooper, but it was probably just as well to be careful. There were so many accidents here in Mississippi. People running their cars off bridges, getting hit by stray bullets, kids pulled under and carried along by freights for near five miles. Lynchings. Murders. All kinds of violence. The South was a volatile place.

"Can we go over what happened?" continued Ned quietly. "Just so I know what's up when people ask me. This is a small town, and you know they will. The newspapers . . . WLBN . . ."

Cooper nodded and started in. "When they called me, that night—I think it was Lucille, one of the duty nurses, who actually did it—I walked over from the house. Daddy's up from Jackson, and they were having a party for some of his friends. A dinner. Mr. Puckett was in the hallway, at the hospital, when I got there. He was still on the gurney they'd used to carry him into the building. But he must have only been there for about ten minutes or so, not too long. They hadn't even had a chance to wheel him into the examining room. I remember there was a little black child. He seemed to be the center of attention, even more than Mr. Puckett. Lucille and the rest of them . . . they wanted that child out."

"When you examined Billy Ray, did he say anything? Was he alert and aware?"

"He was drunk"—Cooper ducked his head when he said this—"and bleeding, drifting in and out of consciousness. We tried to get him focused, but mainly we were concentrated on getting him into the operating room, on stopping the bleeding. You don't want somebody drowning in his own blood. Not right there in the hospital, you don't."

"But did he *say* anything?" Ned insisted. "I mean, did he ask for anybody? His wife, maybe, or his folks?"

Cooper forced himself to remember. "He wanted that boy—Critter, I think his name is—that brought him in. And I think he called out for that boy's daddy, Willy something or other. Maybe Tate. Yes, it was Tate."

"Nobody else?"

"That's all. That's what I recall."

"So he didn't ask for his wife or his family?"

"No, at least not that I remember. He was mainly unconscious, and anyway it wasn't a moment for conversation. Like I said, we were concentrated on saving that man's life."

Ned took that in without flinching. "So once you'd examined him, you decided to operate."

"Yes, we decided to operate." Cooper nodded. "I did. It seemed straightforward enough. We went in. We took out the bullet."

"And then what happened?"

"And then the patient died."

"But you didn't expect him to." Hampton leaned closer, now literally at the edge of his seat. "His wife said you didn't; she sure told that to his daddy. His wife said you came out and explained to her that everything would be all right and that she didn't have a thing in this world to worry about. His daddy and his mama went home with the children. Next thing they know, Mrs. Puckett is sending word out to them, telling them to haul tail back in again because their son is dead."

In the absolute silence that followed, Coop heard the window air-conditioning unit click distinctly to life. He realized he was sweating. "Ned, he'd shot himself; that's why he was in here. Death was always a possibility. I just didn't expect it to occur."

His tone had turned testy. Ned heard this, too. "I know it's difficult for you, Cooper, losing a patient and all. It always is for any surgeon," he said, "but I have to ask these questions for the hospital. This is a tough time for Doctors. You know that. We got more than our fair share of troubles."

He could have been talking to a child—and he was. The very powerful Jack Rand Connelly's child, and he'd best not soon forget it. Cooper saw this realization as it dawned upon Ned's face, and for a moment he hated him for it, hated the placating nature of fear, but the anger disappeared as quickly as it had come. You sure couldn't run around disliking people simply because they thought your daddy was a force of nature, especially when you thought the same thing yourself.

"*Big* problems," emphasized Ned Hampton, "and not just with the schools. This whole integration mess has opened up a great huge can of worms."

"What kind of problems?" Coop actually liked Ned, liked working with him, could not have run the hospital without him. He reminded himself of that fact and forced a smile.

"Outside agitation," said Hampton, and now they both smiled. "Outside Agitation" was the new southern battle cry. "Some folks are coming down from Memphis, they want the Board of Supervisors to let Mid-South Medical set up a new public hospital in the middle of Jefferson-Lee County—right here in Revere, in fact. They want to close this very institution. They're declaring all over everywhere that private hospitals are a thing of the past—in fact, dead already, like dinosaurs."

Cooper said nothing, and Ned continued. He was no longer smiling. "Mid-South is proposing to build the largest public health institution in north Mississippi when Revere's got three private hospitals already—four if you include Charity down in Meridian, where our poor folks can go. With the government behind it, they'll soon run the rest of us out of business. That's exactly what they're aiming to do. It will be socialized medicine. Communism. This country is going to the dogs."

Cooper sat up at attention, listening. He wasn't usually that interested in politics—and this hospital business was straight politics—but he'd had that visitation from the body and now this new thing with Billy Ray Puckett dying on him. He was grateful to let Ned's talk occupy his mind.

"We all know that's been coming," said Cooper. "Even back in the fifties when Daddy took it into his mind to create Doctors. In a poor state like Mississippi, especially if it's mostly rural, you don't need a bunch of private hospitals competing against each other for patients and facilities. Can't keep them up. They're nothing but trophies anyway—at least they are when you come right on down to it. Glorified clinics owned by individual doctors, rich enough to build them. Mark my words, twenty years from now there won't be a one of them left, not down here anyway."

This ruffled Ned. "Twenty years from now is not *now*, and maybe, if you felt that way, you should have told this to your daddy before he used the taxpayers' money to pull up Doctors for you."

"Believe it or not, I tried."

Their eyes met. They both knew that state senator Connelly ran things down in Jackson just exactly like he saw fit. Senator Connelly did not have to listen to anybody.

But Dr. Connelly was fully engaged now, and grateful for it. The body was fading fast. "Nothing can stop the changes coming. We couldn't even if we wanted to, and I'm not sure I want to," said Cooper, but he smiled. "Aside from the obvious—the need to protect Doctors—why are you so against a public hospital in Revere? It can only help. The more sick people we can get to, the better."

Ned seriously doubted the economic wisdom in this particular philanthropic opinion, and his expression said so. "Because 'public' means government-funded, and government-funded means integration! Those folks in Washington are using a carrot and stick on us. Yes, sir, a carrot and stick. With one hand the federals are backing folks like that band of no-account lawyers that calls itself the NAACP Legal Defense Fund, and on the other hand they're trying to trick southerners—and they think we're all just worthless, no-account rednecks anyway, you better believe that, stupid as the day we was born—into working against our own best interests by offering us grants for new schools and equipment and teacher supplements. All we have to do is welcome the darkies into our midst. Take that Hill-Burton Act. All it is, is a way for local government to get federal money for new hospitals as long as everybody promises to be good little boys and girls and allow race mixing. They want to put whites and Nigras on the same floor, maybe even the same room. White nurses having to help out black men! Black doctors able to operate on anybody they choose! It's coming right down to that."

My, was Nathan Bedford Forrest Hampton ever riled up!

Cooper said, "They'd have to get permission first. To have black doctors operating on white patients, I mean. You just can't go up and operate on anybody without his consent. People still get to choose their own doctors."

Though in the end, he knew, everybody would go along with whatever turned up. About this, Ned Hampton was right. Sick people—really sick people—didn't care what color you were, as long as you could help them. Charity down in Meridian had a whole slew of foreign doctors on staff, some of whom could barely speak English, but they were working out fine. First the circumstances changed, and then the changed circumstances changed the people. If nothing else, his own life had taught him that.

"Exactly the point!" exclaimed Hampton, as he missed it. His face above his white shirt collar and neat bow tie had gone quite red. He motioned toward the window, gesturing furiously at something that lay hidden just beyond the calm shade of a giant magnolia. "Look at that uppity Reese Jackson. He's got all kinds of no-account white folks sneaking into him at night. Wanting abortions, needing on-the-sly medicines. White trash up to stuff they don't want folks to know about, at least not decent folks. Supposing Reese Jackson had hospital privileges up on the main floor at Doctors instead of down in the basement where he belongs? He could bring his shiftless, low-life patients on up with him—and not just the black ones. Mark my word, he's arrogant enough to do it, too. He never has shown any hesitation whatsoever in rubbing folks' noses in how he got so rich."

Just like Daddy, Cooper thought. But at least the Connellys had managed to move on, to make *some* people forget where they'd come from; they weren't still in it like the Jacksons were. You couldn't buy your respectability quite as quickly if you were black.

"I hear tell," Cooper interjected, "that Reese Jackson is a pretty fine doctor. Knows what he's doing and all. A good surgeon."

"As well he should be." Ned Hampton sniffed. "All the money the state of Mississippi spent to educate him, sending him up north to college and whatnot. Got a better education than I did! He *ought* to be doing our darkies some good. He just ought not to have profited so much behind it."

Again Cooper smiled, truly enjoying himself now. Gone was the body, gone was the soft, sweet bourbon pull; even Billy Ray Puckett was disappearing fast. Everything nice and smoothed out and smothered over by race. Wrapped up in it. Tied up by it. Bound together with it. Mississippi had barred blacks from its colleges and universities because the United States Supreme Court, right before the turn to the twentieth century, had ruled that the Constitution's equal-protection clause did not really mean that states had to integrate their races and had allowed them to make "separate but equal" provision for them. As usual, Mississippi had enthusiastically embraced the "separate" and totally ignored the "equal." But after World War II, pressure on the legislature to actually *do* something for the state's black citizens grew, and the ever-resourceful legislators came up with a plan to provide equal facilities for its "darkies" by sending the very few who could qualify for professional training to someplace—*anyplace*—as long as it was someplace else, which, politely, meant outside the state of Mississippi. Of course, this new rule had been duly noted on the books but never publicized. Reese Jackson had been one of only six black men to find out about it, and he'd gotten his education. His medical degree had been bestowed, with honors, from Johns Hopkins, and to this day his name was whispered with awe and indignation at the Revere Country Club. Nobody had even been able to find out how one of the poorest boys from one of the poorest parts of this poor state had come to know that this particularly obscure piece of legislation existed.

Reese Jackson was a living legend in Revere.

"Johns Hopkins. We sent him to Johns Hopkins University up in Maryland." *A place my daddy couldn't buy me into.* But Cooper didn't say that part out loud. When he spoke again, he kept his voice neutral. Ned could be right sometimes, even when he was off on a rampage about integration, and Cooper didn't want him to feel slighted and shut up on him, at least not yet. "The good people of Mississippi felt that to be a better alternative than the integration of its medical schools. Better for folks like Reese Jackson to go up north."

*"Better if he had stayed up there, too."* That's what Jack Rand always said. *"Instead of coming back down here with all his changing ways. Bringing trouble. Fermenting trouble."*

But Reese Jackson hadn't minded what Jack Rand Connelly said. He'd come home anyhow.

Ned nodded enthusiastically. "Sure, we need to treat everybody right, and we do that, though you wouldn't believe it by what's on the national news. Our people are happy—at least they *were* happy. They even got their own doctor in that Reese Jackson. Folks got to stick with their kind. We all know that."

"And what do your church members say," asked Cooper quietly, "about 'that'?"

It was only the devil working in him made him say this, and Cooper realized it. The devil and maybe the very last vestiges of the body. But he needed the distraction of Ned Hampton to last just a little bit longer, needed to know he was really and truly safe and that he and Ned were the only ones here.

"What?" Ned looked puzzled.

"Your church members. The ones you worship with religiously each and every Sunday morning over at Piney Grove Missionary Union Baptist Church. What do they have to say about this public hospital wanting to come in?"

"I don't know," said Ned. He'd caught on now, and his face drained color. "I didn't ask them. We don't speak about those things. We don't have time to talk about what's going on now, the integration." He cleared his throat. "We got our songs to sing."

Ned Hampton's singing and where he did it was the talk of Revere and had been for at least three years now. It was generally agreed upon that possession of a melodious voice had been his undoing. When he'd first moved down from Tupelo, he'd joined four church choirs in quick succession—First Baptist, Fairmont Baptist, and Missionary Hill Full Gospel Baptist before branching off and crossing the street to Lane Methodist—but there was no white congregation in Revere that could contain such power, such magnificence. Not to mention Ned's singular choice in music.

Once, after his half-beer-a-night limit, Ned had confided to Cooper that he came from what was delicately referred to as an "irreligious background." His parents did not believe in Sunday churching. They believed in resting up and sleeping in instead. This was a scandal in and of itself throughout the whole county, but it also meant that the standard promises of rural white solace found in hymns like "Trust and Obey" and "Up from the Grave Came a Rose"—melodies that Cooper still remembered, though he hadn't sung anything outside the Episcopalian hymnbook in years—brought with them no echo of youthful reassurance to Ned Hampton. His powerful bass shredded them. His intonations sliced them up.

Then came redemption. Ned's voice hushed reverentially every time he explained what had happened next, his saving moment. One summer evening he'd been out walking and they'd been having a revival over at Piney Grove. You could hear the singing on the night air, catch it on the breeze. Ned heard it; Ned caught it. "A Motherless Child Sees a Hard Time" had been the song, one man moaning out the lead, then scatting it, and the congregation joining in on the chorus. No sound of organ or piano. Everybody clapping out the accompaniment instead. Ned had been mesmerized and intrigued. He'd emerged from behind his tree, gone on inside, and stayed there through "Every Year Carries Off Its Numbers," "Somebody Gone," "Moaner, Where Were You." By the time they got to "While the Blood Is Running Warm in Your Veins," Ned Hampton was hooked. There was enough misery and grit in these old-timey Negro spirituals to hold on to an outsize voice such as his. He felt it. He knew it. He'd found his home and been saved.

He started showing up more and more at Piney Grove, first just to listen to the choir on Sunday mornings and then to sing along with the congregation on Wednesday nights. The music director welcomed him. Ned's was a voice you could use.

Before much time passed, he had joined the choir. Next thing he made himself at home with three other men, all black, forming a quartet that was much in demand at Negro weddings and funerals. White people speculated endlessly about this anomaly. If black people had anything to say, they said it strictly among themselves. Besides, nobody asked their opinion.

Cooper Connelly told his wife, "Ned is the very embodiment of the whole Mississippi contradiction. He's an archsegregationist, and yet he prefers Piney Grove over First Baptist and sees nothing wrong whatsoever with singing all over town with the Warbling Black Birds. Anybody bring it up to him—the contradiction—why, he wouldn't even catch the point."

He seemed to catch it today, though. A muscle in his jaw worked, and Cooper could see his lips clamping tight around words that wanted to spill out. Cooper was even curious to hear them. What exactly would Ned Hampton say? How would he talk back to somebody he thought was spoiled and stupid but still held his job in his hand?

They'd never know. And suddenly Cooper was ashamed of himself for trying to find out, for using Ned as a means to deflect his attention. All in a vain effort, for just a few minutes longer, to keep a dead body from coming back.

He said, "I know you'll do your best by Doctors," placating Ned and calming him on back down, "at the board of supervisors meeting. When is it, tonight?"

The effort was transparent, but it was enough. Ned's mouth relaxed, and he seemed relieved, just like Cooper was, to leave confrontation behind and move on through the day's planned events.

"Tomorrow," he corrected. "Same as your school-board meeting. That's the trouble with Puckett dying right now. It couldn't have happened at a worse time. They were all here, all those poor whites and even a few blacks. I guess Puckett was in that pulp-haulers' union over Macon, the one that white boy from up north started. Blacks and whites . . ."

They were back on Billy Ray Puckett again. That didn't matter to Cooper. Not one bit. Billy Ray was his body, after all. He had made it; he would deal with it. And at least that death had been an accident; of this he was certain.

Ned's voice droned on and on, and Cooper, his gracious self once again, managed to continue smiling his way through the litany of horrors, attend to the few decisions he was called upon to make— *Yes, it was right that the Puckett family meet with him. Set it up with Emily. Have her put it on his calendar*—until he could get Ned Hampton out of his office. Afterward he continued to sit at his desk, as the birds sang, as the air-conditioning carried on its efficient rustle, as another train whistled past, as the sun shone brightly around the edges of his thick drapes.

*Not my fault*, thought Cooper.

Maybe not, but this time it was at least, and most assuredly, his body. He reached for the telephone and noticed, with the clinical detachment of his surgical calling, that his hands were shaking. But not so badly that he couldn't dial in the number correctly, on the second try at any rate.

While the phone rang, he looked down at the newspaper Ned Hampton had brought in with him and laid on the desk. Cooper saw his wife and his father together and smiling brightly up at him from its front page.

"The Honorable Jack Rand Connelly, chairman of the State

Ways and Means Committee, and his daughter-in law, Mrs. Cooper Livingston Connelly, at a soiree at their home, Dunsmuir . . ."

*Evelyne Elizabeth looks pretty*, Cooper thought as the telephone continued ringing in his ear. *She looks happy. So does Daddy. At least that's something.*

How could he have made such a stupid mistake?

IT WAS GOING TO BE a complete and total and utter waste of his time, but Butch Harrison, who had lived the whole of his thirty years in Revere, the last ten of them as deputy to Sheriff Kelly Joe Trotter, knew that it was an even bigger waste to argue with his boss. This was the reason he had survived so long on the job.

"They had to be lazy or dumb or careless, probably all of the above," said Kelly Joe, swigging deep at his black coffee. "Somebody dies over at Doctors Hospital under mysterious circumstances, and those fools don't investigate it. Don't even make a file. How am I supposed to explain that to the taxpayers of this state?"

He was riled, as well he might be. County elections were coming up in June.

Not that Kelly Joe ever had to worry about the competition. Twenty years ago, when he was first voted in, he'd accidentally made himself a legend in one day. Back then elections had been held in early February. On Valentine's Day, after winning what everybody called "a sure-enough squeaker," Kelly Joe had driven up to his house in his brand-new cruiser. He'd rolled on out of the car, a box of Russell Stover chocolates in his hand, pulled out the bullhorn, and shouted on through it, "I'm coming in now, and I want your hands up and your panties down!" unaware—because he was brand-new on the job—that what he was saying was being broadcast to every police station and sheriff's office in the whole of their great state. Kelly Joe was talking to his lawful wife— folks were quick to say it—and they lived out in the county, so there was nobody else around to hear. Still, what happened made him a star in Mississippi. "You'll never again have to spend another cent on campaigning," Jack Rand Connelly had told him. And Kelly Joe never had.

But you got what you trained up, thought Butch. Kelly Joe had made a brief appearance, but most of the deputies down at the hospital that night had been political cronies, buddies of Jack Rand Connelly's, like most all the deputies in Revere. Best as he knew, Butch himself was the only exception. But he'd be danged before he criticized ol' Jack Rand out loud. Instead he took judicious sips of his coffee, determined to speak up only after the sheriff had tuckered safely into his first Krispy Kreme doughnut of the day and the sugar had settled him down a bit.

Butch Harrison, cautious both by nature and by circumstance, was the youngest of a farm family that had moved over to New Hope, Mississippi, from southwestern Alabama when they'd lost their land. He had five brothers, all of whom had recrossed the state line to play various offensive positions for 'Bama's football team. Besides being the youngest, Butch was also the runt of his mama's litter. Together these two circumstances had impelled him to learn to think in a light-footed way. He missed most trouble, if only because he'd trained quick enough to dodge it.

"Seems to me like there's not much to investigate," he said thoughtfully. "The man died unexpectedly. Complications from surgery. It happens all the time."

"Maybe, but the fools needed to make an incident report. Take down some witness information," said Kelly Joe evenly. White folks might be poor, down deep in the county, but they could still vote. "At least pretend they know what they're being paid to do. The fact the department was called in at all, that in an emergency a nurse thought to phone us . . . well, hell, that tells everybody something was up from the jump start. Nobody thinks to call the sheriff if things are running right as they should be."

Butch had to agree with that one; still, he saw the danger and persisted on. He wanted nothing to do with this case, not with Jack Rand Connelly himself likely running defense against it. It was a wonder to him Kelly Joe couldn't see flashing red lights as well.

Butch said, "The only reason they called us was 'cause that Nigra boy, Critter Tate, done brought that Billy Ray Puckett in by hisself. Ten-year-old boy—that was a hell of a distance to be carrying somebody in on your daddy's old truck. Other than that, it was all routine. The nurses were just upset about that child being there, wondering what it was all about. And, naturally, the fact that there was blood. The gunshot wound. They got to call us on that, like they do every time somebody gets hisself shot up down Highway 12 at the Beevis Bar and Grill. It was just routine, and that boy told us what happened."

"Here, have one of these," said Kelly Joe, shoving the doughnut box over and sharing one of his very favorites: raspberry-filled. Generosity like this meant that something was up for sure. Butch felt his heart sinking. "We don't have to do much, just open a little file on it. Let people know we were working for them, that *everybody* in

Jefferson-Lee County gets his fair share of representation. Alls I want you to do is go out there and talk to the widow, see what she knows, then head on over to that boy Critter's house, hear what he has to say for himself. That's all. Ask a few questions; we can open and close this whole case in a day." Kelly Joe's voice turned just a shade placating; he knew that his deputy was no man's fool. "Oh, and you might stop in over Southside. Go see Dr. Connelly himself; tonight, after you've finished up with the others. Get his account. But do it at his house, not at the office, and do it subtle like. Don't want to ruffle more feathers than we need to. We're only doing this because them pulp workers Billy Ray joined up with might start asking some questions. With all that striking going on down there against the mill owners and the trouble blacks and whites always having living along-side each other, somebody might start to think Billy Ray Puckett was intentionally done in. Of course, we know there wasn't nothing like that happened, but if people come on in here, I just want to be able to show them we been working on this, doing our duty. Don't want it being said we been intimidated, or bought out by the mill owners."

Kelly Joe was a man of few words. When he repeated himself, as he was doing now, Butch knew he better haul ass on out of the office.


WHO IN TARNATION *could be intimidated by anything going on this far out in the woods of Mississippi?* Deputy Harrison thought disgustedly as he climbed out of his black-and-white onto grit thick as the snows of Colorado and leading right up to the Puckett front door. The dust of the driveway melded into the dust of what must have served as the small front yard. Not a blade of grass grew on it, but a washtub filled with still-bright geraniums was laid out smack in the middle.

Butch's wife put together a good garden, so he always noticed flowers. These were bright and well cared for. Watered often and pruned. He wondered who took such good care of them—and why they were the *only* things looked like they were being cared for around here.

The house itself was planted on up off the ground on concrete blocks—Harrison thought the river must wash heavy through here in the springtime—and was unpainted. Never had been painted, as far as he could tell. He stepped lightly, watching for weak spots, as he crossed the porch. There were rickety-looking chairs out on it, aluminum and faded vinyl, a big broken-down upholstered chair, a ticking mattress, and a very few scattered, beat-up-looking toys. The deputy could hear a television on in the front room. He didn't look in through the greasy window, though, not a peep. His early home training was still stronger than what they had taught him at the police academy down in Jackson. He knocked smartly on the splinters of the door and waited when nothing happened. He punched it again, harder this time. The television was still going, loud as could be, in the background. Butch didn't recognize the show.

He called out "I'm Deputy Charles William Harrison with the sheriff's office. I'd like to have a word with Mrs. Puckett, if all y'all don't mind."

The door opened with this, and Miss Ruth Ann herself slipped out, surprising Harrison. From the din of the television in the background, he had reckoned he'd need to call out more than once.

He recognized her right away from that television appeal, the one she'd been on just after her husband's untimely demise. But she looked a little better now, like she was maybe getting over the worst of it. She appeared taller, and she'd cut off some of that baby-fine, little-girl hair. Butch remembered her daughter, the feisty one who had knocked stupid Floyd Sobczak's hand off her, right in front of

God and half the folks in Revere, Mississippi. Mrs. Puckett looked a lot more like her daughter today, more than she had when they'd been on television. Butch saw the family resemblance, especially around the mama's sharpened-up eyes.

"What you want?" demanded Ruth Ann Puckett.

"Ma'am," said Butch, removing his hat and minding his manners. "The sheriff sent me out to ask you a few questions—just one or two so's we can set our record straight. I'm talking about the night your deceased husband passed on. Thought we might close the file on it. Maybe set our own minds right as to exactly what happened."

"Nothing happened," snapped out Miss Ruth Ann. "Billy Ray fell down and shot himself with his gun. That's it. It's a sorrow to us, but it's the kind of thing occurs to folks all the time."

Harrison nodded. "Yes, ma'am. I understand this is difficult for you, talking about the untimely passing of your husband and all. I'll only keep you a minute. One or two questions, just to clear things up. If we could find us someplace to talk . . ."

He didn't mean the front porch with all its splinters, but she took it as that. She offered him sweet tea, reaching down beside her to an ice chest and glasses nestled in the cool earth. He was grateful for this. Sipping on sweet tea could keep talk going; nobody expected you to leave till you were good and done. When he didn't move, Ruth Ann Puckett made a slight motion to the porch steps, and Butch lowered himself gingerly on the top one, not shifting around much once he got there. He glanced up to see her looking at him and smiling ever so slightly. She lowered herself down next to him, but not too close.

Butch pulled out a small notebook and took a stub of pencil out of his breast pocket. "You want to tell me in your own words just what occurred? How he got shot?"

"I wasn't there," said Mrs. Puckett, looking straight at him over the rim of her glass. "How would I know?"

Butch blinked. "Right. Now, Miss Ruth Ann—this is just routine—but did your husband have any enemies? We know this was an accident, him falling on his gun and all. We've got to ask these questions anyway. You understand."

"Not that I know of," she said. "No enemies."

"What about that group of pulpwood haulers? Anybody there?"

She said, "Billy Ray had just joined up. Wasn't time enough for him to make much trouble. But they've been here for me since he died just the same. Brought us something to eat every day, helped me get the youngest babies up to my kinfolk in Iuka. I got cousins up there. Nice people, those pulp haulers. Helpful. Even that Yankee guy who started them up."

"That would be Josiah Bixby?"

"Right. That's the one. Used to live with that witch-woman over Revere."

"Do you know who your husband associated around with? Can you give me the names of his friends?"

"Billy Ray didn't really have what you might call friends. He was more of a loner. Spent his time here at home—I mean, over at the trailer—with me and the kids. He was a good father," she added quickly.

"I'm sure of that," said Deputy Harrison, flipping shut his notebook. What a waste of his time! "But he hadn't been arguing with anybody. No trouble?"

Ruth Ann Puckett's answer came out so slowly that it caused Deputy Harrison to pause, stop tucking his pencil away, and turn back to her. There was a ripple behind them, and he turned to see the oldest girl, the one who had made such a spectacle of herself on the television, staring out at them through the screen door. He wondered how long she'd been there, just watching, saying nothing. He wondered how much this child knew.

"Mrs. Puckett," he repeated.

"One time," she said finally, "I heard him arguing with that Willie Tate, Critter's daddy. Nothing to it. Didn't last long."

"Do you remember what they were saying?"

Ruth Ann turned her clear eyes right toward him. She put her glass down, started to get up. "Too far away. Couldn't hear a word of it."

But she was lying. And Butch knew she was.

HE WAS STANDING THERE when the old, rickety school bus pulled up and Critter Tate climbed down off it, staring at him the whole time. The child was holding tight on to a potato sack with holes in it so big Butch could make out the titles on some of the books inside. They were old books. Butch thought he recognized a couple from his own school days over in New Hope. That's the way things were in the South. Blacks got the old school buses when whites finished with them; then they got their old beaten-up books and their falling-apart equipment as well. *If* they acted right and didn't cause a fuss. Butch had been to enough black schools to know that nobody in them knew what "new" meant. So much for separate but equal. He had a sure sense of law and order as well of God's universe and his place, as a white man, in it. But Butch knew bullying when he saw it. And sometimes, just sometimes, when he looked at the television pictures of what was going on over in Birmingham and down in Montgomery—all those folks dressed up in their Sunday best, just like Reverend Streeter over at the River Café— and *determined* to get beat up just so long as they got what was rightfully theirs, he wondered, if he were black and his cute little wife, Lurleen, black, and his two darling babies, Butch Jr. and Ella, black, if he wouldn't have been right there beside them, braving Bull Connor and his attack dogs just so that they had the right to all sit themselves down on a Woolworth lunch-counter chair and have them some lunch.

But that was neither here nor there today. Critter Tate and his falling-apart school books were not the reason Butch had come way out here to the county.

"How you doing, son? Your name Willie Tate Jr.?" he asked. The boy was a little bitty thing. Butch was instantly sympathetic. "Your mama around?"

"In the house, sir," said the boy.

"Would you tell her Deputy Harrison's here and would like to have a word with you?"

The child nodded, but a woman had already appeared on the porch. She had a baby in one arm and another one clinging steadfastly to her skirts.

"Deputy, come on in," she called out. "Critter, bring that officer on up to the house."

Butch gladly accepted the invitation, knowing that an offer of something cold and something sweet would surely come next. He could tell by the neatness of her children that Critter's mama kept a well-running house. She settled him down on a green sofa carefully covered in clear plastic and left him to stare at the obligatory pictures on her wall: a thoughtful black Jesus, a thoughtful white John F. Kennedy, and a very large portrait of Martin Luther King Jr. ornately framed in gold. When the woman came back—bearing a frosty pitcher of lemonade, glasses, and a generous plate of delicious-smelling peach cobbler—Butch noticed that she'd left the other two children someplace in the dark, cool recesses of her little house. But Critter was still with her. She placed him down in a chair opposite the deputy, then moved in another chair from the kitchen, pushed it near the door, and sat down to watch them from there.

"Mighty tasty cobbler," said Butch. And he ate enough of it to show he wasn't just being polite. "Great peaches. Get them around here?"

"*Grew* them here," corrected Mrs. Tate proudly. "Got some put up out back. Give you a jar to take on home to Mrs. Harrison. The quality of the peaches is what makes a cobbler."

No argument from Butch on that. He nodded his thanks and took another sip of his lemonade. Finally he said, "Mrs. Tate, ma'am, I have a few questions for Willie Jr. here. Mind if I ask them?"

Critter's mama shook her head, settled in.

"Critter," said the deputy, "that was mighty smart of you, the way you got Mr. Billy Ray Puckett into Revere so fast that night he got shot."

"Thank you, sir," said Critter, beaming. His television appearance had made him a star. Folks were still talking to him about it. "I knew if I didn't get him to the hospital, he'd bleed to death. Takes forever to get an ambulance out here, if'n we had the telephone to call one."

"You must be a hunter. You know it's not the hole that kills but the bleeding."

"Yes, sir. I know that. My daddy taught me. That's why I took Mr. Billy Ray in quick as I could."

Butch leaned closer. "But tell me, son—what were you doing over that ways anyhow? It was getting on to dark, and the Puckett place is a fair distance from here, a good walk down the road. What you doing so far away from home after supper?"

The boy hesitated, until his mama's voice came to him clearly from her corner of the little room. "Go on, Critter, tell the deputy what you know."

"I was just out there, sir. Walking around. Doing nothing," he said, looking down. "All by myself."

"When exactly did you see Mr. Billy Ray?"

"He was putting up his deer stand."

"In the *dark?*"

"Wasn't dark yet, sir, not when I first saw him. He said he'd got to get it up quick as possible. Said they'd hit on hard times of late and that they needed the meat. Trouble was, he was going at it wrong, sir," Critter said earnestly, and leaned closer. "I could see what he was doing, and I tried to tell him, tried to read him what the instructions said to do. But you know how Mr. Billy Ray is—was. . . . He didn't want to hear nothing about nothing, especially when it involved reading. He can't tell dog from cat if it's written, but he don't want nobody to know it, especially nobody black. He told me his wife had told him all about it, and what she said was what he was meaning to do. I was looking right at the papers, and I was trying to tell him, politely as I could, that things wasn't going to end up the way he wanted, but he wouldn't pay me no mind. Finally I just got on out and left him to it. That's when I heard the shots."

"*Shots?*" Deputy Harrison left off writing.

"Well, yes, sir. Two shots. That's what I tried to tell them at the hospital—tried to tell Dr. Cooper and Dr. Reese both. Nobody would listen. Things were mighty busy."

"You heard two shots? You sure of that, son?"

Critter was sure enough, at least about that, but he had started edging a little away from the deputy. He hesitated and then rushed on to tell about running back to the clearing and seeing Billy Ray sprawled out under the collapsed deer stand. He told him about getting his daddy's truck, half leading, half pulling Puckett into it, and starting out on that long ride into Revere. Critter had gotten his story down pat.

"Anything else you need to say to me, boy?" asked the deputy, still a little puzzled by the idea of two shots. Unless something had slipped past him, which he doubted, Billy Ray Puckett had had one wound. But just to make certain, he'd ask that burly nurse who'd first telephoned them, maybe even Dr. Connelly himself. A gun didn't go and discharge twice when you fell off a stand onto it. In the back of his mind, Harrison had been planning to put Connelly off until tomorrow but decided it was probably better to get this whole thing cleared up tonight.

Critter shook his head emphatically. "No, sir," he said.

"Good boy."

Deputy Harrison got up, and everybody else got up with him. Mrs. Tate hurried into the kitchen and came back with two mason jars of the best-looking canned peaches Butch had seen all season. Shimmered dark brown, like they had a goodly amount of cinnamon in them, which he liked. "Mighty kind of you, ma'am. I certainly do appreciate it."

Mrs. Tate smiled. "Think nothing of it. Hope you got the information you came for."

"You got a right smart boy in Critter, ma'am. A credit to you. He'll make y'all proud."

Butch Harrison had his hat on his head again, was already off the neat front porch and practically off the gray-painted stairs before he turned back.

"Critter, where was everybody—I mean, your parents—when all this was going on? Why didn't you run over and get one of them to drive?"

"No time to find them, sir. I had to get Mr. Billy Ray to town right quick."

"But where were they?"

Critter glanced down for a minute as though he were trying real hard to remember and then looked up at the sheriff with clear, guileless eyes. "Mama and the children were over at Aunt Emma's."

"And your daddy?"

"Well, sir, I don't rightly know *exactly* where my daddy was."

Deputy Butch Harrison always made a practice to be as honest as he could be no matter the circumstance, but, Lord knows, sometimes in police work you got to get dirty. Especially when you were being lied to. He patted Critter on the head, smiled over at Mrs. Tate, and made a big pretense of asking her if he could take a turn around back to check out her peach trees. "Just so's I can tell when I get home exactly what kind they were. I know my wife's gonna want to know that, once she takes a bite of these." He held up the mason jars like a trophy, and Mrs. Tate beamed her consent. But instead of ambling on around to the yard, he doubled right back and quietly approached the porch from behind. He knew boys and their mamas, and he knew that these two would huddle together as soon as the big, bad deputy was out of the way.

Mrs. Tate was already whispering. "Critter, I truly don't understand why you didn't tell that officer you'd gone out to that clearing to meet your own daddy. Nobody was up to nothing. The two of you were only going out frog gigging. Just say your daddy hadn't showed up yet. You couldn't have got him in any trouble saying that."

Critter Tate shook his head, and when he answered his mama, you could hear the wisdom of the ages whispering through his ten-year-old voice. "Mama, this is Mississippi. And if a white man gets shot someplace—anyplace—then no black man needs to be anywheres around it. Daddy wasn't there when I carried Mr. Billy Ray into Revere. That's all them somebodies needs to know."

. . .

BUTCH HARRISON, TIRED NOW, and not a little disgusted, knocked for the second time on the handsome, polished, solid-wood oak of Dr. Cooper Livingston Connelly's front door. He'd rung the doorbell twice before this. Nobody came, but the deputy could hear strains of music—he thought he recognized Ella Fitzgerald singing out something, though he couldn't quite catch the words, and there was laughter. The place was lit up bright as Christmas Day. He knew that somebody was home.

"Might as well be back at Ruth Ann Puckett's," he said to himself, calling to mind the blare of her television, the noise that had shut out everything else. Butch thought about chucking it all and coming back tomorrow. Or, better yet, catching Dr. Connelly alone at his office, but then he decided it was best to get this whole semblance of an investigation over with in one day. Besides, he was puzzled. What Critter Tate had said about that second shot put a new light on things.

The deputy knocked once again and then for good measure yanked on the ornate little bellpull, an antebellum "af-fec-ta-tion" if he had ever seen one, but one which, it turned out, really worked. By the time the eighth chime rang out, the door was pulling open and Deputy Harrison stood gawking at Cooper Connelly's wife.

He pulled off his hat.

Butch Harrison was not a great one for reading the society column in the *Times Commercial*. When he settled down in his Barcalounger with the paper, he generally went straight for the sports pages and then on to true relaxation with the funnies. Only rarely did he glance even at the front page; he got that kind of news off the television. But you'd have to not live in Revere at all not to recognize Mrs. Cooper Livingston Connelly. Tall, blond, a real looker—

wearing high heels in her own house, brandishing her martini glass like a weapon, and shaking her head. Red fingernails, too, and not a nick on them. The kind of hands, according to Butch's wife, that proclaimed their owner's unfamiliarity with housework. Butch was impressed enough by Mrs. Cooper Connelly to take her all in so he could thrill Lurleen with every detail once he made it back home to New Hope. His wife read Miss Dabney's column religiously and would want to know exactly what Butch had seen and where.

"Nobody's ever around when you need them," Mrs. Connelly said, eyes narrowing and looking past Butch as though an errant house girl might be out in the night fooling around in the yard somewhere.

Finally she paused, her pale eyes focused dead on him, and said, "May I help you?"

You could tell from her voice that she wasn't from around here.

Butch switched his hat from one hand to the other. "I'm sorry to bother you, ma'am, but I'm Deputy Charles William Harrison. We're just closing our file on Billy Ray Puckett—that man over Macon died a few days back at the hospital—and I have a question or two left over, a couple of things we thought your husband might help clear up."

"This time of night?" Mrs. Connelly's incredulity was genuine. "We've got friends visiting. Daddy Jack is up from Jackson. Couldn't you wait until tomorrow? My husband will be at his office all day."

A fair enough question. Butch had asked it of Kelly Joe Trotter himself. "The sheriff thought it would be better to just catch him out at the house. Deputies coming into the hospital, asking questions—people might start assuming something was wrong. Might start to talk."

As though they wouldn't talk anyway with his big black-and-white parked on this quiet, tree-lined Southside street. Butch wondered why Jack Rand was up from Jackson. It was the middle of the week, and he usually didn't make it to Revere but on the weekends. Then Butch remembered the articles he'd been reading about the new hospital. He remembered the talk about school integration. Times like these, Jack Rand would be smart enough to spend most of his time up here in his district, not buried down in the capital.

Evelyne Connelly looked Butch over, and then her luscious lips spread wide into a smile. The smile was bright and toothy. Electric. And practiced. You could tell.

Mrs. Connelly said, "I'm sorry. Of course. My husband is here, and my father-in-law, too—up from Jackson. Did I mention that already? Perhaps you'd like to speak with him as well."

Butch wouldn't, and said so. The smile lost some of its voltage at this last. Mrs. Cooper stepped aside and let him in. The interior of her house was much grander than what you would have thought from the street, much larger. But Butch had come to expect this from the few antebellums he'd been called upon to enter—just three actually, in all his career. The Connellys had a marble entrance hall that dwarfed the crystal chandelier hanging from the two-story ceiling and could easily have swallowed four rooms of the little starter house Butch and his wife couldn't yet afford to move out of over in New Hope.

Mrs. Connelly watched him for a moment, still smiling, and then moved across toward a small drinks table near a closed oak door. In fact, all the doors were shut tight, muffling sound. Butch could hear laughter and that singing woman—he was pretty sure now it truly was Ella—but he couldn't quite pinpoint their whereabouts. The only thing he could make out with clear distinction was the *click-click* of Mrs. Connelly's very high heels as she moved purposefully across the polished marble of her floor. She balanced the nearly full martini glass in one hand and didn't put it down as she reached for a decanter with the word "vodka" scrolled on a heavy silver tag. Butch could read the label easily from where he stood. After his long day drinking sweet tea at the Pucketts' and lemonade down by Willie Tate's house, Deputy Harrison was used to being asked if he'd take a little refreshment. He opened his mouth to politely decline what Mrs. Connelly was surely set to offer—he kept to a firm rule of no alcohol when he was on duty—but Mrs. Connelly seemed to have forgotten all about him. Butch watched her top the colorless liquid into her glass, watched her delicately lick her fingers of the spillage, and then watched as she reached for an ice cube, swizzled it around in her glass, and lifted it out again.

Next to the tray, there was a plate of tiny sandwiches, crustless little things about half the size of a bite. She took up one of these, stared at it, nibbled on it. She kept her back to Butch Harrison. She did not offer one to him.

Butch thought, with some amusement, that Mrs. Connelly called herself putting someone like him in his place. He would tell Lurleen about this as well. He could already hear her laughter and her cheerful, "Well, there's no accounting for some people."

"Mrs. Connelly," he said, "your husband?"

She still didn't turn around, but she motioned him to a door. "In there. The doctor's in there. Just knock. You won't disturb him."

She did not lead the way.

The place she motioned to was almost exactly opposite where Butch stood, but he started off, with due diligence, toward it. For a moment, turning back, he saw that Mrs. Connelly had turned back as well and was smiling at him—the same puzzling smile she'd worn when she first opened the door. Deputy Harrison thought it looked well practiced. He also knew you could learn a lot about a man by seeing what he'd chosen as his wife.

"Just knock on the door and tell him you want to ask about that poor thing who died from over in Macon," she sang out, loudly and a little dubiously, as though she doubted that Butch knew his own job. He wondered if she was always like this. Nothing you could exactly put your finger on, just "like this."

His rap upon Connelly's door was a little sharper than it might have been, but the knock was opened by the doctor himself. If he was surprised to see Harrison, or anyone else in a uniform for that matter, he didn't show it. He said, "Come on in. I was just reading."

That seemed like a fair enough statement; at least Harrison thought so, as he looked around. The deputy was a great fan of Mickey Spillane and Louis L'Amour. He had already read a fair number of their books and anticipated reading more. It was obvious Dr. Connelly had him beat, though. Harrison saw every type of book imaginable, scattered everywhere—grimy paperbacks, richly embossed leather sets that smelled of age even from across the room, volumes whose gold-scrolled titles he could not make out, books piled up high in their shipping boxes and with the tags still on them. The only thing they seemed to have in common was their helter-skelter randomness and that this randomness made them look out of place in such a formal room.

Yet, at the same time, the books bound the space together; gave the dark, deeply wainscoted library a focus that Butch doubted it would otherwise have had and isolating this particular setting from the formality of the clipped gardens that led to the house, the sweep of the front hallway, and even from the perfection of the woman who had greeted him at the door. Butch realized that he was in a sanctuary. He had one himself, called it his "workroom," and kept it off-limits to everybody else. It was down in his basement, far away from the everyday activity of his home. But what struck him as odd in this grand haven—so much larger and finer than his own—was not what was here but what his trained eye told him was missing: photographs, family mementos, trophies and small plaques, the simple way-marks of existence that said that life had passed through here. There was nothing on the walls and nothing but books on the shelves. And there were no medical journals, not that Butch could see, nothing relating to Cooper Connelly as a doctor, or as a husband and a son.

Dr. Connelly said, "May I offer you something? A drink?"

He sounded amused. Deputy Harrison decided he must surely be gawking. He shook his head, cleared his throat, lined his face back up again.

"I'm just here to ask you a few questions, Dr. Connelly. Thought I might get them over with tonight—that is if you don't mind. The sheriff wants to call shut to that case with Billy Ray Puckett."

"I don't mind at all. Have a seat. Besides, I imagine my wife has already offered you something."

Butch didn't touch that one. "Just a few questions, sir, that's all."

Cooper Connelly motioned to a low velvet sofa. He was dressed in gray slacks and a shirt open at the neck; a tie and blue jacket were piled near a tray with sandwiches on it and what looked like sweet tea. They were work clothes, not party ones. The kinds of things a doctor might wear under his whites during the day. Ella had started singing again; her elegant scatting drifted in through the closed door. The party still was going on, but without its host—that is, if indeed Cooper Connelly were its host. Butch wondered. Jack Rand's boy did not seem the partying kind. In that, he might be different from his daddy.

Butch had no idea where this notion had come from. But once his mind got hold of it, he knew it was true.

"Billy Ray Puckett," he repeated, settling in. He made brief work of telling what he had learned thus far. It was a cut-and-dried case, he assured Dr. Connelly of this. He ended up by saying, "When you first saw Mr. Puckett, was he conscious?"

"Yes."

"Lucid?"

"More or less. I would say yes. He was in and out, but when he was conscious, he knew where he was and how he'd got there. Knew who he was."

"Out in the hallway, wasn't it? They hadn't had a chance to wheel him in."

"That's right," Connelly said, and nodded.

"Did he ask for anyone?"

"Not while I was there," said Cooper. "Not while I was with him. But the nurse—Lucille—told me he'd mumbled something about that child Critter, the one who brought him in."

"Anybody else? Did Miss Lucille say he asked for anybody else? "

Dr. Cooper paused and thought. "Maybe that boy's daddy. I think she mentioned something about that boy's father. What's his name—Willie Tate? Yes, he said something about him. I remember because Lucille thought it was odd—him asking about those people and not saying a word about his own family."

"Anything specific? "

"No, he asked *for* him, called out his name. At least that's what I was told."

"Anybody else—you sure he didn't say nothing about his wife and children?"

"Not that I know of."

Butch nodded. Wrote this down. "And did you examine him?"

"Of course I did," said Cooper, so sharply that the deputy looked up. The doctor was no longer smiling. "I was his surgeon, after all."

"You saw the . . . what do they call it? The entrance wound?" Butch opened his eyes wide, played the dumb redneck. He loved doing that.

"Yes."

"And the exit wound? Of course, you must have seen that as well."

For the first time, Dr. Connelly hesitated. It got so quiet for a minute that Butch could hear laughter coming at him from the party, even bits of conversation and, through it all, Ella still singing away.

"An exit wound," he prompted quietly. "Did you see one?"

The doctor shook his head. "Actually, I don't recall. I'd have to look on his chart, read what I noted. I only saw Billy Ray Puckett three times in my life—once that night when I performed the surgery and then, briefly, the next two mornings when I made rounds. He seemed fine. Responding well to what was in reality only a routine intervention—not that surgery should ever be taken lightly," he added hastily. "I don't mean that. It's just that I see so many gunshot wounds, accidental ones, especially around now, around hunting time. I would have visited him again; in fact, I was just about to start out on my rounds when my hospital administrator brought me the news—totally unexpected—that he'd died."

"You didn't want to know what had *happened?*" Deputy Harrison iced his words with just the proper note of incredulity. "This was a man you thought would pull through."

"Of course I wanted to know what had happened," snapped Cooper irritably, Jack Rand Connelly's boy after all, "but that's the medical examiner's job to make a determination, not mine, and he was not called in on this. We just assumed heart failure. That's what the attending physician said, and he's the one who pronounced Mr.

Puckett dead. Perhaps it should have gone further, but Mrs. Puckett did not want an autopsy and no one wanted to push it. Push her. She was extremely upset. We didn't want to make it worse. Her situation was already bad enough."

Everybody south of Richmond knew womenfolk were fragile and that, rich or poor, they needed to be protected.

Butch dutifully wrote down what the doctor said. With a pencil stub. In his notebook. He took his time, erased something, and then wrote it all out again.

Finally, "One last question. Did you come across two different wounds in Mr. Puckett? In others words, could there have been more than one bullet in him when he died?"

"Absolutely not," said Cooper Connelly with conviction. "He had one wound to the anterior lower chest, and there were no vital organs involved. His main danger was from bleeding to death, but we stopped the blood flowing before we wheeled him into the oper-ating room."

"Did that child, Critter, mention anything to anybody about hearing a second shot?"

Connelly shrugged. "Deputy, this little colored boy shows up with a white man who's been shot up—you know how things are, how he's going to be treated. It was a wonder they let him in the hospital at all. He was keeping his mouth shut. Mostly trying not to be noticed, if you know what I mean."

Deputy Harrison nodded to the truth of this and then began the struggle up from a deep, down-cushioned seat.

"Good luck at the county supervisors' meeting tomorrow," he said once Connelly had escorted him out of the room, through the vast hallway, and to the front door. The music had switched; it was louder now, with more of a decided beat. Butch could no longer recognize whoever was doing the singing. Besides, he was suddenly weary and anxious to be out back to New Hope. He wanted his wife.

"I imagine they'll be talking about the new hospital," he added to be polite, but his foot was already well planted on the porch.

"Probably," said Cooper, and he smiled. It was amiable—his daddy's smile, thought Butch. Politic. But Dr. Connelly seemed like a nice enough man despite that. For one thing, unlike Jack Rand's, his smile reached all the way up to his eyes. "Everybody's pretty riled up. My administrative assistant came in a couple of days ago talking about how this new hospital threatens to ruin the orderly progression of life down here in Mississippi, and for good. You must know him, name's Ned Hampton. Anyway, ol' Ned was all worked up because federal funds mean integration. The thought of white nurses being called upon to attend to the needs of black men liked to vex him to death. As though the whole thing—the bringing in of this new institution, the changes it will make here, and the *impact* it will have—comes down to a question of race."

"Doesn't it?" asked Butch. "Doesn't everything nowadays?"

The two men looked at each other through the twilight.

"Well, thanks for coming by," said Dr. Connelly, ever gracious, as though Deputy Butch Harrison had been called to his house as a guest. "Let me know if I can be of any further help."

"Sure will," said Harrison. He was halfway down the red brick stairs, halfway between the raucous music behind him and the crickets singing on the evening breeze up ahead, when he turned back. "Tell your daddy I read his last piece in the *Times*. Talking about the schools and what's going to happen. 'Military Avenue will run red with blood before we let the federal government tell us who has to sit next to who.' Did you read it?"

Cooper nodded. The light was behind him, and the shadows

played so funny that Butch could not quite make out his face in the gloom.

"He's something else," said the deputy, "Jack Rand Connelly. A regular card. Been saying the same good-ol'-boy stuff ever since I can remember. Pumping things up. Thing is, times have changed. What you used to be able to say . . . well, folks, at least some folks, might call it asking for trouble. They may not have minded how things were down here when we were the only ones really knew how things went, but now that the rest of the country's paying attention—hey, that's something else again."

"Daddy always wins his election," said Dr. Connelly quietly.

"Just like my sheriff." Butch Harrison could have been aiming for a Mr. Congeniality award. "No doubt about that. None whatsoever. And I guess you can't argue with success. Still . . . the voting ranks might be changing soon, more folks joining in. A different kind of folks, if you catch my meaning."

The deputy's light laughter brought the two men together again, southern white boys taking the breeze on a hot September night, smelling sweet smells on the very pretty porch of one of the prettiest houses in town. But Butch knew that his meaning had been taken. What he didn't know was what Connelly would do with it. Jack Rand was his daddy, after all. And Revere had stayed clear of racial trouble, at least so far. Only thing really happening was Reverend Streeter determined to get heartburn eating greasy catfish over at the River Café. This wasn't Jackson or Selma or Birmingham, and better to leave it like that.

But Dr. Connelly seemed to have his own preoccupations. "This thing with Mr. Puckett seems straightforward enough. Not worth the police expending a lot of energy on it. I wouldn't take it too seriously if I were you."

"Maybe not," said Deputy Harrison, "but I want to send Billy

Ray's gun and the bullet and all the other physical evidence down to the state crime lab in Jackson. Maybe talk to your surgical team, just for the record. That is, if you don't mind."

Cooper shook his head. He didn't mind.

Butch hated to admit it—this boy's daddy was a mighty-big big shot—but the deputy in him told him that something was going on and that he wouldn't be tying this case up by the morning, as he had so fervently hoped.

"You work with the same people all the time, don't you?"

"Same ones," answered Connelly. "Just about every surgeon has his own team, at least in Mississippi. Gil Miller is my anesthesiologist. The nurses change over sometime, but I usually have Sue Lyn Hicks and Janice Newman. I had Sue Lyn and Janice that night, at least I think I did. Drop by my office. My secretary can give you their information—where you can reach them and all."

Butch said he was mighty grateful. "I think this is the best way to go about it, wrap things up, since there was no autopsy. I'm also going to make some inquiries. Got it in my head to see if Willie Tate Sr. owns a 6.5 Carcano. That's the gun Mr. Billy Ray was shot with."

"*Everybody* in Mississippi owns a 6.5 Carcano, Officer. Surely you must know that."

Connelly laughed, and Butch joined right in with him. "You are definitely right about that, sir," he said.

The deputy was on his way now one tired good ol' boy, determined to drag his butt home.

"Give my best to the senator," he said, and then, ever so slyly, "and express my thanks to your gracious wife."

# Chapter 8

"NOW, WHY IN GOD'S NAME does he see his way to writing this mess? That man don't know nothing else but how to create trouble."

Melba had enjoyed her five-o'clock bath and was sitting on her front porch, smelling good and taking in the late-afternoon air. She was also reading her newspaper. Even though she could not stand Jack Rand Connelly—"Really and truly cannot *stand* him," she repeated to Deanie at least once a week—she read his column in the *Times Commercial* as religiously as most folks in Revere read their Bibles.

"Got to keep up with what's up," she said.

Keeping up with what was up was Melba's justification for many of her vices.

With State Senator Connelly, "what's up" was usually murder and mayhem. Or lynchings—always rendered in the plural—down in Money, Mississippi, where he originally came from. At least that was the rumor. Melba's clients talked about Jack Rand Connelly all the time, knew all about him, or so they said. He'd started out his political career as deputy sheriff in the Delta, a poor boy who'd made his money sharecropping, then overseeing, then finally owning, great fine acres of planted cotton. This unlikely progression naturally generated a fair amount of quiet murmuring as to how he'd actually gotten so rich and what part the devil may have played in such a marked transformation. Black people were not the only ones murmuring along these lines.

*"When picking time came, you had to work your people hard. Couldn't take no nonsense."* Jack Rand was still fond of saying this. He loved quoting himself at dinner parties, especially the ones to which he was now invited. *"Getting that cotton in, having to do it, having people depending on you. Why, the necessity of it all would have turned Jesus Christ Himself into a hard man."*

And Jack Rand Connelly was no Jesus, as he'd be the first to admit.

"My goodness," said Melba, hiking up her rhinestone-studded eyeglasses and peering close in to the newspaper.

Jack Rand was certainly riding a high horse today. The little children of Mississippi needed salvation from the fate their government had in mind for them, and he for one was determined to save them.

"School Integration"—the words were writ bold, both in his headline and in his text—"it's heading in our direction. It's what the federal government has determined and will dictate. And it is incumbent upon us to stop it!"

"Incumbent." Melba shook her head in disgust. "The only incumbent that man cares about is himself."

She was so busy talking back to her newspaper—Senator Connelly's was the most popular column in it; whether you loved or hated him, he always got read—that at first she didn't really see the man as he paused at her garden gate. Stopped. Looked around. Still, she was, after all, Madame Melba. She may not have been paying him any attention, but she sensed a presence. Somebody with a question to ask or a need to fulfill. Company. Without looking up, she called out, "Hey, there, don't I know you? Don't I know your people?"

"Maybe," the man answered. "Maybe you do."

His was a nice voice. That was the first thing she noticed about him and the thing she would remember for the rest of her life. How nice his voice was. How kind. How soft. How gentle. Miss Melba Obrenski was drawn to such things.

Lips parted just a curious bit, she looked up slowly from Jack Rand's rantings and ravings to fasten on the face of his son standing right there before her, at the beginning of her brick pathway, his hand poised just an inch above her white-painted gate. She could make him out clearly, see that he was smiling. The smile was small, and it was slightly quizzical. The second thing she would always remember about him was that smile.

In fact, she remembered it right then because she had seen it before. She knew this man. They'd met. Melba could see the vague recall forming itself on his face as well, and in his eyes. She had to stop it. Didn't want him remembering their last encounter, not for a minute did she want that.

She prayed to God he wouldn't quite place her.

You could see he was trying, though, and she was too much Melba not to be already saying, "Good afternoon, Dr. Connelly. You over here looking for Reese Jackson?" Because she sure hoped he wasn't looking for her.

Cooper seemed taken aback by her question, a little surprised, as though he really didn't know what he was doing here. As though he should walk away quickly. Melba recognized the look. She'd seen it a hundred times before, in both her varied professions, and the perception of it automatically kicked in a studied response. Miss Melba notched her smile up, gave her shoulders a little wiggle.

"He lives here, you know. Reese Jackson. In that great big house right there."

Dr. Connelly said, "Really?" He didn't turn away. He didn't move on.

"*Owns* it," sang out the Madame. "Owns the one next door, too. Doesn't own mine, though, I own this one my own self." With "my-own-self" coming out as three distinct and stand-alone words.

Dr. Connelly said, "I didn't know Dr. Jackson lived near here," just as a '56 Chevy with muffler problems passed by. Melba could hardly hear him, and when she did, she could hardly believe him. And, Melba being Melba, she just about said so out loud. Caught herself barely in time. Everybody knew everybody else in Revere, and if they didn't know them, they at least knew their business. In Revere, there were only so many places where a rich black person could live. Catfish Alley was one of them; way out in the county was the only other. But sometimes you couldn't tell with white people. They made a habit of not knowing all kinds of very obvious things.

"He's not home now," called out Melba the all-knowing. She snatched off her glasses and raised a very pretty hand to ward off the sun. "Wife's gone, too, over to Meridian shopping. Mr. Reese is still at his office. Always is. Want some sweet tea?"

"Actually," said Cooper Connelly. He was still at the beginning of her pathway, and they were shouting, ever so slightly, back and forth. "Actually, I was coming from a meeting at the school board, and thought I might go over and have a look at Hunt School. I'm on it, you know. The school board. Anyway, my car broke down on

Main Street. Just stopped working. I decided to leave it there. Came on anyway, on foot. I happened to see your sign. I must say, it's pretty arresting."

"You might say that," said Melba, blushing and hoping he wouldn't get her quick joke.

He cocked his head. He hadn't heard her! Melba let out a small sigh of relief.

"Sweet tea?" she repeated.

Thank goodness for good home training, given long ago but still coming automatic. Because, for once, without it, Miss Melba Obrenski would have been at a loss for words.

Though not for curiosity.

Dr. Connelly said that he would like some tea—in fact, that he would like some very much. It was a hot day, too hot for October. "Things aren't cooling down like they should."

Melba nodded. "They sure aren't," and noted that the doctor did not walk up her path with the purposeful step of a man who needed to be anyplace else real soon.

*Lonely,* Melba caught herself thinking. She recognized it instantly, at least on the people—women in the daytime and the men that had once come at night—who made their way to her front door. Loneliness and fear and heartache had formed the basis of her very tidy living, and she had long ago stopped questioning who should feel them and why. You never could tell. Life was like her former business—you just took what came at you and worked with it, at least until there was no more working left to do.

He was a mighty fine specimen of a man. Melba'd thought so the first time she saw Cooper Connelly, and she still thought so this day. Lately she'd started to forget just how good-looking a good-looking man could be. Probably came from so many years of closing her eyes to what was going on over her, of what was going on in her body, of trying to keep that part of her out of her mind. But the sight of Dr. Connelly was bringing it all back. He was a looker, all right: nice slim build, tan slacks, a tie, and blue poplin blazer properly buttoned even on this hot day. He must have been at least forty, probably only a couple of years younger than she was, but his hair was still bright as a halo. In fact, the sight of his fine figure and his fine hair made Melba glad she'd put on her new white capris and the nice green silk shantung blouse that brought out the sparkle in her eyes. She always dressed up, it was her custom, and God had certainly rewarded her good habits today!

"And caramel cake," she said as he neared her, "just a little piece, so as not to ruin your dinner. I'm sure a little piece won't hurt."

Cooper nodded. Said, "Thank you Miss . . . "

"Melba," said Melba, automatically, pointing to her sign, the reason he'd stopped, the reason he was now on her porch in the first place. "That's me. I'm Madame Melba in the flesh."

"Miss Melba," he said.

"Sit right here." She fluffed up bright chintz pillows on her swing. Then she remembered who he was and who she was and added, "Want to go inside? Take your tea in there?"

Dr. Connelly would probably care about his reputation. A white man this far across Main Street—two blocks—would be noted for sure.

But he said, "Outside's fine. You've got a mighty nice garden. I appreciate the chance to look at it."

"Thank you," said Melba. "Gardening's my pastime, not my profession. I'll get the tea now. It won't take me but a few minutes."

She was rapidly getting over the shock of reading about Jack Rand Connelly, feeling strongly against him, and looking up to see his son standing out there, as though he'd popped, full-fleshed like some male Minerva, right out of her mind.

She was having what she called a Madame Melba Moment.

Melba couldn't wait to find out what he wanted, so she could tell Deanie all about it. They would gasp over and pick out the strangeness of anything he might say to her; marvel on the quirkiness of life. They would whisper over serendipity and mysticism and Ouspensky or whoever else they were reading that week. But mostly Melba would be struck by the fact—though she would not say it, even to Deanie—that a man, *this* man—had come to see Madame Melba. And that, perhaps, he had not come for the usual old things.

She bustled back, teetering in on her favorite wedgies and after having spritzed White Shoulders through her hair on her way out. She balanced a tray cluttered with dark tea and ice cubes tinkling away in tall glasses, with neatly squared sections of cake, with cloth napkins, with forks that were mismatched but real silver, and with the new watermelon coasters she'd bought over at Woolworth's because the look of them cheered her up. The tray was covered with a crocheted doily. It was so cluttered there was no room for anything else. She sat the whole thing down on the glass-topped, wrought-iron table and then settled herself on the swing—but not too close to Dr. Connelly. Melba did not want to be the cause of scandal from the street.

And then she waited. Quietly. Patiently. Because no one came to Madame Melba by chance. Though they might not say what she expected them to. Dr. Connelly didn't.

"You don't look much like your picture," said Cooper. There were a few crumbs on his mouth. "The one out there."

She knew just what he meant—the woman on the sign was about five shades darker than she was. Melba wanted to raise her little chin and say, "Hey, that's me, all right," which was what she usually retorted, even to Deanie. She did not like anybody implying that she was not black enough to be good at her profession.

Instead what came out was, "I took that out of a magazine. *True Confessions*."

Connelly nodded. "You're much prettier than that woman. Softer-looking," he said. "This is mighty good caramel cake."

They sat in total silence for a moment, Melba marveling at what she'd just so easily said and the elegant Dr. Connelly quietly chewing. He smelled good. Melba liked a man who smelled soap-clean.

He finished the cake, put his plate down. "Do you work spells? Stuff like that?"

It was a sudden question, totally unexpected, and there was deep Delta in his voice.

"Depends," said Melba, "on if you need one worked. Or if someone put a spell on you. Normally I don't go in for that kind of nonsense. Folks do everything out of their own thinking, the force of their will. There's nothing else in mumbo jumbo but bad human will. Actually, you look like the type should know that."

Dr. Connelly laughed at that one, just as Melba meant him to do. No doubt about it, she knew her business. But then he looked at her, straight at her, with his clear, clear eyes, and she was sure he was reading her mind and knew why she'd said what she'd said, to keep him but not his attention. They sat there like that for a long moment. In the end it was Melba who looked away.

He reached for his glass. His hands were steady. "That's a fair assessment. I'll give it some thought."

It was getting darker now, and lights were popping on up and down the street. Skippy Jackson limped by with Critter Tate and a small pale, white child, a girl. The boys called out, "Good evening,

Miss Melba. Good evening, Dr. Connelly," and both adults waved back. The girl said nothing. She did not smile or look in their direction.

Melba said, "Isn't that the child whose daddy got killed—died— a little while back? The one was your patient. The one who shot himself. Isn't that his child? I thought they all lived down in the county. What's she doing up here?"

And thinking, *Skip must be full ten years old, and Critter with him. They shouldn't be playing with that white girl much longer. Too dangerous.*

Dr. Connelly shrugged, did not appear to be all that interested. "Maybe they moved up to town. The mama found work or something." And then, once the children had passed, "I've got a meeting happening tomorrow."

"School board?" said Melba, meaning to show him that she kept up. "Or is it something to do with the new hospital?"

"Something to do with the old hospital," he said. "With Doctors. A death. The family wants to come around and talk to me about it. That girl's family."

He pointed to the children as they disappeared into the shadows around the Jackson gate.

Melba said, "That's understandable, given the circumstances. Shouldn't take long."

"It's about her father, Billy Ray Puckett. He was on the news. The one you were just talking about. The one who died."

Melba repeated. "With the children. With the wife."

Dr. Connelly nodded. "Wife's coming with her husband's daddy. They'll be in tomorrow, just the two of them. I'll be there and my hospital administrator and, of course, my lawyers."

"Well, with lawyers involved," said Melba thoughtfully, "you surely don't need my services to know how things will turn out. Especially if you the one got the lawyers and they don't."

She need not have said a word. She could tell he was way deep in his own thoughts, in why he had rambled here. He said, "I don't think you work spells—at least not spells like I know them. Potions. You don't look like you'd work with cat's piss or pubic hairs. You don't look like you'd be the kind to crawl around dead bodies. Getting what you needed from them. Using parts of them. Like people say you do."

He said these foul things in a low, cultured voice, as though he sought something in trying to shock her. Shocking Melba was a hard thing to do, and she was not easily offended. She'd had her life, and she'd lived it. But still, there was a devil in Cooper Connelly, and Melba saw it snap through him. Darkening his eyes in the darkening night.

"Can't help what people say," said Melba, "but maybe I can help you. Care to try me?"

"Now, the woman on your sign, she looks like that," said Cooper Connelly, again within his own thoughts and not responding to hers. "I've been studying her for a while now, each time I drive past. And I drive past often. Back and forth. She's got something in her—that's a woman looks like she could get you anything you wanted. Only got to look in her crystal ball. Conjure it. You got a crystal ball in your house, Miss Melba?"

Melba shook her head.

"Got a Ouija board or tarot cards? Anything in there can tell you the future?"

"I got myself," said Melba proudly. "Don't need nothing else. And, like I said, that stuff don't work nohow."

Still Cooper Connelly went on. "Got any way of getting rid of ghosts?"

"Exorcism," said Melba stoutly. She was a good Catholic who went to mass at Annunciation Church every Sunday at noon. "And, of course, there are always prayers for the dead. That usually does it. You can *always* be rid of what's dead."

Cooper laughed, and his laughter broke the spell that had bound them together. Melba hadn't known it existed until it was gone, until the street sprang back into life around them and night birds started calling. Until children yelled good night to each other, until news programs floated out through lace curtains and open windows. Until moths caught at porch lights and a few last mosquitoes buzzed unseen but not unheard.

"You say Reese Jackson stays over there," said Cooper, motioning. "I've always been curious to see where he lives, to know just what it looks like. I've heard about his house before."

"It's a big one," said Melba, matter-of-factly, "and everybody on this side of town is proud of him. At least he's got that. Everybody carrying such pride that he's part of us."

"He's got that," said Cooper, looking through late roses and through the branches of an opulent crepe myrtle at the enormous, porticoed, exuberant, shiny-bright house next door.

They said their good-byes, Melba relieved that he hadn't gone into the time she'd come into his office, what she'd needed, and with the strangest sensation—another true Madame Melba Moment— that this was one man who would find his way back. But for what? Now, *that* was a question.

# Chapter 9

IT WAS COMMON AROUND THE HOSPITAL to see both its doctors
and its nurses still in their medical whites, out and about, walking
purposefully along the surrounding streets. During Revere's brief
winter, young nursing students from the Women's College of Mississippi would wear dark blue capes over their uniforms and laugh
when these billowed out in the harsh winds that blew up uninter-
rupted from the river and the Delta. The administration encouraged
this. Doctors Hospital was a revered institution, but it was also a
friendly one, part of a neighborhood that included small shops and
children playing on magnolia-lined pathways and drugstores where
you could get a nickel soda at the counter— if you were white.

Situated as it was on Main Street—the dissection between the
north part of town and the south—Doctors was so close to the river
and so high on a rise that you could look out its east windows and be
hypnotized by the gentle flow of the Tombigbee. Ruthie Puckett had
done nothing but watch the gentle surge of its waters in those last

long moments when they wouldn't let her near Billy Ray any longer. Once they realized he was dying. She had told this to Billy Ray's doctor when he came to speak with her. She had told this to Cooper Connelly when he had called her last week.

Today, though, Dr. Connelly stood at a window one floor higher than the one that Ruthie had stared from and watched Mrs. Puckett and her father-in-law get out of their truck, look both ways, then cross the street. Coming to see him. Rob Puckett, dressed in a light gray suit that Cooper imagined still smelled of the dry cleaners, had chosen not to swing his battered Ford into the hospital parking lot. Neither had he selected one of the nearby parallel slots, though there were plenty of these available for him as well. There was no trouble finding parking in Revere, even this close to such a grand and busy place as Doctors Hospital. Instead Big Rob had driven around the corner and eased into a spot far down from his destination. Cooper saw him do it. He pulled in to a lonely street with enough, but not too many, people on it. All black people, Cooper noticed. The Pucketts, county folk and not particularly knowledgeable about Revere, had inadvertently slipped into the colored part of town. Parking there was a mistake. Rob Puckett realized this just a little too late. You could see it in the way he looked around him and in the stiff stride of his walk. He was a pure-dee Jack Rand Connelly man and had no truck with colored people. Cooper wondered how he'd taken it when his son signed up with the pulpwood haulers' union. Lord knows, black folk abounded in that thing. The woman beside Rob Puckett looked straight ahead, oblivious of her surroundings but not of her destination. They were coming to see Cooper. He had called them himself.

Ned Hampton hadn't wanted him to do this. "Let them come to us. Make them *ask* for what they want." But Cooper had insisted on

talking to the Pucketts, had sat alone in his oak-paneled office, with
all its antique furniture bought by Jack Rand and shipped to Mississippi from Evelyne Elizabeth's growing-up house in Virginia, had
dialed their number and asked for Mrs. Puckett, the younger Mrs.
Puckett. Cooper had just started his apologies—the most awkward
of moments for both of them, he imagined—when her father-in-law
had taken the telephone from her and started talking himself.

"All we want for ourselves is some answers here," Big Rob had
said. "Just some answers."

Listening to the man, Cooper doubted this. He knew that his
lawyers—or rather the lawyers for Doctors Hospital—doubted it
even more than he did. But Billy Ray's daddy's gravelly voice was
insistent, repeating the same words over and over again: *Answers,
what happened, why my boy died.* Ned called it his personal dirge. The
way Big Rob said it—his insistence—was not pretty and called to
mind questions about Mr. Puckett's motives. Looking at him, Cooper nodded briefly to the wind outside his window. No use arguing
about motivation.

Ned was on the other side of the room, welcoming the lawyers.
Together, as a group, they kept glancing toward the door. Ned would
not be at all impressed by the Pucketts' trip into town, their dress-up
clothes. "You know that kind, always trying to chisel the money."
Ned might be a regular fixture at Piney Grove Missionary Union
Baptist Church, but there was no way in the world he would ever
have considered going to the Mighty Victory Pentecostal Taberna-
cle. He stayed away from poor whites.

"Dr. Connelly," said Ned, all deferential courtesy, from behind
him now that the lawyers were safely here. "The Pucketts are downstairs. They're on their way up."

Cooper affixed a smile to his face, tested it for tautness, and turned again to the room. He fully expected to see the body in there, grinning back at him from amid the lawyers and the hospital personnel and the whole wide beauty of the conference room—the only place, besides the waiting area, big enough to hold an entire production meant to impress. But the body wasn't there; at least that was something. Maybe its presence wasn't needed to scare him. Maybe he was already scared enough.

When the knock came, he walked quickly over to answer it, ignoring his lawyers' scowl and the brief shake of the head that came from Ned Hampton. They had told him to let the Pucketts knock twice. Keep them waiting, if just a little bit. It was crucial for the negotiations. Cooper didn't care. He wanted this meeting over with. He wanted things back the way they had been. He wanted the Pucketts out of his life.

"Mrs. Puckett," he said, "Mr. Puckett. Please come on in."

They entered to a room of beaming lawyers and a smiling Ned Hampton, all acting as though they had encouraged Cooper in his courteous behavior. There was a crumpled piece of paper in Rob Puckett's hand; no doubt he'd had someone write down directions to the conference room. Insisted they write them out, in his own way, just as surely as he had insisted upon this meeting. He strutted in purposefully enough but then held back. Looked around. Eyes getting big and then narrowing. Cooper thought how much he reminded him of his own daddy, Jack Rand. They were both men brought up to know their place in a state where the placing of folks—and not just racially—was taken very seriously. Both determined to have something but then, once they got close to it, suddenly remembering just who they were, where they came from. And Billy Ray's daddy's place clearly was not here, not amid Doctors Hospital's welter of visitors, patients, orderlies, nurses, doctors, and of course surgeons, all imbued with learned efficiency and a certain saving grace, all busy about their heavenly errand: the saving of lives. In fact, it was his daughter-in-law who nudged him forward, who whispered, "Go on in, Daddy Rob. They been waitin' for us, and we're here."

Everybody nodded real polite to Mrs. Puckett. They knew who she was. The television appeal had made her famous. They all stood up when she came in. She was the only female in the room. Even the stenographer was male, Ned Hampton's final touch. He wanted to ensure that this example of southern womanhood realized right off that this was a man's domain, that men would make the decisions, and that she'd be protected as long as she did what they said.

Cooper watched her make a silent count—one, two three, four five six, seven men—a full five of them lawyers. The only two not attorneys were Ned and himself. Even the stenographer was said to be working on his legal degree. Cooper already knew this, and Mrs. Puckett would learn it quick enough. The lawyers were dressed alike, too, in lightweight dark suits, white shirts, and striped ties, just as identifiable and uniformed as Billy Ray must have been when he pulled on overalls each day, whether he was working or not.

"Ma'am?"

Cooper stretched out his hand to her, knowing he must look just as concerned and helpful as he'd looked the night he'd come out of surgery to tell her that Billy Ray was going to be all right. The look was natural to him, as were the reassurances, though he seriously doubted she'd believe any more of these, at least coming from him. Still, she couldn't very well get away from him, not at his hospital. She hadn't been able to the night her husband died, and she wasn't able to do it now. She gave him her hand. Connelly held on tight.

He led Ruthie and her father-in-law to two seats at the long, polished table that dominated the room and where the others were standing. The chair he held out for Mrs. Puckett was delicate—rickety, even. The country boy in Cooper still used that word. Chairs starting off in Virginia—they had never really adapted to the humidity in Mississippi, and they made all kinds of polite, squeaky protests as the company settled back into them again. For a moment this was the only conversation going on in the room, and then Cooper Connelly cleared his throat.

He said, "Thank you for coming in, Mrs. Puckett. We're sorry to have to bother you at a time like this, but we thought it was better to go on, get everything out of the way. If I might just introduce my colleagues . . ."

Of course he could. He went around the table left to right.

"This is Mr. Meade MacLean, Doctors' chief legal counsel, and his associates, Mr. Hunter Franklin, Mr. Brian Talcott, Mr. James Babcock. . . ." He hesitated a moment, forgetting just who the last man was.

"Hays Levington," prompted Meade MacLean helpfully.

" . . . and Mr. Hays Levington."

Everybody nodded, real polite and murmuring "ma'am," somber now, not grinning. The moment for grinning had passed.

Ruthie Puckett nodded back, obviously scared as could be. Even to her untutored eyes, this many attorneys meant Doctors Hospital definitely saw what lay before it as a legal problem, not a medical one. Cooper could see sweat glowing on her forehead.

Rob Puckett said, "We come here cause we want to hear about my boy's dying. We—his mama and me, his wife, too—want to know just exactly what y'all have to say happened. The two ends of the story just don't pane together—his dying after Dr. Connelly made a point of telling us he was okay."

*"Going to be just fine. Came through the operation well. Just a day or two now, and you can take him home."*

Beside him, Ruthie nodded away, and everybody else in the room nodded right along with her, looking concerned.

Big Rob took this interest as a sign to continue, "Dr. Connelly here"—he indicated Cooper with a wave of his hand—"come straight out of operating on my boy that night he was shot and told Ruthie and all the rest of us that the bullet had gone right through him clean like, said they saw wounds like this all the time during deer season. 'Folks are forever falling out of the stands onto their firearms and hurting themselves. Lots of blood,' says Dr. Connelly, 'but not much real damage. Nothing to worry about.' Next thing we know, my boy's dead."

"Of course we are all saddened by your loss," Ned Hampton broke in. He glanced briefly at Meade MacLean, not at Cooper. "Devastated by it, really. That's why we asked you here—to answer any questions you might have. To be of service."

"Next thing we know, Billy Ray's dead," repeated Big Rob, leaning forward. "Just like that, and this seemed strange to me, strange to his mama—why a whole hospital filled with doctors and nurses and emergency-like folk couldn't have figured out something was going real wrong."

Ruth Ann cleared her throat and said, "What happened?"

*Yes, indeed, what happened?*

Naturally, the only person who could reasonably answer this question was the attending surgeon, and all eyes turned expectantly toward Cooper Connelly. Even beefy, self-assured Meade MacLean glanced his way.

And Dr. Connelly said, "When your husband was brought in, Mrs. Puckett, we did the usual preliminary tests and X-rays, but only what we felt was absolutely necessary. Our goal was to get him into surgery quickly and stop the bleeding. Your husband's vital signs weren't great, but they weren't that bad either, considering the circumstances. Although the wound itself didn't seem dangerous, the bleeding from it was, if that makes sense to you."

Obviously, Ruthie was expected to agree that this made sense to her, and she did.

"The bleeding needed to be stopped," Cooper repeated. "You can see the wound itself on the X-rays. That is, if you'd care to see them."

"I would," said Rob Puckett, speaking right up. "I'd like to see everything you've got."

"Certainly," said Cooper. "They're right here. Seeing them—the X-rays—will explain the trajectory, the problem that we had with it. I've got the X-rays right here. On the basis of the information they showed me, I thought I was facing a pretty straightforward procedure. The bullet had gone through the lower right chest—you could see the hole it made—but no vital organs had been punctured. Even though he was slipping in and out of consciousness, Mr. Puckett's heart still seemed to be pumping strong. Of course, as I said, there was that bleeding."

The air conditioner clicked off, and you could have heard a pin drop in the room's deathly silence.

"But the bullet had done more damage than we . . . than I thought," said Cooper Connelly. He was looking right at Ruth Ann, and for a moment it was just the two of them, instead of this large and formal chamber filled with fine furniture and lawyers and Ned Hampton and, worst of all, Billy Ray's daddy. Just the two of them, like it had been that night.

"I'll show you now," he said to her.

He pressed a button on the table, and across from them, on the wall, a large oil painting started to slowly rise from its fixed position. It was a hunting scene with riders dressed in red coats on horseback, a single fox, a pack of dogs. Very precise. Very ornamental. Nothing like the kind of down and dirty shooting Billy Ray Puckett had been about to embark on when he died.

A lit screen lay behind the painting, and Cooper Connelly carefully positioned an X-ray over it. He took his time.

*That's Billy Ray,* thought Ruthie, *that's him.* She saw the shadowed images of his sternum and rib cage and of his heart. A sudden brightness suffused the effigy and set the ghost heart beating—boom, boom. Ruthie gasped before she realized that it was only the angle of light that had done this, or a trick in Cooper Connelly's movement. She shut her eyes tight, popped them open. All was quiet once again on that X-ray. Her husband's heart had stopped its beating, and he was still dead.

"You can see how the bullet entered," said Cooper, pointing.

As if on cue, the lawyers took over from there.

"Meade MacLean, head counsel for Doctors Hospital," he said, introducing himself yet again, but this time getting all the way up to shake hands, first with Ruthie Puckett and then with her father-in-law. Making sure everybody knew just who he was. Pumping his name right into their minds. "Mr. Hampton asked me to be here, just in case y'all had any questions. Doctors wants me to lay to rest all y'all's concerns."

He fried them with his smile, while his assistant, a younger version of himself, right down to the gee-whiz, aw-shucks look on his face, opened up a bulging briefcase—brown leather, just like Meade MacLean's, only newer—and produced one page of a legal document, brief and to the point. The point being that it had a big, official-looking check paper-clipped onto it. MacLean reached over and took the document and the check into his hands without once taking his eyes away from Ruthie's. His face twinkled at her. Cooper was watching her, too, and so did not miss the slight up-and-down bob of her head. She had children, she had responsibilities, she was living with Billy Ray's parents. She needed money to move on.

This fact had not escaped Meade MacLean's attention. When he spoke, his voice was thick and twanged as right as wholesome buttermilk. "We know that the death of your husband was a grievous loss to you, Mrs. Puckett, a terrible thing. And even though no one at Doctors Hospital—not the nurses, not the X-ray technicians, not the anesthesiologist, and most certainly not Dr. Cooper Connelly— in any way takes responsibility for the tragedy that has befallen all y'all, we all do realize that this unfortunate situation has left you in the equally unfortunate situation of having children to provide for and Mr. Billy Ray's parents to look after."

Big Rob tightened his lips, agreed with this.

Meade MacLean spoke on with great solemnity, and while Ruthie was obviously trying to listen to what he said, to hear the explanation for all this, her attention kept sidling back and forth, back and forth, to that check on the table.

"It's for five thousand dollars, free and clear, with no taxes on it either. All yours," said Lawyer MacLean helpfully. "Something to tide you over until you can get on your feet again. Maybe help you bring your younger children back down from Iuka."

This last was meant to assure her that, just like God, Meade MacLean was all-knowing, or at least privy to all that needed knowing.

"Only thing we need is your signature, that's it. Right here on this line. Five thousand dollars is a lot of money. It can take you a long ways."

It could buy them a house, get them out from under the Puck- etts. Ruthie, hypnotized by that possibility and loving it, was already reaching for the pen.

"I was *greedy*," she would say later, "and needing that money. Wanting that check so damn bad."

But before she could quite touch it, Billy Ray's daddy reached across and put his hand over hers, and his was so heavy it stopped her own hand dead. "Got to think on this first," he said. "Maybe we ought to talk things through with Mr. Kelly Joe, see what he's come up with, before we start up signing anything. Can't just be taking any kind of money from y'all. Money comes at a price. We're still waiting for the autopsy to come up from Jackson, so maybe we ought to just see what it says first. Maybe we ought to talk to Kelly Joe before we call ourselves signing anything. I hear he's got his deputy nosing around, looking after things. Been out to see us. Been other places as well." Glaring at Cooper.

Ned Hampton was quick on this. "What's the sheriff got to do with this? Nobody's talking *criminal* here."

"He's been out to speak with my daughter-in-law, sir," said Rob Puckett. You couldn't miss the mean way he cut through that one word, "sir," but Cooper had spent most of his boyhood surrounded by poor people, both black and white, and so he caught the quake in Puckett's voice, the fear in it. Again the thought occurred to Cooper that this was not Rob Puckett's place, that it was not his daughter-in-law's place either, and they both knew it. Yet here was where they found themselves—in a room filled with men they had only read about in the flat pages of the *Times Commercial*. Meade MacLean was the city attorney, as well as lawyer for the hospital, and he wrote the city's bonds. He was *always* in the paper. And all of this while sitting on a chair that probably cost more than his house was bound to have an effect on Big Rob Puckett.

"Talked to her once. Then he came out and talked to me and my wife. Been over to that colored boy, Critter Tate, and *his* mama. All this talking's got to mean something's up."

"I don't see what one has to do with the other," said Meade MacLean. Cooper was silent, still standing with the pointer in his hand, and so was Ned Hampton. Ruthie glanced over at them, her eyes wide with wanting, needing the money and needing Doctors Hospital to give Billy Ray's father a reason they ought to just go on and take it.

Big Rob struggled up to his feet, the chair squawking and protesting. "I think we should wait," he said, looking at Ruthie but talking to everybody else except her. "See what happens. That's what I think the sheriff would want us to do. He says there's talk of digging Billy Ray up and sending him on down to Jackson so the state medical examiner can look him over. Says there might even be an inquest. Things like this . . . well, you never can tell."

This last, about a possible inquest, was news to everybody in the room. But they were all big boys—big enough to handle any new threat of an inquest.

Rob Puckett politely helped his daughter-in-law up from her chair. "We'll talk more when we know more."

The check still lay on the gleaming table, and even as she was shepherded toward the door, Ruth Ann could not keep her eyes from darting to it. Cooper saw this; he knew Meade MacLean did as well. When Hunter Franklin moved to take the check away, Meade stopped him, but he said nothing, only nodded to the Pucketts as they left the room and closed the door behind them.

The others sat there immobilized for a moment, and then Meade McLean began swiftly gathering up his things.

"He'll be back," said the lawyer. "Wanted more. He just needs time to think things over. I know that kind. Been around them all my life."

Truth was, Meade MacLean had been hustled up north at an

early age—sent first to Choate, then on to Princeton and Harvard Law. Summers up north, too, at camps in Maine or in the upper Adirondacks. When he'd come south, his father and grandfather had dutifully handed over the most successful law practice in northeast Mississippi and gone off to spend the rest of their lives fishing. Meade lived in the old Armitage House with a gracious wife from Mobile and three sons the spitting image of their daddy in more ways than one. Cooper wondered how a man like this could possibly understand what was going on in Rob Puckett's mind. How could he really know "that kind"? Or perhaps it was that greed was universal. It bound in knowledge all classes and races, a universal binding. A fact of this life.

Cooper asked, "But what about Mrs. Puckett?"

"Oh, she's the one wants the money," said Meade as beside him the younger attorneys sagely nodded. "More than he does. And she'll be the one bring him back. You can mark my words on that one. She'll be the one bring him back."

Ned lingered on once they'd left. He stood beside Cooper at the window, watching the first early leaves on the ground as they swirled, caught on the wind coming up from the river.

"Puckett was prepared," Hampton said quietly. "He knows something's up. People don't just give away five thousand dollars, not unless they think they need to. Not down here. They'd rather fight it out. I imagine Rob Puckett will be hanging around at the Melrose Inn tonight, telling everybody how smart he was to turn down more money than he's likely seen altogether in his life. Because something's up. Because more is coming."

But Ned left the implication dangling. He had other, more important, fish to fry.

"There's a board of supervisors' meeting tonight," he said, still talking about the new hospital. "Think you might be able to make it this time?"

"You better go," said Cooper. He started to turn off the lights, clearing out his things. "You know these things better than I do. You can make the case."

Ned hesitated. "It looks strange that when we're over there begging and pleading for favors, the head of the hospital's not alongside of us, doing his share of the bowing and scraping, asking for his place on the dance card. The boys on the board feel like they're being jilted—that it's me and not Dr. Connelly himself asking for their hand."

It was a feeble attempt at humor, but Cooper smiled at it anyway. He'd been born to be polite.

"You handle it, Ned. I've got—"

"A school board meeting tonight."

"An important one. Things are heating up. But we still might be able to make some changes."

Ned said, and not for the first time, "You need to leave that can of worms alone. Nobody's going to thank you for what you're doing, not the blacks and certainly not the whites. Credit's going to go to the wrong people—it always does—and you're going to be left high and dry. Meetings are a waste of time. My meeting. Your meeting. All meetings. Nothing ever accomplished, just a terrible wasting of time."

## Chapter 10

IT SEEMED TO DEANIE that autumn was absolutely the worst time for Skippy's school functions—they had always been an ordeal for her—and of course by school functions she meant school sports. Autumn was the time for the high-school football games on Friday nights. All Revere went to them, blacks and whites to different schools, but everybody showed up. Deanie was expected to show up as well, with Skippy. She had no choice. She had to sit there and see all the other children running, not just the ones on the field. Skippy always limping along beside her. Reese never there.

Everybody else out, though. The games were popular, the top small-town entertainment. Things looked good this year for the Frederick Douglass High School Wildcats—who had, until 1960, been known to one and all as the Revere Colored High School Wildcats. They'd won everything so far against the black high schools of Macon and Ripley and Starkville and Holly Springs.

Deanie drove up, as always, already smiling and waving. Already

calling out, "Hey, how you been doing?" Already with the knot forming around her heart.

Lyle Dean Jackson loved summer even more than her kids did.
Everybody gone on vacation, and she could stay in her house as much
as she wanted. She could slide on over to Melba's when Reese wasn't
around. She could go to downtown Revere as little as she liked.

"Hiding out," Reese called it. Deanie called it that herself. Hiding out since what Reese referred to as the "incident." He did not
call it an accident. Which it had been.

She stopped the car, still smiling and nodding. Got out. Automatically went around to help Skippy out, then stopped herself.
Skippy was ten now, no longer the defenseless toddler he'd been
when the "incident" had happened.

But it was hard. The whole thing was so hard. Deanie gathered
their blankets, their sandwiches, and the thermos of hot chocolate
she'd brought along even though the weather was still so warm. She
pretended that this was why she had come around to Skippy's door
in the first place—to pluck these things from the back of the car, to
make sure she had not unthinkingly left anything behind. To make
sure she had not been distracted. She reached down to make sure she
had stuck the candy right at the top of her purse—two Three Muske-
teers bars, because these were his favorites. She did not want Skippy
to be hungry, to want for anything. Lyle Dean loved her son.

"Here, Mrs. Jackson. Come on up here."

It was Reese's nurse, Eloise, calling out to her, bony, light-skinned,
goodhearted Eloise. Sent out on each of the twelve Friday nights of
the season—not including playoffs—to save a seat for Deanie and
Skippy on the bottom rung of the bleachers and to make Dr. Reese's
excuses. His emergency-appendectomy/paperwork/twins-coming-
early-out-in-Macon excuses. Reese had an emergency for each and
every Friday night that football was played.

"Skippy!"

"Deanie!"

"Miss Lyle Dean!"

"Mrs. Jackson!"

Every black face in town, smiling at her and knowing what had happened eight years and three months and eleven days ago, but no one—not one single person—had ever spoken a word to her about it. Had never even said they were sorry. Reese had let it be known quietly that questions, even condolences, would be a torment to his wife. Reese Jackson was revered here. His version of things was enough. What this meant was that nobody actually had ever asked Deanie what had happened.

This is what had happened: She'd been distracted. Running late. Trying to get Brendan over to Hunt before school started at eight. They'd still been living in that cute little house over on Tenth Street, the one with the short snatch of a drive and the fence. She'd put Reese Jr.—still toddling but already his daddy's pride and joy—on the porch. Mrs. Turner, the woman who helped her, could see him easily from there. Deanie herself would be right back.

Distracted. Only distracted. She'd forgotten her keys. Ran in to get them. "Get into the car, Brendan. Hurry on up!" The keys in the ignition. The starter. The engine. Her foot off the brake. Her foot on the gas. The car in reverse. The bump—so small she might easily have missed it. Worse, passed over it again with her front wheels. Except for the screaming. All of them screaming. It was the scream-ing that, mercifully, stopped her dead.

Three years at La Bonner Children's Hospital up in Memphis. Ten operations. Waking up, month after month, to Reese crying in the night.

"Here, baby, let me help you." Right there beside her son. Set-

tling down on the bleachers. Deanie was solicitous, paying attention. Now that it was too late.

"It's a miracle!" they told her. Finally. After. The doctors all
happy. "A miracle!" They'd saved the leg—a stretched-out, misshapen, toddler-looking leg that Skippy would limp on for the rest
of his life. But the saving had changed them. Had changed Reese Jr.
into Skippy, a name that had no connection to them and that one
of them had had to make up. It had changed Deanie. Oh, how it had
changed Deanie. And it had changed Reese into someone his wife
was still trying to make it up to and to please.

She'd do anything for Reese—except give up Melba.

For the *life* of her, Deanie could not give up Melba. Their talking. Their book reading. Their afternoon stories on the television.
Reese had insisted she stop seeing her friend—and sometimes he had
*really* insisted on this, in his most no-nonsense, in-charge, Dr. Spencer Reese Jackson voice, and Deanie had tried to stop. Owing him
so much. Loving him. Wanting to please him. But eventually, every
time, she'd find herself slipping back through the garden, through
the fence, back over to Melba's.

"It's because," said the Madame wisely, "you know I'm the only
thing in town not under Reese Jackson's sway."


"MISS MELBA," SAID SKIPPY BESIDE HER. The game was over. Douglass had won 29–6, and the excitement had died down. All around
them colored folks, almost all of them nice people, laughing and
talking and going into the night. Deanie always waited. She had her
ritual down pat. Stay until the field cleared, until most everybody
had left—that was important—then give Skippy his second candy
bar and start the slow walk across the field to the car. She was at the
part where she reached for the candy when he spoke.

"No thank you," said Skippy, repeating, "Miss Melba."

"Miss Melba what?" This time he had gotten his mama's attention.

"Miss Melba said I need to cut back on my sweets."

"Oh, she did, did she? And when did she say all that?"

"Two days ago, when I went over there."

"Went over there?"

Of course there was Reese to think of, his hot fury that she had let that neighbor woman contaminate her son. "That hooker," he'd tell her, maybe even raise his voice. Deanie did not want that. But there was also something else, a frisson of jealousy. Deep inside her. *This is my boy, my family, my devotion, my life. My self buried here. It's not for anyone else.*

"Why did you go over there?"

"I'm ten years old now. Got to think about my future. And about the future, Miss Melba's the expert. Says so right on her sign."

Deanie said, "Over to Melba's."

Skippy said, "Daddy don't know."

His mother nodded once, sharply. She was furious with Melba. Not telling Reese was one thing. Not telling her was something else again.

Sarcastic now, "And what did she tell you?" Meaning, *What did she tell you that I couldn't tell you, or your daddy couldn't tell you, or anybody else couldn't tell you? Better than Melba. Who don't know nothing for her own self.*

"First off," said Skippy, sitting up a little straighter, "no sugar."

His mama said, "No sugar?" Candy bar still clutched tight in her hand.

Skippy nodded. "No sugar."

*"Boy you too cute to be letting yourself go so at ten. Look at your daddy. He played sports before, that's true, but he don't play them now,*

*and he's still mighty good-looking. Don't run around like he used to—too busy—but he still manages to keep himself up. In this world, the way it is, you just got to learn to keep yourself up. There ain't nothing can stop a man knows how to keep himself up. Next, you got to decide what you want and grab hold onto it. What it is you supposed to do. Madame Melba can't tell you this. The future can't tell you. You got to figure it out for yourself. And you can do this because your daddy did it, he mapped out the way, and you are your daddy's son. You are Reese's own child through and through, looking just like him."*

It was so funny, because the two of them, Skippy and his mama, were out there alone under the moon, under the stars, and yet Lyle Dean could have sworn Melba was right beside them. But it was Skippy, talking in Melba's exact same crazy, slightly lispy New Orleans voice.

*"You not what happened to you, boy, and you got to move on out from behind it. Ain't no excuse for an excuse."*

A perfect imitation of Melba. Deanie glanced over, amazed, and there was the Madame: relentlessly optimistic, wagging a ten-year-old finger, chewing on gum. Skippy had even thought to move his glasses on top of his head.

His mama busted out laughing. "Where'd you learn to do Melba like that?"

But Skippy wasn't listening. *"Got to move on. Got to leave it behind us,"* he said. *"You got to do it too, Mama. It was an accident. It's over."*

And this voice was Reese. And there was forgiveness in it.

## Chapter 11

"EVERY TIME I COME OVER HERE, you're reading Daddy's column in the paper."

"Can't help it," said Melba, raising her rhinestone glasses. "Your daddy's right fascinating. Evil men always are. Like snakes."

"I wouldn't call Daddy evil," said Cooper, settling in on her white wicker porch rocker. "It might not be the best word."

"Give me another adjective, then," said Melba, showing off her knowledge. "I'll be glad to use it."

She pulled up the paper again, starting reading aloud.

"'Military Avenue will run red with blood before our white children are forced to learn their ABCs with Nigras! Don't matter what the federal government says!' Every editorial Jack Rand Connelly writes seems to begin or end with those words. And using the word 'Nigras' in this day and age and in a public forum—why, it is not to be believed!"

Cooper did not say a word, so Melba continued, "Folks say your daddy worked double duty to get you appointed to the school board so you could siphon all the tax money off to build up a new white academy down the highway."

"Who says that?"

"Black folks say it."

"That's what's being done all through the South. I mean, putting up these segregated schools," said Cooper. " I'd like to see things work out different here in Revere."

"It's hard to imagine they will, though," said Melba, looking out into her peaceful garden. "People—and I'm not just meaning white people—don't like change. It's not in their nature. They don't like to give up what they think they know, what they have. And certainly they don't like to look back and examine how they've done things. They don't like that one little bit."

Cooper Connelly picked up a cup, sipped some tea, and then said very quietly, "I remember you now, from when you came into my office. You're one of my patients."

"Not a patient," said Melba, a little too quickly. "I never came back."

She put the newspaper down, felt her lips tighten. They had moved away from the general topic of integration, and things were getting personal now.

"You should have," said Dr. Connelly "Anything could have happened. All that bleeding. You could die from it, played out your heart. Surely someone must have told you that."

This last was not a question.

Melba stared back at him even though she knew what he must be seeing, knew that *she* was peeking out. Hard mouth, hard eyes: living proof that she was a little girl who'd walked some mean streets and could turn mean in a minute. A girl who wanted everybody to know she could take care of herself. She'd always been like that, scared of weakness—anybody's weakness, but especially her own.

"You should have come back."

"I couldn't." But then suddenly she realized that she *could*—yes, she could tell him. And so she did.

It had not been as easy as she'd once thought, leaving bad habits, starting anew, and she had been lonely at first. Before Deanie had moved in next door, and Mr. Reese. It was the loneliness done her in, and she knew it, plus the pull of old habits. And the fact that there were men about her, always, everywhere, up until now. Until she'd come up with her new profession, until she'd come up with another way she could be Madame Melba for true. Now she felt protected, with Deanie, with other women around her. But back then . . . well, it had happened, and it had happened again. And the baby thing had happened, and just like with the sex, she had gone on, not thinking, and done what she had always done before. With the herbs and the harsh plants—they were the first things she had planted in her garden—the things that her mother had taught her, and her grandmother. The things she'd never read about in her books. But this time it had been different, and the bleeding hadn't stopped. Even after she knew there could be no more baby there, that the baby had been flushed away and bled out of her, even after she knew there really couldn't be any more life in all that red—she had just kept on bleeding and bleeding and hurting and bleeding some more. So she had slipped in late at night to Doctors, had walked herself into the emergency room. She went to a white man because she lived in the black part of town, much in the same way gossip had it white people went to Reese Jackson: with shameful things, things they wanted to hide. And Melba was ashamed of the bleeding, ashamed of the way it made her feel dependent and needy and out of control. It had been a very brief visit. Actually, she had stopped bleeding right before he got to her, still in the examining room but already out of her street clothes. She could feel the stopping. Told Cooper Connelly she didn't know why she'd come in the first place, but he had insisted. Wanted to help her. They both remembered how he'd wanted to help. Warmed up the speculum, even, examined her carefully in her private parts. Told her she needed to stay on in the hospital for a few days. Went to find the nurse to have her admitted, but while he was gone, Melba had gotten up, got dressed, got herself home. And even though a bill never came, she had sent money around to satisfy it later.

"You should have come back," Cooper Connelly repeated. "Let me make sure everything was all right."

"Years ago now," said Melba, staring out into the twilight.

He, medically trained, actually looked taken aback by that, as though he'd never considered such a foolish notion. "Come on in again. We'll run some tests."

"No trouble now." Melba shrugged. "That's over with. Things changed for me that night."

It was slowly dawning on Melba why this man had actually come up on her porch, and it sure didn't help one bit that he had been nice to her before, didn't help one bit that he was kind to her now. He remembered that scene at the hospital, and he thought she was weak; he thought she needed his help. Melba prickled under the notion.

But she sure couldn't act uppity about it and argue, at least not right here on the street, where anyone could see, so as usual she took a sure refuge in coquettishness. She wiggled her shoulders and pulled out her come-on smile—all this to distance herself from him just a bit. Too close. Too close. Go back. But the truth was, she liked having

Cooper Connelly around, liked having somebody sitting next to her. Now that he was no longer talking about her sickness, his quiet, little, unexpected visit had gone back to being the high point of her day.

She offered him more tea and more cake. He shook his head, said, "No, thank you, Miss Melba, but it was mighty tasty." He set down his glass and his plate, and the shift of the swing drew them a bit nearer. His elbow brushed against Melba's bare arm. She smelled the cleanness of him.

"Guess I better get on over to the hospital, make my final rounds. I'll be back another time."

"Sorry about your patient," said Melba, yet again. It had become her customary way of saying good-bye. "A real sad situation. All those children, a truckload of them."

"Terrible," said Cooper Connelly. He had his hat in his hand, had that look of going on his face, but then he turned back to Melba.

"Can you do that?" he asked, gesturing toward her sashaying sign. "Read the future? Know what's going to happen. Know *what happened* and how things will turn out?"

It was the same question he'd asked her the first time he'd come.

Now, normally Melba had her stock answer—a little of this, a little of that—meant to keep the customers intrigued and happy. She was raised on the streets of New Orleans and knew every trick, some of them nasty. But Cooper's gaze was full on her, and the truth was between them now. After all, he'd been her doctor on that dreadful, terrible, lonely-filled night.

"People come here," she said, a bit warily, "but I don't tell them their future. They know that already. Inside. Being listened to seems to bring it out of folks—what they know is going to happen, that is. If I pay attention, and I usually do, in the end they're the ones end up telling *me* their future. Everybody knows their own life. We all know every last chapter and verse of it. At least we know it in our hearts."

The two of them stared at each other for a while, nobody smiling, until Cooper finally settled into his straw hat once again. He said, "I like the way you smell, Miss Melba. What's that you're wearing?"

She was perky on the mark. "White Shoulders," she answered. "My mama wore it for special."

"My mama did, too," said Cooper Connelly. "At least that's what my daddy tells me."

He was off the porch, down the stairs now, but Melba, the little crystal-ball reader, wasn't at all surprised when he turned around one last time.

"Thanks again for the tea. I might come back again—that is, if you don't mind."

And really and truly, how on earth could she mind?

## Chapter 12

COOPER KEPT GOING BACK to Madame Melba. Initially, as he had the first time, because he actually wanted to see Reese Jackson's house—where he lived, this other doctor. This was something Cooper never had done before in all the years he'd been in Revere and lost in the bottle and heard his friends at the country club talk about Dr. Jackson's fine mansion. Its uppitiness. Making fun of it—almost. Cooper found out it wasn't so bad—the house, that is. It looked a lot like his house, only not quite so big. And there were toys on the lawn—a bicycle, a football. And sometimes he thought he heard laughter deep inside it, children's laughter—though he couldn't be sure.

Not like his, Cooper's, house at all.

One thing for sure, Reese Jackson was not there, not at home. Not today. Cooper was almost certain of this. It was too early for a doctor to be home, too much to do, unless he had other important things to attend to, like Cooper had at the school-board meeting.

He'd been turning away from taking that first, furtive look at Reese Jackson's house, had passed it on the street, when he'd discovered Melba, almost hidden away in that small cottage. Initially he had stopped to see a sashaying sign, to smell sweet flowers, to hear a bright, clear voice. But this was at the beginning—the very, very beginning.

Now he came because he wanted to, liked coming around in the afternoons, and he had stopped making excuses about it, too, both to her and to himself. He was likely to show up anytime but especially on Tuesdays, right after the school-board meetings, which were becoming plenty acrimonious anyway. Coming over to Melba's kept his mind off things, kept bad thoughts and bodies and ghosts away. Besides, he didn't have to explain things to Melba. She found out all about what was happening on the news and in his daddy's column.

"You better be careful," she told him. "Folks are getting fired up."

"It's just southerners being bombastic," he told her. Still, he was touched, and less by her words than by the way that she said them. After all, Evelyne Elizabeth pronounced the very same words to him every damn day.

"*Folks are getting fired up.*"

Cooper said, "Everybody knows that once the federal government gets behind something, people just have to knuckle under and accept. Secession's been tried and found wanting."

As usual, Melba's polite chuckle followed his stale joke. They were sitting on Melba's porch, in her wicker swing and seats, drinking hot tea and eating coconut cream cake. The air was getting chilly. Steam rose from their teacups. Melba's next-door neighbor sat with them. Lyle Dean was her name, the pretty wife of Revere's one and only black doctor. A woman Cooper had never met.

Deanie Jackson chuckled right along with Melba, though it was obvious to Cooper that she just wanted to fit in and be polite. She looked a little bug-eyed. Who knew what stories they'd scared her with when she was a young thing growing up in Iowa, where her family was the only integration in town? He'd probably seen more black folks in his life than she had in hers, maybe thousands more. You couldn't imagine that many black folks in Iowa; it wasn't like here. In Mississippi, black folks were everywhere—in the streets, in the fields, in the houses helping out. More than likely, Mrs. Jackson had heard all her growing-up about Rebels, wild and whooping. Killing folks. Lynching every black man they met. Well, you couldn't pretend life here had always been pretty. You couldn't pretend folks hadn't been strung up. Cooper knew, firsthand, that they had.

He said, "We just got to work up a plan. The New Year will be bringing the new ways. We've seen what resistance has done—up in Oxford, down in Meridian, over in Alabama. The earth has shifted, and that's just all there is to it."

Melba said, "You the only white man I know holds that opinion. There may be others, but you the only one I know of says it out loud."

"I imagine they show up at the school-board meetings, eager to air their take on things," said Lyle Dean as she eased her way into another piece of cake. Cooper wondered how she kept her figure. "I bet it's not a pretty sight."

"Why don't you ever come to the board meetings?" asked Cooper.

"Because the school board's not going to make any changes," said Deanie levelly, "at least not willingly. The NAACP will. That's where I'd go—that is, if I went anywhere, which I don't." She raised her head, daring him to ask questions.

"Folks know already what's going to happen!" cried Melba.

"They just going to start their own white school system here, same as they have all through the South. The Seg Academies. Everybody's taxes paying for them, but only some of the everybodies are able to go. Or else they gonna close the whole system down so nobody can go to school. They'd rather deprive their own poor white children than let little black children get on in this life."

Deanie said, "Don't nobody care about poor white people. They gonna suffer in this mess, too."

"Revere can be different," said Cooper. His voice was hoarse. He'd insisted on these very same things not an hour before over at City Hall, where they'd had to move the meetings because the space could handle more people. "We are too poor a state to close down our schools or to fund some makeshift system of private education. We must make things work."

"Or else?" said pretty Deanie.

"Or else we can expect the same dark pictures coming out of here as are coming out of Birmingham and Selma. Pictures that will mark us. Pictures that will take generations to fade from people's mind. We all got to come to the only logical conclusion, and that is that we all just got to get along."

Melba and Deanie looked at each other over their teacups. They both had had firsthand experience in "getting along."

Even at this late date, with forced school integration waiting for them, if not in this coming year then in those right behind, ways to escape it still carried through people's mind like a bright kite on a windy day, and they showed up at the school-board meetings eager to air them. It had met twice the past seven days—last Thursday as well as Tuesday—and the first threats against Cooper had been whispered into his house via the telephone. Evelyne Elizabeth was not amused. She thought black people should stay in the place God had put them—which was as far from her as they could get. Unless they were cleaning up. Her little joke always tended to elicit more laughter than Cooper's weaker one about the failure of earlier attempts at secession; at least it did among the people she frequented. It would still be a week or two before Mrs. Evelyne Elizabeth Connelly showed up at Madame Melba Obrenski's door and so, in a sense, started frequenting her as well.

Ned Hampton told him next thing you knew they'd be burning crosses on his front lawn. Cooper knew that burning crosses weren't the problem. He wished this were an issue that could be laid solely on the Klan and thus dismissed from polite sensibility.

His own daddy was firing things up in Jackson, stomping through the legislature, prophesying that the streets in Mississippi would run red with blood before a black child and a white child would sit down side by side to learn their ABCs, all the stuff Melba so religiously quoted. Writing articles every week for his friend, Lancelot Wiggins V—known as Quint—the owner and publisher of Revere's *Times Commercial* and president of its White Citizens' Council.

Jack Rand Connelly had seen this mess coming for years; he had friends over in Alabama. They'd told him all about that sorry-ass Martin Luther King Jr. Jack Rand and his cronies called him "Jun-yer" for short. He'd tried warning Cooper, told him to steer the school board through its problems. You had to remember who your real friends were and act in their interest. That's why he'd worked the appointment for Cooper and made sure he picked up the presidency as well. It was amazing to him that Cooper hadn't listened and couldn't or wouldn't give a reason why he was doing what he was doing. Said he didn't know why he was doing it himself, and Jack Rand believed him. At least that's what Cooper's daddy said to Cooper's wife. Cooper heard them talking. State Senator Connelly had a voice that carried. When other people—those few who had the courage—besides Evelyne Elizabeth asked him anything about it, Jack Rand just shook his head.

Calls from the senator's new office in the new Capitol Building to his son were pungent and to the point. Jack Rand was an ol' Delta boy, and one who'd started out as sheriff of Monroe County during some very bleak times. He'd never been known to mince words. Cooper had to take his daddy's calls whether he wanted to or not; his secretary would not be stopped from putting them straight through. Jack Rand Connelly was a living legend, as much a Mississippi hero as Nathan Bedford Forrest and just as likely to be written of in the state's history books. Besides, Cooper's secretary, Miss Hilda, had a daughter in second grade over at Stephen Lee Elementary School, and she'd be horsewhipped in harness before she'd let that precious child sit next to some dirty black boy in spelling class. Who knew what that might lead to? She put Jack Rand's calls straight through. Some mornings you could hear Dr. Connelly shouting at his daddy all the way clear out to her desk down the hall. She told the other secretaries about this. Dr. Connelly shouldn't go around disrespecting his father. To a woman, they were all on Jack Rand's side.

Then there was that mess with Billy Ray Puckett. A silly thing at first, a mistake, but now it seemed to Cooper that Billy Ray might be settling in to linger with him for a while. Just like the body. One thing Cooper knew for certain, though, after having grown up with Jack Rand—just the two of them—and watching his daddy move up from sharecropper to county sheriff to become one of the richest, most powerful men in the state: Folks had their price, pure and simple. The Pucketts had their price. He had his price. Even the body had a price. You just had to wait until the bill was presented and hope, if you were lucky, that it was something that could be paid out in even dollar amounts. Cooper was still waiting to find this out.

And he had discovered he preferred to do his waiting on Miss Melba's front porch, talking with her, or with her and her friend Dr. Jackson's wife, about a little of this and a little of that. They could pass a pleasant evening discussing whether Truman Capote's book *In Cold Blood* was really fact or mainly fiction; whether they had ever seen such an intense shade of autumn spider lilies anywhere other than east Mississippi; whether Dr. Streeter, with his dressed-up self, was ever going to be allowed to eat his lunch in the River Café. Cooper enjoyed this kind of chatter. He enjoyed Melba. She was a change.

In the old days, given this kind of pressure—or any kind of pressure, frankly—he'd have been on the Jack Daniel's by late morning. Him and the sun both easing into full shine together; "elevenses," Evelyne called them, coating the word with the sweetness of her sugar drawl. At the very end, of course, he had started much earlier than eleven. If he were home, as he often was then, his wife would tap at his door with just the tips of her red-painted nails and bring in the ice and his sweet bourbon, then sit there beside him like a good mama, watching while he took his medicine down. This was their ritual; it had gone on for years, since even before they were married. Although more than once, toward the very, very end, he'd found himself with the bourbon in his hand, not knowing exactly how it had gotten there, and with his wife, Evelyne Elizabeth, nowhere in sight.

Other times he knew exactly where the bottle came from. He'd go into his office at Doctors, shut and lock the door, and gently ease it from the bottom drawer in his desk. He kept the drawer unlocked. In theory, anyone could have come in, opened it, learned his secret. No one ever did. Still, Cooper tensed up each and every time he slid this particular part of his desk open and heard the sly splinter of wood against wood. This was just as silly as could be. Who was there to hear him? His secretary was a good three doors away. He realized that *he* was the one who did not want to hear him. The thought eased up on him one day that he was starting to drink like Evelyne, sipping a little at a time, but all day long. At least she was a woman, a barren mother. People could feel sorry for her. She could, and did, accept their pity. But Cooper was a rich and powerful man, the son of a rich and powerful man. There was certainly no excuse for his bad behavior. He could not think of one himself.

And he was tired of searching out motives, wanting, and not finding, excuses for the obvious contrarieties of his life. Thank goodness Miss Melba was not one given over to reason. "I act strictly according to the way I feel, my intuition," she had once told him, and she did. She never asked him why he stopped by, and this saved him the energy of having to come up with an excuse for ending up so often at this little white cottage, hidden deep in the shadow cast by Reese Jackson's house.

That is why they sat together—the two of them often, the three of them sometimes—and watched as the weather gradually chilled enough for Melba to cut off her little electric fan and bring out a light blanket. He ate her homemade cakes—the caramel was especially good, though he liked the devil's food and the orange dream, even the coconut, almost as well—and watched the changes in her garden. She had those strange spider lilies, flowers that told you, if you knew Mississippi like he did, that things were finally cooling off and true autumn coming at last. He had never seen this flower anyplace else. Cooper watched as geraniums and daisies and mums gradually gave way to violas and pansies, hardy sorts that could last through a frigid winter. He drank sweet tea with lemon that gradually changed from being iced in clear, deep, frosted tumblers to being warmed in the ironstone cups Melba'd picked up at the Piggly Wiggly on

First. She'd told him this, proudly, herself. He'd noticed that Melba did not often venture far from her house. Cooper thought—and it was a surprise to him—that probably she had gone out to buy new cups just for him. There were a lot of things happening in Cooper's life that he couldn't date, couldn't place. But he remembered the day that they switched to hot tea, he remembered those cups. He remembered the flowers, the smell of leaves on grass, and the quiet whispers of two women reading and talking. He knew they'd move inside eventually—the weather would force them to it—but for now he liked sitting here, rocking and talking to Melba or to Melba and her best friend. He talked as much as they did. Once in a while, he talked more, and he laughed. But it wasn't like he had to say a word; he could just sit silently, as he was now, hearing and thinking and watching.

Watching the same folks pass by, day by day—mostly, but not totally black folks, walking back and forth to Catfish Alley, in work boots or sneakers, tottering past on very high heels—Cooper eventually got over his fear that people might see him from the street.

"THAT PUCKETT GIRL and her mama's moved up into town, living in an apartment," said Lyle Dean. This was her way of changing the subject away from school segregation. "She comes over to play with my Skippy and his friend Critter when he stays at my house on the weekend. That girl and her mama are the strangest folks in this town."

"What child you mean?" said Melba.

"The little Puckett girl." Lyle Dean spoke through sugar-cookie crumbs. "You know, the one whose father died a while back."

If she knew or remembered what part Cooper Connelly had played in the sudden demise of this father, she did not say so.

Melba said, "I wonder why."

"Nothing but poverty down there in the county," said Deanie knowingly. "Not much better for whites than for blacks. That woman's got a family to see after now. Somebody told me the rest of those children got sent up to Uekey."

"Iuka," corrected Melba and Cooper together. Melba added, "It's a small place up in the north part of the state."

Lyle Dean nodded. Like Melba, she always liked to learn new things. "Hardly says a thing. Critter told me she pretty much stopped talking when her daddy died; only speaks out when she has to. What a shock! That's probably why her mother brought her up here to Revere."

"Bless her heart," said Melba reaching for more tea and taking the opportunity to admire the bright new shade of Tangee nail polish she'd picked up yesterday at the Woolworth's. Scarlett Lady, it was called.

Lyle Dean dutifully glanced over at Melba's nails, as she was meant to, and nodded. "I hope things work out."

"Oh, eventually they will," said Melba, passing around the cookie plate and then taking one for herself, "in more ways than one. Schools too, one day. Only thing is, why should white folks want to change what works for them? Most people aren't that brave. White folks aren't."

"Aren't you white?" said Lyle Dean. She kept her head low. She knew she was looking too sly. Melba liked talking about race in general; she did not much care to discuss her own race in particular, and Deanie knew this.

"Maybe," said Melba.

"Maybe it just has something to do with integration being the right thing to do," said Lyle Dean. "Maybe that's the reason."

They were back to it again. As in the rest of their town, their state, their country—all conversational byways seemed to end up at the integration place.

It was a minute or two before Cooper spoke. "The reason we have to change is because separate but equal does not work. It never has, nobody even thinks it does. Maybe it can in the North, where everybody's not thrown together so helter-skelter, but here in Revere, in Mississippi, it's a whole different world. Blacks and whites just aren't separate; down here you have to separate them. We've always been too physically close, working in the same cotton fields and drinking out of the same RC Cola cans. And sharing what little we had—sharing the air we breathed and with only the air between us. You can't say that about life in the North. Lots of white people up there have never seen a black person, unless they were watching them on TV. Black people are icons up north—and icons can change one minute to the next from good to bad to good again. You aren't real. You aren't *people*. But down here black folks are people. During the worst of the times, everybody still speaks to everybody else when they pass on the street."

Lyle Dean looked like she might want to defend Iowa and its ways, but one glance from Melba stopped her.

Cooper said, "Have y'all been over to Hunt School lately?"

Of course Lyle Dean had—Skippy went there—but Melba hadn't. She hardly went anywhere.

"Well, you should go on over. It's half full of kids—just like Lee School's half full. Two separate buildings to maintain, and even though they don't really care about the black one, it still costs them money, and the money's draining out."

On and on he went, pleasantly spelling out reasons why segregation was essentially over, why the old concepts no longer could work. Melba doubted that any of these were the true reasons Dr. Cooper Connelly involved himself with the changes. She wondered if he questioned his own motives as well. But it didn't matter. What did matter was that having this fine man with his fine manners on her porch was better than watching *As the World Turns* or reading Flaubert anytime. Still, Melba was hardly romantic. Where she was now, she'd been in the past. She knew what was coming. "The End" was just taking its time.

# Chapter 13

"WELL, HE HAS HIS OWN IDEAS," said Deanie as they watched him drive away after one of these visits.

Melba said, "He does that."

"Wonder where they came from?"

"I don't think they have much to do with this school-integration business. That's just how they're appearing. It's what he talks about when he's here, what he's doing, but what he's really up to is something else again."

"What would that be?" asked Deanie, instantly curious.

Melba jiggled her head around. "Could be anything. Something he's hiding from. Then again, it might just be sex."

They both giggled and blushed. Even after all these years, sex—the talking about it—was still an exotic topic between them. They each kept that part of themselves to themselves, or at least most of the time they did. Much to Lyle Dean's relief. She didn't want to

actually know what Melba had been up to in her "previous life" and
to find out that maybe Reese had been right about her all along.

She said, "Dr. Connelly's mighty fine-looking, easy on the eyes,
but I still think it's hypocritical of him, coming over here to talk
about integration. Schools are one thing. They're not part of his life.
He doesn't have children. The country club is something else again.
I wonder if he'd ever want to see *that* integrated."

The Jacksons were both firebrands when it came to education,
and Mrs. Jackson felt she had held her tongue long enough. "You
work hard all your life, and they put your children in someplace
like Hunt. Make them go there. There's not a white doctor in this
town who'd send his children to the same school where Reese Jackson has to send his. Windows knocked out, paint chipping off the
walls—lead paint, too, more than likely. Reese does what he can,
buying books and even pencils and papers for the children themselves, for their teachers, but most blacks in Revere are poor as field
mice, and there's only so much a person can do. No wonder Reese
hates them."

"Hates who?"

"White folks. Always has, always will. And he's right to do it.
Just look at your friend Cooper Connelly. He's on the school board
talking integration, but Lee School's the one gets the money, not
Hunt. That's how it's always been. That's how it always will be. Jack
Rand sees to that. And mark my words, deep down and in secret,
Cooper backs him up."

"He doesn't!" cried Melba, surprised at herself. After all, Deanie
was her best friend. She came by every day to check on her, and
Melba got lonely. "He really wants to work this thing out right. He
just hasn't figured out exactly how to do it yet. Besides, even if he
is white, he's doing every bit as much about integration as Reese

is. The whole world knows Reese Jackson cares about nobody but Reese Jackson—not really, not underneath."

"He cares about his patients and his family!" cried Lyle Dean. "He cares about me."

This could be a fight coming, and they both knew it. Deanie's lips tightened, and her hands went to her hips, but Reese was gone all the time and she knew it. Instead Melba, her friend, was here, and by now she knew how Reese always wanted things just so and that lately his temper had started to flash up out of nowhere. Deanie had told Melba these things herself; it didn't make good sense to start acting uppity now.

So Lyle Dean settled down on the porch swing beside Melba and wrapped herself tight in Melba's wool shawl. Casually she said, "Why don't we ride over and see where he lives? He comes over here all the time, seeing what's going on. Maybe we ought to see what's going on over there, too." As though the thought had just occurred to her.

"Over where?"

"Southside. Where Cooper Connelly's house is."

Melba was already shaking her head. "We got no business on Southside."

"Maybe you don't," said Deanie, "but I pay my taxes. I got a right to go anywhere in this town I please."

She reached over for a sugar cookie, let the thought lodge its way good into both their heads.

"We could drive on over there for a hot minute," said Deanie. Although the idea had been percolating around in her mind for a while now, she was still thinking it through. Deanie was very "attached to her house"—that's how Melba described it—with the beauty of it, with making it even more beautiful. And so the loveliness of Dunsmuir had always nicked furtively at her attention on the infrequent occasions when she could find an excuse to drive past.

Reese, Lyle Dean's expert on all things southern, had spelled it out for her early on. "No use you driving into Southside. Black folks don't usually go into the white part of town without a reason, and you don't look like nobody's maid."

"We need to study it," she said, excited now. "Reese's nurse called me right before I came over; one of those Mims boys from over West Point's gone and mangled up his hand in a cotton gin. Probably drinking still whiskey when he did it; that family's noted for great women but some mighty weak men. Reese went right over, and he's going to be late getting home."

"*A very late night for Dr. Jackson.*" Eloise, his nurse, had sounded sincerely sorry when she told this to Mrs. Jackson on the telephone.

"Nice man, Cooper Connelly," said Deanie, changing her tune now. "Nice car. Bet the house is nice, too. And it's still light enough we might actually see something. Aren't you interested?"

Melba said, "But what about Skippy?" Deanie hardly ever left her child actually alone.

Lyle Dean looked right straight at her. "I think he'll be all right. He's ten years old now. We won't be gone long."

For a moment her last words just lay there, clear and curious on the chill evening air, surrounded by laughter from the Franklin children playing across the street and the rumble of a cement truck rolling up from the highway onto Main. Still Melba said nothing, and Deanie didn't breathe.

Finally Mrs. Dr. Jackson insisted, "It might be fun to see that house. They say it's one of the best-looking places in Revere—a real, white-painted, column-porched, magnolia-laden antebellum."

In truth she'd been reading about Dunsmuir for years. Not only was it pictured every April on the front page of the *Times Commercial* during Pilgrimage, when all the faded blossoms of the Old South flowered once again, to be trooped through by the curious and the nostalgic, but Mrs. Cooper Connelly was a very lavish hostess, especially when her father-in-law was in town. She was always in the papers. She was always doing something extraordinary and swell.

"But we'll stand out over there," gasped Melba, clutching at her fire-engine-red angora sweater, as though that blazing piece of fluff were the whole of their dilemma.

"Not you," said Deanie. "You look white enough, you'll fit right in. It's me that's the problem. But it's getting dark out. People will be having their dinner. Nobody will see us, and we'll see everything"

Melba still looked doubtful. She hardly ever went anyplace; not being able to see her own picket fence made her uneasy. "Are you sure about Skip?"

"He'll be fine. Critter's staying with us for a few days, and he's with him. That girl Janet Puckett is over there, too. They've been laughing and giggling. All up to something, but they hush up every time I come into the room. Must be some little-kid secret. Come on, let's do it. Revere's not big as a minute. We could have been there and back by now."

She waited a beat, and then this did it. "Melba, you got all those women coming over here from Southside getting their fortunes told, trying to figure out what their husbands are up to. Don't you ever wonder what they live like?"

"I know what they live like," said Melba. "They tell me, day in and day out."

"But Cooper Connelly's wife never comes over here. She's not the type. Perfect women like that—they make up their own future by controlling it just like their past. They don't need you to tell them what's in store." Deanie's voice turned wheedly.

Melba shook her head, and she was still shaking it as she got up from her own swing and followed Deanie back over to the Jackson driveway and to the Jacksons' second car.

Thank goodness it was a tan Buick, a nice vehicle but simple, the kind that wouldn't stand out on Southside. This was reassuring. Deanie Jackson did not believe in ostentation. She read *Town & Country* magazine and left flash to her husband. Deanie went to the door and called out instructions to her son and his friends. This took a minute. Then Melba and Deanie got in and drove off. Like guilty conspirators, they did not say one word to each other.

Since Cooper Connelly had started coming over with his gray slacks, blue blazers, and striped ties—"rep" ties, Deanie had told Melba gently, correcting her when she'd called them "reb"—Melba had begun paying attention to what she called "normal style," seen that it was vastly different from "Melba style," and for the first time in her life had noted the discrepancy. It was that old chameleon stirring up in her again, and she knew it, that urge to fit in.

Secretly, and without saying a word about it—hardly even whispering the thought to herself—Melba had started making comparisons between the way she looked and the way her good friend, Mrs. Dr. Jackson looked, with the smooth way Deanie walked and moved and with the discreet colors she wore. She'd seen a definite difference between the two. Nothing clashed on Deanie. It never did. Take right now, for instance. Lyle Dean's straight brown hair waved down to meet her soft tan sweater, which in turn waved down to soft tan slacks. Exactly the same color! Absolutely perfectly matched! Deanie had two little pearls in her ears and two matching real gold barrettes keeping the hair back out of her eyes. The only other piece of jewelry she had on was THE RING—THE NEW RING she'd gotten after Reese stopped being so poor. There was nothing out of place on Deanie, and there was nothing that was too bright. Melba's heart thrilled that this perfect confection—so like Jackie—could be her best friend.

Melba never had been one to care much about what she wore or how it went together. She'd always had things other than clothes on her mind. She was paying attention now, though, and saw, with some dismay, that even hidden away in this car, her green pedal pushers and red top stood out like Christmas neon. Her crimson-painted nails shone black. Riding slowly along this muted, tree-lined street in this muted car and beside the muted perfection of her best friend had not managed to tone Melba herself down one bit. This was a melancholy thought.

"You should be working over at Miss Pearl's Dress Shoppe," she told Deanie, even though she'd never been in Pearl's in her life. "They'd love to have somebody like you—somebody who reads *Vogue* magazine and knows every name in the social column of the *Times Commercial* and where folks live and when their house was built. Pearl needs somebody like you over there."

Deanie laughed. No use working. She had a full life already, what with watching out for her son and taking care of her husband. After the incident, she and Reese had mutually agreed, without saying a word, that the best place for her was at home.

Besides, "Black folks can't even shop at Pearl's," said Lyle Dean, "much less work there. I've heard she's lightened up a little lately—lets you come in and get stuff as long as you don't ask to try anything on and she can wait on you when she wants to. Pearl acts like she's doing you a favor to take your money. Reese told me he'd rather send me up to New York or Washington to buy my clothes—or at least down to Meridian, where they have good black shops—rather than put up with that nonsense over there."

"Things are changing," said Melba. "This school business is just the first step in a long mile. You can mark my words on that. Look what's happening in the rest of the country."

"Doesn't matter," said Deanie, peering out through her car window. "Reese would pitch a fit if I shopped over at Pearl's, and he'd up and die if I worked there. You know how he feels about my staying home with Skip."

"Brendan's already out the door, and Skip may have been hurt, but he's getting on. He's getting older. Got his own friends and his life," said Melba quietly. "Pretty soon you're going to be staying home with your own self. Besides, Reese don't rule the world. Pearl's one of my regulars. She comes in like clockwork every Sunday morning, right after she drops her kids off at First Baptist for Sunday School, in that hour before I go off to mass myself. I could put in a word for you, tell her you've got an aura that will bring her good luck. That would do it. Down deep, Pearl's not all that prejudiced, she's just doing what she always has done. Plus, she's practical, a good business-woman. She knows there's only one color in this world that really matters, and that's green."

They both had a good laugh at that one.

Deanie pulled up at the red light on Main. Once it changed and she crossed over, it was just a hop, skip, and a jump to Cooper Connelly's house. Melba's heart was hop, skipping, and jumping already. She could feel it. My goodness! She covered this pounding with a frenzy of words.

"Reese did well to put his new clinic over on Main Street," said Melba, "right in the shadow of Doctors Hospital. He sure knows how to show those crackers what's what."

"I don't know," said Lyle Dean, watching for stop signs, looking straight ahead. "I can remember when we first came here and he had the little office, the one that used to be the Blanchard's store. It was out there on the corner in Sandhurst, black folks all around it. In-the-town folks, county folks—so many of them, but all of them from around here. Nobody comes to Mississippi from some other place. At least the two of us—you and me—are the only ones I've ever known who did it. Maybe Dr. Connelly's wife; they say she came down from Virginia. Other than us, most people are going the other way. Heading north. Reese bought the Blanchard store and spruced it up—painted it white, put out green shutters—but it was still really teeny, and he didn't like me driving over there where he was. The kids were so little, and it was a rough part of town. Streets weren't paved. Back then who was caring about black folks and what they needed? But sometimes I had to go over there anyway—if I had to take the lady who worked for me home. Mrs. Turner. She adored Reese. Just adored him. Still does."

"Every black person in Revere admires Reese Jackson," piped in Melba, "even those out in the county. Maybe especially those. He is their doctor. Folks are devoted to him."

Lyle Dean said, "Mrs. Turner sure is. And one day it was raining. I put the kids in the car. I was taking her home, and we had to go right by Reese's office. The rain was coming down hard, cats and dogs. You could barely watch out of the windows, so at first when I looked out, I thought I was seeing things. I remember wiping the fog away and looking again. They were still there—all these people, snaking out the door of Reese's little storefront office. That line reached around the corner and halfway up the next block. Sick people—why else would they be coming to see a doctor?—standing on this crappy, broke-up sidewalk, under umbrellas in the rain. Sick people. Loving him that much. Trusting that he cared about them and could make them well. I never can forget it. He just means so much to our people. He's a symbol for them, a hope."

IT WAS THE LITTLE THINGS you first noticed when you passed from one side of Revere into the next, and the changes were subtle. If you were talking, you might miss them, but Melba and Deanie were no longer talking. They were looking around.

First off they noticed how the streets got brighter. Magically. Right away—as soon as you crossed Main Street. The reason for this was that the light fixtures were no longer shoddy aluminum and they were no longer few and far between. Instead they were now made of filigreed wrought iron, and all the little bulbs in every one of them worked. There was also a great quantity of these ornate beauties. The sidewalks were trim, and they were even. Pansies and evergreens sat in decorative tubs, nicely placed. Prominently displayed on every corner were elaborate, black markers announcing this as the Historic District.

"I guess nothing historic must ever have happened down where we live," said Melba.

Lyle Dean said, "Our municipal taxes at work."

Deanie took her foot off the pedal, slowed down. It was agreed between them, but never said, that they should take their time, see everything they could. Who knew when they'd have the opportunity or the excuse to come this way again? And it wasn't just fear of the police or being thought trespassers that concerned them. Say what they might, they both knew that Revere was a small city, a place where just about everybody knew everybody else or at least knew about them—a place where Deanie stood almost no chance of being arrested. Any policeman on the street would know who Mrs. Spencer Reese Jackson was; most would have known her car on sight. It wasn't that the city would look at them oddly; it was that *they* looked at themselves oddly, as they stared at these sights, as they drove down these streets, as they ventured into this life.

Leaning close with her nose against her own window and peering over Deanie's shoulder so she could see out hers, Melba stared.

No matter if the houses were well kept or decrepit—and there were old antebellums falling apart, even on Southside—what they were made of was the same. You peered through identical windows into the same deep-colored rooms, where you saw the same portraits on the walls, soft light stroking out the outlines of silver frames on dark furniture. There was the smell of wood fires in fireplaces, heavy on the air even though it was too early for them and still would be for a few more good weeks. And if you listened hard enough, all along the street, you could pick out the sounds of pianos being practiced or played upon, as the case might be. Melba, whose experience, though vast in certain areas, was extremely limited in others, looked out at the scenic show before her and grinned.

"I've never been in his house," said Melba to Deanie, to whom, of course, this fact was obvious. What Melba didn't say, what she just now realized, was that she hadn't been much in anybody's house at all since she'd come to Revere. People came to her, even Deanie. In fact, Melba realized now, this instant, that without television she wouldn't really have any idea how a normal person might live.

Deanie slowed up. "That's it. That's Dr. Connelly's house. The one sitting catty-corner to the street, behind the gardenia bushes. The one that's still all dark inside. I recognize it from the Pilgrimage brochures."

Deanie whispered on, but Melba closed her eyes and pressed her face tight against the coolness of the car window before she opened them, very slowly, once again.

Reese Jackson always told anybody who would listen that the only new thing that had happened in Southside since Civil War times was that the lots themselves—surveyed large in a time of slave labor—had been broken down and smaller Victorian houses had sprouted up between the old mansions, just like wild roses might do in the shadow of oak trees. But the antebellums still dominated, and they were still the house of choice in this house-proud, river-sitting town.

"My great-great-great-granddaddy, Emmet Leigh Hunt, built the home place for his bride, Susan Rayburn Millport from Millport, Georgia, in 1832," was the way the town's gospel was cited in chapter and verse and information gently given, whether or not the information was always true.

Cooper wasn't like that. He told Melba once, "My daddy gouged Dunsmuir out of Raintree Hairston one night when they were playing poker and drunk—at least Raintree was drunk. Of course, Mr. Hairston expected my daddy to give him back the house the next day. That's the way gentlemen do. Mr. Hairston found out my daddy was no gentleman."

Now Melba whispered, "Which one is it?"

Deanie lowered the window just a bit. "That one there."

She wasn't laughing now, and neither was Melba.

"My goodness," she said, real low.

It surely was one of the biggest houses Melba had ever seen, even bigger than most in New Orleans. And something about it reminded Melba of New Orleans, of the orphanage on Nashville Street where children wore faded blue-and-gray plaid cotton uniforms and followed the nuns in orderly ranks from place to place. Melba had her-

self tried out living in the orphan home once or twice, so she knew
it well. She had to crane out of Deanie's discreetly lowered window
and try to be a little discreet herself. The fact that only two people
lived in this whole place was truly remarkable to her. And there
were only the two of them—Cooper and Evelyne Elizabeth. But Jack
Rand, of course, stayed there on the weekends. After all, it was Jack
Rand's house.

Deanie said, "Dinnertime, and that place looks dead as a door-
nail. I wonder where they could all be."

She sounded eager to really know, and awestruck; Melba could
hear it in her voice. She, on the other hand, was glad nobody was
home. She could feel a place better when there weren't a lot of
people around, causing interference, and Madame Melba liked to
get her perceptions straight.

Because *something* was there, or someone, hidden just behind
high walls and gardens and the perfection of manicured wiste-
ria vines. Something that called out to Madame Melba, the little
crystal-ball reader. Something Melba could sense but wished she
couldn't. Something slightly different from the eighth-day wonder
this whole place was made out to be—a graceful image of porticoes
and columns, of fresh white paint and gleaming black shutters, of
outbuildings and old slave cabins just visible through the filigrees of
the wrought-iron fence or over the brick wall.

Looking at the immensity of this mansion, Melba recognized,
and quite suddenly, how very little she knew about Cooper Connelly
and that his attraction to her, which she had mistaken for interest,
was probably due to the fact that she was so totally and completely
foreign to his regular world. He could confide in her, drink her tea,
and talk to her about school integration because she and they would
eventually fade from his life, but this before her, where no interest

was shown in such matters and no encouragement given, would remain. In fact, she realized that more than likely this was the reason
he came to visit her and that she satisfied a need within him that
was more visceral than sex. She listened to him. But, as with sex,
when this exigency was met, he would disappear as quickly, and as
completely, as her clients in New Orleans had done. She was essen-
tial to his life right now for the reason that she was not integral to
it. Talking with her would spare him from talking about unpleasant
circumstances with a wife who was not sympathetic to them, with
friends who opposed them. The schools in Revere would integrate,
and probably sooner rather than later—about this Madame Melba
had no doubt, and neither, she was sure, did the people who opposed
both integration and Cooper Connelly at this moment. Eventually
integration would come, and there would be the moment of dis-
ruption, as there was when one thing made place for another, and
then the longer moments of getting used to it, but these times would
pass. Somehow or other, and more than likely imperfectly, revisions,
even revolutions, were eventually absorbed. And when this happened, Cooper would return to this house and to the wife and the
friendships hidden in it—his life—and although they might never
know the things about him that Melba knew, what they did know
about him would be what he considered to be important. She was
as necessary to his real life as one of the columns that bolstered the
structure of his house—interchangeable, one giving way to another,
each thrown out and replaced without emotion when their useful-
ness was done.

Just then, as she stared, a silent switch was turned somewhere,
and full, unexpected light spread out from the deep veranda that
guarded Cooper's house. Both Melba and Lyle Dean gasped at the
sudden irradiation. Melba waited for a moment, with Deanie be-

side her, but no other thing about the house changed; there was no answering glow from behind the lace curtains. Whatever lay hidden within them was quiet, deep and dark. Keeping to itself. Melba glanced around, at the other neighboring houses—at their firelight and candlelight, at the flickering of their television screens. Its very emptiness made Dunsmuir appear just as out of place as she was, with her bright clothes and her polished nails and with her curly red hair tinted a color that had no precedent in nature.

Deanie said, "I wonder where Dr. Connelly went. I mean, after he left you. Not home. I don't see his car. I wonder."

"Spook house," said Melba. "Looks like nothing but ghosts live there."

Deanie said, "Let's go on home." She turned on her ignition slowly, but with purpose. "I want to show you something. Quick, before Reese gets back."

"Thought you said he was out in the county. It takes a while to get back from there."

Deanie looked out the window, then switched her gaze to the rearview mirror.

"Home," she repeated, not answering about Reese. Something in her voice stopped Melba from saying anything either. The light on the Connelly veranda continued to radiate toward them, a scolding finger, warning that coming to Southside had been a mistake. That black folks, especially black women, should stay put and where they belonged.

Mrs. Spencer Reese Jackson shook her head, shut her eyes to it. "Got to show you something," she repeated to her friend, Madame Melba Obrenski. "And I got to show you tonight before Reese gets back."

Her lips had thinned out to a fine, polished line.

Melba nodded, but this was just to get along. She knew that even with his tantrums and his controlling ways, Deanie wasn't at all frightened of displeasing Reese Jackson. His tempers blew over, and Lyle Dean had worked out more than one way to wiggle out from under his domination. Not like a lot of women, who were actually scared witless by their husbands—scared they might hit them, scared they might lose them. Melba should know.

"Let's get on home," she said, trying to bring back the laughing mood they'd started out with when they'd crossed Main Street and adventured to this foreign place. And it did come back for a little while—at least part of it did, as Deanie slipped the car around a corner and then another and headed them on back to their part of town. Melba had an old Irish grandmother—her *real* grandmother, not just one of the women that had helped raise her up—who always said she was glad to see the last of something. Melba knew what she meant. She was glad to see the last of Dunsmuir's quiet perfection. To see the last of the perfect life Cooper—no longer *her* Cooper—actually lived.

"Going home," she said aloud again.

They cruised down Fifth Street talking and laughing, quietly at first and then with more gusto, about Christmas coming in just six more weeks, about the way the nights were already starting to cool.

"Gonna be a cold winter, a long one for sure."

Melba was thinking just this when she saw Reese's long white car easing up the River Road, as ostentatious as ever, as sure not to be missed. Still, he should have been missed, or at least attempted to be, because the highway from West Point did not end in this part of town, and the road from Macon did. And Deanie had said Reese would be in West Point, that he would be working on one of them drunks from down there. As she glanced over—quickly and furtively, through her cat eyes—at Lyle Dean, she saw that her lips were no longer tight and she was smiling. If she had seen her lying, and most probably cheating, husband, she didn't let on, didn't miss a beat. Deanie was looking straight ahead, talking a mile a minute about some house they were passing and who had bought it from whom. Talking so fast that Melba wondered if she'd seen Reese's car after all. But she was a wife, thought Melba, like Cooper Connelly's wife, and she was protected. She could close her eyes to what she was actually seeing, and, like magic, she could make it disappear.

At the Jackson house, though, where they would normally have said their good-byes and Melba gone her way and Deanie hers, Lyle Dean reached out for her. Melba was moving so quickly to her own house and to her own thoughts that at first Deanie's hand caught only the hem of her sweater. It was enough. Melba could not wiggle away; Deanie held her too tight. Lyle Dean let the sweater drop, and the next thing Melba knew, Deanie was holding her by the elbow. She had a strong grip.

"I want to show you something, in my house," she said. "I told you that. I meant it."

Actually going into Deanie's house was as exotic to Melba as going over into Southside. It had always been Deanie coming to her. This kept Lyle Dean's relationship with her husband at least pretty clean. On the rare moments when he insisted, "Absolutely I do not want you hanging around with that woman"—usually when he was irritated about something else—she could tell him that Melba had never set foot in their home, that she had rarely really spoken with their children. That she was Deanie's friend, and she had no part in their lives.

Until tonight.

"My house," insisted Lyle Dean.

Usually, like her husband and children, she came out through the back of her house, going to her car or over to Melba's. It was just more convenient. But tonight she purposely led Melba to the front, where the lights were all blazing. Their footsteps rang loudly against the brick of the walkway and on the stairs and on the wood of the veranda itself. Deanie had to fish through a huge batch of keys to find the right one, wiggling them one after the other in the brass lock. Melba heard the faint sound of Skippy's television coming from upstairs; it was Saturday, and he was watching *Gunsmoke*. She wondered if his little friends had gone.

Once the door swung open, the light from the Jackson house blinded Melba. She, who lived in a dark house and was childless, imagined that children must just leave lights blazing wherever they passed. Or else that Reese Jackson did not have to encourage economy within his family. Then again, why should he?

The sheer abundance of the light was such that at first Melba was not aware that Deanie was watching her, that she was holding her breath.

She nodded. It was then that Melba looked around.

And found herself transported right back to Southside; this time actually inside it and not just looking in from the street. She saw the delicately glazed apricot walls she had seen on the other side of town, the oil paintings that had grown dim with age, the polished silver, the neat pile of huge, expensive books on art. Her feet sank deeply into the rich carpets—carpets she knew came from far-off and foreign lands—that lay against the patina of river-oak floors. Deanie marched ahead, flinging open doors onto rooms that were already brilliantly lit.

Melba stared, truly agog.

"Why, it's a white person's house," she said finally, accompanying her words with a good bit of breath, "but not just any white person's house—a rich white person's. Wealthy. Like the Connellys' or Judge Mayhew's. A Southside, rich-folks, fine-and-dandy house stuck right here smack in the middle of Catfish Alley. Why, it's probably even *better* than Dunsmuir inside."

Deanie watched her closely, and she nodded.

And in that moment, with Matt Dillon calling out for the bad guys to come on over with their hands up and with the brightness of artificial light all around her, Madame Melba saw suddenly and completely and with witch certainty why she and Lyle Dean Jackson were such good friends.

"Honey, you just as out of place in this world as I am."

Deanie nodded. Shook her head.

# Chapter 14

WHILE DEANIE AND HER CHILDREN were used to going in and out of the back of their house—maybe because it was closest to where the cars were kept—Reese Jackson, on the other hand, had recently taken to using the front door almost exclusively. He could not have explained why if anyone had asked him—though his actions were seldom questioned—but coming in the front door reassured him. All that polished brass and wood, and beyond that all those real wool carpets—"Carpets, not rugs." Lyle Dean did not hesitate to correct him, once she'd learned something new herself—and fine French furniture, real pieces, that looked like they might have come right out of *House & Garden* magazine, which some of them had. Deanie had a knack for doing things differently.

In the old days, until he made it a point to come through the front, he might go for weeks without seeing just how lovely his house was, moving from the kitchen up the stairs straight to bed. He was that busy.

But Reese was convinced, and probably with reason, that he lived in the most absolutely beautiful house in all Revere, Mississippi, the most faithfully restored, the most truly magnificent. Although, of course, he could not know this for certain; too many houses were forbidden to him. But he imagined it to be so, and during hectic days he loved to think of Lyle Dean in it, climbing up ladders to brush a rainbow of colored stain on the walls, rubbing steel wool along the baseboards to make them glimmer, sitting in her sewing room with yards of costly silk fabric she'd ordered from New York or New Orleans to make sure the white curtains at the windows billowed out and then billowed out some more.

Reese had what he'd always wanted. A wife, Lyle Dean, sitting in his house, making him a home. His secret, and as much as he could, he managed to keep Lyle Dean to himself.

It had been a long day, even longer than most, and Reese Jackson was glad to be home. If the truth were known, one never spoken because it was so true, Reese Jackson did not particularly care for his children. Their experience was so different from his experience that he found no connecting link to it, not even a sense of pride. Instead he loved his wife and loved his ornate house and loved the home she'd made for him in it. He loved the fact that she was in it.

His mama, Hinkty—God rest her soul!—had done the best that she could, but mainly she'd spent Reese's growing-up years in other people's houses, taking care of their children. This left her precious little time to take care of her own. Reese, who had what he liked to call "almost perfect recall," could not remember a day when she had been there to greet him when he came home from school. Not even sick days. When Reese was sick—and he was a sickly child—he stayed home alone. Mother away working, no father in sight—this was existence in the part of the rural Delta where Reese Jackson grew up, and the reality for poor people was the same whether you were black or white. If you were lucky, you lived by your aunts or uncles and grandparents, and most people were lucky. Reese and Hinkty, on the other hand, lived by themselves. Yet, first trailing on behind his mother and then later in the books he read, Reese had glimpsed another existence, and over the years he had watched this existence grow and evolve within his own mind until it leaped out and became his reality. He called it the Dick and Jane life, although he said this aloud to no one. Not even his wife. This alternate reality had been presented to him in tattered copies of the Bobbsey Twins and the Hardy Boys as well—series after series all bound in books so old and greasy and decrepit that the school system considered them a health hazard for white children. Reese had not minded. He even read Nancy Drew. And what he saw within those pages marked him, made him want to be in a place of great cleanliness, of order, of food on the table when he wanted it, of attention, of abundant affection, of needs satisfied. He wanted that life. He wanted that home, and, as with everything else he'd ever wanted, Reese Jackson managed to get it.

They didn't entertain much—he was too busy—and Deanie had not found many friends here in Mississippi, though she'd been here for years. Except for the flowers everywhere—he chose those; he sure liked him some flower prints—it was Deanie who kept the house up, Deanie who kept herself up. She read magazines like mad.

Lyle Dean stayed home, just where he wanted her, and she did not waste her time. Recently, now that blacks had sparked a revolution, other groups had jumped on the bandwagon as well. There were even faint rumblings about women working, developing themselves. Reese said all the right things when this subject was broached, and he encouraged his daughter in her quest for a law-school degree. He would pay for anything he was called upon to pay for, but inside he was having none of this notion, at least not in his house. His mama had worked, and it had done nothing but kill her. Reese's unselfish desire was to save his wife from that fate.

Reese walked through the downstairs. He left the dark-paneled, French-doored areas in the front—the living room, dining room, his study, the library, the breakfast room, and three other rooms he hadn't been in for years—heading straight to the kitchen. On top of everything else, Lyle Dean was a great cook.

His mama had not liked Lyle Dean one bit—even before the incident. She was always complaining that Deanie didn't work. "She could at least teach school. Help you out some." Reese didn't need any help, and certainly he did not need any money; he had known what he wanted and still did: to have sweet Deanie as his own sweet secret, to hold her all to himself.

Reese pulled off first his tie and then his jacket, looked up to the one lone light flickering at the top of the long reach of his stairs, and sighed. Then squinted his eyes, which furrowed his forehead. Something was amiss.

Clues were everywhere. First off, Lyle Dean had stayed upstairs, hadn't come down to greet him at the door. Also, there was no comforting smell of dinner coming from the oven, no piece of still-warm pie laid out seductively on the side counter. His wife was mad about something—could be anything—and Reese had to decide if he wanted to get into it with her tonight. They had separate bathrooms; not for the first time, Reese wished they had separate bedrooms as well. He was tired. He did not want to fight. He had other, more important things on his mind.

*You never knew what people might be up to.* The thought was in and out of his mind in a flash, but it was there long enough to shake Reese Jackson.

He started climbing the stairs.

His very pretty wife—and Reese still thought this about Lyle Dean, even after all these years—sat propped up in their bed, surrounded by all kinds of flowered, lacy pillows and staring straight at Johnny Carson. She never took her eyes off the television screen, even when he came in and plopped down beside her extra hard on the bed, just so she'd know he was there. She knew already.

"What you watching?" he asked. With measured precision he took off the rest of his clothes, got up and hung up what needed to be hung. He kept his back to her. He didn't want her to see what might be on his face. He walked to the closet, taking his time, knowing that whatever it was, was coming. Unlike her husband, Lyle Dean did not believe in secrets.

After a while she said, "Strangest thing."

Safe in the closet, Reese started breathing normally again. Once she'd opened her mouth, the truth would come flowing out through the floodgates. She couldn't hold back, not from him. He'd find out real soon what it was worrying her.

"Strangest thing," Deanie repeated, "but that white doctor Cooper Connelly's been coming around. I see him on the street all the time. I see him over next door, visiting Miss Melba Obrenski. I see him watching what's going on here."

So that was it. Reese let out a sigh.

"Free country," he said. He was going to the bathroom now, with his folded underwear and his neatly balled-up dirty socks. "Men can go anywhere they want to, and they do. Lots of time they come over to see trampy types like your friend Melba, women like that. I tried to tell you about her. You just don't understand how things are."

When Deanie didn't answer, Reese looked out slyly through the bathroom door. Once again her full attention seemed to be fixed on Johnny Carson's golf swing and his jokes, even though she'd eased down the sound so low with the remote—one of the Jackson's many new gadgets—that Reese was certain she couldn't really hear a thing.

"Men," continued Reese, striding back into the bedroom, "tend to go into anyplace they want to. It's the hunter in them, and they are like that—predators. Free to roam any damn part of the forest they please."

"That what you were doing over Southside tonight?" his wife said, eyes still full forward. "Staking out your own part of the forest? Looking for some woman to prey on?"

Quick as a flash, there she was, sitting straight up in her bed and staring right at him.

Without a word Reese proceeded back into the bathroom, where he now took his time. He made sure his wife could hear him washing his face and brushing his teeth. He made sure he gargled his Listerine extra loud. And all the while he was thinking.

Now, Reese couldn't say he was really scared—not yet—but he was a good bit uneasy. The memory of what he'd actually been doing, why he'd been coming through Southside, was fresh in his mind. *That woman. Seeing to that woman.* No use trying to explain things to Deanie. Not that thing, at least. For an instant Reese's unease raged up until it really was fear, really was anger. And he thought, *What in God's name does this woman want with me?* Meaning his wife. The thought came to him to bring up the Neiman's bill or the Saks bill or the Dillard's bill—he had any number to choose from—to complain about her extravagance, which he normally encouraged. Start a fight. Start a rampage. Explode every thought of Southside right out of her mind.

But Reese hadn't gotten where he was—all the way out of Money, Mississippi, and on to the top of the heap—by losing his temper. He never argued with Deanie, not if he could help it, and the Good Lord knew she never argued with him. She'd worked too hard to get him, or at least he'd let her think this. And she liked the life they had together; she didn't want to let him go. It didn't make sense for them to waste their time arguing, so Reese, ever practical, had developed certain ways of dealing with his wife.

He showered, slipped into fresh glen-plaid pajamas, and then eased on out into the bedroom once again. The silent television set was still running, and Lyle Dean's eyes were still glued to it.

Reese chose to plop down, not on the bed itself this time but on one of the brocade chairs that were near it. He heard himself saying, "What's that you said?" Against his better judgment.

She was ready for him. Lyle Dean got up, walked deliberately over to the television, and blacked out the picture. The silk of her lace nightgown made a nice swishing sound, and when she moved, the lace on it curved around her breasts and her sweet, sweet ass. No flannel pajamas for his wife. The thing he liked about Deanie—always had—was the girlish way she handled herself, how she was female more than feminine. Her mama had been like that, too. Even after all these years of marriage, both Jacksons still showered and cuted themselves up before heading to bed. Reese was still eager for Lyle Dean. Lyle Dean was still eager for him. Reese knew this. He could tell it. Other women did not interest him in the least.

"What were you up to tonight?" said Mrs. Jackson once she'd settled back in among her pillows and was good and ready for what was coming. "On Southside. Why were you way over there?"

"Baby." Reese fixed a look of pure-dee pain on his face. "Didn't Eloise call you? That girl—I swear I'm going to get me a new secretary if it's the last thing I do. I told her to tell you I'd be over in Macon. That woman." Reese sighed in exaggerated exasperation. "Some man got his hand caught in a cotton gin—a patient of mine. I had to run right over and attend to him quick as I could."

"She said you'd be in West Point," said Deanie, still holding strong. "But anyway, how did that get you over on Southside? I wasn't aware that Mrs. Sarah Berryman or Miss Lilla Franklin had started laying out cotton fields behind their rose gardens."

"Wasn't on Southside," said Reese easily. "Where'd you get that notion?"

His eyes were as big and bugged out as hers were. He hoped they looked as innocent, too.

But just in case, he decided to take the offensive. "Anyway, what you know about Southside? Black folks can get themselves in trouble going over there after dark. Ever heard of the boogeyman coming to get you? Or goblins and vampires? Except they're called the sheriff and his deputies in this town."

Reese's wife did not laugh.

"I was over there tonight, around seven," said Deanie, real quiet, "and that's where I saw your car inching down the street."

That was strange—his advantage. Lyle Dean had a thing about not going where she wasn't wanted. She must have had a powerful reason to cross over Main Street. Things started to click together in Reese's mind, forming a way out, a map of escape.

"Just what were *you* doing over there?" he repeated.

She ducked at that but was still ready. "Looking at the houses. There were a couple of those big old places they always talk about during Pilgrimage. I decided tonight was the right time to do that, to see what I'd always wanted to see."

"Pilgrimage don't come up 'til April. What got you so fired up you just had to *see things* tonight?"

"I saw you," said Deanie, staring straight at him. "That was enough."

Reese tried another tack. "Where'd you say that dumb thing works for me told you I was going anyway?"

"West Point."

He sighed. Edged some more exasperation into his voice. "Just goes to show you. That girl don't know the difference between Macon and Mayhew; Mayhew's near West Point, Macon ain't. She's from over in Reform, Alabama, herself and still hasn't managed to figure her way around Mississippi. Can't tell the difference between north and south."

Deanie didn't say anything, but she did start to look hopeful. Reese knew she wanted him to come up with something she could believe, something that would make whatever was wrong right. He did his best for her. "I got finished up with that Mims boy quicker than I thought and took the time—on my way back in to check in at the office—to go over and call on old Frank Rogers. You know that white man owns the big furniture store over there on College Street?—that's the one. Actually it was the wife I needed to talk to, but I had to get to her through him. I operated on a woman worked for them—Miss Nellie Trayham. Hernia problems. She has to stay on in bed for a week or so, and she was scared of losing her job. Asked me to go over there and make things straight with them. Might not believe she was truly sick if it was coming from just her. They got a daughter getting married pretty quick, and this isn't the best time for Mrs. Trayham to be off working. I told her I'd stop by, calm them down a bit. Help her hold on to her job."

Most of which was true enough. Reese glanced over at Deanie, then made a big show of easing on over onto the bed, fluffing up his pillows, and snuggling in under the covers. When he sighed, he made sure he sounded mighty weary.

"He was there when you got there, Mr. Rogers. It wasn't like you called on Mrs. Rogers—Miss Karen—by yourself?"

At least she was worried about his welfare. He could tell that in the choice of her words.

Reese didn't say anything, and Deanie waited a minute before she continued. "You can get yourself in some serious trouble messing around with white females. Look at what happened to Emmett Till, beat to death for just looking at the wrong woman the wrong way. Look at what happened to Gent Higgins, just two months back. They put him in jail, and that white man he worked for with him. And he wasn't just any white man—he was rich. And why? Because that white man sent him over to a white house to pick up a radio needed fixin' at a time when the white man of the house was at work. They say there's a written-down law against that. The blacks here may think you're God incarnate, but there's many a white person doubts that. I hope it's not white women you've fixed on, Reese. I hope it's not white women making you change."

*Making you change.*

Reese almost laughed aloud with relief, but he would come back to this later. Other women! *White* women! When he had Lyle Dean.

"No women," he said, and then quietly added, "I ain't got nobody in this life except you."

He eased a little closer, all the time thinking. Finally he said, "That's not like you, going over Southside at night. You never go anywhere after dark by yourself. That bad thing, Melba, must have talked you into seeing something. You're a doctor's wife now, well known in this city. You'll find yourself with a bad reputation hanging around with her. What would Reverend Petty think if he saw you two together on the street?"

Deanie shrugged. She was totally relaxed now. Reese could feel her skin warming to him through the sheets. Reverend Petty had changed the subject for them, brought them both back from Southside to the haven of their bed.

"Can't stand that man," said his wife, sighing and snuggling up. "Ought to be ashamed of himself the way he carries on. Calling himself a man of religion and the most lecherous thing walking the streets of this town. Ought to be more like Reverend Streeter. At least Reverend Streeter has his cause."

"*Determined* to eat at the River Café."

Lyle Dean nodded. She could have gone on and on, and usually did, about this man who was not her preacher and about whom Madame Melba had told her a great deal. Tonight, though, this was not necessary. Both Deanie and her husband had gotten what they wanted from their conversation; each had been reassured by it, and they were ready to move on to other things.

As he reached for the warmth and the safety and the comfort he had always found in his wife, Reese Jackson could not help his sigh of relief. Yet again tonight he had found that things could work in his favor, that they could level out, and that his life could still continue puffing along serenely upon the track that he had so carefully laid out for it.

# Chapter 15

AS LUCK WOULD HAVE IT, Deputy Butch Harrison looked up from reading Jack Rand Connelly's weekly column in Thursday's *Times Commercial*, where he'd been ranting away against the federal government and school integration, which was definitely—at least according to Deputy Harrison—on its way, when he happened to glance out the window of his cruiser and see Ruth Ann Puckett walk down Fourth Street, holding on tight to her little girl's hand. He was grateful for the diversion. It was one thing to read about war in Vietnam, another to think battles might be starting to erupt in your own hometown. And Deputy Harrison definitely believed that if they didn't come up with something soon, war was what they would eventually face, right here in Revere, Mississippi. He'd never before seen so many rebel flags floating from houses and shop windows and pasted on the back of truck bumpers. There was even talk of secret meetings—Klan meetings. Even Ol' Man Puckett was rumored as attending, though you'd think he'd still be too busy mourning, what

with his son dead and all. Harrison saw the danger with the Kluckers but Sheriff Kelly Joe Trotter said leave them alone. Couldn't stop
folks, black or white, from gathering together, had to give time to
time and wait until the shit hit the fan to do something. And sooner
or later it would.

Harrison halfway agreed with this, but the situation, about integration, still worried him, and he was glad to see Mrs. Puckett. He'd
been thinking about her for days now, wondering how he might get
her over to Revere to ask her a few more questions. There were still
one or two things he needed to find out. He'd tried going over to her
place, out there in Macon, once or twice more, but he never had
seemed to get hold of Miss Ruth Ann on her own. Big Rob Puckett,
for all his Klan meetings, seemed always to be there instead, and Big
Rob would get him talking about a fourteen-hand deer he'd shot
down near Ackerman or how good Mississippi State was doing in
the SEC this year. They'd go on and on. Actually, that was probably
just as well. Deputy Harrison wanted to talk to Mrs. Billy Ray about
certain particulars he'd recently been hearing. Rumors. Things maybe she didn't want her in-laws to know.

He studied the two of them, Mrs. Puckett and her little girl, as
they came on, innocently, toward him. They didn't know they were
being looked at, you could tell. The daughter said something, and
the mother laughed. Deputy Harrison noticed how Miss Ruth Ann
had put on a little weight. She didn't look as tentative as she once
had. Her oldest child had changed, too, since those early shocking
days in September, since the television appeal.

Neither of them seemed as threadbare as Harrison had expected;
they didn't seem nearly as bad off as Ol' Man Puckett and his sullen
wife. Didn't look as disgruntled and mad. Deputy Harrison recognized the tweed coat Miss Ruth Ann had on—his wife had bought

the same one just last week. She'd got it from J. C. Penney's over on Market Street. It was a smart little thing, not too expensive but not cheap either. He wondered, with some interest, just where Miss Ruth Ann was getting her money. Harrison had made it his business to ask around, and so he knew that the appeal with WLBN hadn't been that successful. Still, people were real nice in Mississippi, real generous. Probably some nice church folks were helping this young widow get back on her feet.

The little girl intrigued him. Harrison squinted closer so he could get a right good look. He remembered her well from the TV. She was certainly feisty, you could tell it, a skinny little thing, with that wired look that said she was always poised to fight back. Some females were like that. They were born to challenge, and they likely died that way as well. The mama had relaxed some, but the child didn't appear to have calmed down one whit since the day her daddy died. She was still every bit as skittish as a forest squirrel during hunting season, something that just naturally scented out danger. Harrison wondered. Was it her daddy's passing made her like that?

He'd heard the other three young ones had been sent up north to Iuka, to some childless relatives on their mother's side. Harrison knew that most weekends Miss Ruth Ann took the Greyhound up to see them, and she always carried Janet with her. Never let her stay with the Pucketts by herself. The few times he'd actually seen them together—usually the mother shooed her away when she saw him coming, just like she had the first time—they had been holding on tight to each other, just like they were doing now. Certainly, you could understand this, after all that happened. Yet and still . . .

What he'd heard about those children hadn't been good.

The Pucketts were close enough now that Harrison should climb on out of his car, and he did this. Ambled over and waited on the sidewalk where they had to pass. He saw the recognition on Miss Ruth Ann's face when she looked up from her daughter and recognized him. But what could she do? She had to smile, and she did.

"Good morning, Deputy," said Mrs. Puckett.

Harrison touched his hat. "Miss Ruth Ann," he said, "and Miss Janet. Weather's turned cold, but y'all both looking mighty fine today. Springy. I'm glad to see y'all seem to be getting over your loss."

With these words Harrison saw the woman shrink, right before his eyes, into the same scared and befuddled little thing he'd first seen on TV. He had been in law enforcement for many years now—first over in Georgia and then right back here in Jefferson-Lee County—and he knew there were some folks, even folks working the good side of things, who lived with the kind of fear he was pulling out of this young widow woman right now. Mostly they were black folks. You got this reaction all the time from them, even from the blustery ones like Reese Jackson. People who had grown up in Mississippi during a time when they had had to get off the sidewalk if a white person passed and yet had *seen* all the changes and so *knew* things could change—to this day, years after the start of the bus boycott over in Montgomery that had turned the world upside down, if a white person came up on them sudden like, unexpectedly, you could almost touch the fear on a black person, cut through it with a knife. It was that palpable. In his line of work, Harrison had drawn that reaction time and time again. He knew some law-enforcement folk who got off on this cheap kind of power. He was not one of them. Mrs. Puckett's anxiety did not make him happy; he didn't quite understand it. He could have come up to her to talk about anything, might even have good news for her or if not good news—and that was a stretch, considering the circumstances—at least something of interest. You'd think a widow woman would want to know how things were going with the investigation into her husband's death, might even be flattered by it; that would be normal. Ruth Ann Puckett had never asked.

She stood there shaking her head at him—just a little, probably without even realizing what she was doing. Obviously, she did not have one bit of interest in anything he might have to say. Didn't want to hear it, didn't want to know it. Wanted him out of her life.

"Miz Puckett," he said. "How you been doing? Been meaning to look you up. If you've got some time on your hands, we could go on over to the River Café here, get ourselves a cup of their good coffee. They got that chicory stuff from down Louisiana. There's a good soda fountain, too, for Miss Janet. Sweet things—cones and soda pops and malted milk shakes. She might like to sit on up there, and Miss Ruby can watch her while we talk. Wouldn't that suit you, honey? Want something sweet?"

Miss Janet didn't look like it would suit her one little bit, but Harrison hadn't expected that it would. He took Janet's mother's arm and guided her gently but firmly down the street to the café's screened-in door. Ruby had just gone through her daily ritual of turning away Reverend Streeter—still fully suit-coated and with a starched white shirt and snappy yellow print tie. Harrison wondered where he'd got it. It looked awful nice—from the whites-only lunch counter, and she shook her head when she saw the deputy sheriff.

"Y'all ought to do something about this harassment, like they do over in Birmingham and down in Jackson. Y'all ought to persuade that man Streeter to eat on home and stop asking for trouble. We don't want him here. I hear his wife makes the best cornbread and butter beans in the state—my cook's been trying to get her recipe for coon's ages. Streeter needs to stay on in his own house to take his meals."

Harrison nodded and kept nodding. What was there to say? Like everybody else, Ruby was just letting off steam before the inevitable happened and Reverend Streeter sat down at her counter to take him some lunch.

Janet sidled right into the booth beside her mother, telling the waitress, "Don't want nothing. Not even water. We not going to be very long in this."

She was the one sat opposite to him, positioning herself so squarely in Harrison's face that he had to turn his head and strain a bit to look at her mama. They were an odd pair, this mother and her daughter. As one puffed up, the other diminished, just like they were on some kind of invisible seesaw, pushed up and down by a bonded middle; the mother said nothing. Harrison half expected Janet would be the one to answer his questions. He remembered quite clearly how she'd looked the day her daddy died, when he, and all the rest of the town, had seen her on TV.

"Two coffees," he ordered, "and one water." He thanked Christine, the waitress, with grave politeness when she put the coffee and the water down in front of them. Nobody but Harrison drank a thing. He blew, he sipped, he shook his head. He watched their light eyes watching him.

Finally he said, "How all y'all getting along since the funeral?" General like. The introduction.

"We've moved on into town," said Ruth Ann quickly, "with my mama. She took us in for a time, since it's just the two of us. I'm looking for work."

"The other children still up in Iuka?"

"Still there," said Ruth Ann, "Until I can get me a job and some money."

Harrison studiously kept his eyes off her new coat as he said,

"Must be hard trying to find work in Revere now for someone never worked before. First cotton went, and now the manufacturing jobs are drying up, and that's true all through the state of Mississippi. Economy's changing. At least that's what they tell me. Now you got to know a pure-dee skill before you can find you a job."

Ruth Ann Puckett nodded. "Can't do a thing without training." She agreed with him on that.

"Not anymore," said the deputy, still sipping and watching. "I hear Billy Ray lost more than his share of jobs when the mills shut down. Tried to find work all down where y'all are and couldn't. That must have been why he joined up with them pulp haulers."

His widow nodded again. She took up her cup. "He wasn't trained in anything. Didn't stand a chance. I mean to get me some education so I can go on out and make a better life for me and my kids."

"What you thinking about doing, Miss Ruth Ann?" asked the deputy politely.

Janet was staring at him real hard.

Her mama said, "I haven't quite figured it out yet. They have this new LPN program over at Doctors. It doesn't make full nurses, but close. They say it's integrated, black and white, but that don't make me no never mind. I been thinking about starting up over there. Maybe they'd take me on as a nurse's aide to start with, until I saved up some money. That is, if I can get in."

Harrison almost said, *Hey, Doctors'll pay for any dang thing you want. From what I hear, you got a powerful little case going. They'll be begging you to take their money soon enough.* But then he realized that her father-in-law must have said the same thing to her and probably more than once. Rumor had it Big Rob Puckett had been interested in getting at some money even before his son was decently put down. Everybody knew he'd been the one to urge Ruth Ann to take the kids on television, and some folks even said he'd drug her over to Doctors Hospital and had themselves a fine talk with Cooper Connelly and his expensive lawyers. That must have been right before Miss Ruth Ann and her daughter decided to move into town.

Letting his mind float in this manner brought it to some intriguing outlets, but Harrison decided it was probably best to continue paddling down his original stream.

"Sad times when a man's forced to leave one job after another," said the deputy, steadily sipping. "Makes you mad to think somebody's got to cut out from his own home and land and stuff up there around Ackerman and come on down here, live with his folks, just to find work, just because he wants to take care of his family."

"We were important to him," said Ruth Ann. She was sitting a little straighter now. Her child was still watching.

"You must have been, for him to join that newfangled pulp haulers' union and work right alongside black men and such. I heard he didn't much like them."

Ruth Ann swallowed. She put her coffee cup down, and now both the Puckett females were staring at him, wariness dulling the slick, smooth surface of their pale, pale eyes. Mrs. Puckett cleared her throat. She said, "That's not true. Billy Ray'd worked with black folks all his life—we all had, every year picking cotton down in the fields. I was doing it the day he died—working right out there alongside Willie Tate's wife over at Mr. Shelton's. We didn't have nothing against nobody. Billy Ray didn't. All of us is the same."

Well, *that* was something.

"And your children working next to her children," said the deputy. "County lets the schools out for the last two weeks in September, makes sure the cotton harvest gets in."

Ruth Ann just looked at him.

He sipped again, not particularly enjoying their rapt attention, certainly not enjoying their fear. "I can understand Mr. Billy Ray's interest in the pulp haulers and all. He needed the money. Y'all needed to eat. The only thing is, he had other friends. Powerful connections. Folks say Mr. Puckett was in the White Citizens' Council. Your *husband*, that Mr. Puckett. Prominent folk. You would have thought one of them could have found him something a little bit better to do."

Ruth Ann didn't say a word, didn't make a motion. She let Harrison continue on with what he had to say.

"Citizens' Council people," he continued. "Well, you know what they say. Seems strange Mr. Billy Ray would associate with them during the evening and then be up working right alongside black people during the day."

Billy Ray's widow said, "He had to do that to fit in here. To make a living for me and his kids."

"That" could be anything: the Citizens' Council, the pulp haulers' union, or something else entirely again.

"But he didn't *like* doing it," insisted the deputy. "Heard he got into fights with Willie Tate, heard it was a black-white thing."

"That stuff's calmed down," said Ruth Ann quickly. Christine came back with refills for their cold coffee, but Mrs. Puckett waved her away. The waitress didn't offer to refill Janet Puckett's water. The glass was just as full as when she'd left it.

"Still," insisted Harrison, "for a man with Mr. Billy Ray's sensibilities—a member of the council and all—it must have been a powerful blow to have to work with black men, and on an equal footing."

Ruth Ann measured her words. "Willie Tate has his ways. He

don't believe in bowing low. They say he never has done, but he means well, and he knows what he's doing. There was no way there could have been a union down there of just black men and no way they could have put one together with just white. The mill owners would have had us fighting one against the other, just like they always have, because it benefits them. Using one of us to wipe out the other and telling us we were Communists if we believed in anything else. The only way we could win was if poor folks banned together against rich ones for a change. Everybody had to be in together on this. Billy Ray knew that. It was the only way for him to get out."

Harrison continued to stare at her over the rim of his cup. "But he still fought with Willie Tate. From what I hear tell, there seemed to be some kind of continual conflict there."

She seemed to ponder this. "There were things Billy Ray had always believed in. You can't change a man overnight. But he was *trying* to change, and I think Mr. Tate realized that."

*A white woman calling a black man "Mr." Now, that's interesting.*

"Which is why Willie Tate didn't report your husband to the sheriff down in Noxubee County when they had their scuffles."

"The law folks wanted trouble," said Ruth Ann, "because y'all are in with the rich, and the mill owners are just itching for the blacks and whites to fall out. They were instigating for it, and Willie Tate was smart enough to see right to the heart of the matter. Joining together in the pulp haulers was the only way for poor folks to get out, to get over. That was the reason he didn't want trouble. You know how things are down here. He didn't want trouble for that reason." Ruth Ann hesitated. "At least I imagine that's why Billy Ray decided to stay clear."

Harrison nodded. "Makes sense," he said. He motioned to the waitress. "Miss Christine, why don't you tell us what kind of pie you've got over there in that case? I got me two nice ladies here who might like some, and I sure want a piece of that fresh apple myself."

IT WAS STRANGE, he thought later, ambling on back out to his car, how Ruth Ann Puckett had taken up for Willie Tate. Actually, she'd defended him just as much as she had her own dead husband. Harrison wondered, as he turned the key in the ignition, if she realized just how much she'd actually told him. Lies mostly, but with some gleams of truth sparking through.

First off, Billy Ray was not the picture of family rectitude and goodwill his wife painted. Harrison had heard about the conflict with Willie Tate—it was almost impossible to keep secrets in a town the size of Revere—and there were other rumors. Things being whispered about Billy Ray Puckett, making their own quiet circulation. Things folks didn't like saying out loud. Then, second, came the fact that Miss Ruth Ann had come right on out and admitted that her husband belonged to the White Citizens' Council. God knew there was pressure enough on him to do it; three-fourths of Revere's lawyers and bankers belonged. Good for "bidness," most of them said. Harrison already knew this; the FBI made sure that he'd gotten all that information. Groups like that had been infiltrated for years.

Still, sitting there in his car, letting it run idle, Harrison puzzled over the fact that Ruth Ann had so readily admitted her husband's involvement with the council. He'd never before met a wife to do this; truth be told, most of them didn't even know if their husbands belonged or not. Women had to be protected in the South, and besides that, the council was almost as secretive as the old Klan. The only logical explanation that came to Harrison was that Miss Ruth Ann had done this—and it wouldn't be the first time—to divert suspicion away from Willie Tate by making things more Billy Ray's fault. Harrison wondered hard at a white woman willing to do something like this to protect a black man. Was it possible Willie Tate could have something over her?

Harrison—a churchgoing, home-loving, family-loving man—had his own private theory about this, a theory that had been hatched and fostered by years working in law enforcement both over in Georgia and now here: Black men were scared crazy of white women, and with reason. He'd seen Negroes who were not afraid to take on a white man and beat hell out of him, take his turn down in Parchman if he had to for doing it. But he'd seen that same Negro lower his eyes and back away if a white woman said one word to him. Talking to a white woman could mean sure death. Observing this time and again, thinking on it, had led Butch Harrison to the remarkable conclusion that while your average black man might not be scared of white men, most each and every one of them was scared of white women. And it didn't seem to matter who the men were. They could be big and burly, rich or poor; he'd seen the same fear on the face of the man who taught English literature at Jackson State as he had on one from down in Noxubee County who had trouble scratching out his own name. Harrison couldn't blame them. Years gone by now, and everybody still remembered what had happened in Money to that poor kid, Emmett Till—that unlucky son of a gun who had come south from Chicago to spend time with his mama's folks. And his wasn't the only sad story. A lot of tales came out of the Delta, and they were still coming.

Once, he and Sheriff Kelly Joe had gotten drunk and started mumbling over that Till case. They, neither one of them, never did think that woman had told the truth when she'd said that young boy—fourteen years old, mind you!—had come on to her. Even seeing her picture in all the newspapers, seeing her grinning righteously from the television screen, you just had the feeling that she wasn't quite right. Something *wholesome* was missing from her. Something good.

"That woman's lying." His own wife had said it as she came back into the living room wiping her hands on a tea towel from doing the dishes. "Lying right through her teeth."

Nothing to do about it, though. Emmett Till was dead, and that lying woman was still living.

But that hadn't been Harrison's investigation. This one was.

LATER, LATE THAT AFTERNOON, Ruth Ann whispered to the man, "I thought about Billy Ray when I put the last of the black pots back in its place beneath the sink, behind the checked curtain, on the shelf. Back home, when we had a home, I was a mess. Billy Ray was always complaining that I never kept up behind the kids. But now, in my mama's house, I find myself becoming as obsessive as my mama. I'm snatching glasses out of Janet's hand before she even has a chance to finish her milk. Wiping up spills before they hit the linoleum tiles; the whole place—all three tiny rooms of it—is starting to smell just like Clorox bleach."

The man opened his mouth to reassure her, but Miss Ruth Ann wasn't paying any attention to him.

"You know, I didn't mean to move up here into town so quickly. I thought it would be a mistake. But one day that deputy came out to the house, looking. Always looking. When he left, Billy Ray's mama called me over. She said, "I reckon you better get on out of here and take that daughter of yours with you." She never looked up from the television screen. She never turned the sound down."

Ruth Ann finished her careful ministrations and walked over to the apartment's window, watching the leaves as they danced down the street. She yearned for a cigarette, just like her mother. She was turning *into* her mother, her greatest fear.

But that wasn't going to happen; Ruth Ann was determined. She shook her head vehemently no and glanced over at her daughter. She did both these things together, at the same time. Janet no longer perched on the end of the couch looking at the Bugs Bunny cartoons. Instead she was looking at her mother. Their eyes met, blue to blue, as Ruth Ann shook her head again, slowly this time. Then they both looked, once more, at the man.

## Chapter 16

ONE DAY, OVER AT MELBA'S, Cooper came to the conclusion that they should hold the next school board meeting at Hunt School. Sitting with her, the whole idea dawned upon him between one sweet thing and the next.

"It's Hunt School itself, the way it is, run-down and all," he'd said to her. "That's the problem. Who'd want to send their kid to a place looking like that? No white parents and no black ones either—only thing is, blacks don't have a choice."

Melba hadn't understood a thing he was saying, at least not at first. This hadn't bothered Cooper. He'd enjoyed taking on the task of explaining himself to her. He liked the way her little face turned up to him and the way understanding finally lit up her eyes. Talking things out with Melba made the solution clearer to them both.

And it was so simple.

"It's the school," he repeated, getting up, pacing around. "Cracked windows, old paint. Halls smelling like stale food and cheap disinfectant—not to mention all that glass on the playground, the litter." He went on and on. "We got to shift the focus here. We got to stop seeing school integration as a philosophy and start seeing it as a problem—and a problem can be solved. We got to change our approach to see this thing done right."

*A problem can be solved.*

He loved the sound of these words, loved the catchiness and the rightness of the phrase, but he was very careful, after Melba's, where he said them. He did not take them home to Evelyne Elizabeth and his daddy. Instead he put them in the street—and on billboards, and in both the black and the white newspapers, where he took out ads at his own expense.


NOW IT WAS COLD AND DRIZZLING—threatening full rain—but folks had turned out anyway. When Cooper drove up to Hunt School, there was no room for his car. He parked three blocks away, down almost to Melba's, and hurried on. He kept himself from looking in her direction and from wondering if she had come. She never went anywhere anyhow, especially at night, so he doubted it. He hurried down the sidewalk, raindrops glistening against his shoes and along the bottom of his pant legs. He watched his step. The pavement around Hunt was rugged, as they called it here, which meant that the street crews hadn't gotten around to fixing it lately. The crews were mostly black, but they took care of the white part of town first because they were paid to do this. Cold rain now, and winter right behind it, but still and all they had a pretty good-size crowd. Mostly black; he noticed this as soon as he got into the auditorium, and this was all right, what he had expected. Hunt was their school after all, but still there were enough whites—about one third—to make the evening interesting.

Cooper looked around again, quickly, from black group to white and then back to black again. He watched as they self-segregated, not just the whites but the blacks, and he wondered if that would ever change. If there would ever really be a difference in this lifetime, or even in the next. And everybody so damn careful—blacks not looking at whites and whites not looking at blacks. Everyone waiting. Everyone just slightly outraged.

School integration meant trouble, and it had meant trouble in the North as well as in the South, and the folks in this auditorium were ready for it, resigned to it. They might turn out and they might listen, but deep down they knew that somebody would have to bleed to make change happen, and underneath—black and white—they held stubbornly to this. Cooper, the healer, marveled at their obstinacy.

Even Reverend Streeter, who normally looked so calm, seemed restless and fed up, and that pretty Miss Lyle Dean was there, Melba's friend and Reese Jackson's wife, and she looked as defiant as the rest. She sat talking politely to Reverend Streeter, who then spoke to Reese Jackson with great awe and respect. Cooper was touched by the sincerity of it. At some point, he thought, Dr. Jackson must have saved Reverend Streeter's life or his wife's life or that of his child, so great was the deference. Then again everybody knew that black doctors were the gods of the South.

But there was nothing for it. Things would not change in this school auditorium and in Revere overnight. Cooper felt the crushing weight of this knowledge in the way the blacks still moved automatically to the back of the auditorium in their own school. Even the small group that moved into the front row, Reverend Streeter and the Jacksons included, did so self-consciously—and yet they had the whole of that vast front to themselves.

It would take more than a mandate from the federal government to make a difference. Still Cooper felt the buoyancy of his plan.

"Hey, Dr. Connelly!"

Annette Carroll was looking up at him, smiling, hers almost the only smile in this tense and hushed room. But it was wide enough, with two holes staring out at him from where her front teeth had once been. Was she seven years old now, or eight? Hard to remember. Time just seemed to fly on by. But Cooper remembered her actual birth clearly, like it was yesterday. In Revere there was no such thing as a strictly surgical practice—it was too small a place—so he'd always done a little bit of everything, and he liked birthing babies, always had. He remembered Annette, though, because she had been such a wanted child and one who almost did not make it. Cooper could still see the fear on Louise Carroll's face as they wheeled her into the operating room for the cesarean. He remembered her husband and saying to him, with great confidence, "They will be fine."

And they were.

The Carrolls took Annette with them everywhere, always had. Louise had left off teaching second grade so she could stay home with her. Annette was with them tonight, her first appearance at what was soon to be her new school. She was only a slightly pretty girl and dressed in the old-fashioned way in which late-in-life parents seemed to always clothe their children. Even at her young age, she looked odd in her smocked puff dress with matching plaid ribbons in her plaited hair. Black patent-leather shoes, ruffled nylon socks—all so old-fashioned. So precious. So caught in time.

The Carrolls were among the most resentful of the plans for school integration; they told this to Dr. Connelly when they met him on the street or at the drugstore. They told it to him every chance they got.

Henry worked over at Revere Power and Water in middle management, not likely to go on much further at his age. And now with

Louise not teaching, they wouldn't be able to make the financial cut when the new segregated academy, Legacy, opened its doors. But for all the resentment, Cooper was counting on people like Henry Carroll. His plan called for them.

Decent people, who might do the right thing in the end.

Waiting for the meeting to begin, smiling down at the little Carroll girl, Cooper thought of Janet Puckett. He'd never laid eyes on her in his life, at least not until the day her father died, but now she seemed to be everywhere. He'd see her from Melba's porch, playing with the Jackson boy and Critter Tate over at Dr. Jackson's house. They were ten years old, not older, and there would soon be a stop to this mingling. Cooper wondered why her mother even still allowed it. Most white parents stopped it by age six—at least with their daughters they did this. Cooper wondered if Janet's mother was here, or her grandfather. He had seen the mother only twice, and both time briefly, but he found that he could remember everything about her, even her name—Ruth Ann. It surprised him that it popped so readily to his mind, came right into it, really. He had been very conscious not to think about the Pucketts at all. Cooper shook his head. What had happened had happened then. It was not happening now.

He smiled again at the Carroll child, nodded at her cold parents. Looked around for Melba, who was not there. But then neither was Evelyne Elizabeth. Of course, he hadn't discussed the meeting with her or with his father. Cooper told himself that he did not tell his wife because he knew she was not interested; he did not tell his daddy because he was down in Jackson, out of town. But Jack Rand had found out, naturally, and he was here, sitting by himself in the back of the room, a smile on his face that was no smile at all.

Most of the time, Cooper loved his daddy. No doubt about this in the world. As far back as he could remember, it had always been the two of them—his mama had died when he was little and remained now a small, silver-framed picture in his daddy's room. No use talking about her, and they didn't. As far as Cooper knew, she came from poor folks over in Alabama, folks who did not have the right to vote in state elections over here. Folks of no use and soon forgotten by Jack Rand Connelly and his ambition. And his son, Cooper, had never investigated them, never sought them out, although he'd always meant to. Too busy playing football at first, and then he'd married Evelyne Elizabeth, practically right out of college, and the notion of introducing her to a passel of down-home, worthless, no-account relations—again, he'd been too busy. He wondered about them sometimes. But it was his daddy and that river-apparition, sneaking-up ghost that had been the constants in his life.

Cooper stared down at the white pages he held in his hands, making a show of going through nonexistent notes. In the end he would be saying the only thing that could be said, and they all knew it, even his daddy, though Jack Rand would die before he'd admit that things had changed and were changing and would doubtless continue to change. By now everybody in town knew this, no matter what they all said out loud.

"They all" were his friends and neighbors, though neighbors might have been the more apt description. His friends—those he knew from the country club, his father's cronies, the people whom Evelyne Elizabeth met for lunch—were not here. They had no intention whatsoever of sending their children to integrated schools. White ministers in brick Baptist churches said integration went counter to God's order; this meant that those rich enough could hide, with clear conscience, behind His word. Tonight they were holding a parallel meeting of their own to start Legacy, which would soon

take its place among the other publicly funded private schools—
the segregated academies—that were springing up throughout the
South. They were making serious provisions to put up a bunkerlike
building—corrugated and with few windows, very much like what
Cooper was in now—in a town where the type of edifice one inhab-
ited was noted with keen interest and respect. Normal criteria of
stateliness and grace would not apply to the new academy; the fact
that it existed at all—a refuge—would be criterion enough to ensure
it immense popularity.

Cooper had driven by the soon-to-be Legacy. He'd done this
on purpose, not three weeks ago. The site was well outside the city
limits and in the county, quite near the spot where Mid-South would
put its new hospital. The federal government, with all its righteous
inevitability, was behind Mid-South, too. Cooper's own secretary
was talking about Legacy. She had one daughter, and that precious
child needed to be protected. But Legacy would cost money. Cooper
imagined she would be asking him for a raise real soon.

He felt a nudge from beside him, "Time, Cooper. I think everyone's here who will be. Your daddy's back there."

Butch Berry, mailman for a good section of Revere, was sitting
on the Hunt School stage right beside him. Short and stocky, Butch
had a face that clearly suffered from too much sun. He lived in a small
bungalow on Eighth Street and Fifth Avenue, near enough to Cooper's
house so that he could have walked over there if he'd wanted to.
Question was, why would he want to? Berry's house was actually
near the black part of town—only the beginning of dirt roads separated it away—and he had three children, all junior high–school
age. Unless things changed drastically, they would be routed to this
very school come integration. They would be "going to Hunt"—a
racial slur that had been slung out mindlessly for the last thirty years.

Back in June, Butch had been what they called a foregone conclusion for school-board president—that is, until Jack Rand Connelly had worked magic and Cooper had ended up getting the job in his stead. By then integration was beginning to be taken seriously. No one hated race mingling more than Jack Rand, and no one could be counted upon to oppose it more vigorously, yet with the best store-bought manners, than his country-club son, or so everyone thought. Back then Cooper had shared the general opinion. Something had changed in him, though, shifted, turned upside down, jerked him around, and he would have been at a loss himself to explain why it had happened or to trace its beginnings. One day he'd just looked up and found himself committed.

Cooper got slowly to his feet. Beside him on the stage, next to Butch, was Mildred Younger, a sweet lady who was their secretary-treasurer, and William Bellford, their school superintendent, who had echoed for years Jack Rand's declaration that school integration would arrive in Revere only over his dead body. Well, it was on the way and William Bellford was still breathing, though with perhaps less fire.

Cooper said, "Nice to see all y'all again. Seems like we've been at these same meetings for weeks now. My wife told me I got to be careful not to wear the same tie twice in a row. Folks might remember it, stains and all."

A splattering of laughter greeted him. Nervous laughter, but still laughter; it promised hope, if he could mine it. Both the blacks and the whites were looking at him, if for no other reason than not to have to look at each other.

"In just a few weeks, on January tenth, when public-school classes reopen," he began, "we can have a change here in Revere that few of us, black or white, ever imagined possible. Some of us were so oblivious to what was happening, the conditions—I know I was—that we never even dreamed of it at all. Next January tenth, in this same school, black and white children can sit down together, for the very first time since Reconstruction, and they can learn their lessons side by side."

There was a sound then, from both parts of the room, equally and merging together. A sigh, a whisper, a motion; Cooper could not tell what the sound was or what it meant. He continued, "Since the civil-rights movement, since the beginning of the changes down here, Mississippi has become a known commodity. At least people think they know us. Towns like Philadelphia and Money—towns we hardly even knew we had ourselves—have become famous all over the world. The bloody and despicable pictures coming out of these places has defined us, and will continue to define us for as far into the future as I can see, at least until the end of my lifetime. We will never get away from those images of black men beaten and murdered and lynched, thrown into rivers and holes, and of white men—and white women—laughing while they did it. Taking photographs of themselves with their Klan hoods off and their faces out there in the light. Proud of themselves, wanting the world to crow along with them. Bad men, translating our state for others into a language that most of us here do not speak.

"For all our faults, and they are many—and believe me, I share in them all myself," said Cooper, "how many of us have here have lynched or murdered? How many of us have consciously thought ill? We just didn't pay attention. We just did what was easy. We went along because this is a poor place and we need cheap labor, or black folk were different, or who was going to clean our house or watch our kids or take care of us if we didn't keep Aunt Roxie and Uncle Jimmie down, and then their children down, so that our own children would be protected and taken care of like we were? Laziness and greed and entitlement got us here—none of them virtues—and we have let them open us up so that now only evil men define us. Only evil men. Only evil. And this evil is not the truth—at least not all of it. It *does not* define us."

He moved out from behind the podium, right to the front of the stage. Reverend Streeter was staring up at him, and Deanie Jackson—this much he had expected—but Betsey Williams was paying attention to him, too, he could tell it, and Cleveland Richardson had stopped shifting around in his own seat and was watching—wary, but watching.

"And what happens if we don't? Why, the whole world will use our malingering against us. Industry will use it as an excuse to boycott our state. Making us poorer. The rest of the country will use it as an excuse to continue to look down their noses at us. Worse than that, we will deprive our own children. There is no way this state can support both a private- and a public-school system. We cannot afford to siphon off money for Legacy just because we want to maintain a style of education we have grown used to. All our children will lose. In the end they have always been the loser. We must have just one system—support that one system—and we must pull together to make that one system work.

"It's time we—all of us here in this room—defined ourselves, and with this integration thing we have the chance to do it. This is a small town, we all know each other, so it isn't a question of dealing with something alien to us—like we would have to do if federal troops came in here, like we would be doing if they put up martial law in Mississippi as they've threatened. We just have a problem. The government's plan calls for Lee High School, our white one, to become upper school for the whole city and for all children in middle school to take their classes here at Hunt—and Hunt is pretty awful. We all know that. But we can fix it." He took a breath. "I'm proposing this to solve our . . . problem. That when school gets out for Christmas break, all the parents, black and white, join together to bring up Hunt School, to paint its walls and its flooring. To clean up the glass off its playground. To make it the kind of place where we really want to send our children and where we *will* send them. We have this chance to remake Mississippi differently and to remake ourselves differently as well."

He could have gone on. Now that he had started, the ideas just seemed to flow, but the silence surrounding him told Cooper that, at least for tonight, he had said enough. He was starting to sound preachy, and since most of the people before him were Baptist, they heard good preaching all the time, better than his.

He went back to his seat. He waited. He was expecting questions—how they could do this, what needed to be done. Problem solving. Figuring out how to make something impossible work. And he was excited by the prospect. He could respond to what they asked of him. After all, problem solving was what he did best. Satisfied complacent, even—he was not at all expecting what came next.

"And what about my son, you goddamn nigger lover! What about my boy? What's his place in all your scheming and prancing around?"

The voice, in that stillness, seemed to come out of nowhere. And at first Cooper thought it was Jack Rand who had spoken; the words seemed so like him, so dramatic. So like what his daddy might say to his boy. But Jack Rand was still sitting at his place in the back of the room, his eyes still on Cooper, his lips still smiling that strange no-smile smile.

As though Rob Puckett and his fury and his hatred did not exist.

"Your nigger-loving ways killed my boy, and I mean to prove it. Think you so smart? Think all we got for ourselves is a 'problem' here? You ain't seen problem, not like I'm fixin' to make you. Murdered my boy, you did, and think you can just bold your way through it. Think taking folks' minds off of it with this integration nonsense will just make letting my boy die go away. Talking all this mess about nobleness and problems, and all the time you just as black as sin your own self. Don't care a thing about Mississippi. You just doing all this to impress a white-nigger whore!"

On and on he screamed, as Cooper stood to take it. He saw Jack Rand look up from the back of the room, waiting for eye contact. And his daddy was shaking his head, his politic way of telling his son not to give up, there still might be time. Cooper saw the hope on Jack Rand's face—just a slight flash of it—and knew that same hope must be on his own face as well

Still time. All was not over and lost. He, Cooper, could give this up. He could give up this notion of integration, or at least the notion of him leading the chase for it. He could go back, go way back, pick up the fallen string and wind his life into the neat ball it once had been. He could tell Jack Rand he'd been right all along. He could tell Evelyne Elizabeth he was sorry for having inconvenienced her and then buy her something nice. And his friends—no, but he realized it was his daddy he wanted. It was his daddy he wanted real bad. He wanted the two of them to put this whole mess behind them—to be able to talk Ole Miss football and Mississippi politics as though the unpleasantness of this night, of Big Rob Puckett ranting and screaming, had never occurred. And more, even more, than that. The body. Billy Ray's death. The investigation. The inquest. Jack Rand was so powerful, so powerful, so powerful. He could take care of it. Every single bit of it. Jack Rand was his daddy, after all.

Cooper watched as somebody grabbed Rob Puckett, pulled him

away, but not before he'd finished having his say and not before he'd
done his damage. They had not intended to stop the damage, and
so it was done. People got up, scraped their chairs back quick, turning away from the spectacle, turning away from the out-of-nowhere
violence, turning home. But by tomorrow what had happened here
tonight would be the talk of the town. *Can you believe what that man
said to Cooper Connelly, and with Jack Rand sitting right there? You have
to remember, it was his son and all died. . . . A black woman—had you
heard?*

*A black woman. A black woman.* Melba Obrenski *now officially
classified—at least for the moment—and somebody saying, "Well, I knew
it all the time."*

Nobody would care about his plan for school integration, not
with a hot topic like this on their minds. Cooper stood there waiting, watching everyone leave, even Jack Rand. He'd be waiting for
Cooper, though—at the house. As would the body. No doubt about
the fact that they'd both be there for him—and Evelyne Elizabeth,
of course—and Cooper did not doubt it one bit.

Politely, he thanked those who had stayed around to receive
their thanking or to show support: the janitor and Miss Cleo Lee
Norcross, who was the very nervous, very shy principal of Hunt
School. She shook her head when Cooper got up to her and said,
"No, I'm the one should be thanking you," but she did not look in
his eyes.

Outside it was still raining, just pouring down, but he barely
noticed. Because, as soon as he came out the door, what he did see
was Melba—the talked-about, speculated-over, indiscriminate-race-
bearing Melba Obrenski—running on toward him with the biggest,
brightest, most welcome umbrella Cooper Connelly had ever seen
in his life.

# Chapter 17

MELBA WOULD SLEEP WITH HIM, if he wanted her to. Naturally, Cooper knew this and had known it for quite some time. Besides that, he'd heard the rumors about her. People might not know what race Melba was, not really, even after what Rob Puckett had said, but the rest of the news about her was all over town in whispers and conjectures. Cooper knew the speculations about her past, if not her present, and he had reason to believe what he'd heard. She had once been his patient, after all.

And Cooper had a powerful attraction to Miss Melba and had since that very first day on her porch. He was drawn to the old-fashioned smell of her, to the way her skin glowed in the light. He loved that she wore White Shoulders perfume, his mother's perfume. Jack Rand had kept an old bottle of it on the vanity table that had been left untouched in his bedroom, in their house back in Money, either as a shrine to the woman he had married or because he'd been too busy to get it taken down. Cooper did not know the reason. It didn't matter. In his mind, the vanity, the perfume, and Melba were linked to the mysterious woman in a fading photograph whom he had barely known.

He found himself thinking a lot more than was seemly about whether he should take Miss Melba Obrenski to bed. He had questioned nothing for so long that this questioning itself was heady to him, a diversion that would surely vanish once he actually had made up his mind.

Evelyne Elizabeth was his wife, and he had always remained faithful to her, or, if not to her, at least to their life together. Their Dick and Jane life, with Daddy, of course. Since they had met, right out of college, he had never slept with anyone else—not the kind of thing he would admit to his religious friends, who thought that a married man sleeping with other women was, at most, a pardonable sin. Still, Melba was different. She made things different. Which was why on Sunday, the very next morning, he found himself on her doorstep yet again.

They'd moved, with the coming of nippy weather, from her front porch into the living room of her little house. It had taken some time for Cooper to get used to it—the continuous red light shining in the hallway had struck him as odd, as did the statues of the Madonna everywhere—but he'd forgotten about them soon enough. He liked the fact that Melba's chintz-comfy place was so full of things and so snug; it seemed to wrap around him, to cocoon him inside. For the first time, Cooper Connelly, the doctor, understood why people swaddled newborn babies. There was a sure comfort to being hemmed in tight.

Another thing that intrigued him was the way Melba always looked just a little startled when he came up, if not with her words then with a move of her body or a quick, slight blink of her eye. Yet she could not really be surprised to see him, not really; she always had food at the ready. She was obviously expecting *someone*. That someone might as well be him.

"Is that your natural hair color?" he asked as they came into her house and left another dreary day outside.

Melba laughed out loud at that one.

"Honey, I don't even know what my natural shade is anymore. It's been hiding out under Clairol from as far back as I can remember. I doubt even God remembers how He made me anymore, at least originally—bless His heart."

"How's your work coming?" asked Cooper.

"Fine enough," said Melba, pealing off purple silk gloves. With all these changes in her appearance—which he summed up in his mind as Melba toning herself down for some unknown reason—he imagined he'd be seeing beige gloves on her soon or, worse yet, white.

She'd just gotten in from the Catholic church, she told him, and so God was still very much on her mind. God and what she'd cooked up for dinner.

"You go to mass today?" she asked him. "Over to St. Peter's?"

St. Peter's was the Episcopal church on College Street, the one Evelyne Elizabeth had selected for him when she same down from Virginia. Otherwise he'd still be over at First Baptist along with everybody else.

"Didn't go," said Cooper. "Thought I'd go for a walk instead. Your flowers still are looking mighty fulsome."

It was only November, but already the weather people were talking about snow up in places like New Hampshire. Winter might be coming, but you couldn't tell this by Melba's garden. She had had mums blooming, bright splashes of yellow and orange, and she'd put out the deepest purple pansies Cooper had ever seen, threading them among the mums until the colors were breathtaking, marvel-ous. No matter how busy the ladies were who came to visit Madame Melba for advice, they were never so preoccupied that they couldn't stop and ask her about her flowers: how she'd done this, where she'd gotten that. Women even talked about her garden when they came calling at his house to spend their afternoons with Evelyne Eliza-beth, saying, *Did you see? I wonder how she does it? A witch-woman for sure*. Women whispering together about her now, and at Cooper Connelly's house, with the same guilty intensity with which men might have whispered about her in the past. He'd heard them do-ing it and didn't blame them. Cooper could have, but did not, come visiting just for the brightness of her flowers alone.

"Staying for lunch?" she said to him. "I've got plenty."

Although lunch wasn't his reason for coming, Cooper nodded yes. Evelyne Elizabeth, who had gone to church, had something to do afterward and would not be straight home. She'd told him about a cold chicken in the refrigerator, and there was bound to be some-thing to go with it—collard greens, shucked corn preserves, things that had been done up during the week by the cook. Things gone stale by now.

Instead everything seemed fresh at Melba's. For instance, she had herbs growing on the windowsill because there were a lot of things she was used to in Louisiana—basil, for instance, and fresh dill and tarragon—that you couldn't find here in Mississippi. She'd explained all this to Cooper, like he would be interested and un-derstand her, which he did. She added that it was always best to be prepared. You never knew what you might end up needing as you cooked.

She'd outdone herself today. Shrimp rémoulade and roast chicken with a special stuffing of cream cheese and chicken livers and mush-rooms that was straight out of her new Julia Child—she showed him the recipe in the book—and green beans with lemon sauce and her grandmother's homemade dinner rolls. Her *real* grandmother. She emphasized this. Cooper thought she had the oddest habit of pulling relatives out of her orphaned past, but he was too much the gentleman to mention it to her, and nothing ever stopped him from eating every bite she put on his plate. She was too good a cook for him to care where it came from.

Melba led him into the parlor afterward—he carried the little tray with her cream and sugar on it—and let him light the log she always kept stocked up in her fireplace. She laid the coffee cups and the apple tart she'd made on the table before him. She let him cut his own first slice while she poured the coffee and put in the little sugar and cream he liked. She no longer asked how much he took of either, just stirred them in herself. Cooper let her do it and sat back satiated and content from her meal, to enjoy her slow, small movements.

She said, "That's the first time I ever saw your daddy, over at the school-board meeting. I saw him when he was coming out. All alone. Funny, when I think of Jack Rand, I think of an entourage, a parade behind him. All these stuffed-up, mean white men thinking just like he does—excuse me for the 'mean.' Still, he was the only one over from the big houses on Southside, but I sure didn't expect to see him there, even if he is your daddy. Must have come out to show his support."

Cooper grunted. He realized he was uncomfortable speaking about his daddy with this woman—not his daddy's actions but his daddy himself—and this surprised him. He talked about everything with Melba, things he never could make himself bring up at home. But he didn't want to talk about his family, he realized. Not that life. This was the place he came to get away from all that. He grunted again, stirred more sugar into his coffee, cut himself another small sliver of her pie. Hoped that she would get his message.

She didn't seem to.

"Or else," she continued, "it's because those white people over at the school vote for him, and he could be losing that vote now, and he's too smart not to realize it, with all the changes coming. What they gonna say when Jack Rand Connelly can't help them? When what Jack Rand Connelly tells them only makes things worse?"

"It's not Daddy's fault what's happening," Cooper said quickly. "He didn't make all this mess."

"Oh, didn't he?" cried Melba. Her eyes had narrowed, and she was looking at him tight. "People like the Carrolls and the others. People like Billy Ray Puckett's pa. I wonder what they're going to do now they know the battle's over. The schools are turning colored. Jack Rand's boy says so himself, integration is on its way. And when that changes, everything changes. It's the end of your daddy, and he knows it. Blacks got the vote now, and they sure not going to waste it on him. He's got to hold on to those scared white voters or he's done for. He needs more than Ned Hampton behind him. He needs more than one somebody watching out for his interests."

"Ned works for Daddy. He admires him through and through."

"Maybe. Right now," replied Madame Melba. She knew a little bit about human nature, and it showed through in her voice.

Cooper reached for his empty coffee cup. It gave him something to do.

"Your daddy thinks you're working against him," she said quietly. "He's taking this personally. He thinks you want revenge."

For a moment, and in total silence, Cooper just stared back at her, at the new Melba, toned down and very pretty but still with streaks of brilliance about her, still able to draw the truth out of him with the friskiness of a kitten picking at a bright red ten-cent-store string.

"I've got a story to tell you." He listened to the words as they came out of his own mouth.

But Melba was hot on her subject—his trifling father—still mumbling on and looking disgusted and shaking her head. For once not listening.

"A story," Cooper Connelly repeated, "about this boy I knew back when I was Critter Tate's age. A boy I knew. My friend."

This got her attention. Melba put her teacup down and leaned closer. Her eyes opened wide again, and Cooper could see her breasts rise softly as she breathed. She was right with him now. He had found that, generally, most orphans were interested in other people's history, in their stories. Cooper was interested in these things himself.

"Something I want you to hear." There were a lot of other things he might still have told her, but Cooper decided to tell Melba this particular story today. He didn't have any special reason for doing it; he just liked the way her brows furrowed together as she listened to what he had to say. Those little lines forming, just right at the top of her nose, reassured Cooper that she was paying attention, that she was really interested in all the new, strange, so-unlike-the-old-Cooper things he had to say.

Melba just looked at him, not moving. When she got like this, Cooper had the strangest feeling that she knew him and knew already what he was about to say next, that there really *was* a Madame Melba. She was wearing a new brown sweater, and Cooper liked it well enough; it lightened her eyes to the exact shade of the caramel icing she put on one of her good, old-fashioned cakes. She'd done something to her hair, too, toned it down a little and let out some of the curl. He liked the new style well enough, but he missed the redder Melba—the brighter hair and the brighter, fluffier, flashier sweater, too. Cooper had no idea what was behind all this rearranging; he only hoped she wouldn't change herself too much. He liked Melba as she was.

He said, "I guess up till my mama died—I was two then, that's what they tell me—we were dirt poor. Of course, that didn't matter. There wasn't nobody wasn't poor where we lived back then. Except, of course, for the few rich planters, and nobody saw very much of them. They owned the land, and you worked their cotton, and they didn't care what color you were, black or white. It didn't matter, you were just dirt. In fact, back where I come from, deep down in the Delta, they'd let black folks come into their house, raise up their children. They'd never let a poor white person in that close. At least that's what my daddy always told me. He hated colored people. Called them niggers to their face. Only trouble is, my daddy genuinely loves the poor. And black people are mostly poor, no two ways around that. It's a dilemma to him.

"There was no way out. The rich ones—the plantation owners—kept everybody else away from us, anybody who might want to build up some industry along the river and suchlike. The big landholders wanted things to stay on like they always had been, with tenants and sharecroppers and season pickers. They wanted new slaves.

"But my daddy, Jack Rand Connelly, was different. He just could not put up with what they were telling him, with what his place in life was." Cooper chuckled fondly. Shook his head. "Must have been the Irish in him, made him so rebellious, so fighting and scrapping. Made him so determined and smart.

"First thing off, he got himself elected sheriff of all Leflore County. Sheriff in a place like that . . . well, that is a powerful position. It's easy, being an official, to come on stuff folks don't want known, that they might be obliged to you for keeping hidden. Next thing—and this part I remember—we were living in a fine, big house and we had ourselves acreage. Soon enough we were hiring tenants of our own. And season pickers."

Cooper paused to look at Melba, who still sat motionless, except for the slow, rhythmic movement of her breasts. She was leaning toward him, so close that he could smell the goodness of White Shoulders on her.

"My daddy only owned a few small farms back then, but they were his, titled free and clear. Whites and blacks—everybody used to come over and work for my daddy during cotton season. They let the kids out of school. And Daddy'd be in that field, working right alongside them. Everybody swigging cola out of the same RC Cola can. But my daddy never let me out in the fields with himself and the others. It was something he just didn't like. 'Got to be different. Got to get yourself an education. Got to be your daddy's pride and joy.'"

"You make your cotton fields sound like something out of Isaiah," scoffed Melba, and she was too much Melba not to say it. "Blacks and whites working side by side together, in Mississippi, like the wolf and the lamb. I been reading your daddy's column in the paper for years now, seeing him on TV, and I can't recall one kind word he ever said about integration. About black people either. Not one word."

"He'll be forced into it," Cooper said to her. "Daddy can bombast all he wants to out of Jackson, but there's no going back to the way things were. We'll never be back there ever again. Once things have tipped enough, you can't stop them spilling. And things have tipped down here for sure."

Melba was curious. "You couldn't ever have been really poor like you say. Poor stays poor, at least where I come from, and poor boys don't end up going to medical school and living in fine houses. They don't end up owning their own hospitals. How in the world did your daddy make it over?"

"I told you," Cooper said shortly. "He was sheriff of Leflore County, back down there in Money."

Melba let this linger with her coffee. She'd heard all about Leflore County and Money, Mississippi. Everybody had. Emmett Till had made them famous.

"When my mama died, he made up his mind that I would be a doctor, a surgeon," said Cooper. "Doctoring is always a respectable thing to do. I can remember him telling me that. It is a fine profession. As far away from dirt as you could get. He said this over and over to me from the time I was two."

He looked over at Melba, expecting that she might challenge him on this like she had on everything else that morning, but she nodded and said, "I can remember things, too, from when I was a child. It shocked my mama all the time, the things I could recall." Considering her circumstances, other people might also have been shocked by what two-year-old Melba was seeing and remembering as well. Cooper smiled.

He said, "He was just always all for it. I was, too. There's something noble about being a doctor, helping people. I liked that part of it. I just couldn't . . . *get* it. The science part. First the math and then the science, and how can you be a doctor if you don't get the science? But once he'd turned his mind to something, my daddy was always a go-getter. He used what he had. Him being sheriff, he helped a lot of people out of their trouble, and one of these was the county school superintendent. There were rumors about how this man spent his free time. Honky-tonk places, moonshining operations; in short, he was someone who required the law to turn a blind eye. Anyway, this man made it his devoted business to see I got the school help I needed to make this dream we were dreaming—me and my daddy—to make this dream come true. My grades were always right where they should be. My *grades* were.

"You might say he took a special interest in my success," said Cooper. "The school superintendent made sure I got the best tutors, fresh out of college, up on all the news in the way of the medical science, but I still couldn't get it. Not even the simple grade-school biology—the tadpoles on the riverbank, the way plankton swims around and grows. It just didn't interest me. I liked history, how this country was settled, the kind of stuff that meant nothing to my dad. The teachers and then the tutors tried over and over again to make me understand, but I just couldn't. Daddy was a much younger man then, a widower bringing up his only son by himself, and my teachers—mostly young ladies—took a special interest in me. It was all very romantic. So they tried real hard, but I just could not put it together. What they were telling me with what I was seeing on the page. And everybody was looking at me—the teachers writing out those A grades, the superintendent, my daddy. All looking and thinking, 'Why, this child's got the best opportunities in the world, and still he cannot do it. What on earth is wrong with this boy?' I was ten years old and already a failure. That's when I met this kid."

Melba's forehead puckered, she moved closer. She loved stories, *especially* about children. Cooper had her totally now, and he knew it.

"He had come in to help his mama bring in the cotton. I don't recall I'd ever seen him before, not hanging around, but then he was just a little kid from the county, probably with rickets and such; he was mighty thin. And I had my own friends. Daddy might associate with everybody, but he didn't want me doing the same thing. He especially did not want me playing with those kids came up to work the fields. Probably I'd seen this boy for years, just not *seen* him, if you know what I mean. Until I came upon him that day reading my book. Handling it."

*Making his acquaintance with the inevitable for the very first time.*

"The boy was littler than I was, skinnier. It was some time before I learned we were the very same age, born just a few months one from the other and some two miles apart. I would discover all of this later. What I saw right then was that this child—someone who worked in the fields for my father—was touching my things. My things. And my daddy did not like foot-dragging. When you came to his place to work, you did what he paid you to do and then you got yourself home. No talking. Naturally, that's before Jack Rand became a politician. He was just interested in making money back then. So I had a mind to charge straight on out from the trees toward this intruder. I was going to give this boy a piece of my mind. Beat sense into him. But something stopped me, dead in my tracks, and I stood there. Quiet as a deer.

"It had to do with the boy's movements, or rather something in the lack of them. In his stillness. In his reverence. In the mystical way he held on to that book. And his face . . . well, I knew right off that my face did not hold that same rapt expression when I was looking at that very same page in that very same book. It was science, you see—field science, my nemesis. I had just thrown the thing there, disgusted, when I'd finished up for the day.

"The boy paid no attention to me, and so, when I moved, I was able to come right up on him. If I'd been my daddy, there'd have been a whupping for sure. But this kid did not know I was there until I got so close I could see exactly what he was reading. What he was into.

"'Hey, what you doing?'

"My, did that child jump right up.

"And he liked to run off when he saw me, but I was too quick for him. I wrestled him down and then beat up on him for good measure, so as to get his attention. Once we exhausted ourselves, I took him on round to the back of the house. Told him he looked like he needed something to drink. We held the hose out, one to the other, and I was extra polite. I was already formulating in my mind just what I would do, and I didn't want anybody spotting us in the front yard and running the information on down to my daddy. You see, I knew that this boy was different, and I don't just mean hungry different, even though he was hungry, all right. *I* was hungry, for that matter, and determined to get what was in that book so's I'd be a hero to my hero of a dad. And I could see that boy had the spark. I could see it on him, even when I didn't even know what I was seeing. It warmed me, though, warmed me right up and rolled me right over. I wanted some of it for myself. 'Hey, you understand this stuff?' I said to him, pointing to the natural-sciences book.

"You could see his mind working through that fear of my daddy, that primal push to run away and a sort of natural curiosity that held him to me, a feeling that was all around him. Something you could almost touch. I could see the battle but even back then I was enough Jack Rand's son to realize when a war had already been won.

"That book had won it for me—its newness, the mystery of what it had to say.

"'Understand anything at all?' I asked him.

"He said, 'Parts of it. A little of it. I think I do.'

"I said, 'I think I get parts of it, too.'

"And that was that. Somehow, without saying a word to each other about our intentions, we made a decision to put our two parts together. We spit on our hands and shook on it. We were both so eager. He picked that book back up. He was the one who carried it.

We walked it on down to the river, and that's how we started working it out.

"It was a brand-new book, and it marked me the way that boy had cleaned his hands and dried them on the grass before he opened it. We sat there all evening, until it got way too dark to see a thing. He went to the county school. Naturally, they didn't have nothing out there, not even good teaching, not in his school. A devoted teacher, but she'd never spent one day in college in her life. On the other hand, I had the books. I had the trained teaching. I just didn't *understand* a thing. But what I did have was a good memory for words, and it was the words and the books I took down to the river. I could repeat them to him. He was the one who could put what was in the words with what was in the books. He could make them both come alive. That boy would squint up his eyes, read a little bit, and then he'd explain back to me just what I had said. And this time I'd get it, or at least enough of it. We both started understanding things we'd never even thought of before, and it was magic. Plain and simple magic. One minute you don't understand a thing, and the next minute it comes clear to you.

"Pretty soon we moved on over from science and we worked out our English and history. I was on surer ground with these, and I wanted him to see that I could show out as well—because he was so good at it. So smart. So naturally and wonderfully talented. Much better than I was. He wasn't particularly interested in anything except the science, but he would listen to the rest. He had to be polite, didn't want to make me mad, because I might run off with my books and then he wouldn't get what he wanted, what captured him. How to do it, how it ran—this was what interested him. One by one, year after year, I brought all my books down to the river and we helped each other, because it worked out well for the both of us. Together—

that boy and me—we patched us out an education. I loved that I could finally learn what everybody so expected me to learn, and for that reason, the relief of it, I suppose it made me love that boy. Pretty soon we were spending all our free time together. Sneaking off. Hunting and fishing. Going, just the two of us, deep down into the Delta, off there, with only the night to catch us. Yet the learning was the most important thing—it's what bound us together—and all the time I was learning, and so was he. All the time."

The silence around the two of them, Melba and Cooper, was so marked that not even late birds chirped through it.

Finally Melba whispered, "What happened?" She was a woman who loved this kind of story, a woman who had always been singularly attached to the happy ending, and she felt one coming on now.

For a moment Cooper paused, as though considering. "What happened?" he repeated. "Why, I went on to medical school."

"And the other boy? What did he do? How did he turn out?"

Cooper turned so he was looking straight at her. "That boy died. Right there on the river. He died there."

This was true enough, but now Cooper discovered he did not want to go deeper into this story, did not want to dredge it up, not even with Melba, his secrets sharer. Jack Rand knew what had happened. Knew all of it, or almost all. That was enough. Cooper got to his feet, almost knocking over coffee and cake and newly bought cups in his rush.

"Got to go home," he said. "My wife will be there. It's Sunday, and she might be expecting me."

# Chapter 18

MADAME MELBA LIKED HER STORIES, and she was watching one of her favorites—*Brighter Tomorrows*—when she heard the tinkle of her little front doorbell. Initially she was tempted to ignore it. Things had just turned very interesting on her television screen. For the very first time, Brad was consulting Zelma about the paternity of their youngest daughter, and all this while that doofus Charlie Henderson, a true villain, snuck out through the side gate. Melba did not want to miss the outcome. And she had promised Deanie, who was shopping down in New Orleans, that she would not; they'd both been praying for months now that Zelma get the comeuppance she so deserved. The bell sounded a second time, just that slight tinkle. Melba had a good half mind to keep on watching her story; to call out to whoever was on the front porch that Madame Melba was not at home and that they should stop around later.

But winter was on its way and bringing high heating bills with it. Plus, there were the changes Melba was making to her appearance;

she was finding, much to her amazement, that the upgrade from bright reds to beiges and taupes did not come cheap. Ultimately it was this money need that made her change her mind, that got her up from her comfortable sofa, took her away from her favorite story, made her put her glass of sweet tea in the kitchen, and head on out to her front door.

By the time she got there, the woman—because her visitors were almost always women these days—had turned and was walking back up the neat brick path that led through Melba's garden and to her front gate. Right away Melba opened her mouth to stop her and then hesitated again, watching the erect way the woman walked, listening to the clip of her suede shoes against the bricks. Melba could have decided right then to turn back to her story, back to the order of her day as she had laid it out. Clients only in the morning, that was her rule. Still, the call of new clothes and, with them, a new Melba was too strong for the chameleon in her. She opened first the front door, then the screen door. She heard herself call out.

"Looking for me?"

Now, Melba liked doing what she did for a living, at least most of the time. She made sure she never did anything to harm anybody— no spells or vengeance or suchlike. There was Mrs. Du Berry across the state line, over in Alabama, who handled that sort of thing. Most of Melba's people just came for reassurance. They didn't care about making anybody else's life miserable; they just wanted to make sure that *their* own lives moved along well. Going to Melba's was like reading through your morning horoscope in the paper—something you did on your own, something you might not have wanted other people to know about—and Melba liked that. She didn't mind being somebody's secret.

At least that's how most of her clients were. This new woman was different, and Melba saw the difference as it paused, altered its course, and returned slowly up the garden path. And she was dazzled by the difference, by the sheen of this woman's white gloves, the drape of her navy blue skirt, the luxury of her cashmere jacket— all more perfect than those worn even by perfect Deanie. Yet, like Lyle Dean Jackson, she was the kind of woman who captivated the mockingbird in Melba, who brought out the chameleon, who played at the mirror pool of admiration and imitation that lay deep within her, the same pool that had changed Melba from what she once had been into what she was now.

"Come on in," she called.

A breeze played against Melba's extravagant sign, sending it back and forth, and both women gazed at it before turning to face each other.

Mrs. Cooper Livingston Connelly was much prettier in person than she looked in the newspapers, but even there, in grainy black and white, she had been lovely. Standing here, staring back at Madame Melba Obrenski, she was beautiful indeed. The flawless gloves and the quality suit were topped off by the equally perfect blond hair and the requisite blue, blue eyes, just barely lined. Still, there *was* something of the photographic about her, as though she were continually poised, smile ready, should a camera pass by.

She was not smiling now. Mrs. Cooper Connelly's eyes were cold, her fine skin drawn. Obviously, she did not relish having to come to Madame Melba's, and Madame Melba was trained to notice such things. Yet there must be a reason she had come here, and that reason must surely be the same for her as it was for everyone else. *Someone loves me / doesn't love me,* or else someone is interfering with the healthy flow of my life. Always the same.

The woman said, "I don't think we've met. My name is Evelyne Elizabeth Connelly. May I come in?"

Melba had her explanations at the ready. Without realizing she was doing it, she'd been rehearsing them over and over in her mind since the very first day this woman's husband had shown up on her porch. *Not my fault. No sex. Nothing happened.* But, right off, this was a lie, because something had happened between her and Cooper Connelly, and Melba knew it. *I think he's just lonely.* But who was she to say this to a man's wife? Mrs. Connelly would think it was sex for sure then. Any woman would who was told this excuse for a man's taking sanctuary. The dismay of this thought hit Melba with a ton of bricks, and for a brief, intense moment she closed her eyes and willed herself back to her couch, back to her story, willed her door shut. Willed herself happy. Motioned for Cooper's wife to come on in.

"I don't give potions," said Melba, only because this was her standard greeting. "I don't cast spells."

"Good, because I don't need either, not really."

This time Mrs. Connelly did smile, though briefly, but it was the brevity of her smile—hard and quick in its passing—that was the first indication to Madame Melba that something could be going on here of which she was unaware, something that had nothing to do with her.

Melba said, "That kind of stuff never works."

Though sometimes it did, and she knew it.

Again Mrs. Connelly smiled. She took off her gloves to disclose a ring the likes of which Melba had only glimpsed within the glossy pages of *Vogue* magazine or in *Harper's Bazaar*. It winked wickedly at her—a large, marquise-cut diamond surrounded by emeralds, a ring quite sure of its own worth. The kind of thing you could safely wear around the streets only in a town the size of Revere. Married, it said, and forever, as it kept this woman within the warm halo of a husband's care. And not just any husband but *Melba's* own husband—that is, Cooper Connelly, her dear friend. Still, what could she do? She was Melba.

"That's sure a nice ring," she said.

She led Mrs. Connelly through her chock-full, red-tinted hall-way, into her overstuffed living room, and sat her down on the couch. Evelyne removed her other glove slowly, finger by finger. She glanced confidently around Melba's small parlor, let her eyes stay for a moment upon the television playing along mutely in the corner, where Zelma screamed silently, over and over again, and then Mrs. Connelly glanced briefly at the painted statues of St. Theresa and St. Jude—the twin saints of the impossible.

"Would you like some tea?" Melba asked her. "Something sweet?"

Mrs. Connelly shook her head. The only thing she wanted from Madame Melba was what she'd come for.

"A man," she said. "I want to see if he loves me."

Melba almost, but not quite, said, *Of course he loves you. What man wouldn't love having a woman like you for his wife?* Instead it came out as, "Loves you?"

"Well, of course he loves me," said Evelyne Elizabeth. "It's just that our situation is complicated."

"Complicated? What could be complicated about loving your husband? Look, if you think there's some other—"

"It's not my husband I'm in love with," corrected Mrs. Connelly quite calmly. "It's . . . well, you should know that. You're the fortune reader."

But the idea that Cooper Connelly's wife did not love her hus-band had left Madame Melba Obrenski at a loss for words.

They sat there for a moment with the television still flickering, until Melba walked over and turned it off. The absolute silence was worse, though, at least for Melba, because it brought very uncomfort-able thoughts with it, temptations. *Maybe, just maybe, if this woman could love someone else . . . If she would leave Cooper . . .* Because deep down within her, Madame Melba knew that Cooper Connelly was not the kind of man who'd leave a wife on his own.

"Do you want to tell me about it?" she said.

The woman laughed. "I thought *you* were supposed to do the telling." The Tidewater accent of her youth flowed gracefully through Mrs. Connelly's voice. Like Melba herself, she didn't sound like she'd started out in Mississippi. "And give me something to make him want me. That's what people say you do."

"I don't do spells or potions. I already told you that."

"I heard you make exceptions," said Mrs. Connelly. She waved an expressive hand that took in all of Melba's pretty things. "I heard that people can get anything they want from you."

"You been told wrong," said Melba, but her mind was quickly foraging through the list of her clients, people who snuck up to her house from Southside. She really didn't do anything wrong, not really, but folks had been known to exaggerate, and nobody, except Deanie, really knew Melba. She was far from her home and with no people nearby to defend her. A woman. Folks thought they could say anything about her they pleased.

"For a price," said Mrs. Connelly, leaning closer.

"I thought you said he already loves you," said Melba sharply, and then, to be reassuring, she added, "I'm sure he does."

"It's complex, though." The woman let out a sigh and sank back prettily into Melba's down couch. "And there's nobody I can talk about it with, not really. No one I know who could understand the feeling."

She sighed again, looked at Melba, and this time she became like any other woman—in love with a man and dying to tell. And she could tell Madame Melba. She'd feel safe with this strange, race-less woman who was so different from herself; talking to someone like Melba would be, to her, like not saying a word to anyone else.

"You see, my husband . . ." began Mrs. Connelly. "Well, we married young, but I never—he never really was the right one for me. It was always this other person. Even before the wedding. Always, from the very first minute I saw him, but I was already engaged to Cooper. I'd already promised Daddy Jack that I would marry Cooper. And so Cooper became the way I could get to him—could get to this other one. The one I wanted."

*This is all about Jack Rand Connelly's money.*

Madame Melba shook her head, her mind working. Wanting to know, to have this small triumph over the man she loved and who continually and carelessly talked about his wife to her, yet at the same time, and for his sake, not wanting to hear what this wife had to say. For an instant, Melba held her breath, believing, as superstitiously as any of her many Louisiana grandmothers, that by not breathing she could hold back the worst. She wanted to stay on this side of knowledge—in the place where she believed Cooper to be happy in his home—because this was a haven, where all her listening and her little smiles and pats of encouragement were innocent and just part of the only safe relationship she'd ever had.

But now, and for the first time, she let herself ponder the fact that perhaps Cooper was not living the life her own mind had so carefully constructed around him—with that perfect wife, that perfect home, all of that good. Instead now she was coming to believe that something a little dark—maybe something a little bit New Orleansy, even—was going on, something Cooper himself was unaware of, or else surely he would have spoken about it to her himself.

"Not that anything's happened. With the other man, that is," said Mrs. Connelly, "at least not yet. Or rather nothing serious. He's kissed me once or twice through the years. Short kisses, but on the lips, on the mouth. I know he's just holding himself in. I can feel it. Holding himself back because, you see, there's my husband. They're friends. Best friends. Business friends. And there's just nothing we can do about him."

"Friends?" echoed Melba. Then, quick as a flash, before she could stop herself, she said, "What's his name?"

And before *she* could stop *herself*, Evelyne Elizabeth answered, "Meade MacLean."

And Melba said, "Meade MacLean? That beefy old fart? You'd choose him over *Cooper*?"

And that was that.


MRS. COOPER CONNELLY'S BLUE EYES took on a cold glitter that was hard enough to match that of her impressive diamond ring.

"My husband's just acting so stupid," she said. "He could do anything in this world he wants—his daddy's seen to that—and he chooses to waste his time getting involved in this school-integration mess. And right now, right this minute, when Mid-South Medical wants to come in and run Doctors Hospital out, after we've spent so much time building it up. Cooper should be taking care of his own business, of his interests. That's what his daddy says. That's what Mr. MacLean says as well."

*As though Meade MacLean would ever really threaten his liveli-hood—and his relationship with Jack Rand Connelly—for her, as though he thought of Evelyne Elizabeth Connelly as anything more than a flirt.*

Inside herself, Melba tut-tutted. Meade MacLean indeed.

"They're the same, the hospital and the school system. The same thing," Melba said, quoting Cooper and then blushing. "They both come down to the same integration fight."

Evelyne Elizabeth ignored her. She had obviously not heard this line of reasoning in her own house. Mrs. Connelly said, "Folks won't speak to me over it—friends, even. The people in my bridge group and my luncheon group at the country club don't want to hear a thing about it. Folks who think they can get away with it cut me on the street. They truly do. And Cooper *will not* listen. I cannot speak a word to him on it. He comes home—when he does come home—goes into his study, and stays there closed in with those packed-up books for the whole night through. His daddy and I have both tried talking to him, told him he's going to lose everything, and over a bunch of little nigger kids determined to go to school where they know they're not wanted. What's more, they will take all of the credit to themselves. So will their parents. Cooper is a rich man. They won't care what happens to him in this whole mess. Why, if it wasn't for Cooper's daddy and what he's doing down in Jackson, there would not be one person who would be still speaking to us, at least not one of our friends. And I'm just fed up and tired, and I don't want him anymore. I haven't really wanted him for a long time. Not in that way. Not in any way. At least now that Cooper's acting so unreasonably, turning everyone against him, there might be the chance for me to get somebody else."

That was a slip, something she had not wanted to bring to Melba's attention again, the reason for her visit. Evelyne Elizabeth giggled, but Melba did not mind. By now she had heard enough to know that this woman was living the same kind of fantasy with Cooper's good friend that she, Melba, was living with Cooper himself. *He would want me . . . He would have me . . . If only . . .* Both of them dreaming their lives away.

Melba pulled her dress closer. "I don't know quite what you want with me."

Outside, she could hear the sound of traffic on Catfish Alley. You could hear everything, if you just listened. You could hear the squealing of children, and you could tell the difference between a passing car or a truck when the light changed on the corner. You could even know, by the click of Miss Mae Flower Webster's heels as she walked past, that the working day was over and that night was coming on fast. You could tell a lot of things, if you were listening.

Melba had spent her whole life listening hard, and so she knew things you could do—wicked, nasty things—to get a man where you wanted him. About this, Mrs. Connelly had guessed right. And Mrs. Connelly wanted something wicked, something nasty. You could see it in the eagerness that still shone on her face and was only half hidden; you could read it in the brightness of her eyes. There was no accounting for taste or for people. There was also the small fact that if she helped Mrs. Connelly get what she wanted . . . why, Mrs. Connelly might move out of the way and give Melba what *she* wanted. A spell, a potion might do this. After a fashion.

And yet even though she knew better—the weakness of all women!—Melba could not help thinking to herself that what she felt for Cooper was somehow different from what his wife felt for his best friend—that is, was something better and with more hope. Again she thought of Mrs. Du Berry, that woman with the huge road signs out on Highway 69, the ones Melba had stared up at when she first came to Revere because Mrs. Du Berry's results were guaranteed. She specified that out loud and clear. But Melba's life had taught her that they weren't, that there was nothing certain. A spell might last five minutes or five years or even fifty, but that old way of doing things always broke down in the end.

"I'm sorry, I can't help you," said Madame Melba, and there was real regret in her voice.

She watched Mrs. Connelly's bright lips—she used Revlon's Cherries in the Snow, just like she did, Melba would swear it—move into a surprised O, then settle once again to a firm, hard line. For perhaps the first time since she'd come calling, she looked directly at Melba.

"They tell me my husband's been coming round to see you," was all she said. It was enough.

She reached into her alligator bag and pulled out a ten-dollar bill. Melba did not want the money, but Evelyne Elizabeth would not feel safe unless Melba took it, and a woman who felt unsafe could do anything. Experience and her own life had taught this to Melba time and again. So she took Mrs. Cooper Connelly's money, and she thanked her, and then she took her to the door.

Nothing left for it, *Brighter Tomorrows* was finished. Melba would have to wait until tomorrow to see if Zelma had gotten her just deserts. Instead *The Noon News* was on, and something must have happened downtown. Something important. Melba saw pictures of the courthouse and the hospital, saw Floyd Sobczak appearing concerned and eager, saw him talking to a crowd of fierce-looking white people on the square. There were no black people in sight.

*Same old school integration*, she thought. She turned off the set.

# Chapter 19

NED HAMPTON HESITATED, his hand poised right at the polished mahogany door. This wasn't his problem after all—at least it wasn't now that he'd called Jack Rand and Senator Connelly had said he'd leave Jackson and come right on up. This meant that there was nothing more he, Ned, could do about things, the disaster of them, than what he had already done. He'd just break the news to Cooper, and the two of them would wait.

Cooper's office was a mess. It was obvious Miss Evelyne Elizabeth hadn't been in lately to dust off the pictures and order things up. File folders were scattered everywhere. Papers—medical charts, even—looked like they simply lay where they'd strayed. Boxes of books here, too, just like what Cooper had at his house. Ned shook his head at what he considered the indulgence of it. *Spoiled boy,* thought Ned. *He's gotten everything he's always wanted. This hospital, all of it, and it's all about to go down with him.* And then he remembered what Jack Rand had said, had promised. He was coming, and Jack Rand Connelly would sure as hell order things up.

Cooper motioned him over to the only chair that sat junk-free and empty. He was on the phone, talking to Miss Evelyne Elizabeth. He was not smiling. But his talking gave Ned a chance to gather his thoughts.

He'd waited until nearly lunchtime to make the call, just to be sure he could get Mr. Jack Rand on his private number and that they could talk. This probably wasn't such an enormous problem, not something that could not be easily fixed. At least that's what Ned said as he started in on the conversation. He kept his voice low. In fact, if there hadn't been the threat of that new hospital, if he hadn't thought they were somehow behind all of this—Ned was a firm believer in conspiracy theories, especially when they involved the federal government—he would have handled things by himself. He'd been called upon before. "Handling things" was something he knew how to do.

But the fact of the matter was that the threat of a new and public hospital had grown from being merely a conjecture to becoming a pending event. That, plus all the ruckus about integration, especially what had happened last week over at Hunt School—Ned could barely pass through the halls of Doctors Hospital anymore without somebody asking what Cooper could possibly have been thinking— well, it was just better to bring old Jack Rand in.

Thoughts collected, mind set, Ned waited patiently until Cooper got off the phone. At least the place no longer smelled of bourbon. Ned was grateful for that.

"Ned," said Cooper, sounding all cordial. "I been missing you coming around."

Ned wondered how anybody could sound so hearty and happy on a day like this. Couldn't this man sense the bad news coming? Wasn't he interested? This boy had a bubble that needed to be pricked.

"Been busy," said Ned. "We got back the reports from the state coroner down in Jackson. Your daddy's on his way home."

"Really," said Cooper, a statement not a question. *So that's what kept you this morning. Talking to Daddy before talking to me.*

Ned blushed. He reached down to brush at a small speck of lint that was marring the perfect crease in his flannel trousers. Now that it was November—heavens! Almost Thanksgiving—he'd switched uniforms into the one that would get him through winter until the arrival of spring. Gray pants, blue blazer, three identical sets and all ordered down last year from Brooks Brothers during their post-holiday sale.

"I took the liberty of calling up your daddy. I thought he might be able to offer us some help. It's best to bring him into this before things get out of hand."

"Did you read what he wrote in the *Commercial*, his latest column?" asked Cooper. "It's on page one. I'll quote it to you from memory: 'We will not give in. We will not give in. I will not allow white children to sit beside their African counterparts. This will not happen. Not in my lifetime.' African counterparts. That's what he called them. Like they had no right being here."

"He's just bombasting," said Ned, determined not to be ruffled. "You know how your daddy is. He's telling people what he thinks they want to hear. Election's coming up. Folks have their notions. They want to hear him say it don't matter one bit to him that his own child—'flesh of my flesh,' I think was the way he put it—is involved in this nonsense. Jack Rand's still going to be here to uphold states' rights and maintain moral and godly order."

Cooper got up and went to the window, looking, without realizing it, toward Melba Obrenski's house. Last few times he'd called, she hadn't been home. "I'm sure my daddy and God are exactly of one mind on this."

Ned waxed indignant. "Why, your daddy's been in the same pew at First Baptist—either here or someplace else—every single Sunday of his life."

"Exactly my point. Have you heard what's been coming out of the pulpit at First Baptist? If I'm not mistaken, the preacher himself said he'd go to jail and live alongside idolotrous heathens before he'd let his precious babies go to a mixed school in Revere, Mississippi. I mean, why do we live in the South if it's not to send our children to segregated schools? It's certainly not for the education itself. But then again, the Right Reverend Stanley Desmond has no intention of going to anybody's jail over this. He's one of the prime organizers of the new academy. Using state funds and county money to open it up—now, how's that for a moral order, and a legal one, too?"

"Cooper," said Ned.

But Cooper wasn't finished. "You been down to Jackson lately? Been into the new Capitol Building? You should get on down there if you get the chance. They've got the pictures of our Mississippi state legislators on the wall. Rows and rows of these pictures, all these white men. You know the thing I noticed? Just how sour-looking they been getting. Not the ones from the teens and the twenties—even the ones known for being in the Klan—but the ones coming up now. Starting in the forties, all these white men looking just so mean and unhappy. My daddy's picture's up there, too. I guess that must say he's mean and unhappy as well."

Ned said with great patience, "Cooper, I don't think you understand. We do not have time to be dealing with philosophy here. We've got bigger problems to head off now, things that hit closer to home. While you've been so busy with this whole integration mess, hell-bent and determined to antagonize anybody that might help us, Mid-South has hunkered down and got on the move. They've been smooching up to the board of supervisors, trying to get permission to build here, and it looks like they might have it. I'd be surprised if you had a friend left on that board, the way you've been acting. School integration might be being rammed down their throats—probably you're right about that—but they don't want to have to take their medicine from one of their own. In fact, if the truth's told, they're starting to think you're *not* one of their own. You won't have a friend left in this town, at least in the decent white parts of it, if you keep traveling down the road you've taken. They won't rest until they ruin you; things are handled that way in Revere, and you know it. Folks might wait awhile, but in the end they'll make you get what they think you deserve. And if you don't realize that, your daddy surely does. And Miss Evelyne, too, if I might add that. I think she's worried about you, as well she might be. We got the news on that Billy Ray Puckett autopsy down in Jackson. Looks like you might have killed him."

It wasn't for nothing that Nathan Bedford Forrest Hampton was the only white man in his all-black church. Ned liked being the center of attention. He'd got Cooper's full attention now, and he knew it, mostly because he hadn't really had Cooper's attention for weeks.

Ned said, "They—and by 'they' I mean the state coroner—say things didn't come out like you said they did. Billy Ray Puckett didn't die like you made out he did."

"Which means?" Cooper bristled and stared right at him, Jack Rand Connelly's boy all the way—but not quite his daddy, so Ned wasn't scared. He knew that Jack Rand would stand with him on this one, and he'd say he was doing it for Cooper's own good and not for himself. A lie if Ned had ever heard one, but Jack Rand, with his black suits and his skinny ties and his raspy, aw-shucks, Camelstrained, deep-drawling voice, would be their only hope in this particular situation. He was the one who could help them hold on to Doctors. The problem was, Cooper saw too many sides of the picture. You had to be like Jack Rand and stay focused, right or wrong, to make it through, to make sure life continued sailing along on an even keel. This was the difference between the father and the son.

"First off, according to this here report"—Ned waved the papers he'd brought in with him—"seems like you were right about the bullet. It was military surplus, shot from a 6.5 Carcano rifle. You can buy that gun anywhere you want, order you one from the Sears-Roebuck catalog for seventeen dollars plus shipping. It's all over down here. Everybody over fifteen's got one. Billy Ray Puckett had his. From what I hear, his daddy has him one as well. Gun was right—problem was you missed some important bullet damage. The state coroner's office said it nicked Mr. Billy Ray's liver. They said—not in writing, of course—that a competent doctor would have caught this, all that blood seeping. He said—again, just between him and me—that there was no way even a halfway competent doctor could have missed it. Yet there is no mention of this in your report. In fact, what you wrote down was awful vague, at least when it's read up close. No specific mention of the liver, and the liver—well, hell, that's always iffy. Always worth mentioning." Ned allowed himself a small shake of the head. "It appears, at least to them down in Jackson, that you sewed Mr. Billy Ray up to die."

"A liver wound?" said Cooper incredulously, and then, "Why, that's almost a death sentence."

"The coroner understands that—maybe," said Ned. "What he don't understand is why you didn't at least mention it. Why you didn't make any attempt to stop the bleeding. It looks almost as if you wanted him to die."

All of a sudden, the only thing you could hear in that room was the sound of the grandfather clock ticking, each tick loud as a backfire, and the sound hypnotized Cooper. Each second delineated and time running out fast. And then, of course, came the body, all of a sudden, seeping in on the efficient sounds of hospital activity that broke, once more, against his office door. Billy Ray Puckett was dead, too, now—a new body—except this one was really and truly his fault, no doubt about that, and it would stay his fault forever.

"Coop?" said Ned. And Cooper imagined what he must look like. For the first time, Ned sounded upset.

"Did the report say anything else?" Dr. Connelly asked. "I guess it doesn't matter. Probably I should read it myself."

Ned hesitated. "Well, not officially. At least not yet, but there seems to be something wrong with the trajectory of entrance."

"The trajectory of entrance?" repeated Cooper. Ned's way of talking half medical could be confusing. "You mean the way he was shot?"

"Yes, that. It's odd, they can't piece it all together. Davis Pilkington, from down Jackson, told me the angle's a tad too low for the wound to be self-inflicted, even counting in the deer-stand fall. It's *possible,* he said, but he'd like a little more time to figure the whole thing through. Said he'd work on it on his own, but it wasn't really a reason to hold back on the report. He knew we wanted to get on with this. More than *likely* it was self-inflicted. But . . ." And he hesitated. "That close up—should have been powder burns. He's checking that again. Thinks there could have been two shots. One going off first and then Billy Ray's gun when he fell on it."

"What'd he think, some other hunter maybe? Somebody who just didn't step up?"

"Or didn't know he did it," said Ned Hampton. "Or did it deliberately. From what they're telling me at church, those Pucketts weren't what you might call quality stock. Not a lot of folks liked them, at least not a lot of our good colored people. You see how the old Pappy's been acting. You can tell the type from the daddy himself. I heard what he said over at that Hunt School meeting. Word about that's been all over town. I wouldn't be surprised he's working hand in glove with those folks over at Mid-South. Wants what he calls vengeance for his boy. I still can't believe he wouldn't sign for that check."

"He wanted more," said Cooper quietly, "and he must think he can get it."

"Only two houses over there, the Pucketts' and the Tates'," Ned said thoughtfully. "And things are different, not what they used to be. Used to be our colored folks put up with the word 'nigger,' just like they stepped off the sidewalk so's a white person could pass. All that's over. The Negroes don't hold truck with stuff like that anymore—white people messing up." He paused. "What they find out about powder burns—that could seriously change some things."

Cooper interjected quickly, "It's my fault. Powder burns or not. I'm the doctor missed the damage."

"I wouldn't be too quick to take on responsibility, not at this moment. It would help Mid-South's claim greatly if they could get you reprimanded, could make out you were an incompetent surgeon. You'd take Doctors with you if you went down right now." Ned turned away from Cooper to look at the ranks of his family pictures.

"We need to go through all the reports again," Ned continued matter-of-factly. "This isn't about Doctors Hospital at all. A mistake was made, but it very clearly could not have happened if that man hadn't fallen on his gun—or been shot. We should look at it from both angles. Keep that train on track and keep the attention off you and Doctors Hospital and what went on that night. Drunk as a skunk—I mean, that man Billy Ray Puckett. I just know that's what happened. Jack Rand knows it, too. That's why he's coming up."

Ned rolled on. "And it don't make that much difference what actually went down. What we got to keep folks tuned to is that the *bullet* was his fault. We'll just right out say, but quickly, the rest was human fallibility—take our licks for missing that nick and hope it goes down like that. These are no-account folks, and you're a good doctor, done a lot for this community and well known. A liver wound's a death knell anyway. Most folks know that. Billy Ray Puckett would have died with his old drunk self out in the forest, would have bled to death if that child Critter Tate hadn't drug him on into town." Ned shook his head. " I always knew that boy was nothing but trouble."

They looked at each other for a long moment, and then Cooper turned back again to the window. It was still such a beautiful day, sunny and almost ecstatically bright; in this part of Mississippi you never could tell about the weather. One day in January it could be seventy degrees and the next one twenty-five. Things could change that quickly, from one minute to the next.

"It's this damn school integration, that's the culprit," said Ned from behind him. "Got you thinking every which way but right."

"I made a mistake. I missed something I should have caught. That's all." But it wasn't all, and Cooper knew this. "I did it."

Ned was thinking. "What we got to do is to make it somebody else's fault. Critter Tate brings him in here, saying Billy Ray plumped down on his gun—nobody says a word about two shots, at least not then. That's because no gun under heaven goes off two times if you just fall out on it. Somebody started out lying—at least they did if the medical examiner is right about the powder burns. That's the angle we've got to focus on, build our story around. Yes, that is certainly what we have to do. Jack Rand will help us. Writes opinion for the newspapers himself. We got to keep the focus off what happened in the operating room. We got to stay on what went wrong in the first place. The bottom line is, that silly poor white-trash man shot his own self, and in the liver. All this talk about a second shot . . . why, it's too late to be thinking about that now."

Cooper glanced back, just briefly, over his shoulder. Ned was nodding so hard and so hopefully that he felt compelled to nod right along with him.

"Yes," said Ned, still bobbing away. "I'm going to go right over to the sheriff's office. We can talk this out—make sure he sees the right thing in it. We can make this town take it our way. Your daddy can take care of the rest, up here and down in Jackson. If we work together and keep our heads, we can weather this storm."

Cooper was all for that. He could see a light flickering for him as well.

"The only thing is," said Ned, and it got so quiet in Cooper's office that once again you could hear the faint laughter of children playing out at recess at Jefferson Davis School, four blocks away. "The only thing is, you got to stop it with this school-integration thing. You got to stop that nonsense right now. Too many folks who count are against it."

Cooper said, "Not black folks." And just that quickly felt his hope fading away.

"But they don't matter, and you know it. They'll get the vote, and they won't use it. We'll go through all this trouble integrating schools, and they won't come up to bat for you. You know how they are. Just look at Reese Jackson. He's got his and he don't care about nobody else. Pays his annual dues to the NAACP and then don't do a thing. Over at my church, the young ones are already starting to bad-mouth him. Everybody knows Reese Jackson should be the one heading up the school board, fighting this fight. It's *his* people going to benefit."

"Blacks weren't allowed anywhere near the school board until a month ago," said Cooper. "How could he be president?"

Ned said, "You always making excuses for that man."

Cooper shrugged and turned back to his window. Outside, through the glass, the day hypnotized him with its breezy leaves swirling in a lazy southern way and with enough grass still left on the square to bounce back sprightly from underfoot. Sunlight and green grass in November always did do him some good. It came to Cooper suddenly just how much he loved Mississippi—the bad of it, the good of it, its cadence, its manner. His daddy was considered the down-home boy, but Cooper always had known he was the one who just plain appreciated this place best. He saw folks on the street saying hey to each other, black and white people friendly in a way outsiders could never imagine. And he saw something else. Those children were there. Critter Tate, Reese Jackson's youngest child, and that Puckett girl—Janet was her name. He remembered her, though he could not have thought of Reese Jackson's child's name to save his life. And it was odd, because the children were not playing, or at least the girl was not. She stood still as a statue, staring, and the force of her gaze, the fear in it, pulled Cooper's gaze right along into hers.

# Chapter 20

REESE JACKSON LOVED WHAT HE DID for a living even though he might mouth off and make noise along with all the other blacks about the conditions down in the basement of Doctors Hospital. Calling them deplorable. Calling them a disgrace—which they were. Normally Reese operated in a dim, freshly painted room, deep in what he called the "recesses." The dimness he could live with; it was the rest of the floor made him mad—and mad at Cooper Connelly specifically. Folks crammed three and four into the little rooms, people—old ladies!—stacked up along the corridor. No doctor to visit with them except Reese and the occasional appearance by Dr. Special Connelly, as Reese secretly called him—the owner of the hospital, who never stayed long. But the truth was, when he picked up his scalpel, Reese Jackson forgot where he was. Forgot about everything else except the job that was his.

And things could have been worse. Here at Doctors, Reese had enough nurses, and that was a blessed relief, although most of them were LPNs. And he had his fair share of the new sample medications from when the pharmaceutical salesmen came round. And the food was actually better downstairs than it was up. "Bland" meant something different to coloreds than it did to whites. Ned Hampton might push to cut back on expenses, but fees were the same whether you were upstairs or downstairs; only the salaries were less. On the few occasions when Reese had to push for what he wanted, he usually got it. There were four private hospitals in the surrounding area, and Doctors, at least for blacks, was the best. Hospital integration would come with the building of Mid-South—and they would eventually build it, Reese believed; he had strong respect for the determined inventiveness of his federal government—but he doubted, even with integration, that, personally, things would be much better for him there.

When he'd first come back to Mississippi from Johns Hopkins, Lyle Dean in tow, he'd commuted down to Meridian and worked in the colored section at Charity to make ends meet. It had been an education for him, after studying in the North. A true welcome-home, coming in the form of a rusty sterilizer, of outdated medicine, of chipped paint. He remembered, and well, one memorable occasion when a rat ran across his foot just as he made it through to a ruptured appendix. His hand had not flinched. He was that good a surgeon. But shit like that . . . well, you never forgot it, never overlooked that this was a white-folk way of telling you that you didn't matter, that whom you were trying to help didn't matter. That's what Reese told his kids, his wife, and anybody else who would listen. You saw it, all right—you just didn't *focus* on it. Not if you wanted to get ahead.

And Reese had wanted, still wanted, and surely would always want to get ahead. Besides, conditions were better at Doctors than they were down at Charity—you had to give it that—and they were better at Charity than they were down on the Delta. Black folks were just never going to get what they needed in Mississippi. You simply had to make up your mind to that.

That was the reason he did not actively protest, why he did not stop operating at Doctors, where he was bringing in a considerable amount of revenue, even though he had to do his cutting and pasting, as he put it, in the basement. He was reminded of this often by Revere's two black lawyers and one black banker, none of whom made nearly as much money as he did. Not that making money mattered to Reese, at least not as much as most people thought it did. Mostly he liked the intangible things that money bought him—the prestige, the deference, the feeling that he mattered. And of course he doted on the operating itself; this was important to him as well.

Reese just loved to heal, to make things better. Not being one given to introspection, he had never actually explored the feeling and consequently did not have words with which to share his passion, even with Lyle Dean. But then again there were a lot of things he did not share with Lyle Dean. She was a woman. She needed his protection.

People could complain all they wanted about the hospital, and Reese complained right along with them, at least for a few minutes until he got bored, but they were lucky enough to have Doctors here in Revere, and he knew it. And he was lucky to be on its staff. Folks should see how black folks were operated on in Meridian and Jackson—that is, when they were lucky enough to be able to go to a hospital in those towns. There was many a black doctor down there who still had to take care of his patients in his own home, right on up to the end, just like they did deep down in the county. He'd even had to take a few of his patients right on into his house when he'd first got started, before he'd built up his clinic, before Jack Rand

Connelly had constructed a fine, modern hospital for his only boy. And at least at Doctors the lights worked. The sterilizer might not be new, but it sterilized. It wasn't rusting.

"Sutures," Reese said, and Eloise handed them over. Actually, they were in his hand before the words were quite out of his mouth. That was the benefit of working with someone for so many years. Things were changing, but Reese was still partial to many of the old ways. His nurse—and she was always the same nurse, Eloise Simmons; at Doctors everybody had his own permanent surgical team—operated with him here in the mornings, then walked on down the street to take care of patients with him at the clinic in the afternoon. They made a good pair. Most days they broke for lunch together at Sallie's. He trusted Eloise implicitly. Reese knew there were things she would never tell.

Some of his patients—modest old women up from the country and the grandchildren they were raising to be just like them—would even say they were going uptown to take in Miss Eloise and Dr. Reese. The two of them together were a little marriage of sorts. Not that Eloise was his type. Reese cocked an eye at her as she wiped the sweat from his head. She was too bony and tall, too awkward and silently devoted. Besides that, she wasn't Lyle Dean.

Reese took one last careful look, then sewed Silas Tucker on back up. He was the kind of doctor who made it a point to remember that he was working on people, not cases, so Silas was Silas to him and not just his latest ruptured appendix. Just like Reese's children were children to him and not merely the bafflement that they actually were. He was ever so slightly intimidated by his daughter, Brendan, and scoffed—only to himself, never even to Lyle Dean—about Skippy's lack of physical discipline. No matter the incident. No matter what had happened. No matter the limp. Skippy needed to take his own life into his own hands—confront it, overcome it—and if he did that, then his daddy could help him. Reese had told the boy this, over and over again. Skippy was just self-indulgent. That boy ate way too much. On top of that, lately he'd taken to spending all his time out in the yard and, worse, in the streets with Critter Tate and that little white girl whose father had died. Reese would catch the three of them watching him, even his own son, and it unnerved him. He wanted his son to stay away from that girl. White girls could get you in trouble. Reese should know.

"Time to close up," he said to Eloise, "and take us some lunch."

Together they cleaned up, put up, climbed up the stairs and out into the sunlight. And they were halfway to Miss Sallie's Luncheon-ette when they heard the shot.

## Chapter 21

THEY CALLED IT A WARNING. At least that's what everybody who read about it in the paper—or saw it on the news or heard about it later—called it. Melba, who was standing right there when it happened, knew that there was nothing warning about it. In Mississippi you shot what you aimed for; that bullet aimed for Reverend Streeter was meant to do harm. Once she got started, she told this to Deanie over and over again, though actually she was so outdone—her heart palpitating and all—that it took her a while to even get the story out the first time. After that, it came easier.

"I was over at the River Café," she told Mrs. Jackson, "just coming out as Reverend Streeter was coming up. Determined, as usual, on his daily battle for integration."

They both could have laughed at this, but they didn't out of respect; the truth was, the River Café had been integrated years ago, and by Melba herself. It had been her first stop, when she'd arrived in Revere and still had young, towheaded Mr. Obrenski beside her.

Christine had served her without batting an eyelash, and they could not undo this action and decide to not serve her, even once suspicions about Melba's actual racial status had taken root, grown, and flowered.

Because of this, Melba made sure she took her lunch at the River Café at least two times a week.

"Sitting in," she'd say to Deanie, and they'd laugh. Melba made it her business to make sure the places she'd integrated—like the River Café and the main floor of the Princess Theatre—stayed integrated. This kept her busy.

So there she was, literally, right beside Reverend Streeter as the bullet sliced through him. Later, much later, she would tell people that she was so close to him that she could almost hear the slug whizzing by. She just didn't know what she was hearing, not then.

"Just missed me. Almost got me. Almost got that silly waitress Christine, too."

At first Melba actually thought it was a backfire—loud and nearby and calling her attention. She pivoted to the sound, but there was nothing moving in the distance. She was sure of that. Nobody running, nobody looking like it might behoove him to escape. Just the slow carryings-on that accompanied everyday life on Revere's town square: children playing, people getting into their cars, people driving away. There was nothing strange in the distance. She would tell this to the city police and the sheriff and finally the FBI when they came, polite as ever, to interview her at her house. But of course she hadn't known what she was looking for, not then. Reverend Streeter, always the gentleman, had slumped down quickly and silently, and she had not yet noticed that her new straw and black patent-leather shoes were planted firmly in his blood.

But because she was confused and looking out into the street rather than right beside her, it was a long moment before Melba realized what had really happened and that it had nothing to do with a vehicle's faulty exhaust. After the shot there was one moment of absolute silence, that moment of innocence when no one knew where the bullet had come from or what it had done. Melba heard a mockingbird singing right through it and the sound of slow traffic moving up the street. She heard both of these things before she heard the screaming all around her and the beginning, low exclamation of Reverend Streeter's moans.

*"We been telling him not to do it. . . ."*

*"Old Jack Rand Connelly said this was going to happen, this very thing. . . . Blood flowing."*

Just fragments of conversation as Melba bent down, down, trailing the hem of her chiffon polyester flower-print dress on the ground. In the blood all around her. In the blood.

"Oh, Reverend Streeter. God bless you, sir."

Because, really, this was all for nothing. This bullet, this blood, this crying and screaming and moaning were all about the River Café, integrating it, and she had already been eating there quietly for years.

"Oh, Reverend Streeter," she repeated, only because there didn't seem a thing else to say. She gave him her hand. He held on tight. And then the funniest thing happened: Melba thought she might help him, and not just in the Madame Melba way of giving advice. She might actually stand up and holler. She might use what she knew, actually stand up and fight back for once, if not for herself then at least for Reverend Streeter, who was lying there beside her, bleeding and yet holding on so tight. Melba knew she could do it. She, right there, could start yelling out directions, calling for ambulances; she would ally herself, a black-white woman with these black and white people who, like she, were slowly realizing the shifting, the monumental happening, the change that could ride on a bullet slicing air. Melba thought, *Why, I could be a heroine or a savior.* The vision of herself stepping out of the shadows, giving orders, and for once taking control lasted only an instant, but it was a clear vision, silver and bright.

*Melba the heroine! What would Cooper Connelly think of that?*

She held on to Reverend Streeter, but she glanced around quick. Horrified, hoping no one had seen those mean-natured, selfish, selfish thoughts upon her face. That no one else could see like Madame Melba could see. She was ashamed of herself.

At the door to the River Café was its cook and owner, red-faced, crew-cutted Bill Hairston, looking sorry, and behind him his wife, who worked the cash register—she was the one who had refused to let Reverend Streeter in every single day—and his two waitresses and the cook from the back, who was black. All looking so sorry, now that the truth of what had happened was sinking on in. Their expressions—all except for the cook's—would change later, but for that moment they were the same. The blacks', the whites', Melba's—all united, all dismayed, all sorrowful, and all frightened. All seeing this poor man laid out and bleeding in the street, all seeing the future.

But then the crowd parted, and Melba's vision of being Reverend Streeter's savior was still so vivid within her that she was certain other people, the black people, had seen it within her and that's why they moved away. Not being from there, not being rooted in the culture, she did not see it as the reflex movement that it was.

"Reese?"

At first Melba thought that Reese Jackson had somehow come up from behind her—his clinic was just across the street, after all—

that he was calling out to himself, announcing his presence. At that moment the accent seemed the same to her; it carried the cadence of every other voice in the city, and so Melba did not turn to it. She kept her hand in Reverend Streeter's and so this time was watching him as the words came again. "That you, Reese?"

"Sure is, and I've brought Dr. Connelly with me."

This time Melba did look up—and smiled at Cooper Connelly without thinking, before she realized this was exactly the wrong thing to do. Not with Reverend Streeter bleeding onto the sidewalk and in such obvious pain, not with everything that had happened and the people all around them and the crying in the background and the moaning up close. Still, she couldn't help herself, and she smiled, bright as sunshine, for an instant when she saw him, and he smiled back. But then, the next second, there was Reese Jackson in the flesh right beside her, elbowing her away as he had a right to do. Melba got busy trying to get herself up off the pavement with some grace. Cooper and Reese Jackson were bent over Reverend Streeter, the white people moving away, now that help had arrived, and only black people around them. It didn't matter, not to Reverend Streeter, not to Reese Jackson, not to Cooper Connelly. They could have been the only three people left on that earth.

"Seamless," was the way she would afterward describe their work together, first to a very interested Lyle Dean Jackson and then to various representatives of law enforcement. "Must be something they teach them up there in medical school." But when she was there, on that sidewalk, what Madame Melba actually saw was something else.

Cooper Connelly, breathless still, and Reese Jackson knelt together beside their patient, Reese gently talking away as he cut off Reverend Streeter's worn suit coat, the three of them just going on, laughing softly, shooting the breeze.

Reverend Streeter said, "I been wanting to eat in this place since I was a boy."

Dr. Jackson said, "Well, you ain't quite made it in there yet, even after all these years of trying."

Dr. Connelly said, "And you sure ain't missed much."

Reese working and Dr. Connelly, reaching into his—Reese's—medical bag just like it was his very own. Handing him gauze. Handing him scissors. Whatever he needed and not fumbling, knowing just exactly where it all was.

"Nothing much," said Reese. "Bullet barely nicked him."

"Must not have been good Mississippi shooting."

A Mississippi joke, and all three of them laughed.

Melba just stood there a little apart, watching Reese's black hands reach out to take what they needed from Cooper's white ones and watching Cooper go unerringly through that medical bag. She kept her Madame Melba eyes trained on Reese Jackson, on the swift movement of his hands, on the way they took what they needed from Dr. Connelly. She listened to the sound of their voices, both rich and Delta soft, and then to the crisper accent of Reverend Streeter, who was from Revere. She began to understand.

"The young folks, they just don't want to do this work no more," whispered the reverend. "Sitting in on folks, until they break down and give you what you come for. The ones who would do it are gone over to Birmingham, gone down to Jackson and Montgomery. They said nothing much was going to happen over here in Revere, no changes. The freedom riders done come and gone. We been left to ourselves."

"I guess they were wrong," said Reese Jackson. "Anything happening in Mississippi, at least until school integration, going to make the national news. You going to be in your house tonight, Reverend

Streeter, and hear what happened to you broadcast on NBC." He handed the scissors back to Cooper Connelly. Reese was in charge here; this was his place. He was the one who Melba heard say, "He needs to go over there. Get this taken care of." Motioning toward Cooper's hospital with his head.

And Cooper nodding right along with him. "Take him on over to Doctors. It's going to be fine. Reverend Streeter's going to be okay."

Melba, calmer now, thought, *Well, maybe*. Cooper got up, gave Melba his hand, and she was so near him. Eyes-meeting near him, so that he could pass on his secret before the world bustled around them again.

Then he let go and her gaze wandered to the edge of the crowd, where the white people stared and where a man's slow movements caught her attention. She could not say why and so did not say so to the police or to the sheriff or even to the FBI; besides, all she was talking about was just a glimpse. She didn't recognize him, thought he could be anybody. Bandy-legged, clad in work khakis, a white man, and, leaving out Cooper, there were no longer a lot of these in her life.

Except this man was staring at Madame Melba, just as Cooper had stared at her—intensely and passing on a secret. She looked harder at him and thought that maybe she actually had seen him before—maybe once or twice, maybe a quick peek, but she couldn't figure out where it had been, and he wasn't saying. Having Madame Melba's attention seemed enough for him. She watched him turn, walk down the street, put his hands in his pockets. There was no longer a gun in them.

"Being a doctor is a mystical business down here," Cooper had once told her. "A power. Anything's a power when it's all about life and death." Trouble was, Melba couldn't remember the rest of the conversation, whether they had been talking about white doctors or black doctors, whether Reese Jackson's name had come up.

It didn't matter. The thought brought her back.

"Not too bad," said Reese Jackson. He acted like he was talking in general, not to anybody in particular, but Melba heard the words as he passed right by. "Just winged him. He'll be fine once we get the bullet out."

Like magic, out of nowhere, hands reached down to lift up old Reverend Streeter and carry him beneath the turning maple trees to Doctors Hospital. He never had fainted; pain hadn't even dimmed his bright little eyes. He'd been talking to the doctors, laughing with them, even. And because Cooper Connelly was with him, he led the group of black men who carried Reverend Streeter through and into the front door. It was Cooper Connelly's hospital, after all.

People were beginning to drift away now, black with black and white with white, and now that they were, Melba heard police sirens coming from over on Main Street. She imagined that Sheriff Kelly Joe Trotter would not like that they had moved the victim without his consent—or maybe it wouldn't matter. Maybe he would think better Reverend Streeter—who must surely have known this was coming—than somebody else.

Some few people—the curious, witnesses, or good citizens— waited for the police to get there to air their tale and give their report. Most others, including Melba, were already busy about their business, hurrying away. The police would find her soon enough, and she knew it. She'd been too close; she'd seen too much. But for now it was the violence itself that seemed to scatter them all, force them away as though by witnessing it they had become part of it. Or that it had made them part of itself. Melba quickened her step, wanting the snugness of her garden and of her house and the deep peace of the river running through the distance.

# Chapter 22

SHE WAS WAITING FOR HIM when he drove up, climbed out of his car, walked up her pathway, knocked upon her door. Waiting for him.

"I knew you would be," said Cooper Connelly.

Melba did not offer sweets or tea. She did not talk about what had happened that afternoon, did not ask after Reverend Streeter. She knew he would be fine. And she did not touch Cooper, did not rub against him; she kept her distance from him. Instead she led him deep within her house, to a hallway that he had never seen before and where the flicker from her red lamp could barely reach them, and she waited for what was to come next. It was very late at night, and outside, it was cold. She felt the cold clinging to him. It had come with him into her house.

Cooper said, "I saw you there. I saw when you understood."

"It's because I could hear you," she said, "from my porch, when you two would go down to the river, when you would talk there.

I couldn't understand exactly what you said, but I could hear you laughing. I loved the sound of the laughing and the words, but they could have come from anyone. I didn't know it was you two, not then."

"It's him," said Cooper, "Reese Jackson, the one that I told you about."

Melba sank to the floor, running her back against the wall and he sank down just beside her. "I know that," she said and had actually known it for quite some time now. She remembered last autumn, hearing their voices coming from the river, carried on the wind up the banks and through her screen door. Cooper's voice, his and Reese's. Funny how you could hear their similarity when they were together—the same accent, the same soft slur of their words.

"We were growing-up friends," said Cooper. "After that first day, we just got along. And there was nothing stopping us back then. My daddy did not like colored people—most people like him didn't—but it was an automatic thing with him, a general conception. I didn't think he had anything against Reese in particular, at least not then. And—when we started—we were still at an age where we could be friends. Colored girls and white girls would have been separated by then—we were ten—but folks have pretty much always let boys do what they wanted. Even my own daddy did this. Oh, once in a while he'd say, 'Leave that Nigra boy alone. Pal around with your own kind.' Mostly he just let us be. My grades had come up. I was playing ball, keeping myself out of trouble. Not much of an object to worry about for my daddy.

"Later on, though, he started really disliking him some Reese Jackson. Daddy'd figured it out—how I was doing, my new understanding—and he didn't like being beholden to nobody black. He did not like the idea that there was a black child roaming around on his land that was smarter than his own child and was instructing him. Back then—before he took hard into politics—the only thing going for Daddy besides our little acreage was the fact he was white, and surely black was never supposed to be better at anything than white.

"So Reese and I kept on our way discreetly—so as not to upset my daddy or Reese's mama either, for that matter. She had a hardworking life, and she would not have wanted any nonsense—no white person mad at her, no white person having speculations and running off at the mouth. Reese was always very careful not to give his mama one minute of trouble, but we kept on with our ways anyhow. We'd be reading our books, learning our lessons, but there was always plenty of other time fishing in the summer, swimming, playing bat ball. We were both of us way into sports. Frog gigging—in fact, it was frog gigging got us in trouble.

"We were fourteen years old by then—that summer—and we decided to go on downriver. It was just something you did, quiet and peaceful, and there were these jumping frogs, and you got your gig—your forked stick—and you caught them and bagged them. We loved doing it. Who knows why? And, like I said, it was a peaceful undertaking, and Money, Mississippi . . . well, our home was in Money, and it was no longer that way. Peaceful.

"Our town—teeny as it was—had sent two black men off to war against Hitler. They'd come back with what my daddy called 'notions,' and these notions just simmered away until one day there was this scuffle. Seems one of these men had not got off the sidewalk like he was supposed to when a white woman walked past. Seems some white men didn't like this—but that's all it amounted to, a scuffle, something that would surely pass. I didn't think much about it. I don't think Reese did. Nobody did. 'That soldier boy just needed to learn him some manners, that's all,' said my daddy. He told this to the men that came calling. I heard him tell one of our neighbors, some man come to visit, that that boy needed to take himself on up north, that was all.

"I'm telling you this to let you know how quiet everything was and how settled, how it was nothing like what happened with Emmett Till—with the noise and the clamor and the national news. Yet there must have been something. I must have sensed something, heard something from all those men—Daddy called them his constituents, even back then—all these white men coming over, milling around, standing around in front of our house. Whispering to my daddy. Our neighbors. People like us.

"So Reese and I took to spending most of our time at the river—so much time there, reading and thinking and staying away from my house. One day we just decided to go on off."

Cooper shifted, and even with her eyes closed Melba knew he had turned and was now facing her. He brushed against her shoulder, the first time he had ever touched her, and she left the dream of his story for a moment to puzzle at this, to gauge its meaning, to keep this new development alive by warming it with her attention.

He said, "Frog gigging is a wonderful thing to do—that is, if you are determined to harness your attention. It requires preparation. It requires travel. If you want to do it right. Reese and I wanted to do it right. First up, we had to choose our night. You can't gig on a full moon—frogs'll see you for sure if you come in on them with that much light. You have to wait until the moon is new. You have to spit on your hands and sell your soul to the devil and hope that the stars aren't shining bright. You have to choose your branches and pare them down—and not just any branches but sharp ones, those can make you a two-pronged gig. You got to get your bag ready. You got to activate up your killer instinct.

"So off we go, into the darkness. There are a lot of rivers around

Money—the Yazoo, the Cold Creek, the Tallahatchie. We chose the Tallahatchie. Don't ask me why.

"You have to understand, Miss Melba, that everything's different down in the Delta. The land is flat, rivers run deep and wide. They are great and mighty things. It takes a long time to get really into them. I think we started out by nine that night—I was just fourteen, but I already drove my daddy's pickup. Sometimes I'd even drive him in it. River wasn't just there, like it is here. You had to head for it, and we did that, down many a back road. I had snuck us some beer, and Reese had cigarettes. Pall Malls. Unfiltered. Hey, we were men! And I was just so grateful to be away—away from the house, away from those men on the porch. I think it took us about three hours' driving to get where we were going. We loaded down our boat, wetted up our bags—you got to do that to frogs, got to put them in a wet bag once you kill them. Don't want their skins to dry out.

"Like I said, you got to do it on a dark enough night, and you got to run a quiet boat. Noise will drive the frogs off. Light warns them that you're coming. You got to sneak up on them, catch them unawares. That's the whole secret of frog gigging: You got to take them by surprise." Cooper's hands, as he showed her this, traced darkness.

"And we were having a good night of it, a glorious night. Drinking our beer, whispering out our nonsense talk about what we wanted to do, about being doctors, whispering speculation about what the cotton crop might do come September. The frogs were all croaking away, innocent and stupid, on the bank. Not scared of us one bit. I was looking toward them. That's when I saw it."

Melba, who had experience in these matters, had the strongest urge to reach over to Cooper, to run her own trained hands where they were needed, to stop his words with her lips. She'd done this often enough when confronted with things she did not want to hear, with revelations that might move her from the safe shore of her own feelings. She knew when something was coming, and she knew how to distract it. "Sex," she had said more than once to her dear friend Deanie Jackson, "used beneficially, can be a way to stop all communication. You manage it right, you never have to hear an unpleasant thing from a man in your life."

Melba's whole aim in the life that had taught her this had been her own self-preservation, to hold tight on to the Melba she knew. But now she was in love, and now she listened.

Cooper said, "It was the body, but I thought it was only garbage at first. This was back when folks felt they could just leave anything anywhere—before littering fines came in—things they no longer wanted and such. You might be driving out in the county and see someone's couch just dropped along the highway, see a refrigerator rusting out in the creek with the door still on, where children could get caught. See big bags of garbage just floating along in the river. That's what I thought it was, in all that dark. Garbage. Something to get out of our way so's we could get on with our gigging and our drinking and our smoking and our fun, but even then, right in that first instant, I don't think Reese saw it like that.

" 'Get on away from that thing, Cooper,' he told me. 'Leave it alone.'

"I wouldn't listen. There were frogs on the bank. I could hear them. This thing—this piece of garbage—was in my way. And remember, I was the white one, used to giving the orders. And my order was, 'Help me move this thing on over.'

"We did what I said. I turned the boat toward the bank. Got closer, until I could see that this thing wasn't really garbage, but by then it was too late. We were near enough to see the familiar outline and the subtle change of color on the clothes. The starlight showed them clear enough—faded soft shadings that the river had not quite had time to wash totally away. Not yet. So I must have known it was a body. Reese did, even though it was laid out facedown in the water, its hands out, legs submerged. Caught on some stubble on the bank. A man.

"'Go on in closer,' Reese said to me. 'Shine some light on him. I want to get me a good look.'

"Yet, by then, sounding just as shit-scared as I was.

"But still saying, 'I want us to get a good look.'

"The thing I noticed was how silent the night had got around us. We'd been quiet—talking in whispers—but we had our flash-lights out, and the light had scared the frogs silent. No fish were jumping. No insects—there was nothing. Just us, our little boat, our flashlights.

"When we got close enough, Reese cut the boat motor and reached down with his gig. He called out to me to help him, to pull this weight over, and I did. We didn't touch it, though, not with our hands.

"'Got to see him. Got to see if he's still alive,' said Reese, but of course he wasn't. We both knew that.

"In the end," Dr. Cooper Connelly explained to Madame Melba Obrenski in the dark, "we did manage to get at him. To turn him around. To see him faceup—or what was left of his face. There were no eyes, lips gone; fish had got to them. Only thing still on that man—only thing you could be sure of—was his race. It might be grayed and deaded out, but his race was still there.

"But then, as we got him over, he seemed to shift a little, like he was trying to pull himself over to some firmer land and rise up. I could have sworn I saw his hands, stumped and swollen, clutching, striving to hold on. For just a second—just the smallest, smallest of seconds—I thought Reese might have been right. That this bloated, stinking-dead man in front of us was still alive and that he was using his last strength to come out for us and that he *would* come out for us unless we got ourselves away fast."

Cooper chuckled at this memory, but it was a cold laugh, a sound Melba had never heard from him before.

"After that, we got out of there quick, all right. And you better believe Reese was right beside me all the way. No more talk about somebody still being alive. No more curiosity, thinking we had an end-of-summer story to tell at our schools. We were out of there. But you have to remember, Miss Melba, how deep we were on the river and hours away from where we had started out and from folks—people who could help us. Because of course we thought there would be people who would help us—my daddy was the sheriff. Surely he didn't want no dead folks just dumped out into the water, not on his watch. I mean, he was the quickest lawman in the state when it came to handing out tickets for littering. He always loved him some Mississippi. He always said we had to keep this place up."

What struck Melba now, and what had struck her over and over again as she had worked through the years within her two peculiar occupations, was how quickly people went back—how thoroughly they could be in an old place and how they could take her along with them. Beside her, Cooper's voice rushed out breathlessly and high. Because he was fourteen years old again, setting out for a leisurely night of sneaking beer and smoking cigarettes. Instead there he was with Reese Jackson, running away from the horror of his life.

"We tore out of there. Gunning the engine on the boat and then into the truck—trying to get it started. Desperate to get home.

"'Daddy's gonna help us,' I told Reese, 'Daddy's gonna do something.'

"We were hotfooting it away from that river. I could look over at him and see on his face what mine must have looked like—bug eyes, white lips, and this complete contortion of fear. Running on up to my daddy's house, the both of us so scared we didn't even stop to think about what we should be doing, what we shouldn't. What my daddy might not like."

Melba edged closer, and even though she still could see only the outline of his body and hear his voice through it, she nodded her head. She knew what was coming.

"We even forgot to remember. Daddy didn't like black people—colored people—Negroes—Nigras. No matter what he called them, he didn't like niggers. He especially didn't like them running up into his house. It was just getting on morning when we got there—sun already losing its red in the east, air already thick and hot. Maereen, the black woman who worked for us, was busy cooking in the kitchen. We could see her through the window as we left that truck in the driveway—the two of us—and we tore on into the house like that body was right behind us. Back then it was still behind us both, and not just me.

"We tore right on into the house, and there he was, having breakfast. I ran right over to him and told him about the body. Dead. Floating. Bloated and gray. Reese was babbling, too. I mean, how many times have you seen a dead man going down the river in your life? I just *knew* Daddy was going to do something about it, him being the law around that place and such. He'd call out the deputies, go on out to the Tallahatchie, and dredge up what was wrong. Fix it. Make things right.

"First inclination I got he wasn't about to do this was the way nothing changed. Melba, it was like we weren't even there. He just kept on eating his breakfast—eggs and bacon, grits, coffee and juice, one bite after the other. Not mixing anything up, going clockwise around the plate like he always had. Not looking up. Reese must have noticed first, because he just sort of shut up, started angling a little bit to the door. He must have remembered that this was Jack Rand Connelly and he was in his house. I looked back at Reese in that sunlight with Maereen over at the stove, with her back to us, not turning around once and sunlight streaming through the ruffled, flowered curtains at the windows. And Daddy not looking up. And Reese getting closer and closer to the door.

"And it started to dawn on me why. But wasn't my daddy always the first one saying how other folks thought we were dirt, were ignorant and no-account and didn't know right from wrong, 'cause we lived down here in the South? I said to him, 'Daddy, there's this man dead and floating in the river. You got to come take care of it. Just out there on the Tallahatchie, downwards near Nowatchie. You got to go take care of it.' I just kept saying, 'You got to take care of it,' again and again.

"But my daddy just kept on eating, going around his plate, and my mind had finally caught up with Reese—late as always. But I just kept talking and talking, talking and talking on and on anyway. Mostly to keep my daddy quiet, because by then I knew what he was going to say.

"And he said it. 'What was the man, son?' Like that.

"I said, 'What do you mean, what was he?' Hedging.

"He said, 'What color was he, son?'

"I said, 'Colored. I guess he was colored.'

"Daddy drank at his coffee, wiped his mouth on his napkin, and said, 'I guess we'll go ahead and leave him as he lay. Got no time for niggers and their activities. Got too much to do.'

"Miss Maereen came over and got his breakfast dishes, cleaned them off the table. Daddy thanked her for it, and that was that.

"At least for Daddy it was. For me it was just starting. Reese never said a word against what my daddy did that day, but I could see right off that to him it was all my fault. He hated me for what Daddy had said—maybe for what Daddy had even done. You see, that boy who got back from the army had disappeared. Some said he ran off to Chicago. Some to Detroit. They had a railroad run straight up from the Delta back then, and it was always full of black people trying to get out. That's what folks said—that he took that train. That he got himself out because he realized, coming back home after the war, that while things might could change in Italy and Germany, they weren't about to change down here in the South.

"Thing is," said Cooper real quiet, and this time the sound of his voice and the sound of his breathing came together for Melba—one lower than normal, one harsher—so that it seemed to her he might have stopped saying his words and instead was breathing them out. "I think that's when Reese started to hate me, me and what I stood for. My daddy. All what was happening down here. But by then the bond we had with each other, the need, was so strong that it couldn't go away. We tried that. I didn't see Reese again for the rest of that summer. Once school started up again, though—and it was serious school this time, high school—that hold was still right there, strong as ever, that need. Reese still didn't have the books—I still didn't have the mind to understand them. And so we went on together no matter what happened, no matter what new horror was going on. The two of us kept on sneaking off all the way through high school, all the way up through college. Why, I'm the one told Reese how he could get out and go on up to Johns Hopkins. Still we are together. We never, either one of us, have been able to break that bond."

"Until Billy Ray Puckett," said Melba.

Cooper smiled. It was getting a little lighter now, and Melba thought she could see traces of that smile and not just feel it near her. "Oh, Billy Ray's not going to stop anything between me and Reese. He may be able to stop my practicing medicine, that's all, and maybe not even that, if I am unlucky. Reese and me, we go way back. What he didn't have, I had; what I couldn't do, he could do. The rest of what happened . . . well, it took its own course."

"You could try," said Melba, ever optimistic. "Just tell folks the truth. Nobody could fault either one of you for what happened to Billy Ray Puckett, and you'd have the government behind you. There's really no *law* to stop you from doing what you did, one surgeon switching out for another. And you were doing it for that man's sake. Trying to get him the very best doctor, even if you thought the best doctor was somebody else."

This time the new light was bright enough so she could see his smile, and it stopped her.

"Sweet Melba," he said.

But this was Mississippi, and they knew it, and the dawn of it was coloring both their faces in its rosy light.

"No way telling what's going to happen," said Cooper. "And for what? It wouldn't do any good for either of us to stand up to it, not the way things are down here. It would bring up just all kinds of questions. We've been doing this for years, and surgery is . . . well, what it is. Billy Ray Puckett isn't the first patient that we lost. He's just the first one we lost because we should have known better. Reese is just so damn good at what he does. It's still a wonder to me that he missed that damage. A wonder."

"Reese Jackson is not God."

"In the operating room he is," said Cooper. "Him with his team, me with mine. Everybody loyal. Keeping it quiet because . . . hey, that's what we had to do to go on. I wasn't a surgeon, but I was the one with the hospital, and no white person was going to let Reese Jackson work on them, not knowingly. I can't think of one."

"What's going to happen now?"

"Once Mr. Puckett finds out, he will pursue this. That's his right. He's angry about his son's death, angry about what's going on with the school board. He thinks he's got enough reason to hate me, and he does. Also, it's a way to strike out."

"Strike out at what? He ain't nothing but an old peckerwood."

"That's just the problem. Folks like the Pucketts—they're at the low end of nothing down here. Everybody—black folks, white folks—all looking down on them. Wondering what is wrong with them, that they cannot get on. Used to be poor whites could make themselves feel like they had some standing by roughing up a Negro now and then. Now roughing up a Negro—hey, that's become a federal offense. Taking me on will help redress this, at least in Mr. Puckett's eyes. And he's got right on his side. The mistake was made. Billy Ray died, and we made no attempt to save him. That's the simple truth of it."

"*Reese Jackson* didn't save him. Won't he speak up?"

Cooper looked truly amazed. "And what would be the good of that?"

"I can think of a whole lot of good," Melba said. "Good for him and good for you. Y'all both need to tell the truth about what happened. Get it out in the open. You just made a mistake, and the mistake didn't kill Billy Ray. It was the bullet did that, and the bullet came from his own gun. Likkered up, everybody says it. Why those folks down in Jackson should have run an autopsy on that. Drinking like a skunk. One thing after another. That was his life. Believe me, my ladies have told me. Almost drowned one time because his canoe flooded up. Tripped down the stairs at his house, almost broke his neck. And that's just the times he was sober enough to tell what was going on. Most of the time, he was so flat-out drunk—skunklike, feeble-minded drunk—he couldn't even remember what had happened to him. Billy Ray Puckett was an accident waiting to happen. Falling on his own gun was what did him in. It wasn't you two at all."

"I wish it were that simple."

"But it *is* that simple. Just . . . tell the truth. Tell what happened that night. Tell them what's been going on all these years. You don't need Reese Jackson to do it for you."

Staring at her, Cooper thought he saw contempt on Melba's face. Could be. If so, it seemed odd and incongruous on her, something that might have originated in his own face and was being reflected back to him now.

"Can't do that," he said, fourteen years old again and back down at the river. Waiting for the body to rise up and take him, this time for good.

"Sure you can," said Melba. "Sure you can do it."

Cooper shook his head, got up. "There's still a little time. They still haven't figured out quite what happened. There'll be an inquiry. I'll have to go down to Jackson, take responsibility for my own incompetence. I can do that with a clear conscience. I never should have been a doctor anyway. It's not what I'm good at. With the time I've got left, I can work on this school-integration plan. Try to change some things. Make up for others. Maybe it doesn't have to come out exactly like I planned—the white parents and the black parents working together. Maybe that part of it was just dreaming, but I still think the rest of it—the actual integration of the schools here in Revere—can work."

Melba was not interested in school integration. "You are making a terrible mistake. You cannot let this ruin your whole career. You cannot just throw everything over like that. You *must* fight back."

"No," Cooper said, and he was smiling.

He was smiling and promised himself that one day, after things had settled, he would be back to explain this to Melba. He'd tell her about the lightness he felt, as though the life that he'd lived was finally slipping off of his shoulders. How absolutely right it felt, for the first time, to be looking into nothing—the nothingness of not knowing what was going to happen with the hospital, with his father, with his wife, with his life. One day, after this integration thing had passed, he'd be back and they'd start talking, just like they always had. He knew they would, and this much was certain: In the end, Melba would understand.

She watched him walk down into the early-morning sunlight. Her bright sign sashayed in the breeze blowing up from the river and waved him off. It reminded Melba that a full day lay before her.

"Cooper," she whispered, and she splayed her fingers against the newly put-up storm window of her screen door. But he had disappeared to her, getting into his car. Driving quickly away. Going home.

She pulled her mind from that closed door and looked once more at her sign—so knowing, so darkly painted, so not her. And she made a snap decision of the kind that had taken her out of New Orleans and landed her in Mississippi in the first place.

"I think I'm all played out here. I think it may be time for me to be looking for a new line of work."

# Chapter 23

RUTH ANN WENT ON OUT to the house in the country. She hadn't seen her mother-in-law in weeks, hadn't wanted to. Her father-in-law she'd seen more recently. That's why she'd come.

She sat beside a silent Mrs. Puckett and watched as the men came up to the house and stayed outside on the porch talking with Big Rob. It must have been forty degrees out there—cold as it ever had been in November—and yet they congregated outside on the rickety front steps. They wouldn't come in. Ruth Ann knew they'd been up to no good.

Mrs. Puckett had been more-than-usually talkative. She'd asked about the children still in Iuka, though not about Janet, and then got on to what was really important: why the men came, why she had come to expect them being there.

She told her daughter-in-law how at first she thought she'd ought to be neighborly. She'd offered them porch cushions to sit on and sweet tea. She'd invited them into her house. But her husband had told her firmly, once, that they preferred to take their drink outside. One of them owned a still, and Mrs. Puckett knew he brought corn liquor with him when he came. She looked over at Ruthie when she said this, with a glint in her eye that her daughter-in-law had not seen in a while but understood. After that, Mrs. Puckett had gone back to looking at *Jeopardy!* She must have felt she'd done her duty, warning Ruthie.

And Ruthie was grateful. She was grateful, too, that Janet went to school and didn't get home until past three in the afternoon, and so Ruthie had been able to come out, on her free day, on her own. She didn't want her daughter here. These men hanging around on the front porch dressed in their work clothes and dungarees, talking destruction and violence. It brought back memories of Billy Ray. He'd been a loner, too, just like his daddy, and the only time he'd made friends was when they were talking, just like they were talking today about meanness, about hurting people, about what they would do. About what they had done. About scaring off the niggers and keeping them in their place.

Ruth Ann wanted to shout at them, *Hey, the niggers don't care about y'all! They don't want nothing you got! You white trash to them, just like you are to everybody else!* But of course she couldn't do that, not in her dead husband's house. Besides, she had to plot and plan and bide her time and wait so that she could take care of Janet and bring her other children home. Most of all she had to keep Janet away from these people. They had known Billy Ray. They might start adding things up.

But she was lucky in that these men had somehow decided that Billy Ray was their martyr, though at first Ruth Ann could not make that out for the life of her. Billy Ray had been fighting with most of them since he'd brought his family down from the hills. Still, she was grateful that they thought of her as a dead martyr's wife. It kept them respectful. It kept them at a distance.

It had taken her some time to realize they had raised Billy Ray to sainthood only because they hated Cooper Connelly so much and Cooper Connelly had been the one to operate upon her husband. This must have been a hard battle for them, a trick in their minds, because at the same time they hated the son, they idolized the father—Jack Rand Connelly with his editorials in the *Times Commercial* defending southern womanhood and saying little white children should not have to learn their school lessons in a different way. Christian Principles, Jack Rand called them. These men—Big Rob's new friends—called them that as well.

These lounging, sullen, drinking folks frightened Ruth Ann, but she would just have to outfox them. Lord knows, she'd done it once before in the past. One of them—a small, bandy-legged man, a loud talker—had shot Reverend Streeter. Ruthie had seen him do it. Many other people had seen it as well. Afterward he'd just climbed into a car, driven by another man, and rode off. They hadn't even rushed. By then everybody had been so involved with that poor preacher lying in the road to pay too much attention to the man who had shot him, had bloodied him with a warning shot.

Next time would be different.

# Chapter 24

"NICE DAY OUT," said Deanie from the window, and she meant it. Behind her, Reese agreed. He was running late this morning. Skippy had already gone on off to school.

Deanie said, "Not a cloud in the sky and the leaves still turning. That's the thing about it here—fall and spring can last a very long time. Not like in Iowa, where they come and go in a moment, sandwiched in between real heat and real cold."

She was surprised to turn back and see that Reese had been paying attention. Usually he wasn't, or so she thought. Aware of her only on rare occasions—when she wanted to visit Melba, when she spent too much money, when his things were not arranged just right—that's how she usually got his attention, not with small talk, books, and notions. Still, she felt safe and comfortable with Reese, and always had.

He was smiling at her from the breakfast table over his neatly refolded napkin, his cup placed perfectly in its saucer, his fork laid

just so on his cleaned plate. All part of the order that he had constructed, day in and day out, above the confusion that had once
been his life. She thought what a great man he was—not just a great
doctor—truthful and honest, and she loved him for it and would
have led him right on upstairs again and loved him to death, had
the day and its duties not been already taking them over. Had it not
been too late for that.

So she smiled at him again, and he smiled back at her and then
got up from the table, gathered his things—he needed a new medical bag; Deanie made a note to herself to get him one for Christmas,
something he would continually forget to get for himself—and kissed
his wife good-bye. A real kiss. Deanie was in heaven. Reese was pas-
sionate with her in the bedroom, behind closed doors, but he wasn't
the type to show affection in public, to kiss her like he was kissing
her now. Of course, no one was here, and that made a difference.

"How's Reverend Streeter?" she asked her husband at the door.
Heart still a-pitter-patter.

"Doing good," said his doctor. "Over at the hospital on the first
floor."

Reverend Streeter and his shooting were still all in the newspaper: how he was doing, how he was coming along. Speculation
about who had done this (Outside Agitators!) and reaction from his
family, most of whom were calling upon God to do some forgiving.
This did not include the younger ones, of course.

Something really awful like this happens—a good man, going
about his business, getting shot, and all over integration—why, even
in Mississippi the white people were shocked. That's what Melba said,
and she ought to know, because they came to her, they told her.

Reese turned back at the door. "They say folks over at the River
Café are bringing Reverend Streeter breakfast, lunch, even his dinner, too. See, they could have acted right all along."

He shook his head, the same old fiery Reese Jackson, always ready to fight the good fight, still hating white people, and with ample reason. Not a hand had ever lifted to help him. But a little tired now, and Deanie noticed it, the way he rubbed his shoulder, hoisted his bag. It had been a long, uphill battle. Still was.

If the rumor was true, things were about to get complicated. Although Melba never said a word about it, everybody else told Deanie that the medical examiner had discovered something mighty strange about that man Billy Ray Puckett's dying. Something that Cooper Connelly should not have missed. There was going to be an inquest or an inquiry, Deanie could not remember which. In the past, Jack Rand would have shut something like this up right quick. Nobody could touch his boy, his daddy would protect him, though Deanie had always suspected that what Jack Rand was doing was watching out for his own reputation, his own image. Cooper was what his daddy wanted him to be, and he better stay that way or else. It occurred to her that Jack Rand was probably just holding back, wanting to teach his son a lesson. At the last moment, he'd step in like normal and the whole mess would just suddenly disappear.

Still, the sun shining and the birds singing and Cooper Connelly walking away from Melba's house at an unseemly hour—Deanie had heard all this from her bed—and now her husband kissing her full on the lips had combined to promise a special day for Lyle Dean, and as usual she called Melba first, got no answer, and then got herself dressed. Apricot sweater, beige slacks, rich and lustrous dark brown alligator flats—all this just to cross her winter-trimmed lawn and go on into her best friend's house. And all because she was Mrs. Spencer Reese Jackson, one of the wealthiest, most beautiful, most secure women—black or white—in Revere, Mississippi, and she would play the part.

A woman who loved her husband and loved her best friend.

It took two knocks, but Melba finally made it to the door. She was dressed as well, and not for working. Her toned-down hair lay loose around her shoulders—no turban—and she wore jeans, something she very rarely did. She did not look particularly happy.

"What you up to?" said Deanie, coming on in through the door.

"I'm thinking," said Melba. She went into the kitchen brought out coffee in new ironstone cups. They'd been on special last week around the corner at Piggly Wiggly. Deanie had looked at them herself.

"Thinking," repeated Melba. "It might be time for me to be moving on."

This was news and not at all what Deanie had ever expected to be hearing from Melba, especially after she'd heard Cooper Connelly's footsteps early on. She stirred sugar into her coffee and stared for a second at the mute television screen, gathering her thoughts together.

"Did something happen with Cooper?"

"Nothing happened with Cooper. We just talked. He told me things. Things you should have told me, you being my best friend and all."

Now Melba had Deanie's full attention. Melba was her friend, the only true friend she'd been able to make in all her years in Mississippi, in Revere. *The Guiding Light* was starting, but for the first time neither one of them had use for anybody else's trials and tribulations. They had enough going on of their own.

"Melba, I don't have any earthly idea what you're talking about." But suddenly Melba's red hall light, her small stuffy room, her perennial sweetness, no longer seemed just right. Lyle Dean did not like anger, either from Reese or from anybody else. But it wasn't as if Melba was angry. It was as if Melba was somebody else.

She stood up, hands on her hips, obviously with something that wanted saying. But Lyle Dean Jackson did not want to hear it. A deep instinct told her not to hear it. Something that could change Melba like this—could flint up her eyes and line her lips tight together and drive her into her first pair of jeans . . . well, whatever it was might be something that could change her, Lyle Dean, as well. And Deanie knew suddenly, right quick and right down, that she did not want a thing in her life changed.

"Better be getting on back home. I'll call you later."

Melba's grip was surprisingly tight for such a small woman. Lyle Dean wondered why she had never had occasion to notice this before.

"You not going home until you explain to me why you didn't tell me about Cooper Connelly and your husband."

"Reese—and Cooper Connelly?"

"The both of them together. Why didn't you tell me about them all these years?"

But Lyle Dean was shaking her head and smiling, relieved now that she knew there was some misunderstanding. "What's to tell? You know Reese don't like white people. He hates Cooper Connelly, talks bad about him all the time. Says he's a stupid white boy and his daddy gave him everything he's got."

"*He* gave Reese everything *he's* got," said Melba, and now she really was starting to get angry. Her voice was rising. Maybe the anger had been there all along, not even really hidden.

Deanie pried her hand loose. "I don't know what you're talking about, Melba."

"I'm talking about the friendship between Reese and Cooper—at least Cooper's friendship with Reese. I'm talking about the fact that they grew up together, that they've been real close now for years."

Lyle Dean shook her head. "Melba, you're wrong." Patiently.

Oh, so patiently, just like she was talking to a child. "Reese Jackson does not like white people."

Melba was right there with it. "That's what he says. That's not what he's living." She spit out one truth after the other. Melba nailed Mrs. Spencer Reese Jackson straight to the wall with her words.

And her words *were* truth. Lyle Dean steadily kept on shaking her head, but all the time she was thinking—about Reese getting out of Mississippi, the miracle of it; about Reese at Johns Hopkins; about Reese coming back—and all her thinking was starting to add up. It was starting to outline a picture of something.

"Now he's letting Cooper take the blame for Billy Ray Puckett dying. Reese did that operation. He made the mistake. Reese should step up."

Deanie stepped up herself then. "Are you listening to yourself? Have you forgotten where you are? This is Mississippi. Nothing like that's gonna happen down here."

"It *has* happened, and you know it. Nothing else can do the explaining, at least not once you think about it, it can't. How else would Reese Jackson have got his start in life? He's always telling everybody how poor he was—no heat in the house, tin-roof shack, no books in the schools he went to, no teachers knowing anything. What got him out of there? It sure wasn't Miss Hinkty. You always told me his mama was just as mystified about how her boy got over as everybody else. *Cooper* got him over, that's how he did it. Cooper taught him what he needed. Cooper made sure he knew how to get on out of here so he could get to school. Then, when he got back, Cooper set him up in practice. How else could he have done it? Black folks are poor down here. Black folks could never have paid Reese enough in a million years to get him what he's got. But Cooper had the money, and Cooper paid it out."

"You lying bitch." The "bitch" took a long time to finish. For the first time in her life, Lyle Dean Jackson was speaking with a true southern drawl.

But Melba wasn't stopping. Now that she knew the truth, Deanie had to know it with her. Since they'd met, they'd always shared everything, and now they were bound to share this as well.

"Reese couldn't have done it without Cooper. Then Cooper couldn't do it without Reese. Like Cooper said, they patched themselves together. Made themselves one whole doctor. Made themselves one whole man. It was Reese operated on Billy Ray Puckett. It was Reese who made the mistake that killed him."

Deanie's slap was so fast and so hard that it knocked Melba's pierced hoop—new and fourteen-karat gold—right out of her ear and onto the floor. They heard it clatter against the coffee-table leg, and then there was nothing but silence until Lyle Dean said, "My husband always tried to tell me you were crazy. Crazy and jealous and a loose woman to boot. What kind of person makes her living telling fortunes anyway? If Billy Ray Puckett was left to die, it was Cooper Connelly did it. Cooper Connelly was his surgeon. Nobody's ever going to believe anything else, because nothing else is true. Reese Jackson is a hero. You, and not nobody else, can take that from him." Defending her husband.

"Lyle Dean Jackson, you are such a fool."

*So this is how it ends*, thought Melba. All the years of reading Balzac together, of watching *The Guiding Light* and *Days of Our Lives* and *Brighter Tomorrows* gone—poof!—just like that.

She heard her back door slam shut and the sound of Deanie's expensive alligator shoes going down one set of porch steps and then up another. She listened as another door slammed—a much bigger door this time, and so the bang that accompanied it seemed much louder, even though it came to her from farther away.

Again Melba shook her head. She'd been miserable. She'd made somebody else miserable. She'd evened the score. She was still a little street fighter from the Quarter after all. Race made no difference, which is why she'd never put much account in it. Black or white, it was being poor that mattered, and being abandoned to get out any way you could. That's what had marked Melba; that's what had marked Reese, too—though he would probably never admit it. Growing up with no real house and no real family, with no caring and left by himself to scramble ahead any way he could. Cooper couldn't understand Reese, even Deanie couldn't understand him, really—but, oddly, Melba thought she could. And maybe forgive him. Later. Somewhere on down the line. The thought comforted her.

Settled now, she looked over at the mute television screen and saw that in all the commotion she'd missed *The Guiding Light* and *The Noon News* had started. Could you believe it, they were still talking about Reverend Streeter? There were shots of Doctors Hospital, where he was being treated, and the sheriff came on, looking determined and still shaking his head. Melba thought it was nice of them, still talking about him with such interest. Maybe there was hope for things down here after all.

Then Jack Rand Connelly came on. He was shaking his head, also. Without even hearing what he had to say, Melba started shaking *her* head, too—just like Deanie had done right before she'd been told about her husband. Shook her head. This is not true. This is not real. But it was true. It was real. Her life was changing on this television screen.

Just as there had been no respite for Deanie, there was none for Melba now. She got up, reached out, turned up the sound, but just barely. Jack Rand Connelly's voice whispered through the room.

". . . was shot this morning as he left his house for Doctors Hospital. Shot through the leg and the chest—two bullets. A neighbor heard it. That's all there was. He's been flown to Jackson."

Floyd Sobczak took over from there. His voice muffled. Milking another new drama for all it was worth.

"Dr. Connelly is in extremely critical condition. No motive has been given for the shooting. No one has taken responsibility. But suspicion is centering on Dr. Connelly's civil-rights work, and specifically on his presidency of the school board and a controversial plan he espoused to integrate Revere's schools before the federal mandate. Mrs. Evelyne Elizabeth Connelly said, before leaving to accompany her husband to Jackson, that hate calls had started coming to the house."

The camera cut to a photograph of Dunsmuir, where someone had scrawled Coon-elly along the pristine whiteness of the side wall.

Floyd Sobczak still talked on, but Melba was no longer listening. Her hands were at her ears, over her mouth. She whispered through her fingers.

"Oh, sweet Jesus," she said.

# Chapter 25

NATURALLY, WITHIN HOURS the whole town had heard about Cooper Connelly. Deanie heard about it too, but not from Reese and not from Melba. One of the ladies at her church called and was obviously delighted to tell Mrs. Dr. Jackson something she did not know. Lyle Dean thanked her politely and hung up the phone. She called the school and left word that Skippy should go on out to Critter Tate's home. Then she sat down in her big house and watched while the bright day got grayer and grayer and then darker and darker, until finally it was dark enough.

Deanie came out her back door and glanced over at Melba Obrenski's, heard the creak of the Madame's sign drifting back and forth on the breeze of the river but saw no light there. Should she go over or should she not? But she couldn't go over there now—not now and maybe not ever. Now she had to get to her husband, and she knew where her husband would be.

Doctors Hospital was lit up like Christmas, light spilling out from all its windows and onto its drive. Deanie glanced briefly at the colored entrance—also bright and active—but she did not stop there. She drove her car up to the main entrance, parked in the main parking lot, walked in the main door. She still wore the same apricot cashmere sweater, the same tan wool slacks, the same highly polished alligator flats that she had worn on her visit to Melba. Except for the fact of her blackness, Deanie Jackson looked just like she already belonged where she was only now heading.

She saw a gaggle of nurses at the station, no doctors. They were all shaking their heads, looking worried. Deanie thought she heard the words "Not doing good." She knew they could only be talking about one somebody, but it wasn't the somebody she needed to talk to. No, they were not talking about him. Not yet.

She walked, undisturbed, to the hospital directory, found the number of the office where she knew she would find him, took the elevator, and went straight there.

The door said DR. COOPER LIVINGSTON CONNELLY, the name deeply engraved on a shining brass plate, but of course Dr. Cooper Livingston Connelly was nowhere around. He was fighting for his life down in Jackson or over in Birmingham—Lyle Dean could not remember which—and instead through the partially closed door she could hear the voice of her husband, Dr. Spencer Reese Connelly. No, *Jackson*. Spencer Reese *Jackson*. Deanie admonished herself sternly because she ought to know. After all, she was Lyle Dean Jackson, and she was married to him.

He was standing at the large mahogany desk, deep in conversation with a ginger-haired man whom Deanie had never actually met but thought she knew. The man had a very rich and deep voice, and the two of them were in what seemed to be a rich and deep conversation. At first neither of them noticed Deanie; only one lamp burned, probably because they had started their work much earlier, when the day had still been full, and had not noticed the change in light. They would of course have had a great deal to do, a great deal to accomplish, now that Cooper Connelly was not around.

It was the ginger-haired man who noticed her first. He looked up, blushed, said, "Mrs. Jackson," in the smooth melody that was his voice. The sound of his own name, Jackson, must have gotten Reese's attention. At least that's what Deanie thought, because it was only then that he saw her.

"Lyle Dean?" he said. In the pale light of the one burning lamp, Deanie saw the emotions run quickly across his face: astonishment, stealth, love, cunning, and pride. Pride stayed, as she had known it would.

"Come on in," said her husband to Lyle Dean Jackson. He opened his arms expansively. The other man gathered up papers, nodded to both of them, and left.

"That was Ned Hampton," Reese told her. Settling into a chair and watching her do the same. "He works for Doctors Hospital. He's the administrative assistant. He's the one called me—first."

Deanie nodded, although she had already recognized Ned Hampton. He was a legend down in the neighborhood for his singing, a white man with a black man's voice.

"You heard about Cooper Connelly?" Reese said to her. Again Deanie nodded. "Terrible thing. They don't think he's going to pull through. His wife was up with her folks in Virginia when it happened, but she's down in Jackson with him now. His daddy's down there, too."

Deanie knew her husband well enough to know that now was the time to start making some inquiries: What you doing here? How did this happen? But she didn't. These were the questions her husband dearly wanted to be asked and to answer. The questions Deanie now had for him were different. They were others, and they were important.

"What about Skippy?" he said.

"I sent him out to Critter's."

"But you *never* leave Skippy. Only just that one time when you went over Southside with that Melba creature."

"Maybe that was part of the plan—your plan, Reese—that I never leave Skippy. That I feel guilty about the incident—the *accident*—for the rest of my life. That I stay where you put me, in that big house all by myself, where you could control me. But that doesn't matter anymore." She paused, then said, "Tell me what happened. How you got here."

Reese answered her gladly, plainly excited again to be talking about what he wanted and to leave out all the rest.

"Jack Rand Connelly called me up himself. Called me right up from Jackson when he first got the news. Asked me—no, *begged* me—to take over the hospital. Take it over until what happens to Cooper happens." Reese was keeping his voice low and measured, a controlled voice coming from a man used to control. But Lyle Dean was astonished to see that his face twitched, that tears welled in his eyes. She doubted that Reese himself had registered this particular emotion, but the sight of it did give her a measure of hope that maybe—just maybe—she was still dealing with the man she knew to be her husband.

She said, "What did happen to him?"

"Two bullets, one to the leg and the dangerous one to the chest. Just like the one killed . . . well, that killed that patient of his. You know, the one that was in the newspaper and on the television. The one where they needed help for the family."

"His name was Billy Ray Puckett," said Lyle Dean slowly. "He was *your* patient. I hear tell you was the one let him die."

Reese sat there, looking at her across the large desk, and this was the only way that Deanie knew that he'd heard what she said. No twitch or, worse, hardening of his face into denial, no shake of his head. Nothing. Just Reese.

Continuing on: "First he had Ned Hampton get in touch with me. Cooper was on the way down to Jackson, but he hadn't arrived yet. His father got to the hospital, set up the preliminary surgeon—a good surgeon, one of the best—but there was still the question about what should be going on up here. Ned—Mr. Hampton—can't do it on his own. Not with everything that's going on here in town, the hearings on the new hospital and all. Now, with Reverend Streeter shot and his own boy gunned down . . . well, Jack Rand's in a hell of a mess, and he came to me. He had to come to me to make things right. Begging, like I told you. Lyle Dean, do you hear that? He was pleading with me—a black boy from the Delta, somebody he'd just as soon see dead as alive—and begging me to take over things here at the hospital, at least for the time being. Needing me to make things right. Hot dog!"

Through it all, Deanie sat there, perfectly silent. She'd seen Reese excited before, but never like this. And though she was horrified by him, a very deep part of her could not blame him. She'd been down to Money once to see the shack where he'd grown up, to see the cotton fields he'd worked, to see the folks life had left there. Reese had shot out—that much was certain—had done what he had to do to get over and to bring her and their children and many, many other people over with him. He was a hero, an inspiration, a wonderful surgeon.

"Cooper was your friend," said Deanie quietly, "and yet you kept him as secret from black folks as he kept you from the whites."

"Cooper *used* me," said Reese, and then he repeated it again. "He *used* me. He didn't understand anything they were trying to teach him, and I did. It didn't matter it was me. He would have used anybody; he was just that bound and determined to please his old man."

"He got you into medical school. How in the world else could you ever have figured out that the state of Mississippi would send you to Johns Hopkins on your own? Nobody ever put two and two together on that, Reese, not even me."

Reese snorted. "That wasn't Cooper, that was his daddy told him to tell me all about it. I'm sure about that. Jack Rand always wanted to get rid of me. He always wanted me away from here. Once we found that body in the river—when we were kids, Cooper and I came upon this body of this soldier everybody thought had disappeared, but there he was dead and floating—once we came on that, there was no way Jack Rand could be safe with me around. 'Cause even back then, you know, things were starting their changing. We black folks were getting our vote; we were coming into our power. We could have pushed him out. *I* could have pushed him out."

He sat there for a moment, smiling. Triumphant at the thought of having come such a long way, of having such power over such a powerful man.

"Maybe that wasn't it. Maybe he felt guilty," said Deanie. "Maybe he wanted to make it up to you, some way, for what had happened. For what you'd been through, for what all y'all had been through down there."

Reese looked over at his wife, and there was total amazement on his face, in its ridges and in the compression of its lips. He hated white people, and underneath he had always hated and feared them, even Cooper. But deep within his eyes, way, way deep within them, Deanie saw something else. She saw what it was her husband was actually proud of—that he had protected her, that she had not had to see the things that he had seen, that their children had not seen them.

"Ol' mean white men like that, they never feel guilty. They never change. Only way to make them change is for them to die off." Reese paused, considered. "I never wanted Jack Rand Connelly to like me, but he had to respect me. He had to see that I was worth something. He had to see that I was better at being his son than his own son was. Who you think suggested the whole thing to Cooper in the first place? Hey, that man never wanted to be a doctor. He never wanted to operate on people himself. I'm the one came up to him and said, 'Hey, man, let's do it like this.' He was all happy. You see, he had started drinking in order to make himself do them—the operations—and the drinking made him a menace, and he knew it. He told me so. Nicest thing about my plan was that even down here in Mississippi nobody had to know just what was going on. Cooper would be there while the patient went under anesthesia—he'd be the last thing they saw—then I would come in and take it over from there. Most of the time, Cooper stayed right on in there beside me—these were his patients after all—but sometimes he left me to myself. Only somebodies knew what was going on were his nurse and my nurse and the doctor over from West Point came in to put the patients under. No reason for any of them to talk; they knew that without me working, Doctors would have closed a long time ago. Ned Hampton didn't know nothing was going on—or else he was playing possum. Most important, Jack Rand Connelly knew."

"I didn't know," said Deanie, "until Melba told me, after Cooper told her."

"You didn't need to know," said her husband softly. "You just had to look pretty and love me. Let me love you. Keep me a nice home. That's all you needed to know. That's all you needed to do."

The sound of his words, the falling-apart of their life together, should have registered as something dramatic and tearful with Deanie; that's how it always was on *Brighter Tomorrows*, on *The Guiding Light*, and on *Days of Our Lives*. Instead she felt nothing but a stillness, all around her, in her, and sorrow, every place but in Reese Jackson's eyes.

His tone turned placating. "This works for him, too. For Cooper. And until this recent mess, it would have continued working. For both of us."

Dr. and Mrs. Jackson sat there in silence, even Reese quiet now and deflated, surrounded by the remnants of Cooper Connelly's privileged life: dusty football trophies and medical journals still in their mailing envelopes, tarnished silver-framed photographs of his up-country wife.

Finally Deanie said, "What about him? What about Cooper? Will he make it? Will he live?"

This brought Reese back to himself, and he smiled his most wicked, handsome, devilish Spencer Reese Jackson smile. "Oh, Cooper's gonna be all right. Jack Rand Connelly is a powerful man, powerful enough to send a private plane to bring the best damn surgeon in Mississippi down to operate on his boy—and the best damn surgeon in Mississippi is me."

# Chapter 26

LITTLE DID JACK RAND CONNELLY REALIZE when he said that Military Avenue would have to run red with blood before black children and white children would sit down to be schooled together, that the blood flowing would be from his own son. Still, that's exactly what happened. Cooper Connelly's being shot coming out of his house—and such a nice house, Dunsmuir, of all places—on his way to work at Doctors Hospital, saving other people's lives and then scheduled for a school-board meeting that night, that's what turned the tide. That's what brought people to their senses. This is what folks told themselves, though many of them realized, deep down, that this was just an excuse. Integration was coming anyway, escorted in by the federal government, and Cooper's shooting just gave them justification for compliance.

Most people—white people—still did not want it, but by now Revere was making the national news. Its businessmen, like businessmen in Birmingham and Tupelo before them, realized the gravity of the situation and, to a man, rallied around the gravely wounded Cooper Connelly, and even around the recuperating Reverend Streeter. But of course Reverend Streeter, being black, had an interest in things changing, while the integration of Revere's schools could benefit a childless, wealthy white man like Cooper Connelly not at all. He hovered in and out of consciousness for days and then for weeks. There was talk that even if he managed to hold on to his life—which was by no means certain—he might be paralyzed or even worse.

Cooper's health was a sure topic of conversation and daily bulletins were given by Floyd Sobczak on WLBN each night. But Revere was a small city, deeply connected, and those who had no firsthand knowledge were few and rare. People thought it was his stance and his support of school integration that had been the cause of his misfortune and the cause of the shot. By the time they found out this was not true—that the shooting was totally, or at least almost totally, unrelated to what he had tried to accomplish on that rainy night at Hunt School—it was too late. They'd already banded together in rectitude to do something about things, to make them right.

As it turned out, Cooper got exactly what he wanted. The white citizens of Revere made calls to their black counterparts and proposed that they all work together over Christmas break to bring Hunt School up to code so that the public schools could quietly integrate in January, without the publicity that would accompany the change should they wait for the fall. They would band together as a community as Dr. Connelly had wanted; Peterson's would donate paint, Hemphill Cement would lay the foundation, Military Plumbing would donate whatever else was needed. The list of those willing to commit just went on and on. They found out there were school districts up in north Mississippi that were doing the same thing. It did not make it seem like you were bowing to pressure if folks bonded together or if you had an excuse—and the shooting of Cooper Connelly, his martyrdom, made for one hell of an excuse.

The final planning meeting, with its speeches and its committees, was set for St. Peter's Episcopal Church on a Saturday afternoon, in the very early part of December. Before this, the only thing that St. Peter's had been noted for that involved colored people was the organization, by its Episcopal Women, of a community luncheon on the Eighth of May each year. The Eighth of May was the day in 1863 when news of the Emancipation Proclamation had arrived in Mississippi, and for generations colored people had proclaimed it as their own state holiday. Which meant there were no colored cooks in white homes cooking. The Episcopal Women had felt it incumbent upon them to take up the slack and provide sustenance where it was needed.

But it was also fitting that the Episcopalians carry the burden of this responsibility. Cooper Connelly was one of their own; he, more than his wife lately, had been a regular attendant. Besides that, thanks to a black lawyer and his family just moved to Revere from Pennsylvania, St. Peter's was the only integrated church in town—unless you counted Piney Grove Missionary Union Baptist Church, which had Ned Hampton as a member, and nobody ever did count this. White people never thought of themselves as integrating anything.

The turnout that brisk, bright afternoon was amazing. At least Melba thought so, and she was among them. She had rarely left her house since the morning Cooper had left it, and then only to go to the grocery store once or twice. She saw very few of her clients, even the old ones, even the ones who had been with her since she'd arrived. Deanie no longer came daily to her door. They'd had one more long conversation—nothing rancorous—and that had been that. They both needed time alone, especially Melba.

Like a ghost, though, she lingered and sometimes could be seen in her garden, at the Piggly Wiggly, and, on this very special day in December, at the last organizational meeting of the Greater Revere Integration Plan. She did not participate but sat quietly on the church stairs, listening to energetic talk coming out from the pulpit, enjoying the sunshine, and drawing occasional drags from a filterless Camel cigarette—smoking was a habit she'd recently taken up once again.

"Ain't you going inside there, Miss Melba?"

Melba had not heard the girl come up, but when she looked over, she knew immediately who she was. Knew *her*.

"Aren't you Skip Jackson's friend?"

The girl nodded. "Janet Puckett," she said by way of introduction. "The one who lost her daddy."

Melba patted to the cold stone step next to her. "Well, what you doing here? Mama come or something? Your grandparents inside?"

The girl snorted. "Big Mama don't leave the house, and my granddaddy wouldn't come in here. He's run himself off someplace nobody knows. My mama would have come if she could've, but she's off at the hospital, still taking her training. She's just a nurse's aide now, but she wants to end up by being a real RN."

"Then she'll probably do that," said Melba, automatically optimistic. "Most folks end up doing what they set their minds to."

The two of them sat for a moment listening to the drone of words and preparations coming from the sanctuary. It was pleasant here, and Melba was one who could truly enjoy a pleasant place and its moment and the company that was keeping it with her, even if that company happened to be a little girl. Only one thing niggled at her.

"Well, if your mama and your people aren't here, what you doing here?" she asked.

The girl looked straight at her, troubled blue eyes to troubled green, and then turned away. St. Peter's was brick but not majestic and it had a lovely campus, outlined with now-bare azaleas and with magnolia trees. Somebody had already planted the early pansies. The pansy was the flower that took all of Revere and most of Mississippi through the winter, the one that kept them focused on the springtime coming just ahead. It looked very much like Melba's own garden here—except of course that there was no statue of the Virgin—but Melba had stopped paying attention to what was all around her. She was focused on the little girl now, on her strange, out-of-the-blue presence, on that quick trouble she'd seen in her eyes, on the fact that she reminded her of someone—probably herself.

"What you doing here?" she repeated.

Janet Puckett didn't answer, at least not to that. Instead she motioned with her hand to the church sanctuary, not turning back. "I can't go in there," she said. "Mama goes—not here but to the Holiness folk. She says I should come, too, but I can't. Maybe when my little brother gets back from Iuka. He's coming home soon with the others. I keep thinking we might be able to go in together. If my little brother can do it . . ."

Her voice trailed off, and Madame Melba let it. She knew when to question and when to let go. Besides, she was feeling something, a faint stirring within her, something that had been numbed and banked and shallow since she'd turned up her television that morning after Cooper and Deanie had gone. Coming back now. Coming on strong.

"He's the one knows all about him—him and the doctor," said Janet Puckett after a while. "Mama knows some and Critter knows some, but they don't neither one of them know everything. Not like my brother. He's little, and so he really couldn't understand what was going on but he knew that it hurt me. Mama knew it, too, but she was scared. The doctor tried to tell her to get me out of there, that I was being scarred and ruined, but Mama . . ."

Janet shrugged and looked away. Melba wanted to reach over and hug her. She was by nature a very physical person, had always been so, except with Cooper Connelly.

"So we decided to do it ourselves, me and my brother, and we worked us up some plans. First off, we sawed through the porch steps. Just a plank of it. We knew he came in drunk most nights. His leg went through, just like we'd hoped for, but it didn't do much damage. He didn't break his neck, didn't even break his ankle, only sprained it a little bit. Daddy was back up and around in a day. And still coming for me. Next thing we decided to do was put a hole in the boat. He loved to go out fishing and drinking, drinking and fishing. We—my brother and me—thought if we sprung the leak slow enough, he'd be out in the middle of the Tombigbee and too drunk to see himself back in. He made it though, him and his six-pack. Dripping wet, rising up out of the water, coming for me." Janet paused. "That's when I knew I had to shoot him."

Melba held her breath and nodded. God knows she'd been in a shooting frame of mind herself in the past.

"Mama helped me, though I don't think she knew exactly what she was doing. We never talked about it, but Daddy and all those accidents—my mama is not stupid. She couldn't be going on to be a real RN if she was." There was pride in Janet's voice. "Plus, she was the one took me to the doctor's when I'd be tore up and bleeding. He fixed me up, took care of me. Told mama she had to do something and fast. Daddy had his deer stand, a new kind he got from Peterson's Hardware, and it came with all these new instructions. Naturally, Daddy couldn't read them, but my mama could. She told him all kinds of stuff wrong, and he didn't know it. Probably setting things up so's it would collapse all out from beneath, thinking he'd break his neck or maybe, if we got lucky, he'd fall on his gun. But I'd had enough of these hinkty doings. Only way Daddy was to die was if I was to kill him myself."

Behind them they could hear the organ burst out in a prelude to song. The church, being a church, had probably decided that this was fitting. They would pray for each other, pray for the project, and pray for Cooper Connelly, whose idea it had been, now that he lay fighting for his life down in Jackson.

"That's what I did. I got my granddaddy's gun—it was a Car-cano, just like my daddy's—and I hid in the kudzu, and I waited, and then . . . I shot him. He fell right out of that deer stand, and his gun went off, and the shot must have gone off someplace deep into the bushes and the trees. I've gone back searching. Couldn't find a hair of it. Afterwards, when it was done and I heard him moaning pitiful and I saw all the blood, I felt . . . but by then Critter came up, and I saw him running for that old beat-up piece of truck they had, and I just let it happen. I just let him part help and part drag Daddy into it. But I saw Daddy look right over smack where I was hiding, and I knew Daddy knew what had happened, really happened. And that soon as he could, he'd be coming for me. And that if he ever caught me, he'd kill me dead."

Behind them the congregation stood to its feet, sang lustily. "Amazing Grace" floated out all around them, loud and clear.

"So I waited. Granddaddy told me my daddy would be getting

well soon and coming back. Mama told me the same thing. It was only the doctor who told me different. He told me I didn't have to be scared anymore. Told me he'd taken care of everything."

Even though she knew what was coming, Melba held her breath.

"He came out to the house early that morning, after Mama and all the rest of them had gone to the hospital. He said not to worry anymore, that my daddy wasn't coming back. That he wasn't going to make it. That there'd been an operation and he'd seen to that."

Melba looked out over the land and the trees and the flowers. Then she looked down at the child beside her—ten years old, no more—and she thought of herself. She kept breathing, slowly and deeply, through the numbness all around her. She loved Cooper, and she could understand why he'd done what he did, and she could love this child sitting beside her, and she could love the flowers and the fresh air and the bright sky and the singing coming up behind her. But murder was murder. Wasn't it? Wasn't that true?

Still she said, "Dr. Connelly only meant to help you. He was your doctor, and he wanted to help you. He only did what he thought was right."

The girl looked up, shook her head, and smiled a sweet child's smile. "Oh, Dr. Connelly wasn't my doctor. Mama never would have took me over there. It was Dr. Reese Jackson helped me. Dr. Reese always helped me. It was Dr. Reese told me he'd made my daddy die."

# Chapter 27

HER GARDEN LOOKED STRANGE without the sign, and Melba knew it, especially now that May's geraniums were springing up at what had once been its base. Nothing for it, though; Madame Melba was finished. The sign lay taken down and heaped up on the porch, soon to be joined by the other detritus of Melba's old life as she cleaned it out, gave it away. It was amazing the number of different dishes one could pick up just by shopping the specials over at the Piggly Wiggly. It was truly amazing the number of books one could read with a friend. Melba gazed over at the silent big house beside her, or at least as much of it as was visible through her seven sisters rosebushes. She took her time staring before she turned back to her own cottage once again.

For a certainty, Melba knew when things had changed and it was time to leave them, and things had certainly changed for her here in Revere. Good things and bad things. It wasn't that business was off. In fact, it had been better than ever since Reverend Streeter had been shot and she'd been interviewed on the national news. She was having folks drive over from as far away as Georgia and people calling her from all over the place, wanting to know what was going to occur next, what should they do.

Melba didn't know what would happen, and she told them so. Only thing she knew was what had actually already happened: that the schools had integrated peacefully but at a terrible cost. Terrible for her, at least, and for Reese Jackson and maybe for Deanie. Terrible for Cooper Connelly above all.

Melba sat down on her swing and let her feet dangle. She ran a hand through her hair. Listening to the birds. Listening to the bees. Missing the sweet sound of her own sign on the wind. Determined not to miss Cooper Connelly, and missing him anyway.

It helped that they had not run in the same circles, knew few people in common. She heard the general gossip—that he was finally out of the hospital down in Jackson, that he was living someplace else now, not in Revere, that his wife was up north—nothing more. She and Cooper had not shared friends or acquaintances; they had not shared a life. Not like Deanie and Reese, whose life, what they had built, would probably save both of them, and save them together.

Two mockingbirds flitted out and around her statue of the Virgin, with obvious intentions toward each other that no virgin should find acceptable at all. Melba could not blame them. She had those thoughts, too, and more and more lately. She'd be thinking about Cooper Connelly, regretting all that time talking, wishing she had gotten on with what was what. Thing was, she'd just been going through a phase. It was like her mama had taught her—she was the kind of girl from whom men wanted one thing. And you better give it to them, otherwise they'd just go on and take it from somebody else. Trouble was, she'd been so much out of practice around men—being Madame Melba, which was a womanly occupation, filled mainly with women day in and day out—that she had forgotten her own mama's teachings, what she'd grown up with. Listen. If she'd slept with him, she'd probably be able to put him right out of her mind. That's how it had worked in the past. Anybody she had sex with—whoosh, gone. That's what she'd done wrong with Cooper Connelly—not sleeping with him—that's what kept him on her mind. Only that. At least that's what she said.

Still, she was missing his visits and found herself constantly wondering over him, thinking about him, even when she was not consciously thinking about him at all.

That's probably why she wasn't at all surprised to look up and see him coming up her brick walkway. At first she thought he was just in her mind, a ghost. It took her a moment of his steady coming toward her for her to realize that her brain had not put together this Cooper, because he was not quite the man she'd known before—he was too thin, too limping, too changed. And his smile had gone deeper, gotten brighter as well.

But, being Melba, it was the limp that got to her. She popped up from her porch swing—mercifully not thinking—and ran right on down to him.

"Here, Dr. Connelly, let me help you right on up these stairs."

Just like always, but different, too. Melba came close to him, touched him, held on to him, in a way she never had—could not have—done in the past.

"You looking mighty fine today, Miss Melba," said Cooper, and she said, "Hey, you're looking mighty fine yourself."

After that it took a minute for things to get settled. Melba had to plug in the fan and offer lemonade and cookies. In the kitchen she had to put her hand over her palpitating heart and catch her breath. Finally, back on the porch swing and sitting right beside him, she plucked up her courage and said, "I thought about you. Wondered."

At first he didn't say anything, just looked at her with his clear eyes. "There was a lot to get settled."

"With your daddy?"

"With Daddy, yes. Mainly with Reese, but then with everyone."

"Well, Mr. Reese," said Melba, and she shrugged in the direction of his big, dark house. "He's on a roll now. Your daddy gave him Doctors."

"He was the one; nobody's a better surgeon than Reese is."

"That's what your daddy said—in the newspapers, everywhere. Almost more talk about that than anything else—how Jack Rand done turned that great racial corner."

Cooper shrugged. "It's something I don't understand. Something that needs explaining. And yet I can see my own self that things like this, strange things, happen over and over again. Daddy's like that. Poor people are his cause. He's the one told me about that scholarship got Reese his education up north."

"*Jack Rand* told you about that?" Melba was all incredulous.

"How else would I have known it? Daddy's the only one up on the law. He brought me the paperwork, too. Reese knows it."

"Maybe he was feeling guilty about the body and all, the story you told me," said Melba. "Maybe he was trying to make up to Reese what he'd done."

"Maybe," said Cooper, sipping at his lemonade. "Or maybe he just knew that someday things had to change."

"They changed, all right," said Melba, again looking over her rosebushes at the big house. "Lyle Dean's gone on out and got herself a job."

Cooper nodded. "So I heard. She's working at Pearl's now. Jack Rand keeps me informed."

"Mr. Reese let that man die," said Melba. "He admitted it to Deanie and didn't feel bad about it one bit. Saw that little liver nick seeping blood and just sewed Billy Ray Puckett on up. Said it was a lost cause anyway—a liver wound—but he would have done what he did no matter what. Said that man had to be stopped from hurting that little girl. Deanie had a mighty lot of trouble with that. She thought he should have done *something*, not just left him to die. I myself don't know. He was a bad man, and Reese got rid of him, because he was the one who could do it. He's a god down here. After Reverend Streeter got shot and you got shot and they found out Billy Ray's daddy knew all about it . . . hey, well, the whole official matter, the inquest and all, just kind of disappeared, and Billy Ray's daddy with it. Just disappeared. Deanie knew it, though, and Ruth Ann Puckett and her daughter. I knew it."

Cooper said, "I knew it, too."

"I imagined you did," said Melba, and she looked away.

"He told me himself, down there, right under your house, at the river. Said what he'd seen. Said what he'd done."

"And let you take the responsibility for it."

"It *was* my responsibility. I was Billy Ray Puckett's surgeon," said Cooper, "and Reese Jackson is my friend."

Melba said nothing. She did not even roll her eyes. She sat still.

"My friend," repeated Cooper. "And he is a great doctor. My daddy, Reese, and me—we go back a long ways."

Melba and Cooper stayed as they were for a minute, looking out over azaleas and spring daffodils and tulips and silently thinking about the past.

Finally Melba said, "I guess that's right."

It was a whispered last part; at first she thought he hadn't heard it. Hoped he hadn't, even. But when she looked up, he was looking right at her—thin, tanned, but still Cooper, and smiling the most beautiful smile she'd ever seen in all her whole, long Melba life.

"I got me a job teaching history over in Meridian," said Cooper. "That's where I heard Madame Melba was packing up, that Miss Melba Obrenski was looking for something new."

"It's good changing things once in a while. Keeps a lady like me on her toes."

"Like my wife. I guess things didn't work out for Evelyne Elizabeth here, things I was blind to. She's divorcing me. Moving back permanently to Virginia. What *you* thinking about doing?"

Melba thought for a moment, decided on the truth. "Well, actually, I'm thinking something might happen for me in the flower way. I'm good at growing. A little shop, maybe, something like that."

"Sounds nice," Cooper said, still looking right at her. "And I think I might know just the spot. Might can help you reach it, too."

Now it was Melba's turn to look straight at him—directly, deep down, all the way at and into him. Breathing. Not knowing what she'd find there, but determined. And still breathing. Taking Cooper Connelly in and letting everything that had come before him right out of her life.

"Where?" she said, just starting to get it, but her eyes were already bright and her lips smiling, and when she did this, Miss Melba Obrenski, at forty and counting, was still one hell of a welcoming sight.

"Down Meridian, with me," said a warmed Cooper Connelly, then added, "Legally."

Melba heard him; she heard exactly what he said and what he

meant. One last breath—*whoosh*—and it was over. Everything, all the others, were gone, and Cooper still with her.

"Sounds good," said the last of Madame Melba the Seer.

And from her own brand-new, wide-open, so-sweet world, that little chameleon Melba Obrenski joined in with, "Sounds mighty fine."

## Chapter 28

REESE JACKSON HATED SCHOOL FUNCTIONS, always had hated
them, ever since he was a boy. Except for the sports, which he'd
loved. There was just always so much else for him to do, so many
needy people who hurt for lack of attention—attention he could
give them. By now Reese was sure this was the refrain of his life.

But he knew he'd better show up tonight at Hunt School. "Better be there," Lyle Dean had warned him. "Skip is going to perform."
It had been almost a year now since Billy Ray Puckett's death, since
the other changes, but things were still a little frosty at home, Lyle
Dean still working, no longer always there when he got in at night.
Reese found maybe he didn't mind this so much anymore, or at least
not as much as he'd thought he would. She was still *in* their home,
after all, hadn't left him like he'd once thought she might. That's
what really mattered, which was why Reese Jackson knew he'd better show up tonight.

The sign said it all:

HUNT JUNIOR HIGH SCHOOL
YEARLY TALENT SHOW
SEPTEMBER 10, 1967
ALL Y'ALL COME!

And everybody in town would be there, because this was the first event at the new, fully functioning, fully renovated, newly integrated Revere Middle School. The only thing the same about Hunt was that it was still sitting here in the black part of town.

*Looks good, though,* Reese thought, easing his new car—a swanky Dodge Polaris, sky blue—into a slot not too far from the door. *It should* look good, *all the work we put into it. Everybody working together.*

*Manually* working together. Reese himself had been tucked out in overalls, high on a ladder, slinging paint on a wall. He discovered he was good at it, a hidden talent. Lord knows he should have been; he'd seen Lyle Dean going at it so many times.

Reese ambled on into the school. Saw his wall. Made sure it still looked good, which it did.

"Hello, Dr. Reese."

"Hello, Dr. Jackson."

Black and white both speaking to him, now that he was officially over Doctors—though Doctors was on the verge of closing down, and probably sooner than any of them imagined. Reese knew it. Jack Rand Connelly knew it. The Jefferson-Lee County Board of Supervisors had granted Mid-South Medical Center everything it had asked for—more, even—and now that behemoth of progress and job opportunities was on its way in. A year, two maximum, and Doctors would be closing down, and all the other small, private hospitals with it. Times were changing, and the changes would just continue to seep, seep, seep into their lives. Reese didn't mind, found it didn't matter one bit if the whole hospital was about to shut down right when he'd gotten it where he wanted it. It just wasn't the same without Cooper. Reese was starting to see that Cooper had been a more important part of it than he'd ever thought. He and Melba had left Meridian and gone over to Tuscaloosa near where they say Cooper's Alabama mama had been from—and where he'd gone back to school at U of A. Wanted to be a teacher, at least that's what Reese heard. Melba and Lyle Dean were still thick as thieves, and she passed on the news. Maybe Cooper would come on back over when he finished up. Maybe he'd end up teaching right here at Hunt during its second full year of integration. Reese thought that would be fitting.

He stepped into the crowded auditorium and found himself looking around for his wife. Didn't take long to find her. She'd seen him first and was waving him over. She was surrounded by people and talking away. Herself again. Outgoing. His Lyle Dean, the woman he'd married.

She'd saved him a place at her side. He hadn't even asked her to do it. Reese eased himself on into it, said his hellos, and settled close.

"Skip's the last one," she told him, "the very last one. That means no sneaking out. No emergencies. You got to stay for the whole show."

"I *want* to stay for the whole show," Reese told her, thinking of at least ten other places he'd much rather be and ten other things he'd rather be doing. "I *planned* on staying."

Lying through his teeth, and Lyle Dean grinning at him because they both knew it. But he would stay. Hell, he'd stay anywhere he had to, as long as he could be beside warm, sweet-smelling, fine-looking, comforting Deanie. His wife.

"Good crowd out," he said to nobody in particular. Maybe to Cooper. Cooper had been on his mind a lot lately. Popping in when you least expected him to, and for no reason. Cooper had told him once—maybe twice—about the body they'd found that night when they were deep into the Tallahatchie River, how it would pop up on him sudden like and how it would not go away. Coop was like that now. Popping up out of nowhere. Running himself through Reese's mind.

Reminding him also of things that needed remembering—of his own body, of Billy Ray Puckett. Reese Jackson did not feel one iota of remorse.

"I had to do it," he'd told Cooper down at the river. "Poor folk like that Puckett woman, her little girl. I *know* it was a liver wound, but I wasn't going to take me no chances. If by some miracle that man had pulled through—and I've seen it happen, seen bodies rise up—he would have been after that child and he would have killed her. Sheriff wasn't going to do nothing for them. Oh, once it happened, he would have looked sympathetic, might even have started him up an inquest and such. Of course by then Billy Ray Puckett would have been long gone. And that girl would have been dead, killed off by her daddy, and who would have cared? Billy Ray Puckett was going to die one day anyway. I just helped him along before he could do any more damage to his child."

And Cooper had nodded. Like Reese, he was from here, from Mississippi. He understood.

Mr. William D. Wyndham, the new principal of Hunt—its first white one—came out on the stage, and the whole shebang started: out-of-key singing and out-of-step dancing. Piano and tuba playing that was right hard on the ears. And Reese Jackson just as out-of-his-mind bored as he'd known he was going to be. A merciful break for tea punch and cookies, and then everything commenced up again.

Critter Tate, who was living with them during the week so he could take advantage of the new school system, came out next. He was a magician ("The World-Renowned Alfred Cadabra"), and Janet Puckett was his trusty assistant. Fortunately. Because he could not have gotten on without her.

"Critter, it's the left card. The *left* card," she hissed.

When the hat came off and there was no rabbit in it, she was the one found him hopping nonchalantly off of the stage and held him up.

Everybody got a big laugh out of the two of them—black people still with black people and whites still with whites, but at least they were in the same room and they were laughing together, and at the same thing.

*That's something anyway,* Reese thought, still leery of white people. But he looked, and there was Janet Puckett up on the stage—the once so shy and angry Janet Puckett—and she, too, was laughing and bowing. Laughing and bowing. Reese stared at her for a long moment before looking away.

Then it was Skippy's turn.

His name—"Spencer Reese Jackson Jr., Comedy Routine"—on the program and the boy himself limping out onto the stage. On his crutch. Reese, scowling, wanted to say, *Skip, you don't need that thing.* But then, seeing him, blinking, looking at him again. For a second wondering if this were his boy at all.

Was it possible you could live in a place with someone day after day and year after year and still not really *see* that person? Reese would have doubted it, and he would have doubted it loudly and to everyone he knew. Except for the fact that today he was not quite recognizing Skippy, not quite placing his own son. Skip had changed on him somehow, when Reese wasn't looking. Got taller. Got thinner. Got himself resembling another eleven-year-old boy Reese maybe knew, or else might maybe remember.

Skippy raised his crutch, swung it slowly in a golf swing right to left, said, "Heeeeere's Skippy!" a perfect imitation. And brought the house down.

"He's been practicing," whispered Lyle Dean beside Reese. "All summer long with Janet and Critter. They wouldn't let me see what they were doing, wouldn't let me tell you. They said we all had to wait until now."

Reese watched, fascinated, by the bow-tied, blue-blazered boy before him—his son—as he became Madame Melba Obrenski, became Reverend William H. Streeter, became Principal Wyndham, became Reese Jackson himself.

"Eloise, time to close up now, go over to Sallie's and get us some lunch."

Everybody in town knew Dr. Jackson's precise habits—how he had lunch every working day of his life with his nurse—and everybody laughed, including Dr. Jackson. Reese was relaxing, enjoying himself. He found himself right there in the flow of the thing.

"I think that boy's got talent," he whispered to Lyle Dean.

Deanie was too busy laughing and clapping to talk back.

Skippy waited, let the chuckling die down, and then he said, "Yesterday, during first period, our teacher said to us, 'Children, I want you to tell us how you know your parents love you.' (Trilling for all the world just like Miss Louella Millsaps, his sixth-grade teacher!) 'Just one small notion that lets you know this is true.'"

Skippy paused, looked deadpan into the audience.

"Great timing," whispered Reese to Lyle Dean.

Skippy continued, "Well, Cindy Bates said she knew her parents loved her because they had taken her all the way out to California to

Disneyland even though her mother pointed out to her how much she hated kiddy rides, how they made her sick. And they *did* make her sick; Cindy threw up cotton candy three times. Then Lucas Lurie said he knew his parents loved him because they'd given him a baby brother, just like he wanted and just like they'd promised. Lucas is having so much fun, says he wants another one. This time Mr. and Mrs. Lurie said they don't know. They'll have to give it some thought. Would he like a new bicycle instead?"

Another burst of laughter.

When the last of it died down, he said, "Then she came to me. She said, 'Skip, now tell us how you know your parents love you!'" Skip was still trilling. Folks were still laughing.

Skip got his crutch, ambled with it to the front of the stage.

"I told Miss Millsaps that I just knew my mama loves me," he said—and they were waiting for him now, you could have heard a pin drop—"I know my mama loves me because when I was a baby she ran over my leg—right over it—with her car. She just loved me so much, wanted me near her so much, she just had to make sure I'd never be able to run away!"

A gasp. Stunned silence. Reese could feel it all around him, feel everybody's eyes on him, and on Lyle Dean. This horrible, never-talked-about thing brought to light. But suddenly Reese wasn't paying attention to any of it—to the eyes, to the gasps, to the people—not even to Lyle Dean, who he just knew was now all right. Reese was looking at Skippy. Seeing him clearly. And Skippy was looking right back at him. Waiting for his daddy. Willing his hands to start clapping together. Willing him to start smiling. Willing himself to finally be Spencer Reese Jackson Jr., a great man's son. Willing Daddy Reese to be the first one on his feet.

And once Reese was up, he stayed up, as the clapping swelled around him and all the children trooped back on the stage for their bow. Reese didn't see them; he was too busy looking right at his son. First *recognizing* him fully—then looking through him. Going back. Going back. Back to a time and place where two other young boys grew up together. And played together on the wide Delta. And learned their lessons together on a river. Where they dove deep, deep into that river—that great and glorious river. The river meant to heal us and to make us whole.